PRAISE FOR A DANGEROUS GAME

"Dyer gives us a strong heroine, high stakes, vivid world-building, and gorgeous writing all wrapped up in one package… What more could you ask for?"
Kelley York, author of *Other Breakable Things*

"*A Dangerous Game* is an unputdownable story, a wild ride from start to finish. This is a stand-out novel."
The Literature Hub

"This book is an adrenaline-filled thrill ride from start to finish, where the only time you put the book down is to catch your breath. Addictive, thrilling, amazing."
S.E. Anderson, author of the Starstruck series

PRAISE FOR THE UNTAMED SERIES

"A fantastic dystopian tale. Highly recommended for fans of strong heroines and intriguing sci-fi worlds."
Pintip Dunn, *New York Times* bestselling author of the Forget Tomorrow series

"Dyer writes with an urgency and a rhythm that compels you to turn the page."
Sue Wyshynski, author of The Butterfly Code series

"The pages are packed with vivid imagery, high tension, and an earnest and willful heroine."

Tracy Clark, author of The Light Key Trilogy & *Mirage*

ALSO AVAILABLE FROM MADELINE DYER

THE UNTAMED SERIES

UNTAMED
FRAGMENTED
DIVIDED
DESTROYED

THE DANGEROUS ONES SERIES

A DANGEROUS GAME

COMING SOON...

THIS VICIOUS WAY

THE DANGEROUS ONES
BOOK ONE

A DANGEROUS GAME

MADELINE DYER

INEJA PRESS

A Dangerous Game
Copyright © 2017 Madeline Dyer

Madeline Dyer asserts the moral right to be identified as the author of this work.

First edition, November 2017
Published by Ineja Press

Edited by Michelle Dunbar
Cover and Interior Design by We Got You Covered Book Design

Print ISBN: 978-0-9957191-6-3
eBook ISBN: 978-0-9957191-7-0

The author can be contacted via email at Madeline@MadelineDyer.co.uk
or through her website www.MadelineDyer.co.uk

For Rachael and Sarah

TEN YEARS EARLIER

FIRST, I HEAR THEM IN my dreams.

Long, drawn-out screams. Screams that grab and burn, like fire; sounds that never let go. Sounds that—

"Keelie!"

I open my eyes, heart pounding, and see a figure looming over me. My father—short, red-faced, worried. He grabs my arm, pulls me up. The screams continue, still scorching me.

For a moment, I think it's the Turning. That it's the spirits screaming, that they're reverting to their most dangerous of temperaments, and it's a good job we're inside, else they'll kill us. But then I realize. The screams are human. They're *us*.

"Keelie! Come on—we've got to go, got to leave. *Now*." My father hands me several layers of clothes. "Pack everything quickly. Like we practiced."

Behind him, my mother's shoving everything she can get her hands on into the only suitcase we have. Her hands move so fast. "Owen, get the weapons!" she yells.

Nearby, there's sharp movement—hands and arms reaching for things. Heavy, quick breathing. Bea, my

1

older sister, scoops the baby out of the cot, holds Mila close to her chest just as the infant starts crying. I see the look on Bea's face—how she's trying to stay in control and not panic.

My body jolts; it's happening. Actually happening.

They're out there.

They're coming for us.

Outside, someone shouts. I think it's Red's voice, but I'm not sure—it's distorted by the heavy clog of the engines, the shouts, the screams.

A thousand emotions drive through my body, clash with each other, start to do battle. I know I should be afraid—the fear should be palpable—but I'm not. My body hums with energy. This is it.

I fight to stop a smile erupting across my face. There are times and places when smiling is appropriate. This is not one of them.

An engine rumbles outside, and then my father's crossing the hut. Clanking sounds follow, and I know he's getting the knives.

"It's okay, it's okay," Bea whispers to Mila. But the baby can't understand, and we all know Bea's saying it to herself. "It's okay, it's okay, it's okay."

I pull on clothes—a shirt, a hoody, an outer coat, and dark jeans—straight over my pajamas, then find my shoes, put them on. Then I grab my rucksack, start stuffing things inside. My blanket, spare shoes, a book. A second passes, then I grab my teddy bear—even though I know I'm too old for him now.

I fold Bea's blanket hastily and stuff it into the top of my bag.

"Keelie, take these." My mother thrusts several items into my arms: a compass, a pack of energy bars, water purification tablets, a tub of Vaseline, a bottle of insect repellent, and some antiseptic cream. "Put them in your bag; we've got no room in ours. And be quick. Bea, Mila's food is in Gwen's hut. Grab what you can, and then go—we'll meet you in the woods, by Eighth Branch. Get Mila away before she starts crying. And where's Elf?" She turns away, her face red with the heat, and flaps her hands around her head for a moment.

"Here." The curtain to my right moves, and then my brother's in front of me, reaching for the bottles of water, just as our father hands them to him.

Bea heads out of the hut, her arms wrapped tightly around our baby sister. An empty tote bag hangs from her shoulder.

"Be careful!" I call after her, but I don't know if my words are loud enough, and I wonder if that's the last time I'll see my sisters. My heart clenches.

No, stop it.

I need to stay calm. Gwen's hut isn't far. It's the nearest one to ours, and a lot of Mila's things are in there because Gwen looks after the baby when my mother's hunting and Bea's gathering.

Heart thudding, I squash the new items into the rucksack, realize they won't all fit, and pull the teddy bear back out, place him on my bed.

"Hurry up," Caia-Lu whispers. I look up, see her old, gaunt face. "We have to go now. They're getting closer to this hut."

"Keelie—keep packing!" my mother shouts at me, her words fraught. And then she's yelling more and more stuff, but her words are too loud, and I can't make them out. I stare at her hands, the way they move next to her head. She spins around a couple of times, like she doesn't know where to go next.

"We haven't got time!" Caia-Lu grabs the Watcher Doll from the table and squeezes it hard between her palms as if the red paint on it will imprint onto her skin if she holds it tightly enough.

She's calling upon the spirits to help us, even though she's not an active Seer right now—she doesn't get called to the Dream Land or given Seeing dreams put together by good spirits and the Gods and Goddesses. I pray that the spirits will still help, because we're Untamed, but I know that's no guarantee. They're mostly on our side, but they still ripped my uncle to shreds and then altered time so that the scene played over and over for hours and hours. Some of them just want to torment everyone—whether they're Enhanced or not.

The cries outside get louder. The screams.

"We have to go now!" Caia-Lu yells, and then she's gone, and the Watcher Doll's gone too.

I start to go, to follow her. Wisps of early morning light peak through the window, and I freeze as I see the shapes and—

"Keelie! Pack that stuff, grab the other bag—the one under there, yes. Elf, give me a hand with this."

I shake as I reach for the next bag—as I realize this is real. Very real. Outside, I hear voices, close to our hut. Caia-Lu's and Gregory's.

"Where's the torch?" Elf barges past me, then grabs it from the side counter, spilling a bowl of dried leaves.

"No—don't turn it on," my mother hisses. "They could be right out there. Keelie, look from the doorway. See if Ramna and Sara are ready to go. Be careful. Don't go outside, not without me."

I follow my mother's words, and, a second later, I stand in the doorway, holding back the heavy curtain with my arm. It's lighter outside than in our hut—there's a full moon along with the dawn light, but it mainly illuminates the mist—and it takes my eyes several seconds to adjust.

Caia-Lu stands by Gwen's hut, ten yards from me, her head in her hands. She turns slowly, lifting her face, and, despite the haze, I see the haunted look in her eyes.

"Run, child. Running is the only way out," she shouts.

My chest tightens. I scan the rest of the area, but I can't see far because of the early morning fog billowing out of the semi-darkness. There's another hut behind Gwen's—Nina's—but I can't even see its shape. Nor can I see my aunts, Ramna and Sara. But I wouldn't from here. Their hut is on the other side of the village and—

A scream sends chills through my body.

Bea.

"Keelie! No!"

My mother tries to grab hold of me, but I'm too quick. I move into the half-darkness—toward the Enhanced, are they here now?—and I run, run toward the scream, toward Bea.

Footsteps pound behind me, and energy resounds through my whole body.

"That way!" Red yells, emerging from the dark, the mist, and he grabs my hand tightly, pulls me to the left.

I skid and slam into him, my best friend. We nearly lose our balance, but somehow we slip on the mud, and our weight propels us to the side. I grip his hand tighter, run faster, my eyes blinking furiously, trying to see ahead.

The trees are there; I can make out their outline. And—

And I see them.

Bea and—and the woman.

Red and I falter, stop. I feel his body jolt, and then he squeezes my hand, hard. He's shaking.

They're here. The Enhanced are here.

We're too late.

Caia-Lu told you to run!

Bea's crying, trying to cover her ears and hold the baby at the same time, while she rocks on the balls of her feet. She shakes her head over and over again. Mila starts wailing, and Bea trembles, then tries to make herself smaller, crouches down. I see her eyes shut as she nestles the baby into her lap, then she moves one hand up, covers her left ear.

"It's all right, dear," the woman says, reaching down to Bea with a long-fingered hand.

"No! Don't touch her," I yell. She doesn't like being touched by strangers.

The woman turns to me—mirror eyes taunting—and I gulp. She takes a step toward me. And I'm sure she's going to kill one of us. Me? Bea? Red?

But no, everything I know about them tells me that's wrong. The Enhanced Ones don't kill us. They're not violent people, not murderers—that's what they say. Any deaths in conversion attacks are *accidents* because the Enhanced Ones are programmed to want to *save* us all.

Yet, whether intentionally violent or not, they are still armed. And I don't believe Dad when he says their guns are only for sport. They're going to use them on us, sooner or later.

"It's all right, children," the woman says. "Don't be scared. I've come to save you, my dears. We Chosen Ones will save you all." She smiles brightly and looks toward Bea. "There, there. Don't cry, my darlings. You too can live your lives free from negativities."

Red lets go of my hand and steps toward Bea and the woman. "Bea! Come over here, now."

But Bea isn't looking at Red, and I don't think she hears his words. She's overstimulated; everything will be an overwhelming blur to her.

I dart forward. Mud splatters over my legs, cold and thick and clammy on my jeans, like it's trying to draw me back, stop me going.

"Good girl," the Enhanced woman whispers as I run at them. I don't know how I hear her words—I just do—and she reaches for me.

I duck under her arm as I enter her thick cloud of perfume, nearly gagging. My eyes water.

"Bea!" I hesitate, know that I need to grab her. But she doesn't like being touched a lot of the time, even if she knows the person. "Bea! Come on!"

I look around, and then the woman's reaching toward me, and I ignore the voice in my head and pull Bea up. My sister's arms are locked around Mila, and Bea stares at me for a moment. I push her to my left as hard as I can, and we're moving, my two sisters in front of me.

"Red—" I turn, but I can't see him. "Bea, run!" I shout, but my voice is strained, and it's suddenly got darker—clouds over the moon and—

Warm fingers close around my wrist.

I twist, see myself reflected in the Enhanced One's eyes, see myself captured.

For a second, I freeze. Then I spring into action. I slam my fist into the woman's face, kick out at the same time, turning so I can throw off her center of gravity. But she's strong—too strong—and her grip doesn't weaken. If anything it gets stronger. She pulls me closer, and I turn again, kicking out, adrenaline pumping through me.

Her arm snaps around my body, like a lock. And—

"Let us save you!"

Suddenly, there are more. More people, more mirror eyes. I scream at them, try to frighten them, even though I know it's impossible—they only feel what they want to.

I twist against her body, manage to unlatch her arm from me, and duck as a flash of something gold flies toward me in the half-light. An augmenter? My mouth dries.

No.

No.

No.

I can't take the poison that will steal my soul, fill me with artificiality, and never let me be the same again.

I turn, got to keep moving—but there are so many of them. They work in packs.

"Keelie!"

The scream comes from behind me, and I try to turn—think I see a figure and—

A gun goes off.

I gasp as something big and heavy hits me, and I fall forward, pulled down with one of *them*. I hit the ground hard and roll over, freeing myself from the Enhanced One's weight. Pain flashes through me.

"Keelie?"

My head jerks up, and I taste blood on the roof of my mouth. My tongue feels too big.

Red has the gun—one of the elders' guns. He stands there, with Bea screaming behind him. She's cradling Mila, still trying to cover her ears. She shouts at me, tells me to get up. Red holds the weapon. At thirteen years old, he knows how to use it. We're taught as soon as we're responsible enough. He learned at the age of eight, and, two years later, on my own eighth birthday, I was old enough too.

I duck just in time to avoid his second shot.

My heart pounds. The ground pounds. Everything pounds, and I feel something building up within me—momentum, as if the world is suddenly going to stop, but I'll go crashing forward. I cover my head with my arms, try to hunker down so I'm invisible. Coldness seeps into my body.

They fall around me—the Enhanced Ones. I see them, even though my left eye is pressed against the ground, blurring my vision.

Something wet splashes over me.

I stay still. Listening. Scared.

The screams are louder now. More of them. More of us?

It's all right, I tell myself. *It'll be all right. It'll be over soon.*

And it will end in blood and tears. That's what Caia-Lu has always said; suddenly, I see her face in front of me. Her eyes are haunted, and they're sinking into their sockets, being drawn back, until they're gone. Until there's nothing there.

"Run!" a voice screams. Another voice—my father's. "Run!"

I lift my head, move my arms slightly, try to see. But there's—the air isn't…it's smoke. *Smoke* billows toward me. And there's no one else, Bea and Red have gone. Disappeared. Something hisses loudly, crackles, up in the sky and—

"Run!"

I catapult forward, but I don't know which way I'm going now, only that I've got to get out. Something's on fire, and the vehicles are too close. The engines are running, but why haven't people moved them, driven off? I turn to the left, look toward the hut where we store fuel, see the flames.

"Keep running!"

My legs plow into action before I consciously make the decision. I pull myself forward; gritty air scratches my throat. My eyes smart as I try to see—try to see where people are…my family… I've lost them. Where are Bea and Mila? And Elf—is he in the hut still?

And what about Red?

A woman ahead of me stumbles, but I can't see whether she's one of them or one of us. The air's too thick. It's hiding stuff, making it harder—trying to protect us?

Another gunshot goes off, and I duck, freeze. Every part of my body throbs.

Keep going. Don't stop.

I run again, and then I'm at the woman's side. I see her green shawl, recognize it—my aunt Ramna's shawl. I reach for her hand, and she turns. Blood pours down her face. My stomach squeezes.

"Go!" she wheezes, pointing to the right. "Go!"

I stare at her. Can't. Can't go, can't—

I see the Enhanced Ones looming. Two men with eyes that are too reflective.

Aunt Ramna pushes me, and my legs jump into action as if they're not mine, as if she's governing me with ancient magic. I dart to the nearest hut, pull myself behind it, lean against it, breathing hard. Its hide covering feels rough against the side of my face.

I hunker down, feel the fear in my body, feel it trying to take over.

No. You've got to stay in control.
You've got to run! You've got to go!

I nod, then I peer back out.

More smoke—black smoke. Figures are moving, but I can't tell who they are. My people? Or not? My eyes aren't working properly. They're stinging, stinging too much—there's something in them.

I rub them, but I get more dirt in them, feel my panic rising. A weapon. I need a weapon. I grope about in the dirt, mud hiking under my nails. My fingers grapple at something—a stick. I pull it toward me, but it's flimsy. Still, it's all I've got and—

I hear his scream. I turn, and I see him fall, see it like he falls in slow motion. My friend. My *best* friend.

His eyes roll back for a second, but, then they return, and they're on me.

Help me, his eyes say.

I see the blood around his body, notice the way it fans out so perfectly. A beautiful circle.

My body jolts.

Red.

No.

No.

No.

Nails of ice pierce my soul.

A shadow falls over me.

Your death is already written in the silk of time. You cannot escape it.

I look up and scream.

ONE

"YOU'RE NOT STILL THINKING OF that dream, are you?"

My brother peers at me, concern evident in the way his eyebrows arch above his dark glasses. I'm glad I don't have to see the look in his eyes.

"Of course not." I keep my voice low.

We shouldn't be talking. Not here, not in the heart of New Kimearo, an Enhanced town. Talking is asking for trouble. Rahn would be furious if he knew Elf had chosen this moment to interrogate me.

"Good." Elf nods. He turns slightly, and I see the shape of the gun beneath his shirt. There's an identical one in the back of my waistband. "Our parents aren't coming back."

I grit my teeth as I keep watch. We're standing in the shadows, and there's something about our position that makes me feel stronger. "I know that. You don't need to remind me."

"Are you sure?" Elf pauses, and I know he's watching for movement.

There's still one Enhanced man in the office ahead. Any moment, Yani's distraction should lead him out of the office, and that'll be our cue. I still can't believe Rahn approved a distraction team for this—they're usually for rescues, not raids. Still, I'm curious as to what method Yani will use. Something tells me it won't be the *reveal-and-run* technique. That's too high-risk. We only risk death—or conversion—when we absolutely have to.

Elf moves closer to me. "Because I don't want you getting any ideas."

"Me?" I murmur. My eyes narrow slightly. A cloud moves in front of the sun, casting a long shadow over us and the square. "Me *getting ideas*? Huh."

"I know what you're like. Ever since we met Katya, you've thought your dreams are signs too. And these dreams happening again, *well*...."

My back stiffens a little. "No. I haven't. *I'm* not a Seer." And I'm well aware of the fact. Caia-Lu said that only *special ones* become Seers, those who are naturally more spiritual. The Gods and Goddesses and spirits seek them out and bring them to the Dream Land to give them visions of the immediate future, warnings of conversion attacks.

I don't know why Elf always brings this up. Just because I have vivid dreams and *he* can never remember any of his.

I breathe deeply, thinking about the dream. A lot of my dreams are repeats. Flashbacks or nightmares or sometimes a morphing of the two. This particular one was a nightmare I first had a few weeks after we joined Rahn's group, when we were finally safe. Then it was a semi-regular occurrence for about five years. Since then, it's only been sporadic. Last night was the first time in a long, long time for that particular dream. But it still shakes me up. In it, my mother stood tall, confident, but still, almost like she was frozen, and my father slightly shorter at her side, but still steadfast.

"*Save us, Keelie. Save us.*"

That's what they said, over and over, in my dream. And they looked sad. Sad that I haven't done anything to help them in the decade since they were taken. No, in the decade since they sacrificed themselves.

And it was so real, my dream. *The* dream. I could smell my mother's perfume, see dandruff on my father's shoulders.

Then I saved them. I made them Untamed again. In my dream.

Sometimes, I think I'd rather have more of the flashback-style nightmares of the D'Elinous attack—even if they occasionally merge into a nightmare—than these guilt dreams of my parents that show me what can never be.

But then I remember what the flashbacks *could* show me, and I'm glad it was a fictitious nightmare I had.

"They're gone, Keelie," Elf says.

"I know."

I swallow hard. My left leg starts jittering. I put more weight on it, still it. There. That's better.

Ahead, there's movement in the dealership office: a man walks past the window. The back of his head is to us so there's no flash of his mirror eyes.

I watch the scene for the next few moments. The office is small, freestanding, and Elf and I have sight of the two doors, one at each end. We'll see the moment the man opens one.

"What distraction method do you think Yani will use?" I ask. Energy thrums through me. I want to get up and run in there now.

"Don't know. Something small," Elf murmurs and carefully adjusts his dark glasses. "He only needs to get one person out of the office. Not fifty or more out of a compound. We're probably not even going to hear the distraction. It'll be something small. Something safe. The first we'll know that it's working is when the Enhanced leaves the office."

After a few more minutes of nothing, I scan the area again. The buildings around the office are constructed from a dark gray stone, and they add an oppressive atmosphere to New Kimearo. I'd have thought the

Enhanced Ones would've painted them or something. Maybe pale blue. Or yellow. Peaceful, happy colors. The Enhanced are big on that sort of stuff.

To the left, is a yard full of cars. I know which one I've got my eye on. All we need are the keys. And I know where they'll be.

"Any moment now," Elf murmurs, his voice low. "Any...moment...now."

As if on cue, the door on the left side of the office opens. Elf and I duck back against the wall, let the shadows swallow us completely. I check my hood is up and my glasses are secure. My heart pounds with a fresh surge of adrenaline, and I smile. Adrenaline pounding through my system is what I've lived to feel ever since Caia-Lu told me my death was already written in the silk of time. I don't care how dangerous things get, as long as I'm living.

The Enhanced man steps out. He's tall and wears a well-tailored suit. His eye-mirrors glint under the bright sun, and I shudder a little. Just seeing them— seeing Enhanced eyes—makes me uncomfortable.

I twist my arm around, behind my back, check my gun. The Luger is still there—of course it is. I can feel it against my skin. But there's something comforting about touching it with my hand.

Elf's breath is hot against the back of my neck as we watch the man walk away. He doesn't once look around. Too trusting—they all are. He didn't even lock the door.

"Ready?" Elf asks.

I wait until the Enhanced man is completely out of sight, no doubt going to the far side of New Kimearo— if Yani's distraction is completely successful—then I run. My steps are light; the rucksack on my back contains only the essential things needed on a raid or excursion, and I continually check my surroundings. But I know this area's empty now, and, anyway, Elf's got my back. He's staying in the shadows; if anyone comes, he'll alert me and use whatever means are necessary to get me out of there safely and back to the others at the meeting point.

I can't help but smile as I make it to the door. The handle is cold, like ice, and welcome against my searing skin. I leave the door open.

Inside, the office is dark. My eyes take a few moments to adjust, and I scan the room quickly, picking out shapes from the darkness. Two chairs. A desk. A small coffee table covered in messy papers, coffee-stained mugs, and a potted plant. A small wooden cupboard. And a metal cabinet. My smile gets wider, and I head for it. That's where the keys will be. I know it won't be locked because the Enhanced Ones pride themselves on their honesty—but, even if it is, I've got a couple of Five's hairpins and some sharp, pointy bits of metal. No lock has beaten me yet.

My fingers glide over the cabinet's ornate front as I search for the opening mechanism. I find a lever, tucked up and under some embellishment, and glance quickly over my shoulder. It's still quiet. Eerily quiet. But it's always fairly quiet in the towns and cities. The Enhanced congratulate themselves on their calm, tranquil natures.

A pity that's at the expense of their souls.

I open the drawer. A dozen sets of car keys glisten back at me. We don't normally steal our vehicles from a garage or dealer—usually, we find a car with the key still in the ignition, or we hot-wire one if there's plenty of time—but this was too good an opportunity to miss. A whole dealership with only one man supervising it today. It hadn't taken Rahn long to split up our raiding group, giving himself and Nico the role of backup to Yani's distraction, so I can grab the keys, while my twin covers me.

Just get one car for now, but as many keys as you can carry. That's what Nico said. We'll only be able to drive one car away before the noise attracts them—but if we have many keys, we can come back later and get more. Have to leave it a decent time though, else the

Enhanced will be on red alert. Surprisingly, they don't rekey their cars all that often.

Cars are crucial. But they're also hard to get. Rahn said that when he was little, the Enhanced had many cars, but now that's not the case. Few drive them, and the roads are mostly abandoned today. The Enhanced Ones amass in towns and cities—they don't like being out in the wild—so most don't need cars.

But we do.

Heart beating fast, I scan the keys—they're all neatly labeled—and I pick out the set for the white L200 that we saw behind the dealership office. We've already got three L200s, and there's something about matching vehicles that makes me smile.

I shove the keys into the left pocket of my leather jacket, then slide my rucksack down, so it hangs off one arm, and undo the zip. There's not much in my bag— just my compass, a pack of food, half a bottle of water, and a packet of painkillers. My survival supplies are running on the low side, but there's plenty of room for the keys—and other stuff too. I could take back a couple of the coffee mugs. Bea would love them.

Then I see the Swiss army knife on the desk, only a foot or so in front of me. It calls to me.

I pick it up slowly and stare at it. I marvel at all the different blades and tools on it. And the main blade itself looks savage, like it could do a lot of damage. It's even got a screwdriver. Ever since Red got one for his tenth birthday, I've always wanted one of my own. Into my pocket it goes.

I smile, triumphant, and then reach for one of the coffee mugs.

"Can I help you?"

I spin around.

For a second, I can't see him. But then the floor creaks, far to the left, and my eyes zoom to that corner.

An Enhanced man sits in one of the chairs. He's slouching, so his frame doesn't disturb the chair's silhouette—is that how I missed him? My eyes widen, and I feel the urge within me to kill him. It's instant, instinct. But it's also something that Rahn insisted needed training out of me for my own safety. We kill the Enhanced to protect ourselves—that's the rule. But we *don't* seek them out. Ten years ago, I let my desire to kill them control me. It consumed me. And I haven't killed any Enhanced since Rahn helped me to focus my anger on other less dangerous things.

Now, I stare at the Enhanced man in front of me, and I feel it all: the desire to kill, as if I'm back to being eleven years old, and he's another one of my victims. And I could easily kill him here. I'd still be obeying Rahn—I haven't purposefully sought out an Enhanced to kill. And even our leader says they all *deserve* to die. We should have no qualms about killing them if it means we survive. We just don't hunt them down.

I have no qualms about killing them. They're wrong, unnatural. I hate them.

I breathe deeply. My Luger is in the back of my waistband.

That's when I notice the Enhanced man's face. Not just his eyes, but his whole face. His hair is as black as night—as black as mine—and his skin is light, like soft moonlight. His nose is slightly wobbly-looking, as if it healed badly from a break—odd for an Enhanced One who could use augmenters to fix it—but it gives his expression an air of perpetual curiosity, like no matter what emotions he's filled with, part of him will still look curious.

He's attractive, and I immediately feel wrong for thinking that. What would my younger self say? She'd have already killed him. And when you have augmenters in your system, appearance means nothing.

The man stands, and his mirror eyes seem to get bigger. They make his jaw look even stronger. A gold ring in his ear flashes. His crisp, white shirt rustles as he moves, and I see the tattoos peeking out from under his collar and the edges of his sleeves.

"*Can* I help you?"

I step back, feel adrenaline bolt around my body.

Shoot him!

But a gunshot would likely attract more Enhanced here. They don't use guns, so they'd know an Untamed was here. Drawing more to this office would put me in danger, as well as Elf. Possibly Rahn, Yani, and Nico too.

But this man must already know I'm Untamed—the Enhanced don't steal.

Killing him silently is preferable.

He lifts one of the mugs from his desk and takes a long slurp before licking his lips in a very decisive way. Something about his action makes my heart pound faster. I like it when my heart pounds fast. It tells me this is dangerous.

"I asked if I could help you, ma'am?" He doesn't move, just stays sitting. He smiles.

"Yes." I keep my voice smooth. "You can help me."

Strangulation. That would be relatively quiet. Because I'm going to have to kill him now. Can't have him alerting others and risking my group. Only I haven't got twine in my survival bag.

But Elf has. Can I run out, grab it from my brother, and get back here before this man alerts others? I look over his desk again, see a radio. If I take that with me while I get the twine, my plan will work. The corners of my lips twitch, and I let my rucksack fall from my arm; I'll need freedom of movement.

"And how may I help you?" the Enhanced man asks. There's something strangely mesmerizing about his voice.

The door I came in by is behind me, but the Enhanced is slightly closer to it. If I lunge for it, chances are he'll do the same—and get there first. I know how quickly these monsters can move. The other door's on the opposite side of the office, but I can see it's bolted near the top. I do my calculations fast. The bolted door—

it'd take me three seconds to get there, dragging the spare chair for me to climb on to reach the bolt, and another two to unbolt it. Plenty of time for the Enhanced to stop me. The window's three seconds away, but it's not open wide enough, and I'd have to jump and angle my body sufficiently. I'd need more of a run-up for that than I have, and the Enhanced would have time to grab my foot if I attempted to dive out. I could scream and bring Elf here, but doing so could also bring more Enhanced Ones. And Elf's not as good a fighter as I am.

The door I came through is the only feasible option. Have to hope this man's not in the usual good shape.

I glance at the radio on the desk again.

Grab it and go!

I lunge forward. My fingers close around the fancy radio, and I drag it back toward me, whirling around and—

"I don't think so." The Enhanced man moves quickly. He's by the door in a blink of an eye and shuts it with a click.

I see its key code lock light up. Shit. I don't know the number.

He grins at me.

You're caught, Keelie. Eleven-year-old you would never have been caught.

My chest tightens. No, not caught. Not yet. Beads of sweat form across the back of my neck. I look around quickly. There's nothing I can use as a ligature here. The radio clicks in my hand. I drop it quickly and stamp on it. It makes a crackling sound.

The man steps closer. I try to see fury on his face, but I can't. He still looks curious.

"I know *exactly* how to help you." He smiles.

I lob the set of keys from my pocket at his face, then pull out my gun. It feels good in my hand, and I hold it steadily between us.

"Step over there," I tell the man. "Keep away from the other door." My voice is as steady as my hand.

A DANGEROUS GAME

The Enhanced man puts his hands up slowly. Then he shakes his head. "Violence is wrong." His voice sounds strange. He's hesitating. "You—you need saving. The evil needs to be—"

"Stay back!" I yell, clicking the gun's safety off. I jerk my head to the side. "Get over there, and I won't hurt you!"

But everything inside me is rearing up, and it *wants* to hurt him. To hurt him now. To fire the gun, even if it means alerting more Enhanced. Because it will hurt him. He'll feel the pain.

But, when I was younger, I didn't kill with a gun.

A gun feels like cheating. To me, a gun isn't for killing; it's to scare them.

The Enhanced doesn't move. He keeps smiling. "I can help you."

"Get over there!" My gun doesn't shake because I know the moment a gun shakes, your opponent knows you're not confident. And I need to be.

Calm and confident. That's what my father always said.

"Get other there," I repeat, and make my voice stronger, my words harsher. "Get over there, or I'll shoot you. I'm not bluffing."

The man's expression doesn't change. But what was I expecting? Fear? They can't feel fear. They're abominations. They don't feel anything—not anything *real*. Just what they've programmed themselves to feel and—

He lunges for me.

I jerk my body back, but my foot catches something. I curse as I'm thrown off balance, and something slams into my back. I turn, but the man is on me suddenly, hands crushing into me as he—

I yell out as he snatches the gun and twists it so my sweaty fingers slip from it. I turn and try to grab him, but he leaps away—too fast, too strong. Of course he would be. I curse.

"Swearing isn't ladylike," the Enhanced says as

he chucks my Luger out of the open window. I stare after it, heart pounding. "Swearing is a sign of the evil controlling you. Let me save you." His lips curl into a smile.

"I'll show you something else that isn't ladylike." I punch him hard, aiming under his jaw. My knuckles catch him, but only as he turns, and most of the energy is rebuffed through my arm.

My eyes jerk to the bolted doorway—I'm nearer it now.

The man scrabbles back toward me, but I'm ready. I kick him hard, and I turn, throw my weight backward and duck under his arm as he strikes out. I grab the potted plant from the desk and propel it at him. It hits him in the stomach, and he falters. The ceramic pot shatters when it hits the floor. I'm disappointed it misses his feet, but it produces shards. If I can get one, I'm confident I can kill him with it alone. He'd scream, but I could muffle the sounds, prevent other Enhanced from coming here and finding me and Elf.

I turn fast, head pounding, see the coffee table, and jump over it. I land like a cat on the other side and feel the way adrenaline rewards me. I shove the table at him, upturning it, sending things everywhere, and then lunge for the ceramic fragments.

The Enhanced must realize my plan, because he moves at the same moment, shoving a chair to his right where it crashes into the small, wooden cupboard. He reaches the broken mess first—superhuman speed—and grabs me, yanks me back into the center of the room, away from the dagger-like pieces.

His hand stays around my arm, and I stare at it, aghast.

You really have been caught.

Shit. Shit. Shit.

I can't be caught—can't be converted!

I throw my weight backward, try to throw him off balance, yet he remains strong. Too strong. And I'm still human—properly human. I can use that to my advantage. But how? Need to think.

With his free hand, the Enhanced man plucks my glasses from my face.

His lips twist into a smile as he sees my eyes: his confirmation.

"First time you've seen one of us?" I ask, grinning.

"No."

"Then you should know that we work in packs. Much like you do." I stand taller. "Now, you're going to let me go, else I'll bring a whole army of Untamed in here. All with their guns and violent thoughts and *murderous* intentions. Shall I scream?"

I have no intention of doing so, but he pauses—and is that worry on his face?

"They're just out there." I jerk my head to the window. "Why don't you look? You'll want to see how many there are before I bring them here, yes? You don't like the element of surprise, do you?"

He turns his head.

I punch him and twist around, my whole body thumping with energy. I kick out at him. My foot connects with his shin; the man grunts, but doesn't let me go—he pulls me closer, snarling in a somewhat comical way that makes my lips twitch. Even their snarls are fake. I'm a good fighter—I know I am; I'm the best in Rahn's group—but the Enhanced are upgrading their augmenters, getting stronger and stronger. And this man shouldn't be this good—not with violence, because that's what it is. Fighting me like this is *violent*.

I bring my left foot down as hard as I can, straight onto his foot. At the same time, I throw my weight forward—into him. He stumbles, and I twist, feint a punch with my free arm. He reacts as I want and the momentum throws us both to the left. We crash onto the desk at the side of the room, me beneath him, sending the desk across the floor a few feet, papers flying up. A laptop falls to the floor. The desk's wooden edge digs into the back of my knees as I swing my legs back and forth, kicking him as he leans over me.

The images in his eyes reflect, try to distract me. I look away, breathing hard. He still hasn't produced any augmenters for me yet. That's good. I turn my head, see a biro still on the desk. Can I stab him with that?

But, before I can think, his hand slams over my mouth. I bite his fingers as hard as I can. He withdraws his hand immediately. I try to move, but he's still got me there, he's too strong.

"You ba—" I yell, but the air whooshes out of my lungs, cutting me off.

The man falters, but only a bit. I try to twist around, to see—

I remember the Swiss army knife in my pocket, and *why the hell* haven't I used it yet? I wriggle, trying to get enough room to move my arm, to get it, but I can't. His weight's too heavy, and he's too strong.

And then an augmenter flashes above me: a small vial of blue liquid, an addictive substance that only allows its user to feel good emotions. *Artificial* emotions that clog up a person. The augmenters steal humanity, steal souls.

"It'll be over soon, wild one," the Enhanced whispers. And his voice is dark. Dark and dangerous, but there's something else mixed in there too. Something… Something I can't place, and there's no time to think. No time to remember.

The augmenter is right there.

"No!" I try to bite his fingers again, but he moves them deftly out of the way. I wriggle, trying again to move—to get the knife from my pocket—but he leans onto me more, crushing me.

The look on his face hasn't changed. He still looks happy—*and* a little curious. He's saving me. That's what he thinks. That's what they all think.

He flicks the cap off, and I hear it bounce as it lands on the desk behind my head.

So close.

Inches away. The vial is inches away. And he's closer, leaning over me, his body pressing against mine as he holds me down and moves the augmenter closer…closer…closer….

I ram my forehead into his.

Pain breaks out before my eyes, and he falls away from the desk, pulls me with him. In the second before I crash on top of him on the floor, I see the pain in his expression—pain he shouldn't be able to feel. Or is pain not an emotion, a physical state that they can still feel? Before I can work it out, I land on him, sprawling out onto the paper-strewn floor, and my head whacks down toward him again. I try to stop myself, and—

Our mouths press against each other. Hard. My lips are parted. His aren't.

He tenses.

I freeze.

Get out.

I use him as a board to push myself up, but his hand shackles my wrist. Hot fingers, like rope.

"No," he says, and there's no pain in his voice—the headbutt didn't hurt him much? What kind of augmenters has he taken? "You…you need saving."

"Like hell!" I shove him back into the floor, but he's strong and we're struggling now—an even match? Or has he got the upper hand? And he's going to get another augmenter out for me—any second now.

You can't become one of them!

And I *can't*. They're wiping us out, converting us Untamed, making us all 'happy' and 'perfect'—even 'correcting' our bodies and abilities—destroying what it means to be human: to have flaws, to *live*. Because when they choose what they feel—or when the others choose for them—they're not living. They don't feel the rush of adrenaline at an unexpected turn of events…like a surprising kiss.

They kidnap our people and forcibly convert us because they think they're enlightened, that they know better. They really think they're 'saving' humanity, making mankind better, destroying negative emotions. That's why we're a threat: we can display violence, we can hurt them. Sure, our numbers aren't great, and we can only reconvert them if they've been Enhanced for less than a week—and even then, people aren't the same.

We can't impact Enhanced society that greatly. But we're their reminder that their world isn't truly perfect yet. We exist. That's why they're after us. I'm sure they get a kick out of forcing augmenters down our throats, showing their dominance, that they're the 'greater' humans.

If I become Enhanced, it'll be my choice. Not because some man thinks he knows what's best for me. A man who can't even see that he's exchanged his soul for his lifetime of happiness and security.

I try to yank my body away from him, need to get up and get out. But his grip is too tight, and he keeps me where I am—on top of him. I manage to elbow him, but it's not that effective, barely makes him grunt. I go to punch him, but he blocks it somehow. My breathing ratchets up a notch. His fingers dig painfully into my shoulder. And I know I need to do something *now*.

Then my eyes widen.

When our mouths touched, he froze. I had the advantage then.

I lean into him, grab his head with both my hands, and kiss him hard, ignoring the internal screaming within me. His lips are soft—surprisingly soft—but they're firm too, and—

His grip on me slackens beautifully, and I use the opportunity to push his head back a little, give myself more room. I need to get away, and I'm painfully aware of how on top of him—and *kissing him*—I am. Every part of me wants to stop kissing him, but I can feel the difference. He's not fighting me, not when I'm kissing him.

Keep kissing him.

I do, and I try not to think about *who* I'm kissing.

Except, of course, I do. *Kissing the enemy.* My pulse surges. Oh, if the others could see this! A strange kind of excitement fizzles through me, and I try to push it down. Need to think—need to keep kissing him, keep him distracted. And I need to get away from him. Can I run to the bolted door from here? Would I have enough time to open it? Is he distracted enough? How much of this is he going to feel if he's not taken Lust or Passion or whatever sexy augmenters they have?

He makes a noise deep in his throat, sounds like he's enjoying it. He must feel some of it. Or maybe it's making him feel happy—they all take Happiness in their daily concoctions, don't they?

I kiss him harder, imagining he's Nico. Except this man kisses me back in a way that Nico never has. This man isn't restrained. He's not worried. He puts everything into it.

And he's an *Enhanced.*

His hand moves from restraining me to holding me, gently—just like that. I turn my head slightly, moving to kiss his throat, my eyes searching the carpet for anything that might help when I move to get away. I don't know how quickly he'll recover. I kiss the soft skin at the base of his neck, wonder if I can bite through an artery or something important there.

Then I see it.

The knife. *His* knife. The Swiss army knife. Must've fallen out of my pocket. But that's perfect.

His breathing is heavy as I move my right arm slowly. I kiss his mouth again, his tongue pressing against mine, and fight the waves of shock in me as I feel his body respond.

Time seems to stand still as I move my hand inch by inch, still kissing him. My fingers click as I wrap them around the Swiss army knife.

He moans.

Now.

I pull the knife toward me and manage to flick the blade out using one hand. Then I stab him in the shoulder in one swift motion.

What the hell? His shoulder! You should've gone for the abdominal aorta!

His eyes spring open as his body jerks. "You—"

I yank my knife out of him and catapult away, through the office and—

"Keelie!" the Enhanced man yells.

Part of me falters. He knows my name?

Stab him again! Kill him!

But I ignore the voice in my head. I know when it's time to abandon the plan, when it's time to retreat. Ten years ago, I wouldn't have, but even though Rahn's a pain, I'm more sensible now. And I've got to think of the others.

Is it sensible though, leaving him alive? Why are you leaving him alive?

I push the voice away.

The small wooden cupboard is against the wall, near the bolted door—pushed over here in the fight—and I leap on top of it and slide the door's bolt back before the momentum of my jump sends me to the floor. I grab the door handle, turn it, push the door, and…it doesn't move. Doesn't move at all.

I freeze. Look up. The bolt's definitely clear.

"It gets stuck," the Enhanced man whispers.

I turn my head in a flash. He's sitting up, but he's not coming after me. He's slumped by the desk, blood pouring out of his shoulder. And his eyes— they're mirrors; *of course* they're mirrors, but there's something else too. Recognition?

No. That's stupid.

He doesn't know me. He can't know me. I don't know him. I've never seen him before.

But he knows my name.

"You have to push it harder," the man says. He brings a hand up to his shoulder, and he's trying to stop the bleeding, but he's doing it all wrong and not pressing firmly enough. He's not even looking at the wound; his face is tilted toward me. "The door… Push it harder… It gets stuck."

My shoulders tighten. Like I couldn't work that out myself.

"Your glasses," he croaks, and he raises his good arm, points.

My eyes snap to them. They're on the floor, next to him. If I go to them, he'll grab me. It's a trap.

"Your eyes are beautiful, but you can't go back out there without the glasses on," he says.

And he's looking at me, and I don't like the way he's looking at me. It's too…familiar.

"I'll take that chance," I say, waving the knife.

"Okay," the Enhanced man whispers. "Run now."

Sweat pours down my back, down my forehead, down my arms. I grab the door handle, twist it, and throw my weight at the door. *All* my weight. The door flies open, and I trip over the threshold, land on my knees.

But I'm up in an instant, looking over my shoulder. The Enhanced hasn't moved. He hasn't pounced on me. He hasn't even tried. He just watches me; he's letting me get away.

Why?

But I know I can't think about that now.

I run.

TWO

"WE NEED TO GO!" I hiss at Elf as I reach him, my voice a little too loud than it should be. He's still in the same place, and I pull him away.

My heart pounds. We need to meet Nico, Yani, and Rahn at the meeting place, and then get back to Nbutai. I look back toward the office, expecting the man to come out—or for other Enhanced Ones to appear in the forecourt—but no one does.

"What?" Elf says, his voice low. "Where are your glasses? What the hell's happened to you?"

I try to wipe the still-wet blade of the knife on my jacket as I slow to a brisk walk, keeping a lookout all around. I want to run as fast as I can, but I know that would be a dead giveaway. "There was a bloody Enhanced One in there!"

Through his heavily tinted glasses, I see Elf's eyes widen, and suddenly it's so obvious that these glasses aren't enough—we need ones like Rahn's, even if they do block most of the sun out.

"Did you kill him? Where's your gun?"

Shit. The gun.

I look back. It's there—on the ground, just outside

the window. How didn't Elf see it being thrown out? How didn't that alert him something was wrong? What the hell was he doing?

And now my gun's lying there.

I make up my mind in a split second. I run for it, pocketing my knife on the way. Elf shouts my name—stupid! I skid on the gravel, stooping down to reach it and—

I see his face above me, at the window, and let out a squeak. It's the Enhanced man—*of course* it is. I freeze. His hand reaches out the window, toward me, and he drops something.

Paper—folded up. It lands next to me, blood-stained. Fresh blood.

"Take it!" the Enhanced hisses. "Take it, and you'll understand."

And then he's gone—gone farther into the office and—

"Keelie!" Elf yells.

My heart does a funny loop-the-loop motion. What harm can it do? I pick up the paper and pocket it, then grab my gun, and run back to where Elf's now partly hidden himself from sight of the office window.

"Got the keys?" Elf's staring at me as I tuck my Luger back into my waistband. He hands me the spare pair of glasses from his survival bag, and I put them on. "The truck... Where are the keys?"

I stop, my head throbbing. My hands pat at my pockets, but there's no set of keys there. Just the knife. I curse. Of course, I threw the set at the man. And I didn't have a chance to gather up the others.

I shake my head. "Come on!" I shout too loudly and wince; we still need to be quiet. We need to get away unharmed, uncaught.

We leave. Elf and I both know the drill, and we're twins of the stars: we don't always need to communicate out loud. I just know what he's going to do, and he knows what I'm going to do. We've always been like that.

But he didn't know when you were getting caught.

I push that thought away.

Several blocks away, we slow to a more relaxed walk. The buildings are closer together here, and each wall is lined with windows. Walk steadily, that's what we need to do. Walking in an Enhanced compound is both my least and most favorite thing to do. With every step, I expect them to jump out, to realize who I am—what I am—and grab me. But the thrill of danger it sends through me is like a drug, it feeds me, nourishes me. Its presence says I'm alive, and I *live* to feel adrenaline coursing through my system. To feel the beat of my pounding heart, to know that I'm dancing with danger.

We walk out of the town as if it's the easiest thing to do. The buildings disappear behind us, and, soon, we're back in the wilderness, the wild desert; it always amazes me how quickly the Enhanced Ones' settlements start and stop. There are no outskirts, where the sand-colored buildings become farther and farther apart. It's almost like a line has been drawn, and they build on one side and not on the other.

Elf and I move for the cover of the rocks and low vegetation, walking carefully.

The sun beats down on the back of my neck, and I feel sweat forming. Elf glances across at me, then scans the area again. I do the same. New Kimearo is in one of the southerly valleys of the Titian Mountains. Ahead, the land gets steeper, rising to make the great mountains along the horizon.

We're not far from the meeting point now.

"Right. What the hell happened?" Elf looks at me, a sense of urgency on his face now that we can speak freely.

"I told you, there was an Enhanced in there." I kick at a loose stone, watch as dust rises.

A sideways glance tells me that Elf does not look happy.

"And your gun? It was outside the window. How?"

"He disarmed me. No—don't look like that." I wipe my sweaty hands against my jeans. "He was strong, a better fighter than most. What were you doing? Didn't you see him throw it out of the window?"

He shakes his head. "I went back around the other buildings—thought I heard something. I thought you'd be all right." Then he swears. "I should've gone in there, not you."

"Elf, I can handle it—I got away, didn't I?"

He scowls as I sum up the rest of the events, briefly. I expect him to have some sort of crazy reaction when I talk of how I kissed the Enhanced, but he doesn't. Just glowers.

I check behind us. The town's fading in the hot, shimmering air. It looks surreal.

"Rahn's going to want to know about this," he says after a long moment.

I smile. Now the adrenaline's subsiding, I'm starting to concentrate on how best to tell the tale.

"Don't exaggerate it," Elf warns. "We can tell when you do that, and it just annoys people."

Rahn, Nico, and Yani are already by our vehicle—one of the blue L200s—behind the boulders near First Rock when Elf and I arrive. It's one of our less-used meeting places, an hour's walk from New Kimearo.

Rahn, Nbutai's leader, stands with his back against a boulder, and his arms crossed in front of his chest. The sun dances off his dark glasses. Next to him, Nico and Yani are looking at one of the foxhole radios Three made. Nico has the earpiece against his right ear, and he's frowning. I guess the signal's still not good.

"About time," Rahn snaps as Elf and I join him.

I look in the truck bed and see they've already

moved my motorbike into it. We brought it along and stowed it by the rocks a little way off in case Rahn's group needed a quick exit, so they wouldn't leave Elf and I without an escape option—just as well when we didn't obtain a new vehicle. But they should've waited until we were back before moving it.

"You secured it all right?" I ask, pushing the sleeves of my jacket up. I don't want my bike falling over.

"Of course," Nico says.

"Why'd it take you so long?" Rahn jabs a finger toward me. "We got here ages ago. We were thinkin' you'd been caught and were listenin' out for the broadcast." He shakes his head. "Where's the new truck?"

"Didn't get it."

"You didn't get it?" Rahn tilts his head to one side, slowly. "So all this has been for nothin'?" He jerks his thumb at Yani. "He nearly got caught in the distraction. We only just got out of there in time."

"Keelie got caught," Elf says.

The effect that Elf's words have on the three men couldn't be more different. Rahn scowls and immediately looks back down the slope toward the town, no doubt scanning for approaching Enhanced Ones. Yani takes his glasses off and wipes the back of his hand across his tired eyes, then makes the *thank you* sign to the Gods and Goddesses—presumably, pleased I'm here, not that I was caught. He makes that sign a lot, particularly after the Turnings when our group's made it through the spirits' rages because it's never a guarantee; nothing about the spirits can ever be guaranteed. And Nico rushes up to me, encloses me in a sweaty hug, and presses his lips against my forehead.

I pull back, peeling myself from Nico's sweaty body, trying not to breathe in his stale odor.

"What happened?" Rahn points at me.

I tell them all quickly. My hands still feel oily, and I wipe them on my jeans. "And look." I pull the Swiss army knife out of my pocket. "Got this too—it's even got a tin-opener."

Rahn peers at me once I've finished speaking.

"You *seduced* an Enhanced?" He looks like he might be sick.

I put the knife away and fold my arms. "I did it to get away. Last resort."

"I don't like this," Rahn says. "Why did he let you go?"

And why did you leave him alive?

"And how'd he know your name?" Nico asks, his tone dark. He steps closer to me, and, for a moment, I think I'm in for another hug. "They don't have profiles on us, do they?"

Everyone's looking at me now. I rub my arms. Sand sticks to the fine hairs there, and I try to brush the specks off.

I shrug. "I don't know the answer to either of those questions."

Rahn shakes his head. "You don't know him, do you—that Enhanced man?"

"Of course not. It's not like I meet up with the Enhanced in secret, is it?" I straighten up, and something in my back clicks.

"It's no one we've lost to them? No one who might know us?" Yani asks, but we all know there's no one from Nbutai who's been caught in recent years— there's no one it could be.

"So you didn't get no truck, and you nearly got yourself caught by an Enhanced who knew who you were? That right?" Rahn asks.

I nod, and my hands go automatically to the pockets of my leather jacket again. I pat them down, but there's nothing—nothing but the knife and the folded note the Enhanced gave me. Frowning, I pull it out.

Rahn grunts at me. "What's that?"

"It's what the Enhanced gave me, when I retrieved my gun. He dropped it out of the window. I told you."

"What's it say?"

It takes me a moment to stop my fingers from clenching it. I unfold it carefully. The paper looks old, like it could tear along the creases if I'm not careful.

It's blank.

"Nothing." I show it to them.

"Nothin'?" Rahn shrugs. "Throw it away. Could be a tracker or somethin'. We don't want nothin' that'll give away our location."

"But it's *paper*," Elf says. He leans across and takes it from me and turns it over. "It's just paper. Their technology's not *that* advanced."

"They can make augmenters—that's advanced enough," Rahn snaps. "And what about their sensors at some of their cities that pick up if you're Untamed?"

"Yeah, but that's all that's advanced: anything to do with capturing us," Elf says, his gaze briefly on Yani as the older of the Milton brothers leans against the truck. "Look, the firearms, the vehicles—they're all the same types that have been around for years. They're not developing new ones—or, at least, not many— because augmenters and things that detect us are their main focus." He pauses, and I wonder if he realizes that he's invalidated his own argument. "I don't really see how they could make this paper into a tracker."

"We can't risk it." Rahn grits his teeth. "One mistake, and we're dead. We have to assume he gave that paper to Keelie for a reason. And what's their number one purpose concernin' us? To convert us. Of course they're makin' new technologies to do that, to help them."

"But he let me get away," I point out.

"After you stuck your tongue down his throat." Rahn doesn't attempt to hide the disgust in his voice, and Nico doesn't try to hide the look of absolute fury on his face. "And he still tried to convert you. Just throw that paper away."

"But Three always wants paper—says he needs to draw out circuit boards and make notes on how he makes the radios."

35

"He should know that off-by-heart," Rahn says. "Writin' stuff down is for kids." He glances at me. "Fine. Keep it. Give it to Three." But he doesn't sound happy about it. "Now, we've got to go."

By the time we return to Nbutai, the sky is darkening, and I can only just make out the outlines of the huts. Our village is hidden away in a crook in the Titian Mountains, and the spirits and Gods and Goddesses protect us. They protect all the Untamed—all of us who won't give in to the Enhanced and their 'perfect' lives—and they warn our Seers if our locations have been compromised.

I shut my eyes briefly, willing myself not to be transported back to *that day*. For a second, I see Caia-Lu's face in front of me—she hadn't been active for nearly a year, we don't know why, what she'd done to make the spirits and Gods and Goddesses turn their backs on her, on us. Unless it was something external blocking Caia-Lu? Grief can do it. But Caia-Lu wasn't still grieving, was she? Yet we had no active Seer at D'Elinous; that's why the Enhanced were able to ambush us.

"I don't like it. It doesn't seem right," Elf says. He hasn't shaven for a few days, and he pulls at the short hairs sprouting from his chin. "That Enhanced let you go—even helped you with the door and reminded you about the glasses. It doesn't make sense."

We're in our hut—the one we've shared with our sisters for the last five years after we built the new huts following a bad storm—and we're tucking into Marouska's soup.

Elf points his spoon at me. "What do you think?"

"I don't know."

"Where's your bag? Your survival kit?"

I turn to look. Then I realize it's still in the dealership office. "I must've left it there."

"Was your name on your bag?" Elf says. "Or on anything inside it?"

I frown. "My compass has a K on it. But it was at the bottom of my bag. He wouldn't have seen that. And he knew my name. *Keelie*, he said."

Elf frowns harder. "What about the food-packs? Marouska would've written your name on it so you got the right one."

"But weren't they all the same?" I've got a fish allergy, but I'm pretty sure all the food-packs had bread and dried meat in them this time.

"There's got to be some way he knew your name. That would account for it."

Except that even if my name was on the food-pack, it still didn't leave my bag—not in the time I was in the office. The Enhanced will probably have analyzed it by now, looking for clues as to our location, but we're careful to keep nothing in the bags that links them to Nbutai.

Elf shovels more soup into his mouth.

"So why did he let me go?" I muse.

"And why did he give you blank paper? You still got it?"

I slide the paper from my pocket. I haven't had a chance to take it to the Sarrs' hut for Three yet.

"I don't like this. That man's not acting normally—not for them. Not after you kissed him."

I laugh, folding the paper up. I put it into the pocket of my jeans carefully. "Maybe that's the secret? Seduce them, then they see us as people—you know, people who have their own rights and can live how they want—and they'll let us get away."

"It's worth knowing," a light voice says, and I turn toward the entrance to see Five standing there.

She invites herself into our hut and sits on the edge of my bed. Her long, bare legs stretch out in front of her, and I see the color rush to Elf's face as he so obviously looks away. I know for a fact my brother's interested in Five, but he's got the idea in his head that the four-year age gap is too much, especially when she's older. According to him, girls always want an older man. By that logic, the only girl he believes might be interested in him is Seven, but I can't see that ever happening. Seven's too shy, and Elf's always lusting after the older Sarr sister.

"So, was he a good kisser?" Five asks me, her lips twitching. News spreads fast here.

I shoot her a look, but she just grins, then lies back. She holds up a hand, and I see her nails are painted with the red polish that Elf got her a while ago when he was raiding.

Five sighs, exasperated. "Come on, Kee. *Was* he a good kisser? Maybe if we made them all our lovers we could live harmoniously? Kiss away their desire to convert and all that."

"They're monsters." Elf's voice is quiet. "Touching them…kissing them is *disgusting*." He glances at me. "I'm surprised you had the nerve."

I raise my eyebrows. "It was a matter of life and death."

Elf just shrugs. "Don't go getting any ideas—either of you."

The corners of Five's mouth twitch, tugging the smile out of her. Elf frowns, and she makes an excuse to leave rather quickly.

"What was that about?" I turn on Elf. "Five was only joking—as if *we're* going to become *their* lovers."

"It's not something we should joke about." Elf yawns and places his soup bowl at his feet. "And it's late, no time for chatting and joking anyway. We need to be fresh tomorrow, prepared for anything and everything. I wouldn't be surprised if that Enhanced showed up here looking for you, Keelie. Wouldn't be surprised at all."

THREE

THE UNTAMED WOMAN IS IN a pale blue room, sitting at a table. She's not restrained this time, because these people insist that they are nice, that before it was for her own good. They had to make sure she didn't run before, but now they know she won't.

"Here it is." The man hands the woman the vial, and she tries not to look at his mirror eyes, tries not to feel the fear.

Her fingers seem to stick to the augmenter, but she's shaking. The battle is raging within her.

"Drink it up." Another man beams at her. His teeth are perfect, and he has a silver ring through his left eyebrow. The artificial lighting catches the ring, and a myriad of colors is reflected on the opposite wall.

"Come on. Drink it."

She doesn't drink it. She never does — not voluntarily.

They know what they have to do.

And I don't want to watch.

But they always make me watch.

"Such a shame." The first man shakes his head. "But it's for your own good."

Then he nods.

"Take her to the conversion room. We'll do her again.

She's strong, but she'll succumb to us in the end."

I wake up, bathed in sweat, gulping down air as if I need a hundred times the usual amount. It takes me a few moments to breathe normally.

I look across at Elf, consider whether to tell him. I used to tell him all the time, right after the nightmares started. But my screams also woke him and Bea and Mila, and I couldn't *not* tell them.

I listen. It's still dark—I can't see Elf clearly, but I can hear his deep breathing. He's sleeping. I listen harder, and then I make out the sounds of Bea and Mila breathing too. Mila's eleven now, and Bea's been teaching her the names of the different plants and which ones are edible. Bea's memory is amazing— she knows far more than I do, and she can always remember exactly where each plant is. Or where anything is. And taking Mila out to learn about the plants is something she does most evenings—she prefers to have structure, a routine to follow, when she can.

I sit up slowly and wipe my sweaty hands on my blanket. To my right, I see Caia-Lu's Watcher Doll. It's not a real one now—not a token connected to the spirits, a token to guard us, because it can only be real when a Seer uses it. I don't know how it ended up in my bag when we escaped. The last I saw of it, Caia-Lu had it, and then she disappeared.

I offered the Watcher Doll to Katya once, but she said she had her pendant, said it must be the equivalent; it's only natural that different Untamed groups would have different means of keeping a Seer and their people safe. Katya's pendant keeps her from getting permanently stuck in the Dream Land once she's been summoned there. She didn't need the Watcher Doll—but I think she realized I did. Because, apart from my siblings, it's the only bit of my old life left that's mine. And it's comforting to have it. Even though the token's empty.

I pick it up now and look at it. It's not even a doll, so I don't know why it's called a Watcher Doll—it's the name it's always had. It's a carefully carved wooden ellipsoid with two dents on one side. A ring of bright red paint circles the ellipsoid at its widest point. When I was little, Caia-Lu told me it represented the world, and the ring of paint is the energy around the world that keeps us safe. If I was a Seer, I'd be able to call spirits to the Watcher Doll, to protect us. The *good* spirits, that is. Their power would be held in by the red ring, and they'd be bound to our group to help us all, not just to prevent the Seer from becoming trapped in the Dream Land.

The Turnings happen more frequently here, so I listen to the spirits shrieking and howling fairly regularly. Still, they're around at other times too. They're always around somewhere, usually causing chaos and danger or killing us. Apparently, they appeared shortly after the first humans converted themselves into the Enhanced. But the spirits also help our Seers, help with the visions of the future, along with the Gods and Goddesses. So they're on our side, mostly.

And so the Watcher Doll makes me feel safe—even though I know the protection I feel from it isn't real. Isn't a guarantee.

And the dream isn't real either.

It's my imagination, as always. But, just in case, I don't let myself sleep.

Better to be safe than sorry.

A DANGEROUS GAME

The next morning, I punch Finn as hard as I can, aiming for the soft, fleshy bit under his jaw. My fist connects there at a right angle, and he staggers back. He'll have wonderful bruises there tomorrow, and I grin, then pounce forward. My body slams into his, and I grab his arm, manage to twist it behind his back and use the advantage to shove him across the line.

Pain flashes across his face. Pain and annoyance.

We never hold back with each other, and he doesn't like getting beaten by a girl. That only makes my victory sweeter.

"Okay!" Nico shouts, jumping up. "That's it."

"What?" I yell. "Already?"

"You've beaten him."

I pause for a moment, then let go of Finn, and clap him on the back. It's my attempt at making sure he's all right—although it is a half-hearted attempt. He grimaces and looks at me sideways, a glimmer of something indistinguishable in his eyes.

A little way off, I see Mila sitting cross-legged on the sand, watching. Her face lights up in a huge grin as she sees me looking, and she waves. I smile back. Then she gets up and scampers toward our hut.

I can't wait to teach Mila how to fight properly. I've taught her the basics, but I'll have to wait until she's a bit older to really get into it. I think then the two of us will really connect, that our sisterly bond will grow. I'm only just starting to feel like I know how to treat her as a sister. Before, she was just a small child who I never really felt able to interact with. Stupid, right?

Nico joins us, looks between me and Finn for a few moments.

He doesn't say anything until Finn's gone. Then he turns those big eyes on me. They're the kind of eyes that make Five go soppy, but, for the last few weeks, they've been annoying me. Five says that means I don't appreciate Nico enough, especially given his interest and how we're sort of together.

"You didn't really need to do that, did you?" Nico

42

keeps his voice low and neutral in tone, though I know exactly what he's getting at—because he's always getting at it.

"If you don't like it, you don't have to watch. I'll find someone else to referee."

Nico sighs. "That's not what I meant. I just don't think you need to fight anyone. Not like that."

I wipe sweat from my face with the bottom of my T-shirt. "How else am I going to stay in tip-top condition?"

"There are plenty of other ways."

I kick at a loose stone and watch it dart across the hard ground. "But to be a good fighter you have to practice and *actually fight* people. Lifting weights and running isn't enough. I need to *fight* to get better. And I need to get better."

"You *are* better," Nico says. "You're the best out of all of us. You know that. Everyone knows that. You have been for ages. You're the strongest we have."

"Not strong enough. That Enhanced nearly had me. If I hadn't kissed him—and surprised him—I'd be one of them by now." As soon as I've said the words, I realize I shouldn't have—reminding Nico of what I did to distract the Enhanced will only make his mood sourer.

His expression darkens, and his nostrils flare as he breathes out heavily.

"I need to be stronger, Nico," I say quickly. I shake my head, then flex my arms. I feel pumped, and the energy's buzzing through me. I need to use it. Need to feel my heart pounding. "I have to be stronger. I have to be able to protect myself. It's always the weak ones who don't make it. Survival of the fittest."

Nico grabs my hand. "Keelie, just listen."

"What?"

"I know you have issues with control—because of what happened—but this isn't—"

"Issues with control?" I stare at him.

For a second, I think he's going to look at the ground

and back down like he nearly always does—but he doesn't. Nico raises his head and looks at me straight on.

"I don't know all the details of what happened to you and Elf and Bea and Mila at your old village. But I know that whatever it was, you think it was your fault. You think it was because you were weak—and now you're trying to overcompensate."

Heat rushes to my face, just as tension fills my jaw. "You're right. You don't know what happened then—"

"I know the look of a person whose guilt is eating them," he says quickly. "And this isn't healthy. All this fighting, obsessing about your muscles and how strong you look, it's not healthy—not for a girl."

"Not for a girl?" I let out a shrill laugh.

Nico takes a small step back. "It's not healthy for anyone to be obsessed with fitness as much as you are."

I stare at him, unsure whether to feel bewildered or amazed. Part of me can't believe he's actually saying this. I flex my muscles, flaunting them in front of him. I know I'm stronger than he is, and I also know that it's something he doesn't like. He's one of those people who believes that men should always be the stronger, better gender. Part of me is surprised that he even went for me, given my strength, but now I realize I'm a challenge for him. He wants to break me, make me weaker. If he can persuade me not to work out as much, so that he's the stronger of the two of us, he can say he's conquered me.

"*This* isn't healthy?" I raise my eyebrows; two can play at this game. "Well, I've seen how out of breath *you* get on a run—and how you pretend you're not. And you try to hide it, but you fail, Nico. And now you're jealous of me—because my level of fitness shows you up. You're being a typical guy and trying to control me." My voice is dangerously loud, but I can't stop now. "Is this what it's going to be like if we ever get together properly? You trying to stop me from doing things?" I point at him. "Because you have no right."

Nico holds up his hands. "I'm just saying it's not your fault, and you don't need to prove yourself."

"And I'm saying you need to respect my decision. If I want to fight and train, then I *will* fight and train. You're not going to stop me. How dare you talk about what happened at D'Elinous? You know nothing."

I stalk off, fuming. It's been a few months since Nico and I have had an encounter like that. Most times now, we're good. Well, *more* than good.

Angrily, I push away those memories. Still, he can be a jerk.

"Hey, Keelie!"

I look up, see Five coming toward me. She grins and waves.

"Haven't been kissing any more Enhanced?" she asks. Then she sees the expression on my face and frowns. "What's happened?"

"Nico," I mutter. "That's what's happened."

She sighs and rolls her eyes. "Explain."

I do as we walk back to the huts. When I've finished, I expect some sort of solidarity reaction, but she just shrugs.

"He's just being caring."

"No, he's being controlling. There's a difference. A huge difference."

"You're misreading it," Five says. "Nico's not trying to stop you from doing all your sporty stuff. He's worried about what your motivation for it is. Whether it's harming your mind or something."

I let out an exasperated sigh. "Not you, as well."

She holds up her hand. "Hey! I'm perfectly happy to change the subject—say to that Enhanced man." Excitement shines suddenly across the whole of her face. "What was it *really* like kissing him?"

I groan.

"Was it like—scary? Because he could've converted you at any moment if he'd wanted to. I bet it made it all the hotter too. Gods, imagine if you two fell in love! Think how romantic that would be—forbidden love and all."

"Forbidden love never ends well," I say. "It's not supposed to. That's why it's *forbidden*. And you have a completely unrealistic view of the world. As if one of us would ever be with one of them. Elf's right. It is disgusting."

"I haven't heard you complaining about making out with one of them though," Five says, raising her eyebrows. "I'm right, aren't I? He was a great kisser."

"Well you go and find him then!"

Five smirks. "Maybe that's why you're so mad at Nico."

"What?"

"Because *he's* not as good."

A few choice words come to mind, but I don't give Five the satisfaction of hearing me say them. Instead, I ask about her and Elf. More specifically, when they're ever going to get together.

I give her a pointed look. "I know you're interested. You flirt with him all the time. And it's not really fair if you don't make a move on him."

"More romantic if the guy does it," she says.

I snort. "Yeah, and Elf's never going to do that. I guarantee it. But I'm pretty sure he's in love with you."

Five blushes, and I know I've got her.

"Okay," she says finally. "But I'm not making any promises."

I smile, and I'm surprised to realize how much better I feel. "Deal."

"And one more thing," Five says. "You really look awful, Keelie. Like you've had no sleep for days. Rahn's got you down on the scouting rota for tonight, so I'd go and get some sleep now if I were you. You can sleep in our hut—Dad's gone out hunting with Kayden, and Mum's helping Three with his copper. They're trying to get the coating off it—you know, the one that burns our fingers." She straightens up. "I don't know where Seven is, but she won't mind you sleeping there. We've got the blackout blind up at the moment, so you can get it pretty dark."

I nod slowly. "Why can't I sleep in my hut?"

"Didn't you hear? Mila's started one of her tea parties in there with Esther and Bea. And Mila's singing again. They'll be hours, and you won't get any sleep in there."

I can't help but smile. My youngest sister is amazing at singing, and she sings all the time now.

"Thanks. I'll go to your hut."

A few minutes later, I enter the Sarrs' hut. It's one of the smallest of all the huts, despite it being home to the biggest family. But that's just the way things are around here, especially when Rahn is in charge. It's no secret that he doesn't like the Sarrs.

The blackout blind is in place above the window, and I pull it down, and the hut plummets into near darkness. I feel my way to the corner where Five's bed is—a few blankets on top of a grass mattress—and lie down. Something digs into my hip and I sit up, feeling for something on the mattress. But there's nothing there. I lie down again, then realize that whatever it is isn't on the mattress, but in the pocket of my jeans.

My fingers close around something pointy inside the pocket. A thick piece of plastic—one of Mila's jokes. She's always hiding them in our clothing because she thinks it's funny when we find them at random times. I scowl, then put it back in my pocket at a different angle, and my fingers brush against something else: the note the Enhanced man gave me. I pull it out. I'll put it in my other pocket, away from Mila's plastic stick, and—

Light catches my eye.

Light, from the note.

I sit up. My eyes widen.

I unfold the paper and stare.

Glow-in-the-dark ink?

My mouth dries as I read the words the Enhanced

wrote. Everything seems to stop.

I mouth the words over and over, and I start to feel sick.

I know what happened to your parents. I know what you did.

FOUR

I STARE AT THE PAPER, faintly aware of how my breathing quickens. The letters jump out at me, and I blink several times, still mouthing the words.

I know what happened to your parents. I know what you did.

My fingers are cold.

But that Enhanced can't know. *He can't.*

I look around quickly as unease fills me. My shoulders roll forward, and my spine is uncomfortable.

He's bluffing. There's only one other person who knows what I did, and he's dead.

I know what you did.

The more I look at the words, the more it sounds like a threat, but that's stupid. I curse under my breath. It's just some sick game. It has to be. He realized he shouldn't have let me go and wanted to unsettle me, scare me. Who knows how many notes like these they give out?

Except they don't. I know that. Because they don't let any Untamed get away.

But he did.

And he wasn't acting normally.

49

I press my lips together. There's a metallic taste in my mouth. I fold the note quickly and stuff it back into my pocket. My ears pop as I swallow, and the sudden pain makes me jump. I look around the Sarrs' hut— still can't see anything—and suddenly wish I was in my own hut. At least there, I know where everything is and I'm surrounded by my own stuff. But, here, it's unfamiliar, and it makes me more nervous.

I chew on my lip, then run my hands up and down my arms. I'll burn the note as soon as I can, when no one's watching, when no one can question me.

I lie back down, vowing to put the note out of my head. I need to sleep, not worry about something that's never going to develop any further—because it isn't. I won't see that man again. My eyes close, and I concentrate on my breathing, try to get it more regular.

But I can't sleep now.

I listen to the sounds outside. The voices in the distance. Someone's banging a stone against something. Something metal. I can hear the *bang, bang, bang*. Tinny sounds.

Every time I start to think about the Enhanced man's note, I force myself to think of something else. It doesn't mean anything. I grit my teeth.

At some point, I must've drifted into a semi-sleep, because I'm suddenly aware of Seven gently shaking me, telling me to get up.

I bolt up. "What is it? Enhanced?"

And I look around, part of me expecting to see that Enhanced man again, with his tattoos peeping out from under his crisp white shirt. What if he's here? What if he's told them—told them about me, what I did?

My chest rises sharply.

Seven shakes her head. "It's time to check the lands."

"Oh, right. Yes. Uh, give me a moment."

She leaves the hut quickly.

A minute later, I follow her out. Seven, Esther, and Kayden are waiting a few feet away, all chewing energy bars and talking, but they stop as soon as they see me.

I point toward them. My eyes fall on one of Mila's skipping ropes nearby. "Are we on foot?"

Kayden nods, and the light emphasizes how he's greased back his red hair. "We're checking over that way." He gestures to the right.

New Kimearo's roughly in that direction, though not visible from here. It's a long, long way away, but I feel nervous, threatened.

I shake my head, realize that I'm being stupid. All this tension is what the Enhanced want us to feel. Then they're justified in saying their way of life is best, that we'd feel better as one of them.

As the four of us head off, a couple of the dogs in tow, I have strong words with myself. I'm not going to let that note affect me. I'm *not*.

"You all right?" Esther looks across at me as we leave Nbutai behind. She uses one stocky hand to shield the sun from her eyes, then bats her dog away as the animal jumps up at her.

I nod.

"You look awful," she says. "You've gone all white."

"Hope that doesn't mean you're getting ill," Kayden says. "We don't want another virus."

The last time our village got sick, most of us were out of commission for weeks. Rahn was the only one who escaped the virus, and he'd had to raid New Kimearo on his own for medical supplies. It hadn't been ideal.

We don't talk much more, we just walk. It's one of our regular routes. We check the immediate area for any changes and scan as far as we can see. If anything strikes us as unusual, then we either investigate it now or send two of us back for backup.

Esther's dog runs ahead with the other mutt. I don't particularly like dogs, but I prefer it when we have one or two of them with us. In general, they're better at sensing stuff and noticing if anything's different or wrong.

I half-expect that we'll find something—discover something—this time, but we don't. It's the same as always. There's nothing to make us worry.

And, by the time, we get back to Nbutai, we're all worn out. The terrain was difficult on that route, and the muscles in my calves ache viciously. Bea's sitting with Elf. They're marking something on the dry ground with a stick, maybe a board for a game or something.

I smile, then head off toward the fire. No one's on fire duty at the moment, and I look around. Corin is the nearest, but he's sorting through a bag of belongings, not paying attention.

I take the Enhanced One's note out of my pocket; the flames hiss as I drop it into the fire.

We're running, weaving through the trees. My heart pounds. There are two of them behind us. And we have no bullets left. My parents missed the only shots they had.

"Let us save you—you poor creatures!" one of the Enhanced Ones yells. Her voice is strangely warped, and it's almost as if the words are twisting around my body, trying to drag me back, trying to drag me toward them.

No.

My mother grabs my hand. My father has Elf's already. I look around for Bea. No one has her hand. And she's screaming, veering off, and she's still got the baby—

"They're gaining on us!" my mother hisses. "We can't outrun them! They're going to get us all!"

And they are… They got… I try not to think of Red, my best friend. But they got him.

I heard his scream. And I turned, and I saw the blood. And I still don't know why there was so much blood, because the Enhanced aren't violent. They say they don't want to hurt us.

But I ran. I chose my family over him. But the Enhanced are still after us.

"Run faster! We can do it!"

But we can't. We know it. We all know it.

"Keelie, Eirnin, Beattie; listen," my father says, his breath labored.

My body jolts; he only calls Elf by his real name when it's important.

"Code one," my father says. "We're going to do code one—me and your mother. You must keep running. You have to keep running. And you have to get away."

Code one? My eyes widen. "What? No—you can't!"

I try to stop, but my mother pulls me along faster.

"We have to, darling. Your father's right!" She sounds strange—it must be the adrenaline. It's like a drug, changing everything. Like augmenters do. "The six of us aren't going to get away from this. And we have to save you! Go south— for weeks, go south. There's another group of us to the far, far south. Rahn Eriksen's group—join it! Look after Mila, teach her about us."

"But—"

"No arguing," my father hisses. "You obey us. It's decided."

"At least we won't be dead," my mother says. "We'll still be alive."

But we're better dead than Enhanced. That's what everyone says. That's what Yuma says. What she says, always—

Yuma's dead.

The shock of that realization pulls through me, makes me feel sick.

"It will save you," my father adds, and his voice wraps around me. "Look after Mila for us!"

And then he melts away.

Time stops. Everything goes white, and I know what's coming next. What always comes, and part of me knows I shouldn't be so self-aware like this, in a dream—but I am. I always gain awareness at this point. But only for a second.

Before it changes.

The trees collapse and shrink into nothing. Elf's face twists past me, and Bea urges me to run as she disappears. Enhanced women enter the room, the scene shifting.

The Untamed man—it's a man this time—is tied to a chair. He's fighting the bindings and rocking the chair back and forth as he tries to get away.

We both know it's useless.

He shouts and screams, swears and curses.

Then he looks at me. His eyes lock onto mine, and, for a second, we both see the images that flash through my mind. The blood. The Untamed eyes. The body.

The man nods, and, in that second, his eyes turn to mirrors. Mirrors that reflect the horror on my *face.*

"You're next."

FIVE

I HATE DREAMING ABOUT MY parents, of anyone from D'Elinous. It's *all* in the past, and I can't do anything to get any of them back.

Sometimes, when I have dream-flashbacks to that night, they morph into one of my nightmares. Maybe that's the worst part: that it merges my last memory of my parents, my people, into something designed to terrify me even more, but merges in a jagged, broken way, where nothing makes sense.

Only my own guilt.

I think of my father's words now, how he said to follow code one. He thought it was admirable—and saving his children *was* admirable, an act done with the best of intentions.

But in the end, they didn't have a choice. They didn't choose to surrender, not really. They thought they had to.

I heard their screams.

And that was the last I heard of them. Two guttural screams. Like animals being slaughtered.

Still, I'm grateful it was *that* part of the night I flashed back to this time. The flashbacks that show the time between Red being shot and my family and I running are the worst. The nightmares that I hate the most because of what I saw and what I did.

I groan and roll over, and—

A folded piece of paper is on my pillow.

I bolt upright, heart pounding, and grab it. My head buzzes. I feel strange.

I unfold it. The writing isn't glow-in-the-dark again. It's plain as day.

First, I go hot. Then I go cold.

Me again, Keelie. Meet me tomorrow, at my office, and tell no one. You'll regret it if you don't follow my wishes.

I stare at the words.

He knows where we live. He's been here. He knows.

They all know—they could be coming. *Shit.*

I jump up, covers flying. Elf, Bea, and Mila are here. I see their sleeping forms. Sleeping or… *Shit.* I'm shaking.

I cross the hut to shake Elf awake. He opens one eye slowly. Untamed. I breathe a sigh of relief.

So the man's been in here…but didn't convert them. That doesn't make sense.

"What is it?" Elf sits up.

I look to where Mila sleeps, then Bea—and I see that what I thought was Bea's sleeping body wasn't. It's a blanket all bunched up. Bea's not there.

"Where is she?"

Panic flares inside me. My heart rate speeds up. I glance toward Elf, but he's just rubbing his eyes.

"She'll have gone for her walk," he mumbles, rolling over and pulling his blanket with him. "Left a while ago."

Bea and her walks. It's not unusual. She often goes off alone. But an *Enhanced One* has been here.

I shove the note into my pocket and pull on shoes, rush outside. The Sarrs' hut isn't far, and I barge right in.

"Katya!"

At first, I can't see her, but then all the Sarrs are

sitting up, staring at me. Three mumbles something, and then Katya stands.

"What is it, Keelie?"

"Have you had a dream?" I yell at her. "A Seeing dream?" My heart pounds heavier, I feel sick. "Have you seen anything? Are we going to be attacked?"

Katya looks at me kindly. Her lips curve into a soft, sympathetic smile. "No, we're safe. It's fine. Is it another of your nightmares?"

I shake my head, breathing hard.

Tell no one, that's what the note said. And the last bit—was that a threat? That I'll regret it if I don't do what he's said?

But, he's been *here*, an Enhanced One has been here—

"Bea's missing," I yell, and I don't know why I'm obeying the commands on the note. I should tell them we're all in danger and—

"No, I'm here," Bea says.

I jump, feel my chest go all jittery as I turn and see Bea standing in the doorway. She looks like she's been up for hours, and her ear defenders are around her neck. She smiles, raising her eyebrows—they're high-arching, and, more than once, I've wished mine were that shape. Then she turns and heads back out.

I rush after her, mumbling something to Katya, but I don't think she knows what I'm saying. I don't even know myself.

Bea spins around in a circle, throwing her arms wide. Her shoulder-length hair spins out around her. "I think I'll teach Mila how to make poultices today. The herbs on the eastern part of mountains are ready, look." She shows me her small bag, unzipping it. "It will be easy and—"

"Bea, stop. Did you see anyone?" I yell at her. Her face pinches inward, and I grimace. "Sorry. Bea, can you listen, please?" I try to calm myself, try to speak softly, but I keep looking around, and I know I'm making her nervous. I can't see anyone though. No

Enhanced. And the Sarrs are all still Untamed. So everyone at Nbutai must be?

"Yes," Bea says. "Oh, you got it?"

"What?" I pull my hair away from my face. It's greasy and needs washing.

"Our friend's note," Bea says, letting her bag fall against her hip.

"What? Who?" My eyes widen, and I expect Katya to step out of her hut at any moment. But she doesn't.

Bea nods vigorously. "He looked different though. Now he has shiny eyes. I said I'd take him to you, but he just wanted me to give you the note. He was nice."

My head pounds. "What? Where was he? Was he here?"

"No. Up at…" She frowns, and I stare at her, take in her features.

Elf, Bea, Mila, and I are all mixed race; we all look fairly like our mother, but, out of the four of us, Bea and Mila look most like our dad. You can barely see Owen's resemblance in Elf and me. But it's strong—perhaps the strongest—in Bea, in the structure of her face, how her nose is stronger and her jaw wider. She slides the strap of her bag from her shoulder to her arm, then clasps her hands together. Her face crumples.

"Am I in trouble?"

"Of course not." I hold my arms out to her, offer her the embrace.

She steps toward me. She's taller than me, and the embrace is awkward. We don't usually hug because she doesn't always like touching, but every now and again, we do. Though she often hugs Elf more than me. And Mila *a lot* more.

"He was very nice, Kee-Kee," she says after a moment and steps away.

"But he was Enhanced?" I look at her as she nods, but she doesn't look at me.

"Still our friend though."

My chest tightens, and a cold breeze blows over me. "This is important, Bea. How long did you walk for?"

"The sun wasn't up when I started, because the herbs I was looking for take a while to get to. And the route isn't the most direct. It was a long walk, but Mila needs to know how to make the poultices in case they're needed again. You should know as well, Keelie. I can teach you too."

I look at the sky, then back at her. "So, you walked for, what, an hour? Two?"

She nods, and I stare at her. She went *miles* away. So the man didn't come near the village? But he still came *far* from New Kimearo…looking for me.

"Bea, we're not supposed to leave the village boundaries," I tell her. "Not without telling someone and certainly not alone and without weapons."

Bea looks stricken and starts fiddling with our mother's butterfly necklace around her neck.

My head pounds, and I try to think. The man doesn't know where we live—unless he followed her.

And he will have—won't he? All Enhanced want to know where we live.

"Did he hurt you?"

She shakes her head, eyes on the ground.

"How long ago was this?"

She shrugs, still not making eye contact. "Not long." But her voice is so quiet now, and I know I've upset her. My shoulders droop a little. I didn't mean to.

"Bea? Can you take me there now, please?"

She looks up, but still doesn't meet my gaze. "But he said that you need to meet him *tomorrow*."

"No, we have to go now."

"But it's time for me to make Mila's breakfast."

"Elf can do it."

"But I *always* do it. And I also need to show Mila how to dry the herbs. And Mila's going to sing to me this morning. She loves it when people listen to her singing."

I shake my head and shiver—the old shirt and three-quarter-length shorts I wore to sleep in aren't warm. "Please, Bea, this is important."

"Can I teach you too then? If I go with you now, you'll be there for Mila's lesson and can learn about the herbs as well?"

I nod.

Her face lights up, and seeing the look in her eyes makes me smile.

"Okay." Bea grins and surprises me by grabbing my hand, pulling me along.

We get a few feet, then I look at Rahn's hut. "Wait a minute. Stay right here."

I need a gun. Rahn keeps all the firearms in his hut.

"But you're not allowed in there," Bea whispers, eagle-eyed, before I head off. "Keelie!"

I wave at her to be quiet and pray that no one chooses this moment to leave their hut. I think Sajo's scheduled for fire duty at the moment, but so long as he's still by the fire, he won't be able to see me.

I pull back the drape that hangs across Rahn's doorway. It's fairly dark inside, but I listen carefully; his heavy breathing tells me he's asleep, and I step inside.

The light's not great, but my eyes adjust after a few moments. I look around quickly. He's to the left, sleeping with his mouth open. For once, he doesn't have his glasses on, but I see them on a chair next to his bed. For a moment, I'm struck that he has a proper bed. With a frame and everything. The rest of us have mattresses, if that. But, then again, he is our leader.

On the other side of his hut are several boxes. One has carvings on it. The others have weapons laid out on top of them.

I tiptoe across and grab the nearest Luger along with some ammunition. The semi-automatic pistol makes a scraping noise against the wooden lid as I pick it up, and I wince.

Rahn stirs.

I freeze, look back toward the door. The drape's fallen back down. I grit my teeth, then make my exit, carefully—and as quickly as I can.

Bea's still staring wide-eyed when I emerge. I check the safety is on the gun, and then I tuck the weapon into the back of my waistband.

"Right, come on," I say. "We're going now."

"You haven't got any shoes on," Bea points out.

In my fear earlier, I left our hut dressed as I had been for the night. But there's a pair of shoes nearby that I'd left outside to dry a few days ago, and I retrieve those, slip them on.

Bea frowns as we walk away from the village, looking across at me. "You can't shoot him, Keelie," she says, flapping her hands. "We don't shoot our friends."

Friends, indeed. I snort.

"Just take me to that place, please."

"You're not listening! We don't shoot our friends."

"No," I say. "But the Enhanced aren't our friends, Bea." And looking at her, I know she knows that. And I don't understand.

I grit my teeth. There's a chance the Enhanced is still there—or nearby—and, if he is, I'm going to sort this out once and for all. He is not blackmailing or threatening me into doing anything.

And he is not getting away alive.

Bea and I run for what seems like hours. Amazingly, she doesn't tire much, despite not being in as good a shape as I am.

We've run part of the way to New Kimearo, though the mountains still block the sandy-colored blocks from view. If you didn't know the town was over there, you'd have no idea.

It's nearly fully light now. There are just a few smears of pink across the sky, left over from the sunrise. Everyone will be getting up at Nbutai now. Part of me dreads what they'll say when they realize Bea and I have gone. And when Rahn realizes one of the Lugers is missing. And that I've been in his hut.

And then Katya will add in what I told her, too.

Maybe it's a good thing I mentioned to her about an attack. If they think I've gone off to defend us, they'll send more people, and, if that Enhanced man is still in the area, one of us will find him and shoot him. That's the protocol. If an Enhanced is near Nbutai, that's what we do. And everyone knows it. We can't have them knowing where we live.

But that man didn't want to know where you live.

According to Bea, yes. But there are so many things that don't make sense with that man, and I don't trust him. Hell, he's an Enhanced. Maybe this is a new tactic—to lure us into trusting them and then they get us all in one fell swoop rather than individually?

"This is the place." Bea stops. "The herbs are just over there."

I look around. There's quite good cover here. Lots of boulders and ridges rising. There are a few stubby trees to my right and some low-creeping vegetation that Bea starts telling me the name of. To my left, there are more rocks, some as tall as me.

"Right here?" I glance at my sister.

She sits down carefully on a rock, after using her sleeve to wipe any bits of sand or debris off.

"Bea?"

"Yes?"

"Was it right here where you met him? Where you met that Enhanced man and he gave you the note?" I look around for a moment. We're so far out. I had no idea Bea came this far on her excursions. It's too dangerous.

Bea nods. "Yes. But he wasn't just an Enhanced man."

"*What*?" I frown at her.

"He was our friend."

I peer around, looking hard. Then I study the ground. Footsteps in the sand. I follow them with my eyes and—

Something clicks.

I spin around, pull my gun out, and flick the safety off.

He's there. Right *there*. The Enhanced from the office.

I lift my gun, lining up my aim.

"Put the gun down!" the man shouts, ducking behind a rock. "Violence is not the answer."

I let out a bitter laugh and lunge forward.

"No," Bea shouts, throwing herself between him and my loaded gun. She flaps her hands and jiggles about. Her eyes widen as she stares at the barrel. "No! No! No!" she yells, making direct eye contact with me, and then she moves her lips, like she's trying to say something more.

"Bea, get out of the way!"

"No!"

My hackles rise. My eyes go straight to his hands. I can't see any augmenters, but that doesn't mean he doesn't have them.

The man smiles. "I knew you'd come straight away. I know you, Keelie. And I was sure I wouldn't have to wait until tomorrow."

"Bea, get out of the way now!"

I step to the left, but Bea moves with me, waving her arms about.

"Bea, please, I don't understand."

She continues moving her lips, but without words, and flaps her hands still.

The man smiles. He bloody *smiles*. Even in the face of death, they smile.

"Keelie, put the gun down. I know you've realized it," he says.

"Realized what?" The hairs on the back of my neck stand up even more.

"Realized who I am." He looks so damn amused that I feel irritation rising.

I stare at him. "I don't know who you are."

Bea's bottom lip wobbles, and then she starts shaking, but she moves to the left. I reposition the gun in my hands just as Bea whispers, "It's *him*."

"Who?"

The man laughs, looking at me. "Are you *really* going to make me strip off?"

My eyebrows shoot up. "What?"

He tips his head to the side, then he undoes the top button of his shirt. "I'll show you."

I stare in bewilderment as he undoes all the buttons, as he peels the shirt away from his torso and drops it on the ground. Defined muscles, elaborate tattoos, and—

"See, Keelie, see?" Bea whispers. "It's our friend."

My eyes widen as I see the scar.

The man grins. "I got these tattoos for you. I remember you saying you liked them. Don't you remember that conversation? We were sitting under the trees, with the blue sky and—"

I take a sudden step back.

I remember that. I remember it really well.

But… I stare at him. I try to see him, try to remember and *see* him….

No.

He died. *He* didn't get away. I saw the blood. *He's* not one of them. Not an Enhanced. He can't be.

I shake my head. He's lying. Got to be.

"You're not… You can't be…."

Anyone can get that scar. And the Enhanced will do anything—go to any length in their modifications—if it means winning our trust.

"Oh, I am," the man says. "It's me. Red."

I feel sick as I look at him. Suddenly, I *can* see it. It's him, older, bigger, stronger, but—

No.

It's not him.

They'll do *anything* to get to us. Mind games and—

If it was him, I'd have recognized him right away in

that office. I would've. I know I would've. I *kissed* him.

"I told you," Bea says.

"Now do you see?" The man sounds impatient now. "Have you worked it out yet? Why I let you go? You really didn't recognize me?" He turns toward Bea. "You did, didn't you?"

"Of course. You're our friend."

My lips feel funny, like they're swelling up. Rubbery and strange, that's how they feel as I look at him. As I look at Red.

No! It's not him.

The air around him shimmers with the heat. I look at his body. His naked torso. The tattoos accentuate the muscles of his abdomen and make his chest and arms look…*hot*. I feel heat rush to my face and force myself to look at his face.

I stare at his nose. His wobbly nose that makes him look curious—even now. But Red didn't break his nose. Not when we were younger, when we were best friends, when we'd compete over who got to take Caia-Lu the Watcher Doll when she summoned it for one of the rituals, when we'd goad each other to climb higher and higher up the mountain and over the most dangerous terrain, when we'd argue over pointless things.

But, that night, he fell forward—hit his face. And I saw him, lying on his front, his head at an angle, his eyes on me, with a ring of blood around him that reminded me of the ring of paint around Caia-Lu's Watcher Doll.

And I should've gone to him. Should've gone to all of them.

But I didn't.

"I thought you were dead," I whisper. "I'm sorry." I swallow with difficulty, look for signs of anger in him. Betrayal. Because I know Red, and he wouldn't forget it. He harbors grudges.

But he smiles, no hint of anger on his face. "There's nothing to be sorry for."

"But I left you... I *lied*..." I straighten up, feel sick. That lie. That lie has haunted me, and I've repressed it over the years, forced myself not to think about it whenever I start to.

"I said it's all right, K."

My eyes narrow. *All right*? But the Untamed always rescue the Untamed. And I left him, left all of them.

He *should* be angry.

But he's not.

Of course he's not.

I inhale sharply and reposition the gun, looking at his mirror eyes. "You think I'm going to fall for this? You think I'm stupid?"

"I know you're not stupid. Far from it." He steps closer. And his voice is so dark, so beautiful. Not like the voice I remember him having.

But he's not the little boy I remember.

I look around quickly.

Bea's sitting back on the stone again, but she's watching us. Her fingers are playing with our mother's butterfly necklace, but her eyes are firmly on me, watching everything. I try to give her a reassuring look.

Red—no, *the Enhanced man*—smiles. "I'm not what you think I am. I'm undercover."

He pauses, then steps closer still, so close I can smell his aftershave. Citrus. But with a hint of something herbal. It wraps around me, and when I look back at him—at his mirror eyes—he nods slowly.

"Keelie, I'm still Untamed."

SIX

"WHAT, KEELIE? NO HUG FOR your best friend?" The man looks at me carefully, and I stare back.

I try to speak but my lips feel funny. His eyes are all I can look at now, as if they're magnetized. "No. You're...you're Enhanced."

"I'm not." He sounds annoyed, more like Red, and I hate him for it. I blink and see his body lying in the blood. "The eyes are an illusion. The mirrors are simple lenses. I told you, I'm undercover."

"Undercover?" I echo his word faintly, but it doesn't sound like my voice. "You're not undercover. You tried to convert me! You were that close to shoving augmenters down my throat—"

"And you shoved your tongue down mine and saved the day." He grins before his face turns serious. Behind me, I hear Bea disguise a laugh as a cough. "There's surveillance in that room, Keelie. The Enhanced know the Untamed want our cars. And I have to keep up my pretense. Don't know who's watching me."

I shake my head so hard my neck clicks. A glance at Bea tells me she's still trying not to laugh. I wish she'd look away. I don't want to be thinking about *that kiss* while my sister is watching and very much here.

"You were going to convert me," I say, eyes back on the man. On Red?

But it…it can't be *him*….

Only now that I've seen the scar, it fits. And I look at him, his chest and arms with those tattoos, and feel a strange, warm feeling in the core of my body, a feeling I try to push down.

"Those were duds. I wouldn't have converted you," he says. "Well, I wasn't completely sure it *was* you at first. But then you kissed me, and it was everything I'd imagined since we sat under the trees. And, in that office, my soul recognized yours, and that's when I knew for sure."

"Your soul? How clichéd is that?" I take a small step backward. And I don't know why I do. I run a hand through my hair, trying to process all of this. My eyes fall on his shirt on the ground, then I look back up at his chest. "Put your shirt back on."

"Too distracting for you?"

I press my lips firmly together, but the warmth in me grows. He looks *great*. And here I am with greasy hair and the old clothes I sleep in.

But, if Red's telling the truth and he's not one of them, then this is huge. This is the kind of information we need. My head spins, and I wonder how many of them are out there, the undercover Untamed. The idea nearly makes me explode, and I get that dizzy, excited feeling I get with an adrenaline rush.

"You know, I'm glad you kissed me and then fought to get away," he says, shaking his shirt out.

"You are?" I stare at him, smiling. There are no pockets in his shirt, but what about his jeans? A place to hide augmenters, while he waits for me to trust him?

But you know it's Red, really, don't you? Why don't you want to admit it?

"Made my job easier," he says as he buttons up the shirt. "The duds I had were colored water. Any

Enhanced watching the cameras would've seen they'd done nothing to your eyes, that I had fake augmenters. I wasn't sure what I was going to do next. You made it easy. Authentic."

I stare at him, trying to ignore the way my heart is pounding. "You hadn't thought of what you were going to do if I hadn't kicked your butt?"

"No." His lips stretch into a thin smile. "There aren't many Untamed around here. You were the first one who broke into the office—at least on my watch." He peers at me, gives me a lopsided grin. "You're hotter than I ever imagined," he says, lowering his voice so Bea can't hear. "Gods, K. I can't believe it's you. I mean, what are the chances? We're miles away. Miles and miles." He shakes his head, and then a strange expression takes over his face. "And you're so... I didn't do your body justice in my dreams."

"Your dreams?" I feel myself blush and immediately feel conflicted. I still don't know for sure that this man is Red, that he is definitely Untamed. Especially when his eyes say otherwise....

But he *did* let me go.

And he's not trying to convert me now.

So what do Bea and I do? Take him to Nbutai? But, no, a voice in my head reminds me that that's too risky. We can't guarantee that he is who he says he is. I step back, up against the rock, feel its rough surface dig into my legs. From here, I can see for miles. No one else is around. It's just the three of us.

I look over to Bea. She's tugging at the stained sleeves of her long shirt. She often wears that shirt. Won't wash it much, says it doesn't smell right when she does.

"You all right?" Red asks.

I look at him carefully. "What color was the candle that Ji-Lu got me for my seventh birthday?"

"Purple. And she's called *Caia*-Lu." Red grins. "Gods, Keelie. Didn't think your memory was that bad."

Excitement builds in me. My lips tingle. "And you're definitely still Untamed?"

"Untamed and wild." I think he winks, but it's hard to tell because sunlight keeps flashing from his eyes as he moves his head.

"Stay here."

I head over to Bea, and I try not to smile—not to influence her—as I ask her what she thinks, whether this really can be Red. She gives me a look that says I'm mad. And I really don't like that look, which she knows.

"Of course it's him. I told you. You should've listened to me."

"But he *could* be Enhanced. It could be a trap." I fold my arms and glance back at Red. He looks amused.

"The Enhanced convert immediately," Bea says. "He had the opportunity—before you *kissed* him." A mischievous grin passes over her face. "And he didn't. Ah, I always *knew* you two were going to get together. Right from when we were little, you two were always close."

"We're not together though."

"You want to be." She grins and gives me a very pointed look. "I'll go and see if I can get any more herbs then. Might've missed a few." She winks. Actually winks. I can't remember ever seeing her wink before.

"Okay. Just stay close by. We'll need to get back to Nbutai soon." I shift my weight from foot to foot, but I smile. "I'll go and talk to him some more, see if I can suss him out properly."

Bea smiles as she gets up. "If that's the excuse you tell yourself, fine. But you just want to talk to him."

Her words follow me as I head back to Red. He smiles pleasantly at me.

"Tell me about this undercover stuff," I say, my gaze on Bea as she walks away. Twice, she turns back and grins at me.

"I can't."

I raise my eyebrows and focus on Red. "Uh, I'm

Untamed too. I'm hardly going to compromise you."

"And suppose you get caught and they draw information out of you? You'd send all our work down the drain and give out any names I tell you."

"So you're not telling me anything?" I'm still holding the gun, and I notice he eyes it a little warily now. But I do believe him…don't I? He really is Red…isn't he? And Bea thinks he is. She's good at judging people.

But it's dangerous—I know that. The only people you can really trust are those you live with.

Yet, I want to believe him. And life's been relatively boring in the last few years. Well, pretty much since we got to Nbutai. Rahn stopped me from going out and killing the Enhanced, from getting my adrenaline fix that way, said I could get it through fighting and running and exercise. But could I get it from Red? From immersing myself in this—in undercover Untamed stuff, in secret missions, secret meetings….

And I *am* attracted to Red.

And my death is to be at a specific point—so it doesn't matter what I get involved with in the meantime or how dangerous it is.

"I can't tell you anything," Red says. "I've told you too much already. I have to be careful—that's why I couldn't go with Bea to give you my note in-person. There's always a chance I could get caught, and the less I know about where your settlement is the better." He leans forward, and it's as if the intensity of his mirror gaze increases. "You can't tell anyone about me. It's top secret. I mean it. You can't tell *anyone*."

"Why?" I shake my head. My mind is running through all the possibilities—the advantages this gives us. "You're exactly what we need. Someone on the inside."

"No. I'm not supposed to tell anyone. The more people who know, the more likely it is I'll get caught."

"I wouldn't tell anyone!"

Red smiles. "I know you wouldn't. But if you were on a raid, you might act differently if you saw me. And

I can't afford to have the Enhanced find out. If they do, I'm finished. And then they'll look for the others."

"The others?" I stare at him. At his lips. "You mean this is an organized thing?"

"I work with three other undercover agents."

I straighten myself back up, staring at him. At Red... Red whom I grew up with, whom I cared for very much... My best friend, and now he's—

No, ten years have passed. I need to concentrate on that.

But he likes you. He's been thinking about you.
And you like him.

I blush as I think about his comments about my body and how his dreams hadn't done me justice. And now part of me is wondering whether his lips *always* taste like they did in the office. Whether they'd taste like it now....

I force myself to look at the ground as I focus on his last words.

"Agents? You make it sound official."

"We're more likely to succeed if we treat it as an official job—not something we're messing around in." He gives me a sympathetic smile. "I'm sorry, K. This is the way it has to be."

I stare at him. "So what do you want from me?" I take the most recent note out of my pocket. "Your notes were threatening, Red. They scared me. I didn't know it was you. I thought—"

But I cut myself off.

Part of me wants to tell him about the nightmares—and how I had one the night after I saw him in the office. Because it must've triggered it, mustn't it?

I think about the second note. I hope it doesn't predict another nightmare tonight.

Red smiles easily. "And that was the perfect way to get your attention. You're family-orientated." And, of course, it reminds me of the lie—of my aunts, my extended family I left behind.

I swallow with difficulty, processing his words. He

wasn't really threatening me? *I know what you did.* Just reminding me?

"Why not say it was you in the message?" I ask.

"Too risky," he says.

"Risky?"

He nods. "I had to think of another way. And I thought you'd want to know that I'd found your parents."

I fold my arms and watch him carefully. "You just said you couldn't tell me anything."

He shrugs and looks in the direction Bea went off in. "This isn't part of my mission. But they're safe and well, your parents."

"Safe and well?" I raise my eyebrows. "They're Enhanced."

"Do you want to try and break them out?"

Red's question knocks me off balance, and, somehow, I end up stumbling on loose shingle. His hand shoots out—super quick—and he grabs me, steadies me. His touch is hot against my skin, and I feel something pull through my body, unbalancing me, releasing too much energy.

I look up—see my reflection in his eyes—and he's so close. Close enough to kiss….

Concentrate.

I pull my arm back, breaking our contact, but it doesn't stop my heart from thudding. And why the hell am I feeling like this? What we're talking about is important. I need to concentrate on that.

"They're Enhanced," I say slowly. "My parents are Enhanced. Once it's done, there's no going back."

"But Untamed rescue the Untamed people who've been taken."

"Because it's *before* they've been fully converted. There's a chance then."

I don't like looking at Red, not when it's his face with their eyes. I take a deep breath, force myself to look away.

"And you don't think there's a chance now?" His

voice is rough.

I look at him carefully. When I was little, Caia-Lu told me about an elderly couple her sisters broke out of a compound. They starved them of augmenters until they were running lean, but the couple went mad. They lasted for two days before they killed themselves.

And I've heard other similar stories too. Not ones that end in suicide—that's rare, I think. But ones where the people are never the same. A week in an Enhanced compound is usually the absolute cut-off point. Anything beyond that and the individual is far too addicted to the Enhanced lifestyle. Even then, they're never the person they were before capture. And, besides, it's a week for the strong people. Some don't even last a couple of days before they're fully converted.

I think of Red's mother.

She was Enhanced for three days before she was rescued, but she was never the same afterward—filled with vacant looks, constantly sweating, and addicted to any drugs or alcohol she could get her hands on. That's what the augmenters did to her. She couldn't even be left alone in the village—there always had to be someone watching her.

Or she was tied up.

I remember the look on Red's face each time he saw her that way. Each time he begged her not to take any more of the powder, each time he tried to pry a bottle from her. And he believed it was his fault, that he wasn't enough for his mother, that she hated living with him.

But it wasn't his fault. We all knew that.

It was because of the Enhanced. The withdrawal effects from their lifestyle.

And that was after *three days* in the compound.

Not ten years.

I don't understand. Red knows what his mother was like after she was converted. Yet he thinks we can save my parents?

"No," I say. "It's been ten years. That's way too long." Ten years since I last saw him…ten years since I last saw my parents. Everything happened that night. That fateful night. I press my lips together for a moment. "What? Do you think there's a chance?"

I look at Red carefully, studying him before I realize what I'm doing. Before I realize that my eyes are running over the sharp lines of his face, pretending his eyes aren't mirrors.

Look away.

Red parts his lips slightly. I try not to look at his lips. I also try not to notice the way my breathing gets faster, and how, automatically, I start to lean toward him.

Stop it.

"No."

"So why say it?"

"Because I thought I'd better give you the option."

I look away from him to where Bea is only just in sight. She's on the side of the dip, collecting more plants. She's staring into the distance. I know what she'd want, if Red asked her the same question. And I know that Mila would jump at the chance. She's told me before how she hates that she never knew Mum and Dad.

And Elf? Well. Elf wouldn't want Red trying to get our parents back. We don't often talk about them, but I know my brother, and I know he thinks our parents are lost to us. It's what we're taught after all.

And ten years is a long time.

Too long?

But I imagine Mila's and Bea's faces when I bring our parents back.

And then their faces when our parents are in withdrawal from augmenters, when they're desperate and angry all the time. When they're shells of their former selves. When they're always trying to go back to the Enhanced.

When they're not our parents anymore.

"No," I say finally and look back at Red. I put the gun back into my waistband, then pull my shirt over it at the back. I don't take my eyes off Red as I do it though, as if I've got to keep staring at him. *Have* to.

Red nods. "Good call."

And my eyes devour him. I drink in every little detail of his appearance: how the thick bands of muscles around his chest and shoulders show through his shirt; how the shirt's bottom hem isn't quite flat against his sculpted torso and the waist of his jeans is low, and I can see a teasing glimpse of his hard, flat stomach and the tattoos there. I want him to take his shirt off again, and more, so that this time I can really appreciate him—and part of me is shocked that I'm thinking about Red in such a strong way.

"I can't believe I've found you," Red says. I try to ignore how deep and raspy his voice has suddenly gone, and how it calls to something deep inside me. Because this is pathetic. I'm being like the stereotypical lovesick teen.

I think of the second note. "You want me to come to your office tomorrow?"

But he shakes his head. "Too dangerous. I only wrote that for effect. And because I knew you'd find me out here today anyway."

"Oh."

He grins. "We'd have to be careful, but what about regular meetings? Out here?" He indicates the landscape around us. "Or higher up the Titians?"

"Here's fine," I say. I don't want Red going any farther into the mountains until I can be *absolutely* sure of him. I'm fine putting myself in danger—but not the others. Anyway, part of me wants him all to myself.

I swallow hard, but I can't pretend I don't feel the way my face heats up.

"We'll meet once a month?" I say, wiping my clammy hands on my jeans.

"Once a month?" He sounds incredulous. "Keelie,

we have loads of catching up to do. You have no idea how happy I was to realize it was *you*. You don't know what it's like there, with them—so drugged up on augmenters that they think we're all best friends and everything's perfect. I want to see *you*, Keelie. I want to see you regularly, just to have another conversation with an Untamed person who isn't pretending to have joined the perfect mob, if nothing else."

I think his eyes say that he hopes it won't *just* be a conversation though—but it's hard to tell, what with the mirrors. Still, I fight every ounce of my energy not to smile and grin like a lunatic.

"How's Bea been doing, out here?"

"All right. She's amazing at plants."

"I remember." He smiles. "I saw on your mother's notes they'd diagnosed her soon after she was converted."

"Diagnosed?"

"Autism," he says.

"Caia-Lu always called her a changeling," I say.

Red nods. "And Bea too."

I look across at the horizon.

"So, you and Bea survived. Uh…" He trails off and looks awkward. But I know what he wants to ask.

"Elf and Mila too," I say.

"Shit. Wow." He lets out a low whistle and plays with the strap of his watch. It's very expensive-looking. But Red always did like valuable things.

"Did…did anyone else?" I ask. "Like, with you?"

He shakes his head, and a muscle in his neck pulses. Is he thinking of what I did?

The wind picks up, and I shiver. I look at Red; suddenly, I feel like something's not right, even though I want to touch him. Kiss him. See if he tastes the same way he did. But part of me screams that this man *can't* be Red. That it doesn't make sense. Why would Red be in New Kimearo? We're weeks and weeks away from D'Elinous, our old village. There are hundreds of towns and cities he could've gone to—hundreds that are nearer to our old village. Why would he be out here?

"Is it really you?" The question escapes my lips before I can stop it.

And, suddenly, all these fancies run through my mind; we can be together again. Me and him—best friends. And it'll all be okay, and it'll be like how it was back at the village, and maybe I can save everyone… everyone who was lost to us and….

Red closes what little distance there is between us. "It's me. You know it's me."

He touches my chest, his fingers splaying out above my left breast. His fingertips tap on my collarbone. I breathe in sharply, check that Bea isn't watching from afar, and try to ignore the fluttering within me.

"Right here, you know." His voice is like velvet. Men's voices have always been a weakness of mine; my knees tingle, and it's all I can do just to stand there and look at him. "You can feel it's me, K. I know you can."

A myriad of feelings goes through me. Panic. Apprehension. Anxiety. Disbelief. Excitement.

I put my hand over his, slowly, then pull his away, so he's not touching me there. So we're just holding hands. And that's better, isn't it?

"I'd better go," Red says, but he doesn't let go of my hand. "Can't have anyone getting suspicious of me."

I nod. "So…when are we meeting again?" Something about saying those words makes me tingle. I hope I'm not blushing.

He squeezes my fingers. "I'd like to meet tomorrow. Hell, I'd like to stay with you *now*." I wish I could see his eyes under those mirrors. "But I—I don't want anyone getting suspicious. How about in three days' time?"

I nod. "Same time?"

"Early morning's best. Just after sunrise. Right by these rocks."

I can't help but smile, and he grips my hand tighter.

Part of me doesn't want to let go—it's *Red*, for the Gods' sake!

Right before he leaves, he glances over toward where Bea is. "She won't tell anyone, will she?"

I shake my head, a little annoyed. If it was Elf here, would Red have asked that? "Of course not."

"A secret romance!" Bea's eyes glisten as she stares at me on the walk back. "I saw you two—thought you were going to kiss."

"You saw?" I raise my eyebrows, feeling myself blushing again. My chest swells a little, and I shake myself. "It's hardly a romance! But we can't tell anyone, Bea, about him."

She laughs. "Of course not. Otherwise it wouldn't be a secret."

"No. About *any* of it. Him being undercover. Everything."

She nods, but I distinctly notice the annoyance in her posture. "I wouldn't put our friend in danger. You should know me better than that. But, if you're going to be seeing Red, and if stuff is going to happen, you should definitely end things with Nico. It's not fair to string him along."

"Yeah," I say, wondering whether stuff is in fact going to happen.

By the time we get near Nbutai, I feel strange and jumpy. The meeting with Red keeps replaying in my mind. I can't stop thinking about him, about the danger he's in. Red's right—no one else here can know about him. It'll put him in more danger—as well as whatever mission he's involved with.

But this is huge. I know that. And I want to tell them. But it's something Bea and I will have to keep to ourselves. At least I have her to talk about it with.

"Keelie! Bea!"

I see them waiting, on the outskirts of Nbutai. Rahn, Sajo, Corin, Kayden, Paul, and several more men, all holding guns. Mainly Glocks and Lugers.

"What the hell is goin' on? You stole one of my guns!" Rahn is fuming.

"You worried my wife," Paul says. "And you mentioned an attack, then we couldn't find you."

"And you came out here on your own with *her* to defend us all?" Rahn points savagely at Bea.

I step in front of her, heat flooding me, before my sister can react. "Don't talk about Bea like that."

"Well what good would she be if we were bein' attacked?" Rahn demands. "She'd get overloaded or whatever it is and—"

"I take it there is no conversion attack?" Corin steps forward.

I shake my head. "Bad dream. That was all."

"We went to collect more herbs," Bea says, showing them the contents of her bag, then she starts telling them their names and all the different properties and the types of poultices she's going to teach me and Mila to make with them.

Rahn scowls. "So there's no one out here?"

"No. I just had a very vivid dream."

"Not a Seer, are you?" Rahn looks at me in disgust now, his upper lip quivering.

"No." I keep my voice steady.

Rahn grunts. "Well, you can pay for all the upset you've caused. I want you on cleaning duty for the rest of the day. And then you can look after Finn. He's got diarrhea."

Bea turns to me. "He's got diarrhea?" Then she frowns. "What about our lesson, with the herbs?"

"Forget about your bloody herbs!" Rahn yells. "Some of us have to live in the real world."

"Rahn!" I hiss. Tension pours through me, and I grip my hands into tight fists. "Don't talk to my sister like that."

Rahn snorts. "Don't pretend like you care."

I slap him.

"I do not ignore her!" I yell. "She's my sister—she's a person, Rahn. A *real* person—more of a person than you!"

Rahn staggers back, grabbing at his glasses as they slide askew cross his face. Several of the men step closer to him. But Corin and Paul step closer to me.

I spit at the ground, then glare at Rahn. "That's what I think of you."

For a few moments, no one does anything.

I turn away. "Come on, Bea. Let's go and find Mila."

SEVEN

NEWS OF ME SLAPPING OUR leader spreads around Nbutai fast. People seem divided into camps: some hate me for disrespecting Rahn, and some admire me. A lot of the men watch me carefully now. Attitudes are changing; I realized that when Corin came and collected the Luger from me—he gave me a reassuring nod. There was something about his manner that reminded me of Elf.

"Be careful, though, Keelie," Five says. She's joined Mila, Bea, and I for the lesson on herbs and poultices. "Rahn's going to have it in for you now."

I shrug. "I don't care. He deserved it."

"She slapped him like this!" Bea yells, overexcited, and then demonstrates on the ragdoll that Marouska made for her a long time ago. The fabric's all dirty now, but Bea won't let it be washed.

Mila laughs hysterically.

Five smiles, and the four of us go back to our lesson where Bea tells us all about the different properties of various herbs and the best ways to dry them. Her face really lights up as she teaches us, and Mila stares at her adoringly. Our little sister loves Bea more than anything in the world—Bea's filled in the role of mother for Mila, and there's nothing Bea can do that will make Mila look at her differently. Sometimes, I'm jealous of their bond. But I've got Elf. Twins of the stars.

"When can we make the poultices?" I ask.

"In about two weeks, I think. The herbs have to be upside down in bags for about that long. Putting them in the cab of one of the trucks would work well...if Rahn lets us." I notice her tone drop.

"What about Yani's hut?" Five asks. "His gets the most sun. It's like a greenhouse in there."

Bea's eyes light up, and I smile to myself. A couple of times, I've noticed her and Yani walking together. Once, when Mila and Bea were singing, I found him listening in secret.

I watch Bea carefully as she tells us more about the herbs, still worried that she believed what Rahn was saying earlier—that I don't care about her. But she's sitting next to me now, and she seems happy. I'm relieved. Because Rahn is wrong. Bea's my sister, and I'll do anything for her. Just like I'll do anything for Elf and Mila.

Five leaves to get food at one point and returns with the smoothest soup—the texture Bea prefers. We eat and laugh and talk, and then Bea teaches us some more about the plants, and soon we're all engrossed in it again, and then it's time to get something for our evening meal.

Just before last light, Elf enters the hut. I don't know where he's been all day—he's one of the few people I haven't seen, not since I left him sleeping here this morning—and he grunts at me, Mila, and Bea, then he sees Five. The change in him is unmistakable, and I smile as he suddenly straightens up and musters out a greeting.

"Are...are you having, uh, fun?" He gestures between Five and Bea. Bea's herbs are laid out on the floor, and Mila's doll, Straw Hair—under Mila's direction—keeps trying to eat them.

Five nods, smiling. "Great fun. It's really interesting learning about the medicinal properties of plants."

Elf slips behind me, then sits on his bed. I sneak a glance at him, see that his face has gone red and he's looking at the floor. His hands are tightly clasped together; he does that when he's nervous, and it's so obvious who's making him nervous here.

I see Mila has noticed too, and she sticks her tongue out at him. She does that a lot.

Go on, I mouth at Five, raising my eyebrows, well aware that Elf's following the conversation.

What? She widens her eyes, but I can tell she knows perfectly well what I mean because the corners of her mouth are turning upward.

I stand up. "Bea, you going to take Mila out for her walk?"

"I'm not a dog," Mila says.

"I didn't mean that," I say, looking at her. Then I flick my eyes to Elf and Five and raise my eyebrows.

Bea looks unsettled for a moment. "We normally go earlier..." She tugs at her hair. "But I was teaching you about the poultices and herbs, and it was going really well, so I didn't mind that we weren't going on our walk. But it's a bit too late to leave now. It's already dark."

Elf looks relieved.

"Okay, what about getting Mila washed and ready for bed?"

"I can do that myself," Mila protests, looking very much like she doesn't want to miss the chance of seeing Elf embarrass himself. Which, admittedly, is quite high—when it comes to Five.

"Okay, but why don't the three of us go?" I say. "And, after we're washed, we can look at the stars."

Bea hums as she stands. "Yes. Mila, I'll tell you one of the Old Stories too."

"Don't forget Straw Hair," I say to Mila.

By the door, I grab Mila's pajamas and our thick

blanket. It's a heavy one with the smooth texture that Bea likes. I consider taking the clothes Bea and I sleep in—I finally changed out of mine before Bea's lesson—but I figure that we'll just change when we're back. Only Mila's likely to fall asleep and get straight into bed when we return. Bea and I will probably stay up for a bit longer.

Out of the corner of my eye, I see Elf giving me an alarmed look. He's tense, but Five's about as relaxed as can be, lying nearly horizontal across the floor on her stomach, her head propped up on her hands in such a way that her dark hair fans out over her shoulders.

I grab my new Swiss army knife, pocket it, and steer Mila out of the hut, Bea following.

"Are they going to *kiss*?" Mila whispers loudly.

I smile to myself.

The washing station's not far away. There's not much water left in it, but we all get washed, and then Mila dunks Straw Hair into the water before spinning her around so water droplets fly from her hair all over me and the folded blanket I placed on the ground not far away.

Nearby, Finn sits. I almost miss him in the dark, but once I spot his pale face, I then can't not see it. He doesn't look great, even in this light, and I wonder if we'll all get sick.

"He's really nice," Bea says in a low voice to me as I pick up the blanket.

Mila walks slightly ahead of us, and we follow.

"Finn?" I raise my eyebrows. *Nice* is not a word I'd associate with Finn. He's argumentative, scathing, and he's played some horrible pranks on Seven.

Bea shakes her head and laughs. "Not Finn."

"Who then?"

Her face pinkens a little, and she squeezes her hands together for a moment. Mentally, I go through all the men it could be. Corin's a year younger than me, two younger than Bea, but I've never noticed anything between them. Or would I notice anything? The next oldest guy is Nico. And she knows I'm not interested in him, not really…so could it be him?

"Yani," Bea says, her voice strangely high-pitched.

"Yani?" My eyes widen, and a smile tugs across my lips. Nico's brother. Five years older than her. That's not too bad. Could be worse. About a year ago, I'd briefly wondered if my sister had feelings for Sajo, Finn's dad, and it had made me feel weird. "You like Yani?"

"He's really nice," she says again.

"Oh, you do!" I gasp. "Just think, if you two get together, we can go on triple dates. You and Yani, Elf and Five, me and R—" I cough quickly, suddenly aware that Finn or Mila could be listening. "Nico."

Bea glances at me sideways. "You were going to say Red."

"No, I wasn't."

She raises her eyebrows. "You nearly gave away Red's secret undercover status."

I look ahead to where my eleven-year-old sister is now skipping. "You think she heard?" I don't think Finn's concentrating on us.

Bea shakes her head.

"So, has anything happened with you and Yani?" I ask quickly.

"We spoke two days ago when he filled up my water sack for me, and he wanted to know about why nettles sting."

"Why nettles sting?"

"Yes. That's what he asked. *Why do nettles sting*?"

"And why do they?"

Bea shrugs. "Nettles aren't my specialty. But after that, he asked about herbs. We talked for half an hour. And then yesterday morning he waved to me. Oh, and a week ago he told me he was thinking of walking up to Twisty Rock and wondered whether I wanted to come along to see if there are any useful plants there. I mean, I told him I couldn't because I was going to help Mila skin that desert rat she caught in the snare. But he might ask again."

My eyes widen, and I suppress a smile.

A few minutes later, Mila joins us, and we find a spot to stretch the blanket out on, then we lie down. I fold the remainder of the blanket back over the three of us, so Bea's cocooned in it in the way I know she likes. Mila is between us. Then I point to the different constellations.

"Which one is you?" Bea looks across at me through her long lashes. Part of me has always been envious of her long lashes.

I look up at the stars, find the two bright spots that are always close together. "That one's me on the left. And the other one's Elf."

Twins of the stars.

"And the one above it is you, Bea. See?"

"Where am I?" Mila asks, lifting her hand up and pointing.

"You're that one below Elf and I. See, just there, a little farther down—because you're younger than us. You've been in the world less time, so your star hasn't climbed as high."

"Where's Straw Hair's star?"

"Right there." I move her hand over and point out the brightest star—the one that Nico thinks must be another planet. Yani says it could be the New World, but that's not right. No one sees the New World, not when they're in this world.

"Where are Mum and Dad?" Mila asks. "I want to see them."

I wince. A moment later, I pick out two new stars, fairly near ours. Then the feeling of the earlier anxiety from my talk with Red gnaws at my insides. If I'd said yes to rescuing my parents, would he really have helped me? Found a way to make it work when no one else has? And they've been there ten years… A week is always the cut-off point.

The three of us settle down. Watching the stars is one of our things that we do. It used to just be me and

Bea, but Mila likes it too, and occasionally Elf. We used to do it more before, and part of me feels guilty that I've left it so long.

I smile as I see the relaxed look on Bea's face. Traveling here with her wasn't good. I've never seen her so scared as she was then, and it took her a long time to get used to life at Nbutai and the routine here. But she seems happy now, and seeing her happy makes my heart a little lighter.

I listen to the sounds around us. There's a slight breeze running through the long grass to my right, and a few night insects are humming. Back toward the village, I can hear the others getting ready for bed and building the fire up. Hisses and crackles fly through the air toward us.

I look back at Bea. I smile.

"You said you'd tell me a story," Mila whines. Her fingers curl around my wrist, but she's turning to look at Bea.

Bea nods. "Which one would you like?"

She frowns. "One about…about Straw Hair!"

Bea smiles, then tells Mila one of her favorite stories. She calls them the Old Stories, because they're the ones Caia-Lu would tell us back at the old village, but Bea adapts them so that Straw Hair is the central character. Her memory is amazing.

Bea tells the story for well over twenty minutes, adding in many specifics and details I'd long forgotten. Mila hangs off her every word at first, but then I notice her eyelids fluttering.

Shortly, she's asleep.

I fidget about in the blanket for a few moments, turning so I can see our hut. Whenever Bea, Mila, and I are out here under the stars, Elf usually comes out to carry Mila back. She's big for an eleven-year-old, and I hurt my back once carrying her.

I suppose I'll have to wait for Elf to be ready this time. Don't want to walk in on him and Five. Then I smile, wondering if anything's actually happening in there. It would be just like my brother to ask her about her favorite things or something, and not actually talk—or do—anything.

Then my mind turns to Yani. Is he aware of Bea's interest in him? Even though we live in the same group, I don't really know Yani that well. Nico doesn't speak of his brother much, and Yani's one of those quiet people.

Still, Bea's right, he is nice and he—

The long grass nearby rustles. I sit up and turn toward it, trying to see in the darkness, and—

Something hits the back of my head.

I cry out, my body jolting.

"Be quiet," a voice snarls.

I twist, trying to see, trying to free my hands from the blanket, adrenaline rushing through my body. I hear Bea cry out and—

Pain, heavy, across my head. Again.

White spots fill my vision.

Then there's no more.

EIGHT

THE KNIFE OF MADNESS CHASES me, and I'm running, but it flies faster than I can go. I can't move quickly enough. It's right behind me, cutting through the air, whistling. Trying to get me.

My bare feet slap the ground, spray mud up all over me. I feel it splatter against the backs of my legs. My breaths come in short, sharp bursts.

Need to get away.

Have to get away.

Red's right behind me, and I turn, see the wild look in his eyes as he sees the knife whizzing after me. See the horror on his face as he realizes what I am.

And the knife of madness. It's always there, chasing me, always chasing me.

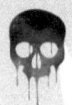

I open my eyes to darkness and stars and the roar of an engine.

I'm in a truck…in one of our trucks? I press my hands against the floor. Wood, uneven. Splinters.

Panic and nausea pull through me, their long fingers grabbing as much of my stomach's contents as possible, churning it all up.

My mind clouds over, and I struggle to think.

My stomach squeezes again.

The surface beneath me moves.

A second later, I throw up.

The vehicle jolts my vomit toward me, and it soaks my jeans. I breathe deeply—trying not to smell it—but the putridity invades my nostrils.

I scramble to the left, trying to avoid my vomit and—

Something yanks my right foot back, hard. Pain, around my ankle. I turn, my vision blurring, and feel my foot with my shaking fingers. My shoe has gone, and there's rope around my ankle, double-tied in such a way that there isn't a knot at my end.

"Hello?" My voice wobbles, and I suddenly feel fear. "Bea? Bea—are you here?"

I blink furiously, trying to see, but the darkness is like a thick fog, obscuring everything, trying to weigh me down, trying to stop me.

"Bea? Mila?"

But there's no answer, and I can't hear anyone else's breaths.

They're not here? Not taken too?

My fingers follow the rope, and I lean forward—my head suddenly aching—and follow the rope until it disappears over the side of the truck and underneath the vehicle's frame. I lean over as far as I can, trying to find the other end, but I can't—and the momentum of the vehicle means leaning farther risks me being thrown out. Being dragged along the desert ground would probably kill me. Too many rocks.

I lean back.

Shit.

Someone's tied me up. But only by one of my feet.

I breathe deeply, know I need to stay calm. I push

my hair back, then tie it loosely with the band I keep on my wrist. Okay. Right.

The truck jolts again, and something falls forward, a few feet in front of me. An empty fuel can. I recognize it immediately. This is one of our L200s—the red one, I think.

Someone from Nbutai has taken me, tied me up.

More pain at the back of my head, and I raise my hand, gingerly feel the two lumps at the base of my skull. Someone's hit me hard. Twice.

When I open my mouth to scream loudly, it makes me feel sick.

I shout anyway, for as long as I can, and I try to see into the cab. But it's dark, and I can't crawl forward enough because of the rope—

Rope.

The rope is likely tied underneath the vehicle, so I can't untie it. I need to cut it. I have a knife—I pat my pockets down, then curse. There's nothing there. Whoever's taken me has got my Swiss army knife.

I swear loudly. Saying all the bad words I know makes me feel better. A lot better.

A few moments pass, and I try to think. But all I can think is that I need to wait, wait until whoever's driving the truck stops. I can't do anything until then.

I curse again.

It takes hours for the vehicle to even slow down. By the time it stops, I feel dizzy, sick, and disorientated. My head is throbbing. But it's starting to get a little lighter now. The light makes it better.

The cab's door opens, and I straighten up as someone jumps out. A man—I see his silhouette, see his large nose, feel the hatred in my blood boil deeper.

"I think we need to talk," Rahn says as he looks over the truck's wall at me. His nostrils flare, and I see myself reflected in his dark glasses for a brief moment. "No one undermines me. And no one *ever* slaps me."

I muster as much strength as I can, trying to ignore my pounding head. "You were out of order. You insulted Bea. You deserved that slap. And where is she? Have you hurt her? What about Mila?"

Rahn tilts his head slowly. Then he lifts his arm up. I see the flash of the barrel before he has the gun against my head.

My eyes widen, and I gasp a raspy breath. He wouldn't…would he?

"You need to apologize." His words are dark. "And you need to apologize now. I mean it. I'm your leader, and you'll treat me with the respect I deserve."

You don't deserve respect. I want to spit the words at him, but I reconsider. I know he's going to force an apology out of me. Or kill me.

"I *will* be respected, Keelie. You will respect me." He tilts his head back, looks up at the sky for a moment. "My father was the leader of our group before me. Of course, it wasn't the Nbutai group then. But he was the leader, and he got the attention and respect he deserved. Me? I was just a child then, people never took notice of me. But that changed when *I* became the leader. And I am not that meek child anymore. I claimed my rightful position, and everyone follows my command. I will *crush* anyone who stands against me." He removes the gun from my head, tucks it into his waistband, then cracks his knuckles. "Now, have you got something to say to me?"

"Sorry," I mutter.

"I can't hear you."

"I'm sorry." I clear my throat. "But you had no right to attack me and drag me out here." I try to stand, to give myself height over him, but my legs are too shaky. The pain at the back of my head throbs. "You're a monster. And where are my sisters?"

For a second, Rahn doesn't say anything. Then he leans in closer, over the truck's wall, so close I can smell his sweat. His face is inches from mine, and I can see every dirty pore in his skin.

"Keelie, I don't think you understand me. And I don't know how you've managed to live in my group for ten years without understanding how we operate. But, in my group, you respect me. You don't insult me. And you've got to be taught a lesson."

Got to be taught a lesson.

There's something about the way he's looking at me that sends shivers down my spine. Maybe it's because I can't see much of his face—the darkness and his glasses are a shield.

I shake my head and stare at my feet—one shoe missing. "You'll never get away with this."

"Get away with what? Teaching you respect?" He laughs. "Your sisters are fine. But *you'll* be lucky if you make it back to Nbutai alive."

His words make me go cold. All the muscles in my face slacken. Rahn laughs, then he steps away. I watch him climb back into the cab.

A moment later, the engine starts up again. He only stopped to talk to me?

He drives me farther out, across the desert. I'm disorientated, and I can't work out where we are. Can't recognize it at all. There are no signs of New Kimearo on any of the horizons—no signs of any civilization, so I can only rule out one direction that we could've taken from the village.

Thinking of Nbutai makes me wonder what my sisters have told Elf and the others. They'll know it's Rahn who's taken me, won't they?

My stomach twists.

I try to stretch forward, grimacing when the rope around my ankle tightens and tries to yank me back. But I keep reaching for the back of the cab. There's a window: I can see the back of Rahn's head. He's definitely on his own in there, and that makes me feel better. I can take on one man easily, as soon as I'm untied. Even if it is our leader.

A minute later, I look around the truck bed again, but there's nothing I can use as a weapon. There's a folded tarpaulin in the far corner that I can't reach, and the empty fuel can rolling around.

I try with my fingernails to saw through the rope, but it's definitely not a quick option. Shit. Rahn's really in charge of me now. And I can't do anything until he unties me.

I lie back and think, wait.

Eventually, Rahn stops once more. It's completely light now.

"Come to have another pointless conversation before we drive on again?" I sit up as he moves toward me, mustering all the confidence I can. "And really, isn't this a huge waste of fuel?"

Then I see the knife in his hand. It's not my knife. He points it at me.

"You know what happens to those who disobey me?"

"You wouldn't." I eye the knife carefully, then Rahn. I shake my head. My hands aren't tied, and, if I lunge at the right time—when he's off-guard—I could get the knife; he's close enough that the rope around my ankle shouldn't be a problem. I just need to distract him. "You wouldn't, Rahn."

"Wouldn't I?"

"No." I keep my breathing even. "Leaders don't kill their own people."

I try to hold his gaze, steady, though I can't see his eyes. His intentions are hidden. He grips the knife tighter, then leans in a fraction closer.

"Know this, Keelie. If there's a second time when you disobey me, I won't be bluffin'."

Bluffing?

He bows his head, and I see his bald spot. He brings the knife down to my foot, hovers the blade above my skin.

I tense.

"I'm cuttin' you free." He half-smiles. He's enjoying this.

He also takes a deliberately long time to cut through the rope, and, under those glasses, I know he's watching me.

"And, if there's a next time, it won't be you I punish." Rahn gathers up the rope, and I pull my foot back toward me instantly. He turns and looks out at the desert. "Perhaps it'll be Bea I take out here. Over yonder. I'm sure she'd like that."

My muscles harden, and it's all I can do not to pounce on him. "Don't you dare take Bea anywhere. Or Mila—or anyone."

"Then never make me do this again. Because, believe me, I'll use whatever means are necessary to annihilate my competition."

Annihilate.

"Get in the cab, Keelie. And don't tell anyone anythin'."

We get back to Nbutai in the evening because Rahn drives in circles most of the way and goes ridiculously slowly. We've been out nearly twenty-four hours and he didn't give me any of the food he'd packed. Once we're out of the truck, he digs into his pocket and hands my Swiss army knife back. I wait for him to give me my other shoe, but he doesn't do or say anything more, just heads off to his own hut.

Elf is the only one who appears happy to see me. He's the only one who rushes toward me, but even his movements are jolty, like he's self-conscious.

"What did he do to you?" His voice is low, and he takes me into our hut, away from the watching eyes.

"Nothing." I look around. "Where are Bea and Mila?"

"They're out gathering with Katya, Alan, and Marouska. They should be back soon. Bea was upset, and I thought sticking to her routine would help. Though they've been out a while."

"Why was she upset?" For a second, I feel dizzy. It's the hunger. "Did Rahn hurt her too?"

"Rahn hurt you?" Elf's eyes are imploring. "Keelie?"

Rahn's words come back to me. *Don't tell anyone anythin'.*

I shake my head, ignore the throbbing at the base of my skull. "No. I'm not hurt."

It takes a hell of a lot to hurt me. And if Rahn thinks he has, then he's wrong. So wrong.

He didn't even scare me. Not really.

NINE

THE NEXT DAY, I BUSY myself with chores at Nbutai and try to ignore the frosty looks a lot of people give me. I don't know what lies Rahn's spread about me, but he must have said something.

The hours pass quickly, and day turns to night. And then I wake up in the early hours, knowing that very soon it'll be time for me to go and meet Red. We agreed to meet just after sunrise. Part of me tingles at the thought of seeing him, and I don't know why.

Well, I do. But I shouldn't think of it like that. It's not going to be the same as before. Ten years have passed. *And there's the small matter of what you did.*

I push that thought out of my head. These first meetings are precious—my gut tells me that—I can't taint them. Just can't.

But, of course, seeing Red again is bound to bring up those memories. But what did I expect? To be able to forget about it? I'm surprised I've pushed it out of my mind as much as I have.

I speed up, walking there quickly with legs that tingle with far too much energy and adrenaline. I've got a new survival bag on my back—one that contains twine among other things—and I feel confident. The sky is lightening; the rest of Nbutai will be up soon. I left a note for Elf telling him I'd gone to check the snares on the far side of the mountains—the ones no one likes checking because of the distance.

I get to the meeting point in enough time to scout the land around it properly and check for any traps. There aren't any. Of course there wouldn't be—this is Red, my best friend. I choose a flat rock to sit on—one that has cover in front of it so I'm not immediately visible—and I wait.

I don't have to wait long.

I see him way before he sees me.

Red walks confidently, but always double-checking the land around him. Sensible. He carries a small rucksack, and an expensive-looking leather jacket is folded over his arm. When he's close enough, I see that he has a skin-tight T-shirt on. It looks good on him. Very good.

But it would look better off him.

I look away quickly, embarrassed, even though I know he hasn't seen me—or heard my thought. I chide myself, don't even know where it came from. I have to keep control of myself.

I wait until he's nearly upon me before I reveal myself.

Red jumps back a foot, brings a hand to his chest. "Gods in hell!"

Seeing his mirror eyes turn to me so suddenly, my hand automatically goes to my knife. It's reassuring to have the weapon on me, but I have to remind myself that he's not one of *them*.

"Keelie?" Red moves toward me, as if to embrace me. His watch—a different one this time—looks like it's made of pure gold, flashes under the early morning sun.

I shake my head. "Show me your pockets. Empty them, and the bag too."

He rolls his eyes—the action is just visible by the tiny

lines that separate his sclerae from his irises. "Really?"

"Really."

"I told you before, I'm not one of the enemy." But all the same, Red does as I ask. He knows I can't be too careful. Neither of us can.

No augmenters are produced from the rucksack. Only a novel in pristine condition, a cap with a fancy logo on that Red looks very proud of, and a—

"You brought a chess set with you?" My eyes widen as I recognize the symbols on the outside of the box, and, immediately, I'm drawn back in time. For a while, Red and I played it nearly every evening. I was by far the better player, but I'd let him win every third or fourth game. Enough to keep him interested.

Red's grin is infectious. "Of course. And I'm going to take you out...piece by piece."

He bites his bottom lip, giving me a strong look, and tingles run over me. I get the distinct impression that he's also running his eyes over me, checking me out, and I hold back a smile. I look good today. Got my best clothes on—the ones that make my body look much better than it does in the garments I sleep in—and my hair is far from greasy.

Stay focused.

"So, how's the undercover stuff going?"

He shakes his head. "I can't tell you anything. For the safety of both of us."

I nod.

"Besides, I don't want to ruin these meetings with boring undercover stuff." His gaze drops down my body, then back up. With any other man, that would annoy me. But not with Red.

"So why are we meeting?" I ask, raising my eyebrows. The corners of my mouth twitch.

"You want me to spell it out?"

"Yes. Spell it out." I smile and feel confident and alive in a way I haven't done in a long time.

Red steps nearer, and, again, I find myself staring at him. He's filled out well. Muscular. He doesn't look like the type of man who works out just to get a muscular body to intimidate people with. He looks like he actually uses his body. And the tattoos on his arms just set it all off.

"You want to know why we're meeting? Why we're *really* meeting?" His voice gets rougher, and there's something in his tone that speaks to me within.

I nod, my eyes darting to his. I try to see beneath the mirrors.

"To play chess," he says, indicating the box.

I laugh, then I see his face. "You're serious?"

"Can't get a decent game of chess back there." He jerks his thumb behind him, and part of me expects to see the distant outline of New Kimearo breaking the skyline. Except it's not in view, not from here.

I push my hair back from my face. I'm hot and sticky.

Red opens the chess set. He's got that gold ring in his ear again, like in the dealership office. "The enemy says chess is the only acceptable form of war as it's not real violence, but no one's competitive when they play. It's like they don't care. You don't know how many times I've dreamed of playing chess with you."

I tilt my head to one side. "You've dreamt of *playing chess* with me?"

Red nods. "Many a night. And you know what?"

"What?"

"I always take you—the queen—with my bishop. And then...it always turns into something more." He picks up a bishop and holds it up, giving me a mischievous grin. "Some of the pieces are really quite...phallic. I wonder what my dream means."

My eyes widen. "Well, you're certainly not shy, are you?" I look down at where the other pieces are. Two can play at this game. My hand seizes the white king, and I place it in his hand. "Is that you?"

"The king? Sure."

"Well, it's a shame you're the weakest piece on the board. You wouldn't have the strength to get me."

"Ah, but I'm the most valuable. The whole game is

about keeping me safe."

I pick up the queen next. "But *I'm* the most powerful. And the king doesn't even do anything. Not really. Whereas the queen gets lots of action."

Red grins.

It feels strange flirting with him. Nico and I don't really flirt. We're both just...there, together. Well, *sort of* together.

Nico.

I try not to think about him. After all, I haven't done anything wrong. This is just harmless flirting. It's not like I'm meeting up with Red for sex or anything.

Of course that makes me think about having sex with Red and—

I concentrate on setting up the chessboard on a low flat-topped rock, forcing all other thoughts to the back of my mind.

Red and I sit either side of the rock, cross-legged. I play white and make the first move, then we settle into the game.

I look up at him after a few moments of playing in silence. "This feels weird."

"Very weird," he says as he takes one of my pawns. "I'm beating you easily—now that's the definition of weird." Then he pauses and looks at me. "I like it out here."

"Me too," I say.

We play several more moves. My hands shake a little. I try not to look at him as I play, but I can't help it. I steal glances at him, and there's something very thrilling about sitting only a few inches away from a man who *looks* Enhanced.

After ten minutes, Red leans back away from the board. "It's difficult undercover, in their cities, towns. I'm a nervous wreck in them, constantly sure I'm going to get caught."

"You didn't look like you were a nervous wreck in the office," I say.

"Good actor." He shrugs. "But I was, under it all.

Especially when I realized it was you." He exhales hard and shuts his eyes for a moment. "There aren't many of us undercover, but a while ago a few converted."

"Willingly?"

He nods and looks pained. I start to reach across to touch his arm, to offer comfort, but I stop myself. I don't think he's even noticed.

"They couldn't handle it. The fear, the nerves. Being undercover made them more…" He wipes his hands on his thighs, then looks up at me again. His mirror eyes flash. "It exaggerated all the typical Untamed suffering. You know, the bad stuff we feel that the Enhanced want to cure us of."

"But it's not *bad* stuff," I say. "It's just part of life. It's part of who we are, of being human."

Red makes a non-committal sound.

I lean forward. "Are you all right? Red?"

He smiles weakly. "Do you believe you're suffering?"

"Living so we can choose to feel real things isn't suffering." I pause, then I do reach out. His hand is cold. "You're not…."

"No," he says. He turns on his smile, and it completely transforms his face. "It's just difficult living with them all the time. It's why I need to come out here, need to see you." He squeezes my hand quickly, then taps the board so all the pieces jump up slightly. "Your move, K."

I turn my attention back to the board, but I can't concentrate—that's the problem—not with him sitting so close to me. Just on the other side of the board. So close, I could—

I see the blood around his body, notice the way it fans out so perfectly. A beautiful circle.

I flinch, turn my head quickly.

"What is it?" Red jumps up, and—because of his sudden movement—I do too, and we're both automatically in alert mode, looking around for the Enhanced.

I narrow my eyes, searching every rock, every

cranny. My knife is in my hand before I realize it.

But there's no one here. And I know why I flinched.

"I don't know," I say. "I just—just got a feeling."

The knife of madness slices deeper, Keelie.

I take a deep breath, but I can see the knife in front of me—the one from my dream, not the one I'm holding. The one that is invisible to most, but chases me.

"You think we've been followed?" Red's voice is low. "Your people or mine?"

I don't answer for a long few moments, just stay looking out at the sand and the rocks. The knife will disappear soon—I hope.

"Keelie?"

"I don't think there's anyone there." But my words don't sound quite right.

I step back, and my foot catches on a stone, and I fall onto the dry earth, feel the sand get into my hair. I groan, rolling over. Embarrassment floods me.

"Keelie?" Red looks amused as he leans down, offers me a hand.

But I don't take it.

I stare at him.

His eyes suddenly look dimmer. The mirrors are fading. He could soon pass for Untamed....

My eyes go to his lips. I wish they wouldn't, but they do. My eyes don't obey me anymore, and I look at those lips. Magnificent. They look full, especially for a guy, and my gaze follows the curve of them. My breathing speeds up.

My hand stretches to meet his, and the contact zaps warmth through me. I pull him toward me, suddenly feeling empowered, in control.

"Kee—" Red stumbles, falls, but catches himself, holds his body above mine, not touching me. And his lips are so close.

Everything stops.

I stare at him, and he just holds himself there. A structure over me. Secure. I can't see the definition of his eyes, but I know he's looking into mine.

After about five seconds—five long seconds in which I'm very aware of him as he hovers over me—his arms begin to shake. I look at his muscles. He shouldn't be shaking.

"Gods, Keelie." He makes a deep sound at the back of his throat.

Then he leans down.

His lips brush the hollow of my neck, tenderly at first, then with a slight force. I feel his tongue there, and the slight graze of his teeth. Electricity runs through my body. I lift my head, push my hips up too. My right hipbone presses into his, and then he lets himself fall against me completely. But gently.

Our bodies meet, and the pull within me gets stronger. My hands run across his back, up and down, and then they're in his tousled hair. I close my eyes.

His knee pushes my legs apart, and I gasp, eyes flying open.

His face is so close….

Just as his lips are about to meet mine, I turn my head away.

Red's eyes widen, and he looks at me. "Sorry, I shouldn't have." Then he moves over to the left and sits so we're not touching.

Neither of us says anything. I listen to the internal raging within me. I wanted him to kiss me properly, to keep touching me. So why did I stop?

I sit up and look at him. "*Why* did you write *those* words on the note? That first one. *I know what you did.*"

I'm totally ruining the moment more than I already have. And I don't even know where that question came from.

"I told you, to get your attention." He sounds a bit annoyed. Or maybe I imagine that.

I fold my arms.

Just drop it.

But I don't.

"You could've written something else. You could've written, *Hi Keelie. It's Red. I'm still alive.* That would've worked. That would've caught my attention."

"Didn't we talk about this before?" He sighs. "You didn't recognize me at New Kimearo—even when we kissed, you didn't recognize me." It sounds like an accusation, and it's something that hurts him, I can tell. "If I'd given you a note like that, you'd never have believed me. No. I had to be careful. Anyway, it worked. We're both here. We're both together... I'm sorry if it bothered you."

How could it not bother me?

"Your note gave me nightmares." I shrug. Maybe I would've had them anyway.

Red sighs, then reaches out. His touch is soft on my arm. "I'm sorry. I just... I thought it was the best thing to put. I needed you to realize it was me. I'm sorry."

He pulls me close, an arm around me. I look up at him.

"Do you get nightmares...about that night?" I ask, and it feels strange talking about nightmares with Red, when usually it's Elf I talk to.

But Elf doesn't know the whole story. He just took my word for it that there was no one left to save at the village.

Red shakes his head, and he holds me, keeps holding me. I stare out across the desert land, my head against his chest, listening to his heartbeat. My eyes fall on our shadows. I can't see where his ends and mine begins. We look like one unit.

And then I realize how close I am to him, and I feel butterflies stirring in my stomach again. I'm so close to him, I could move my head slightly, lift it up, and kiss him.

And he would kiss me back, wouldn't he?

"I can't believe I've found you," Red whispers into my hair.

"Me neither," I say, holding onto every ounce of willpower in my body.

TEN

RED AND I ARRANGE TO meet again, and then I leave quickly, feeling like I'm on a countdown.

No one at Nbutai appears to have missed me, and I tell Elf the snares were empty, then slip into the usual routine: checking stock, doing chores, and maintaining my strength. But, the whole time I do it all, I feel different. Excited? Nervous? Red didn't want to talk about that night, so I don't understand why he hinted at it in his note.

Unless he's as messed up by it as I am and part of him wants to talk about it... He just can't bring himself to actually do it?

I'm almost scared to go to sleep that night, because I expect to be overrun with the nightmares, but, for once, I sleep peacefully. By morning, I feel refreshed. As refreshed and peaceful as Bea and Mila look, still asleep. I take a moment and watch Bea. She hasn't woken up early today and gone for her usual early morning walk. That's...odd. She'll skip other parts of her routine sometimes—if she's run out of time or has got distracted—but the early morning walk is pretty standard. The only other times she hasn't gone out were when she was ill. She says she likes the time when no one else is about, to clear her head before she makes Mila's breakfast.

Elf looks at me as I leave the hut. He's sitting just outside.

"You were dreaming about Red," he says.

His words make me go cold, and, suddenly, I feel self-conscious.

"What—what did… How do you know?"

"You said his name." He pauses and looks up at me with concern. "I miss him too. I know it's different for you, but he was my friend too."

Different for me? Because our families had assumed we'd get together? Because he was the only boy in our group whom I wasn't related to, and therefore from an early age we were pushed together? Because we spent a lot of time together by choice too. Particularly toward the end.

But I don't want to think about that. Not now.

I point to the sky. The pink hues from the sunrise are fading, but there's a strange light. "Do you think the Turning's close?"

"Katya says so." Elf stretches his arms out either side of him, then stands. "We haven't had one in a while."

"Not unusual, not for this time of year."

It's fairly common not to have many Turnings for a while, then suddenly have loads. We're coming up to the end of the slow period now. Soon the seasons will change ferociously fast as the spirits get restless. Thinking of the spirits makes me nervous. No one likes the Turning. No one wants a spirit to feed from them and kill them.

"What's on the schedule for today?"

"Hunting," Elf says. "Yani says he saw game on the other side of Anjazi's Rock late last night. We're going out there shortly."

"Great, I'll get my things."

"No." Elf places a hand on my arm. "Rahn's leading it."

I try not to flinch, try not to show the effect my brother's words have had on me. "And?"

Elf watches me carefully. A muscle in his jaw visibly tightens. "And I don't want him…" He shrugs. "Hurting you."

"Hurting me?" I step back, my eyebrows shooting up. "He won't hurt me, Elf. I can manage myself."

Elf shrugs. "I don't know what went on before… What he did to you—"

"He didn't do anything."

Elf raises his eyebrows, but it's not in a surprised way. It makes him look angry. "He did, and you're protecting him. Hell, Keelie. He took you away, in the middle of the night. The first I knew was when Bea and Mila came running to me, in tears. Bea said you'd gone off with Rahn."

"I didn't choose to go!"

"Exactly." He raises his voice, and I glance toward Rahn's hut. "I knew you wouldn't go off with Rahn, just the two of you—and now you won't say a word about what really happened? That's not like you. Normally, you'd be raging. You'd be declaring war on the man. But you're not. You're not even speaking about it." He pauses. "He threatened you, didn't he?"

I look away. *Not me*, I want to say. But I can't say the words. Rahn made that clear.

Minutes pass, and my brother and I stand here. In the hut, I hear Bea getting up, moving about, and then Mila's high-pitched voice. A moment later, Bea starts humming and then her hums turn to soft song. She doesn't sound ill. Maybe she was tired, needed to sleep more.

Elf exhales. "You're staying here when we go out hunting. No arguments, Kee. Rahn wants a small group—four or five hunters. If you come along, I can just see it, he'd find an excuse for you two to be paired together—alone. He'd… I'm not letting him get you again. I didn't protect you last time, but I will from now on."

"It wasn't anything like that," I say quietly.

"But you won't tell me," Elf says. "What am I supposed to think? You come back, all subdued and quiet."

Subdued? Quiet?

"It wasn't me he threatened," I say.

"Wasn't you?" He looks at me carefully. "Who then?"

I take a deep breath. "He said if I challenged him again or something, he'd take Bea out next time. You know he's never liked her! I can't retaliate against him, Elf. Not if I'm to protect our sister. And I have to."

Elf pales, then grips his hands together in front of his chest.

"Don't say anything to him," I warn. "If he knows I've told you, he'll take that as me trying to cause a mutiny or something. Elf, I mean it. You can't do—or say—anything."

His eyes darken. "Fine. But I'll be watching him."

"You and me both," I mutter.

I head back into the hut and join Bea. She's sitting on her blanket, holding our mother's necklace. Bea was wearing it the day D'Elinous was ambushed. And it's the only thing of our mother's she has. The only thing any of us have.

"You all right?" I put on a cheery face.

Bea runs the necklace through her fingers, feeling each amber bead in turn, then the butterfly in the center, before she slides it over her head. She turns to me, eyes wide. "You look like Mum."

Her words freeze me, and I stare at her for a second. I didn't think Bea remembered Mum, what she looked like, how she smelled, how she always sang to the birds early in the morning. But there's no reason why she shouldn't. Bea's older than me, and just because she thinks differently to us, it doesn't mean her memory's affected. Immediately, I feel bad for even thinking that Bea wouldn't have remembered. I can remember Mum and Dad.

"So do you," I reply, taking in Bea's face.

Bea frowns hard. "But you look more like her…you and even Eirnin. I wish I looked like Mum. Then I'd be close to her too."

"But you are close to her. You're her daughter, her first-born."

"I want to see her, Kee-Kee. I want us all to be together. You and me, and Eirnin and Mila. And Mum and Dad." She looks up at me. "Do you think it will happen?"

I take my time in replying. I don't want to lie to her—shouldn't lie to her—but I don't want to say the words.

I shrug. "Someday, we'll all be together again."

"Someday? When?" Bea leans against me, rests her head on my shoulder.

I stroke her hair.

"Someday, Bea. Someday."

In the end, the hunting party comes back empty-handed. Rahn curses and blames malignant spirits, then storms off.

"You okay?" Elf joins me on the sand, where I'm sitting, watching Bea watch Marouska and Esther play with the dogs twenty feet away. They throw them sticks and squeal with them when they run about.

I nod, watching her. Bea's talk of our parents has made me feel strange all day. Uncomfortable. I never asked Red which Enhanced town he's tracked my parents down to. And what if they are at New Kimearo, or can get there? What if I could see them— see them Enhanced. For years after the D'Elinous attack, Bea regularly asked me when we'd see Mum and Dad again. It nearly broke my heart telling her that we wouldn't.

I look at Elf. "Do you ever dream about finding Mum and Dad?"

My question obviously surprises him because he lets out a low whistle.

"They're dead," he says.

"They're Enhanced."

"Kee, they're *dead* to us. Dreaming about finding Mum and Dad isn't going to help us. Just torment us." He sighs, and the way he looks at me suddenly reminds me of Rahn. For a second, I freeze. Then the resemblance is gone, and it's just my brother next to me. "We mustn't let it affect us now."

We watch Bea in silence as she watches Marouska and Esther run round and round with the terriers.

After a while, Five walks past, carrying a heavy load. Elf rushes off to help her—just as I knew he would—and I'm left on my own again. Left to think about my parents.

But I know I've made the right decision. They're too far gone. We have to concentrate on the people we still have.

ELEVEN

I CAN'T STOP THINKING OF Red. He fills my head, fills every part of me.

And the knowledge of some secret undercover Untamed group makes my heart pound. Maybe once Red's got to know me more and things have settled, he'll tell me all about it, and I can get involved. Yes, I'd love that. I'd love to be an undercover agent too, be in the midst of the Enhanced all the time, living with the adrenaline and the thrills. And we could make a bigger network or something. Work with the undercover agents—because Red will trust me by then—and then we can really start to do stuff. Big stuff. Stuff that will help all the Untamed.

"Hungry?"

I look up, dazed, to find Nico standing in front of me, holding two plates of steaming noodles and sauce.

"Got you extra meat in yours," he says, handing me one of the plates. He digs a spoon out of his back pocket and gives it to me.

"Thanks." I wipe the spoon on my shirt several times, then dig in.

Nico sits next to me, and we eat in silence, watching

everything from the edge of the village. Rahn and a few of the men are discussing something by the fire. Seven and Five are taking the dogs out for an evening run—but I frown as I notice one of the dogs isn't with them.

"I heard Bea wants to go out shooting," Nico says after a while.

I stare at him. "She's never wanted to go shooting before. The noise would terrify her." I can't think of anything worse for Bea.

He shrugs. "Rahn must've got it wrong then."

"*Rahn.*" I curse. Great. Next he'll be forcing her to eat anything other than the smoothest soup and slices of mango.

Nico puts an arm around me. I tense up.

I've never tensed when Nico's touched me before, and he notices, withdraws his arm. After a moment, he gets out a pack of cigarettes. Offers one to me.

I shake my head.

Smoking is one thing I'll never do, though Corin and Nico smoke a lot. But I associate it with Red's mother. How she was at the end, desperate for anything. Anything addictive.

But you're addicted to something too, Keelie. To adrenaline, to the rush. To putting yourself in dangerous situations where you can never be sure of other people.

I stiffen a little. My adrenaline-seeking behavior is controlled. It may look impulsive, but it's careful, planned. I'm careful. I think through all the possibilities before I do something. Yes, *my* behavior is controlled. Red's mother's behavior wasn't. It drove her insane.

I'm not mad. Definitely not mad.

And I think about her now—think about her properly. How she scratched her skin furiously all the time, complaining that it burned and burned. She'd douse herself in Caia-Lu's cleansing lotion every hour or so, but it never worked.

"Help me," she whispered to me once, as I walked past.

Red told me to ignore her, to step into his hut with him, pretend she wasn't there. And so I did.

I ate with Red, and I stared at the smears of mud covering the side of his face, and the blisters on his hands, all the while listening to his mother's moans. Twice, she screamed for Red, screamed for her *wild, unkempt brat of a son*. Red didn't react, not to her, but I saw the look of hurt on his face, and I knew how he felt he wasn't good enough for his mother. Not when she'd been Enhanced and had seen how wonderfully clean and well presented everyone in an Enhanced city was.

I wanted to reach across to hold Red then, to comfort him. But he'd become different in the last few months, different since his mother became desperate—not just for augmenters, for anything, drugs, alcohol, everything. He'd closed off more. He didn't talk as much. And sometimes, there was a look in his eye that reminded me too much of his mother's look.

Once, I saw him holding a bag of fine, white powder. He said he'd confiscated it from his mother, but he turned away as he said the words. I didn't see him the rest of that day, or the next. Two days later, and he was fine. More than fine. Overexcited about everything.

"Hey." Nico draws me into a tight hug, and I let him, though the smoke tickles my throat. I try to get him to distract me from my thoughts. From Red.

And I know I shouldn't be thinking of Red so much. Not when I'm with Nico. And I wanted to be with Nico before, didn't I?

Nico takes my plate from me and stacks it with his. "You all right? You look a bit…."

"A bit what?" I say, defensiveness clear in my voice.

"Lost," Nico finally says.

He brings my head closer to his, then kisses my forehead. His lips feel like slugs against my skin, and I shudder, then pull away.

"Where are you going?" he asks as I stand up.

"I've got work to do," I say.

"What kind of work?"

"Training work." I bring a hand up and shield the low sun from my eyes, then set off. "Going for a run," I call back, immediately knowing I'm not going for a run. But telling him my plans wouldn't do any good. He hates me riding my motorbike, and recently I've stopped riding it as much as I like to—because of him. What the hell?

Nico hurries to catch me up. "But it's getting dark."

"Not really. Won't be fully dark for a while. I've got time."

Getting away from Nico—being on my own—makes me feel better. Makes me feel like I can breathe again. And maybe it's because I feel guilty when I am with him. Because I did kiss Red—at the office—and then… then what would've happened yesterday if I hadn't pulled away?

I grimace.

And I didn't even pull away from Red because of Nico. I breathe deeply as I head back into my hut.

"Going for a ride on the bike," I tell my siblings as I grab my leather jacket. It's not real leather, and it won't do much if I fall. I haven't got any safety gear, much to Katya's and Alan's horror. But I've never fallen. Had a few close calls, once or twice. But that's all.

Mila nods, holding Straw Hair carefully. Elf, examining a radio, shrugs, and Bea tells me not to be long. And to be careful. There's a knowing sort of look in her eyes, and I wonder if she thinks I'm going to see Red now. Something tells me she's keeping track.

I look at them all for a second, then see the Watcher Doll lying on my pillow. One of them's been holding it. I pick it up quickly and return it to its place at the foot of my bed, then head back out. Nico's watching me, not far off. Corin's with him, and I watch as the two of them speak. Then I head for where we store my motorbike.

There's nothing I like more than riding my motorbike. The exhilaration it fills me with is like a drug. Feeling the wind on my face, seeing my shadow with hair streaming out behind me, it makes me feel alive.

And I live to feel alive. I crave it.

This isn't madness.

I take the bike up the steepest path I can. The engine's not that loud—Three modified it for me last year—and its tires kick up dust. I operate the gear shifter with my left foot and the hand clutch with my left hand, then use the throttle—need to go faster, faster, faster.

Everything's better when I feel like I'm flying.

TWELVE

I BARELY SLEEP BECAUSE I'M meeting Red the next morning, and every part of me tingles.

Stop it, I chastise myself. *He's just a friend.*

I try to keep my breathing even, but I can't stop thinking about the way his body felt over mine, and how his lips were so soft against my collarbone.

And why I turned my head away.

Why I stopped it.

When I get up, Bea's already awake and ready to go out on her walk.

"You're going to the same area?" I whisper to her as we leave the village.

She laughs. "Don't worry. I'm only going part the way. Don't want to intrude on your romantic get-togethers."

"That's not what they are," I say.

"So why are you meeting him?" Her eyes flash.

I smile.

When I don't reply, Bea gives me a knowing grin, then heads off to the right, leaving me on the path alone.

Like before, I get to the meeting place first. I try to

sort out my thoughts, my feelings about him, before he gets here. But, just when I've decided that maybe it's not a good idea for us to be together like this, I see him, and it's like my heart doesn't listen.

"Hey, you." I find myself smiling, and I want to touch him, want to kiss him.

He waggles his fingers at me in a way that makes me laugh, and I don't even know why. He looks good today, wearing dark shorts and a gray T-shirt that clings to him in all the right places, accentuating his muscles and drawing attention to his tattooed arms. His legs are muscular too, and I see a gray tattoo with a geometric design extending down from his right knee to his ankle. His left leg is clear of artwork. I look back up at his face, note how is hair is curling a little with the humidity and—

"Your eyes!"

He grins, and the emotion reaches his eyes. Beautiful *gray* eyes. No mirrors.

I stare at him.

"No point in having my disguise in."

Before I can stop myself, I pull him close, my hands on his shoulders. Our faces are inches apart, and I stare at him. Stare into his soul, because that's what it feels like with the intensity of the emotion.

Seeing his eyes, Untamed, changes everything. They set off his face in a new way. He was attractive before, but now he's more so. Now he's on a new level, and I feel a deeper yearning stirring inside me.

"Missed me?" he says, smiling, and the twinkle in his eyes grabs me.

"No." I give him a mischievous grin and turn a little, see my survival bag sitting not far away.

"Not even a little bit?"

"Not even a little bit." But my smile betrays me.

"Another game of chess?"

"Sure."

We set up the chessboard, but this time we play a whole game. I try not to notice how close we are or how the air between us seems charged. A few times, I catch him looking at me in an intense way. He wins, easily. He says he hasn't been practicing much, but it's obvious he has. Or maybe I've lost my talent. It has been years, after all.

After the game, we sit on the sand, our backs against a rock. The surface is hot with the sun's heat, and it feels like little fingers, massaging me through my thin shirt.

We're sitting with a few inches between us, and I look across at him.

"What?" he asks. "Have I got something on my face?"

"Just those kissable lips." The words are out of my mouth before I can stop them. Alarm pours through me. Hell. What am I doing?

Mortified, I look away.

"Kissable lips?" There is a lightness in his voice, and I force myself to look at him again. He's grinning, and I look away quickly, feel heat rush to my face.

I press my hand into the sand, trying to distract myself. But he's so close…too close. I'm too distracted. And I obviously don't trust myself to speak anymore. I mean, why the hell did I say that? *Kissable lips.* Must be his eyes, I decide. Them looking Untamed. Making me giddy, making me say stupid stuff.

"So," Red says after a few minutes. He turns to look at me. "I haven't explained the meanings behind my tattoos to you yet. I think you'll like it. Want to know?"

"Uh, okay."

In one quick movement, he pulls his shirt off over his head.

For a moment, I don't know where to look. His arms have a lot of tattoos, but his chest is *covered* in them, more so than I remembered. A lot more. And not just his chest and arms either—his whole upper body is a canvas to the ornate designs.

"So, this one." He points at the eagle. "That's all about flying and freedom. You know, being able to travel in this world and having all the freedom you can have, but being free." I nod. To me, that's what the butterfly on my mother's necklace represents. "These lines here, these darker lines that sort of clip its wings—that's about restriction. The things you have to do to be free."

"Like being undercover?"

He nods. "Exactly."

"So I'm free and flying, but also got to stick to the rules. See these circles here?" He points toward his left shoulder where a cluster of blue circles have been etched. The shapes overlap each other, and some are darker than others. "These represent the different lives."

"What? Reincarnation?" I lean closer, squinting a little.

He laughs. "No. The different sections of my life. A circle for when I lived with my mum, at D'Elinous. A circle for the conversion attack. A circle for my undercover work."

"So what are the other circles for?"

The look in his eyes seems to get deeper as he makes direct eye contact with me. "Future parts of my life," he says. "Important things."

A strange, bubbly feeling pulls through me as he explains the importance of his other tattoos. I smile, and I look away for a moment, feel like I should at least *try* to calm my racing heart.

"I really wanted you to know about them," he says. "I know you like stories."

Stories. I think back to the ones Caia-Lu used to tell. The one she used to tell most was "The Dragon and the Elf," because it was mine and Elf's favorite, and we'd even act it out. I was always the dragon, and my brother was the elf. It's how he got his nickname, because for several months he insisted he was the elf in the story and would only answer to *Elf*.

"Yeah," I say. "Nothing to do with you wanting to strip off in front of me."

He grins, then leans back a little. "Well, maybe a bit."

"So, are they permanent? Your tattoos?"

"Of course."

"So they're not temporary…like with the Enhanced?"

He shakes his head. "I've never had them do any alterations or modifications on me, just like I've never taken a real augmenter. Nearly did once by mistake though."

"What?"

He smiles, coyly. "It was a close one. My undercover partner realized and stopped me. Thank the Gods." He points at his chest. "Anyway, I got these three years ago. Before I joined the undercover stuff."

"Before?" I stare at his tattoos, following the swirls of blue and gray ink as they create the eagle's wings that spread over the hard planes of his chest and drip feathers across the muscles of his stomach. More heat floods me. "What were you doing? Where were you?"

Gods, so much time has passed. There's so much stuff we don't know about each other.

"Here and there," he says, and I realize I'm staring at him, at his tattoos, his muscles, imagining what they'd feel like under my fingertips.

"What kind of answer's that?" I manage to get the words out, but only with difficulty.

"Mostly traveling. Looking."

"Looking?" I tear my eyes from his tattoos, up to his face. His full lips…and those eyes!

I try to shake myself. It's just Red. My friend.

"Looking for other Untamed. I found a few others." His expression changes. "But I can't say much, for—"

"For the safety of both of us," I finish for him, smiling.

He smiles back. "You looked so beautiful, you know."

"Looked?" I raise my eyebrows.

"When you stormed into my office, fueled up like an avenging angel. Gods, you were brave, Keelie, marching in there."

I smile sweetly. "You know, you could've let me get the keys and leave. I was only going to take the one truck."

"I've got an appearance to maintain." He spreads his arms out wide and his muscles and tattoos ripple. The eagle looks like it's going to fly. "But out here, we have no illusions to keep up. Out here, we can be ourselves."

He breathes deeply, then he turns toward me properly. I feel the jolt that only true, strong emotion can instigate. It runs through my body, grabs every part of me.

And I stare at him. At Red. My Red.

Back from the dead.

He lifts up his hand slowly, and my hand lifts to meet his, like it's automatic, instinct. Our fingers entangle, and I keep my eyes on him. His lips part slightly. His touch gets a little hotter, then he lets go of my hand and runs his fingertips down the inside of my arm, slowly. The touch sends delicious chills spiraling through me.

When he gets to my elbow, he stops, looks at me. And he's leaning forward, closer. And I've leaned closer too. So close.

"I really want to kiss you, Keelie."

My breath catches in my throat.

Red leans forward more, closing half of the small distance between us. "Would that be okay? Just a *small* kiss…."

I nod, smiling, and he kisses my smile. My hands go to his shoulders, feeling his cool skin. And a thousand fireworks explode in my body as I kiss him back.

It is everything that our office kiss wasn't. It's fire and ice and darkness and feeling and intensity. It's everything in me becoming alive and meeting him.

The need to press myself against him—to feel all of him—rises like a stormy tide, so quickly, surprising me. And every bit of control in me disappears, like an elastic band has been cut, and it's now useless to resist.

I kiss him, roughly, hard. His teeth graze against my bottom lip, and I gasp.

I want him, and the sudden urgency within me shocks me. I haven't felt like this before... With Nico, it's—

Don't think about him.

My body yearns for Red's, and it's like a tap has been turned. Desire floods me. I press myself as close as I can, knowing where this will lead. His hands lift my hair away from my neck, then slip down to my waist, and my hands press against his back, his bare back, feeling the way his muscles move as we kiss. As we kiss deeper and deeper.

I push him down onto the sand, lean over him, kissing him. Then he flips us over, so he's on top of me, and I'm drowning in him as he kisses my neck. I can't breathe. I'm losing myself, and, just when I'm sure that I'm lost, Red pulls back. He looks at me, and we're both breathless, both breathing raggedly.

And it's Red. The boy I grew up with. The boy who knows me better than anyone—even Elf.

He slides his hands all over me, and then his fingers are undoing the buttons on my jeans. I feel breathless, and exhilaration takes over and—

Something screeches behind us.

We spring up. My heart pounds.

A spirit hovers ten feet from us.

I suck in air too quickly, then shake my head. Mustn't look at it. Looking at spirits is dangerous, makes them think you're challenging them. My uncle challenged one—a really bad one—and it destroyed him in seconds. But I can't look away—because what if it attacks? And we need warning and...but this spirit is still. It's staying there. Hovering. Not coming closer. Not screeching anymore either. Just...watching us? Watching us with many eyes. Many, *many* eyes. I start to feel sick, and I know I'm looking at it too much—fascinated by its gelatinous-looking tentacles that are semi-translucent yet still seem to radiant a bronze color. And what even *is* it? Like, really?

I glance at Red, my heart pounding. As subtly as I can, I do my jeans back up. Might need to run fast in a minute. "What's it doing?"

"I don't know." His voice is low, tense.

We watch the spirit for a long, long time, and a cold wind wraps around us. And it's strange, watching it while trying not to look at it, not to accidentally challenge it. I press my lips together slowly. I wonder if it could work with the Watcher Doll. I imagine myself capturing the spirit and putting it inside the Watcher Doll, making the token active so it can help protect us.

Only I know that's wrong. Watcher Dolls don't *contain* spirits. They just provide the link between a Seer and the spirits. Spirit boxes actually imprison spirits, and they're really dangerous. No one likes to be trapped.

Go home. The words flit toward us, as if they're in the air.

"Did you hear that?" I look at Red, sideways.

He nods, his face pale. "Guess it doesn't like us being together." He attempts a laugh, but it doesn't sound natural.

The spirit hisses suddenly, and I jump back against the rock.

Go home!

Then it disappears. Just...just like that. Vanished into thin air.

"Has it gone?" I look around, take a step forward, adrenaline at the ready as I search for it. But I can't see it. It's really just gone? I let out a shaky laugh. And—Gods—we've seen a spirit, looked at a spirit, and we're *alive*. It didn't rip us to shreds like one did my uncle.

"Keelie... I'd better go," Red says, and his words sound strange, and he doesn't look like he wants to say them. He takes hold of my shoulders gently and stares at me, his lips parted slightly.

I stare at him. "What? Because of that spirit? We can't let that thing dictate what we do."

He bites his bottom lip with his perfect front teeth, and my breathing speeds up a little. I want to lean in again, to slide my arms around him, to feel his body against mine.

"I have work to do."

"Now?" I whisper, and I hook a finger on his belt and look at him in my most meaningful way.

He nods. "I can't risk being caught."

I let go of him. Take a step back. "Of course." What was I thinking anyway? Were we really going to have sex out here if that spirit hadn't disturbed us? But I know the answer: yes. Because the idea of it is sending thrills through me, and I'm sure Red knows it.

"Tomorrow," he whispers, a certain glint in his eyes as he picks up his shirt. "Meet me, tomorrow. I can be here mid morning. I have to see you again, Keelie. I can't stay away. I need you."

THIRTEEN

I NEED YOU.

No one's ever said that to me before. Especially not a man. And it was Red. Red who said it. And it sounds crazy, but I feel connected to him. So connected.

I meet back up with Bea, and I can't stop smiling when we get back to Nbutai. There's so much pent-up emotion and energy inside me. So much stuff I wanted to do with Red. But didn't.

Because he left.

But he *needs* me. And tomorrow can't come soon enough.

"You look happy," Five says, falling into step with me as I walk through the village. Bea's already headed off to get Mila's breakfast and prepare for her lessons. "Where've you been?"

"Just out." I even nearly feel like stopping and petting one of the dogs.

"Out?" Five raises her eyebrows. "Nico found you then?"

I stop. "What? He was looking for me?"

And suddenly my heart goes crazy. What if he saw me and Red together? What if—

But no. I'm being silly. He wouldn't have gone that far out. He doesn't like walking, prefers staying in the village. I'm the explorer out of the two of us. I'm the adventurous one.

Five nods. "About two hours ago. Super early for him. You really didn't find him? Were you gathering with Bea?"

"Yeah." Something like that.

Guilt seeps in. It's like a black mist inside me, and I know I deserve it. And part of me tries to tell me that it's okay—because I know Red from before, because we're connected. Only it doesn't make it okay, I know that. My head knows that.

But my heart doesn't.

I think of what Bea said.

I need to break up with Nico. Sooner rather than later. I don't want to be one of those girls who cheats on her boyfriend. I close my eyes for a moment, remember how upset Aunt Ramna was when she'd discovered her husband had been having an affair.

No.

I'm not like that.

Five's chattering away to me, but I barely hear her. I mumble that I need to find Nico.

He's in his hut. I realize it as soon as I'm standing outside it, even though the drape is pulled close.

I take a deep breath, then call out his name and push the cover back.

There's a candle burning inside, and Nico's sitting on his bed—a low mattress, of sorts. He smiles when he sees me, but the flickering candlelight adds a sense of ominosity to his appearance.

"Yani's out," Nico says, grinning. That look in his eye. The look I know well. Very well. "He's not going to be back for a while now, though I thought we'd have had longer—where were you?"

"Had longer?" I stare at him.

"For you and me to spend some time together," he says, and he says it so simply. He stands up and takes me in his arms, and it's awkward. "Where were you anyway?"

I scrunch up my nose. "Out with Bea. Um, Nico—"

He kisses me.

Kissing Nico is different to kissing Red. Very different. I shouldn't be comparing them, but I am. I can't help it. I thought before that Nico knew me, really knew me, but now it's obvious that we're not right together. It's Red I'm supposed to be with. I only really kissed Nico that very first time because it just seemed that I was expected to do it—and others had told me they thought we'd be good together. And then it just sort of went from there.

And now we've been sort of together for three years. Well, he even thinks we're *together*—no *sort of* about it, not for him. And how didn't I notice how boring being with him is? How did I think that that was it? Red set every part of me alight—and we were only kissing.

Nico pulls me down onto his bed, so I'm lying down. His hands roam over me, and, when at last his lips leave mine and move to my neck, I feel something like relief.

I shouldn't be doing this.

Bea's right. I need to end things.

"You seem different." Nico lifts his head up and looks down at me, then moves so he's lying next to me.

"Different?" I'm breathing hard, but not because of him. Because of the guilt.

But what do I tell him? I can hardly say I've met someone else. I've got to keep Red a secret.

But isn't he going to notice you disappearing each morning anyway? Someone's going to notice.

Yet I've still got to end things. Before, I didn't think me and Red were going to get together. But we have.

"Nico, I'm sorry."

He doesn't flinch.

"It's all right," he says. His voice is neutral. "I know."

I sit up. "What?"

129

"It's your time of the month. That's why you're not into it. It's okay."

I stare at him. I'm not on my period, but something tells me I shouldn't say that. Because that would give him hope.

I take a deep breath. "Nico." I grip my hands together, hard. "I—I think we need to take a break."

A break? Like that isn't giving him hope.

For a moment, he doesn't react. He just stares at me, his eyes all big and puppy-like. Then he pats his blond hair, almost self-consciously, and makes a strange noise at the back of his throat, kind of like a squawk.

"A break?"

I nod.

"Oh."

I get up quickly, my heart fluttering.

There. It's done.

Except it's not.

A break is temporary.

And what I want is forever. With Red.

Unease clouds me as I stumble out of Nico's hut.

It's amazing how quickly euphoria can be replaced by guilt. Earlier, when I was with Red, everything was perfect. But now it's all a haze. Nico walked past earlier, eyes red-rimmed. I felt the guilt load up inside me, like another portion had been added to my weight.

But what was I supposed to do? *Not* end things?

Only I haven't even done that. Not properly.

But maybe he knows. Maybe he's guessed.

I wipe the side of my face with my hand, feeling irritable. Marouska scolds me twice as I stir the soup—for not stirring it *properly* and letting it stick to the pan—and Corin asks me if I'm okay. I nod, but half an hour or so later, when I'm staring into the fading sky, he comes back, says he's heard about me and Nico.

"What made you do it?" he asks.

Red.

My shoulders tighten. I shrug, try to loosen them. Or maybe I'm shrugging to his question, I don't know. But I don't want to be here discussing Nico. I want to be out there…with Red. Every part of me aches for him, and I know it sounds stupid, but that's how I feel. I really do.

"Well," Corin says after a long time in which I haven't replied. "I always thought you two were an odd match."

"You did?" I turn and look at him. I'm sitting near the fire, my long-empty soup bowl at my feet.

Corin nods. "You're so full of life, and you've got ambition. You're reckless. You love raids. He's just… *not*. They say opposites attract, but…" He shrugs. "I don't know."

But he's right. I realize that as I sit later on in the hut, watching Bea comb out Mila's long, wet hair. Nico and I would never have really worked, would we? We were sort of together for three years, but, when I think about it, did I ever really want to be with him?

No. Of course I did. Didn't I?

But not when you can have Red.

And Red said he needed me.

And I need him.

We're meant to be together. I move to the doorway and look up at the stars. Elf comes and sits beside me, then Bea, then Mila. The four of us, all huddled up. Family.

We could almost be back at D'Elinous.

Things were so much simpler back then.

And everything was easier.

A DANGEROUS GAME

I am in a room, alone.

The walls are gray, drab, and the paint peels from them in long sheaves that are like fingernails.

There's no door.

I'm trapped.

Everything is wrong.

I scream and scream to be let out, and I shout, tell them that I thought I was doing the right thing. That I thought it was okay.

But no one answers.

Alone.

I'll always be alone.

FOURTEEN

EARLY NEXT MORNING, ALL I want to do is see Red—as if seeing him will make everything better—but everyone seems determined to stop me from leaving. I guess it's one of those unspoken rules of the universe. I want to be with Red, and there are one thousand and one things that need doing first.

Kayden has me skinning and butchering a gazelle. He was out hunting most of the night with Three and Esther. I'm anxious to get away, to meet Red, but I can't refuse Kayden's request and draw attention to myself.

Then Bea informs me Elf's been sick, and can I come and help?

Of course I help, and I find we've got no fresh water in our hut. A trip to the nearest watering hole tells me it's dry, and I have to trek farther to the next one. I make the walk alone, lost in thought, in guilt, in that nightmare.

It was a new one, but I can't shake the feeling of unease it's left in me.

I tell myself that I'm only feeling that way because of yesterday—because of Nico—and that soon, things

133

will be more bearable. But, for some reason, I keep thinking of those words that Caia-Lu said to me when I was little: *Your death is already written in the silk of time.* Before, it never made me feel uneasy. Just gave me a determination to live. But now—maybe it's because of the unease that I'm already feeling—I feel strange and uncomfortable. If my death is at a fixed point, then it doesn't matter what I do. I can't stop it. And, up until now, I've really jumped into life. But is life worth fighting for even if it's not going to last long?

And is mine going to last much longer?

I shrug the darkness away and take the water back to the hut, then seek out Rahn. He has the medical supplies, and Elf needs some rehydration tablets.

When I eventually get away from Nbutai and near the meeting point, I know Red has been there for a while. Plus, he has mirrors today, and I stop for a moment.

I slow down, feeling worn but also elated at seeing him. Still, I'm careful, and I make sure it *is* Red and get him to empty his pockets and bag before I sit down with him. No hidden augmenters.

"What's this?" I find an identification card in a wallet in the heap that Red's emptied onto the ground. Robert Yearling, the card says his name is. The photo is most definitely of him. "J&L's Garage: Assistant Manager," I read, straightening back up.

"That's my job there," he says.

"The Enhanced have proper jobs?" I don't know why, but I've never really thought about the Enhanced having actual jobs. I'd always assumed that their only 'job' was to convert us. Sure, I know about the teams they send out, looking for us. But I hadn't imagined they do normal stuff too. "Let me guess, you get paid in augmenters?" Then I frown. "*Real* ones?"

Red shakes his head. "We can buy whatever we want with our wages."

"So you don't need to have any augmenters at all?"

"Everyone gets low-grade augmenters for free.

Same with food, clothes, and accommodation. But if you want stronger augmenters you either persuade a doctor that you need them as the normal ones aren't stopping your suffering, or you buy them with your wages. Or you can buy more clothes, more food, books, DVDs. That's how it's supposed to work. But if you're friends with someone high up, you get nicer stuff anyway as part of the basic care package."

He packs everything back into his bag. There's no chess set this time.

Then he leans in toward me, takes my hand, and pulls me close. I lean into him, feel my knees weakening.

"Are you okay? You're shaking?" Concern fills his voice.

"Fine," I say. And I don't know why I'm acting like this. Why I'm bringing my bad mood here, when all I wanted earlier was to see Red. Only seeing him reminds me of what I did yesterday—how passionately we kissed, and how we could've so easily done more—even though I was still with Nico.

And I haven't even ended things properly.

"Talk," Red commands. He's got some strong aftershave on today, much stronger than usual. It smells like it costs a lot, and it makes me feel a little sick. Red's so used to all these expensive things, pretending to be Enhanced, and my most prized possession is my modified motorbike that's covered in scrapes and scratches and probably wouldn't pass an inspection—if it had one. His clothes are always perfect. Mine are scuffed—even my very best clothes that make me look great looked a lot better when they were newer, and made *me* look a lot better then too. My favorite leggings that used to cling in all the right places are starting to lose their shape.

We're from different worlds.

I sit down slowly, then look at my feet. I stretch them out and wiggle them. Red sits next to me, but he doesn't touch me. Just looks concerned. Even with mirrors in, his eyes look concerned.

"So," I say. "I, uh, had a boyfriend."

Red's head lifts a little. He takes a sharp breath, but doesn't say anything. I see the way his Adam's apple sticks out a bit as he swallows.

"I ended it with him last night." I shut my eyes briefly, trying not to feel as bad as I do.

Except I didn't even end it. *Take a break*, that's what I said. But Nico knows what that means, doesn't he?

Red clears his throat noisily, then looks at me. "You had a boyfriend? Shit." He grips his hands together. "And you ended it because of me?"

Slowly, I nod. And then, suddenly, I'm worried about what he's going to say next. How he's going to tell me I shouldn't have. That I shouldn't have made anyone suspect that something else might be going on, that I might be seeing someone else.

But people break up all the time without a third person being involved.

And Nico and I weren't right. Weren't right at all.

"Wow." Red runs his hands through his hair, makes it stand up like crazy. And I want to reach across and run my hands through it too. I want to be close to him, because I've done all this so we can be together. "Keelie, I—I… I don't know what to say."

I smile quickly. "It's okay—I'm not expecting a relationship from you. Just fun, whatever you want. Nothing heavy if…" I trail off, unsure where to look, and stand up, turn my back to him.

There's a pause, then he stands too, moves next to me.

"You feel it, don't you?" His voice is a whisper that caresses my soul.

"Feel it?"

His face reddens a little, and then he reaches across and touches my chest gently. "In here. You really feel it… Gods, I've dreamt about you for so long, and I've wanted us to be together. And I wondered if you were dead, because I've always been looking for you, and I felt bad thinking all these things about you, in case you were dead. Like that made me sick somehow. But…but it is real, isn't it?"

My vision blurs a little, and I can't believe he's saying this stuff. Or that I'm here, with him. With Red. I picture him as a little boy, how he looked when I was ten and he was twelve. We were playing by the creek, splashing each other. And we were doing it because we'd seen Yuma and her boyfriend doing it. And Red thought it would be fun.

And he pretended to kiss me then.

And I pretended to kiss him back.

And then he *did* kiss me.

I found it funny. He didn't.

He walked away.

But now he's here.

"I feel it," I say.

We kiss, and he holds me lightly at first, daintily, like I'm fragile. But then his grip gets stronger, more certain. He backs me up against a rock, puts his hands either side of me—his arms become beautiful walls around me—and leans into me. His breath is rugged.

I pull him closer, and fireworks go off inside me—and they go off so fast, as if a dam has broken. And suddenly the desire and emotion and *need* floods back into me.

This is Red.

And I want him.

As clichéd as it sounds, we're meant to be together. Since I found Red, everything's been better.

As we kiss, my fingers lift his shirt up. Our mouths part long enough for me to lift the shirt over his head, to discard it, then my fingers are against his skin. And it is perfect.

So perfect.

Steeling myself, I lean back as far as the rock behind me will allow.

"You okay?" His words are breathless, but he looks worried.

"I want to look at you," I say, and I push him away

ever so slightly, just far enough so I can see his chest. His tattoos, that eagle. His muscles.

He grins. "You've no idea the dreams I've been having about you."

I try not to blush, but I know I fail spectacularly at it.

He says that I'm cute, and he kisses me again, more assertively this time. I'd thought there was passion in our previous kiss, but this time—this time it's even more.

"I think we should even things up," he says.

"What?" My word is breathy. I try to reach for him, to pull him back—I want him close again—but he stays just out of my reach, grinning.

He licks his front teeth. "Well, if *I'm* partly undressed…" He trails off, suggestively.

For a second, I wonder what I'm doing. I barely know him. The *new* him. This is the fourth time I've seen him, no the fifth—

No, you grew up with him.

You know him.

He can't be much different.

My lips twitch, and I can't stop myself.

He takes my shirt off, and then my bra. His touch wanders over my breasts, taking the fullness of them in his hands. He kisses each of them in turn, and I shiver, arching my back. My whole body tingles, alive, and I moan, reaching for him, trying to pull him closer, closer, closer.

I undo his belt. He kicks off his jeans, reaching for me.

More kisses, more touches, more undressing.

He swears under his breath, looking at me when we're both naked.

Neither of us can stop smiling as we step up to each other, as we meet.

We lie on the sand, hand-in-hand, and listen. The air feels heavy, like it's full of voices that aren't meant for us. Words, long forgotten—some screamed, some whispered, some cried. The land holds onto its past.

Red sits up slowly and looks down at me. I stare at his chest, his arms, the tattoos. He breathes in deeply, then smiles a smile that reaches his mirror eyes. But I can see beneath them. I can see *him*.

"You're so beautiful." His voice is husky, deep. "Every time I see you, I fall deeper."

"*Every* time?" I raise my eyebrows. "We've seen each other barely a handful of times since…."

"Since we found each other again. Soon, I'll be trapped in your web and there's no place else I'd rather be trapped in than you."

I frown at how inappropriate that sounds, but I smile after a moment.

He leans over me, and my hands go up to touch his chest. His warmth zaps through me. Light catches Red's eyes, and they flash. I feel a thrill within me. Mirrors signal danger. I breathe deeply. I like the thrill. I like it a lot.

"Soon we'll be together properly," he says.

I raise my eyebrows. "We will?" He's going to leave his undercover position? Come to Nbutai? He'd give up his luxurious lifestyle to live in a hut where dust gets in everything, where sometimes we have to walk miles just to get clean water?

"When this is all over, we'll have a nice house together. I'll get you anything you want."

"You think it will be over soon?" I murmur, stretching my neck so I can kiss him.

The war between the Enhanced and Untamed has been going on for hundreds of years. Our people's number is getting smaller—so I suppose we'll lose. But it won't be any time soon. We'll hide in the earth's pockets if we have to.

Red smiles slowly as I finish the kiss. "I love you, you know that, don't you? Do you remember when I first said it?"

I stare at him for a moment, unsure that he can mean what I think he does. Because we were just children. Then I say, "Yes."

"Tell me about it." His voice is even huskier now.

It's a memory I've played in my mind over and over again, even when I told myself not to. But that was because I thought he was dead. I thought I was obsessing over a memory of my dead best friend.

"We were watching those lizards."

"And what were they doing?" His grin gets bigger.

I feel heat rush to my face. I was ten and a half. He was thirteen, just. I didn't understand how he could say it and mean it at the time. Part of me still struggles to understand—he was *thirteen*.

But the way he's looking at me now….

We sit up, and Red pulls me onto his lap so I'm straddling him. We kiss, deeply. I stroke his chest, and his arms slip down around my back. There's something about my bare skin against his that makes me feel alive. His lips leave mine, and then his mouth trails down to my neck. My breathing gets heavier.

Stay in control.

We have sex again, and, this time, I stare at his mirrors the whole time. Before, I savored it—my first time with Red. I wanted to remember every detail. But this time, electricity runs through my body, makes me feel more alive.

I can pretend it's dangerous, seeing his mirrors, and the thrill of it courses through my system, filling me up.

And it's perfect.

I only shut my eyes when we separate, when we lie back on the hot cushion of sand. I feel elated. Elated in a way I've never done before.

After a few moments, our breathing returns to normal rates.

"You know, this kind of emotion, it's what the Enhanced want to feel," Red says.

"What?"

"I was at a bar a couple weeks ago. Some guys were talking about seeing if they could invent a Wild Sex augmenter."

"Wild Sex?" I raise my eyebrows. "But they hate that we're wild. You know, *wild equals bad.*"

Red chuckles. "I guess wildness is good if it's controlled by them." He rolls his shoulders. "The jokes they made though, they were really lewd. One of them even said about having sex with an Untamed instead of inventing that augmenter. Said it would be a massive achievement, and a great way to feel emotion *and* snare a Chosen One: have sex and then convert."

I wrinkle my nose. "This isn't where you reveal yourself to really be one of them and convert me, is it?"

"Well, having sex and not converting you would be a great way to gain your trust, right, if I *was* Enhanced?" He laughs. "But I'm as Untamed as they get."

He trails his fingertips over my stomach in light circles, and butterflies build in me. He lifts his head up slightly, then rolls onto his side, one hand still on me.

"Beautiful," he says. "Just beautiful. Ah, I wish I could see you tomorrow too."

"You can't?"

"Can't get away tomorrow. The next day though. I'll see you then."

We finalize the time we'll meet, and then I blink up at him, his face partly silhouetted by the sun. I start to sit up and—

Voices.

Red swears loudly, and we both jump up, turning.

I see them.

Panic fills me, and I look toward Red. He turns, lunges away from me, grabs his clothes, and then he's off. Sprinting as fast as he can. Leaving me here, and—

And I freeze. Completely freeze. Just stare after Red and—

"Keelie!"

I turn back.
Elf stares at me, thunder in his eyes.
"What the *hell?*"

FIFTEEN

"YOU AND ONE OF *THEM*?"

My brother's voice is blunt and quiet. Behind him, stands Five. She stares at me, her mouth open in a perfect O.

I look around, my heart slamming in my chest, back and forth. Red's running. He's made good distance already.

And I'm naked.

Hell.

I reach for my shirt, grab it with trembling fingers, try to use it to cover myself up.

"You got a gun?" Five asks Elf.

A gun. I inhale sharply. *No.*

Elf shakes his head. "Just leave him. He's going to get away anyway." Then he swears loudly.

My hands shake as I grip my shirt.

"Keelie?" Elf's tone rises a little. "What the hell?" Disgust ripples through the air toward me, like it's radiating off my brother's body. "You and one of them?"

"It's not what you think." A lump forms in my throat. Why didn't Red stay—and why did he have to wear his mirrors today? Shit. Why didn't I ask him about that?

But it was him. *Of course* it was him. Untamed. He didn't convert me.

"Not what I think?" Elf snorts. "It's definitely what I think! Gods, this is…" He wipes the back of his hand across his mouth. "Tell me you used something. That you're not sleeping with him unprotected."

"Of course I'm not," I say, breathless, my heart still slamming away. "We were careful."

He shakes his head. "I feel sick. What the hell would make you do something like that?"

Five's eyes narrow. "Was that *him*? The one from New Kimearo that let you get away?" she demands. "The one you *kissed*. It's him, isn't it?"

My heart pounds faster, faster, faster. I nod slowly.

Immediately, her expression changes. She looks sickened.

I need to explain, but Red's warning flashes through my mind. If I tell them he's still one of us, it could put him and his mission—whatever that is—at risk. That's obviously why he took off.

Five looks disgusted. "I was joking when I said it would be cute if you fell in love. I didn't mean for you to do exactly what I said and go out here and—" Her eyes widen. "You've seen him before. Out here. That's why you dumped Nico."

Elf makes a strangled noise.

I glare at them. "Look, can you both turn around so I can get dressed? I'd rather not have this conversation while I'm practically naked."

"I'd rather not have this conversation *at all*," Elf says darkly, but he turns around, and so does Five.

I pull my clothes on as quickly as I can. As I do so, I scan the area. There's no sign of Red at all now. He really just ran off. Needed to stay undercover. Hell, he can run fast.

"You had *sex* with one of them," Five yells as soon as I say I'm decent. "With an Enhanced One? What the—"

"You don't understand," I say, trying to keep calm. I look at Elf, begging him to understand, see that his face is turning an alarming shade of crimson. "Just listen. He's not… He's not like the other Enhanced. He's fine, really—"

"*Fine*?"

Both my brother and best friend look like they're going to explode.

"Look! I'm still Untamed, see!" I point at my eyes. "Nothing has changed."

"Except you let one of them…" Elf trails off, then coughs violently. When he's finished, his eyes are watering, and he wipes away the tears. "How could you? Gods, why don't you just join them? Join them now, Keelie. It would make it easier for you if you want to be with him—or what is it? Just a conquest for you? Something to prove how strong you are, so you can say you've slept with an Enhanced and still got away Untamed?"

I raise my eyebrows. Part of me can't believe he's even saying that. Just the thought of joining them, becoming one of them—the people whose feelings are artificial, the people who are robotic and devoid of humanity—makes my skin crawl. I clench my hands together. The Enhanced are *wrong*. Being Untamed is the right way of life. The only true way of life. As if I'm going to leave the Nbutai group!

But then my heart drops. The moment anyone at Nbutai hears about this—the moment *Rahn* hears about this—it'll be over. He's going to kick me out. They all are.

Shit.

I have to tell them. Have to. And they wouldn't endanger Red, would they?

"Elf, didn't you recognize him?" I fold my arms.

"Recognize him?" Elf yells. "Unlike you, I wasn't that close. I have boundaries."

My temper flares. "Will you just listen? I can explain

it all. But you two mustn't tell anyone, else you'll mess up *everything*. Promise me."

Five throws her hands in the air. "Mess up everything? You're the one who's messing up, Keelie! How long did you think you could get away with this? I just… Gods. I don't even know you anymore."

Elf watches me, massages his neck.

"I can't believe you did it so close to Nbutai." Five's voice is dark. "It's one thing if you want to play dangerously, but it's quite another if you want to sacrifice us all."

"We're hardly on the doorstep of Nbutai—you can't even see it from here. And he doesn't know where the village is." I grit my teeth. "But will you listen and let me explain? Red's on our side."

"No Enhanced are on *our* side," Five yells.

Elf's face pales considerably, and it's quite a contrast to his previous red hue. He stares at me, then takes a step back. "That man… *Red*?" He's shaking.

"What?" Five looks confused.

I step closer to my brother. I can deal with Five after. "Yes, that was Red," I tell him. "He survived too. And he's undercover. It's a secret operation. He can't tell me much, for my own safety—and his own, and those in his team. There's like a group of them. But no one else is supposed to know, otherwise it jeopardizes their safety. They're *Untamed*."

Elf seems to swallow with great difficulty. He shakes his head, then runs his hand through his hair. I watch as he turns around and looks in the direction that Red retreated. I look too, wonder if Red could be hiding behind a rock down there, or whether he really has vacated the vicinity so quickly, like I first thought.

Five shakes her head, then laughs. "And you believe that story? Actually believe it? Keelie, it's lies. He's Enhanced, and he's trying to get you to trust him."

"If he's Enhanced, he would've converted me. He's had plenty of opportunities, believe me. And I'm still Untamed—still one of us." I nearly bring up Bea seeing him—but I don't. I don't want them confronting her about it in the village, where others could hear.

Five looks at me sadly, shaking her head still. "Undercover Untamed are impossible. We can't pretend to be them. We can't. Keelie, he's got to you, twisted your thoughts. He's got inside you and—" She breaks off, probably realizing her word choice. "We saw his eyes. Mirrors, Keelie, *mirrors*."

"They're fake," I say. "He doesn't always have them."

"No," Five says. "He's *Enhanced*. He's using you—he's using you and your soppy ideas of forbidden love and how exciting and romantic it is in order to get to all of us. You're putting us in danger." She glances at Elf, and he shakes his head. "We have to tell the others. I'm sorry, Keelie, but you're a liability."

My breath catches in my throat, and I spin around. My black hair slaps me in the face, and I shove it away. "What?" My eyes widen. "You're not going to tell the others! You can't—weren't you listening? It'll risk their whole operation, and then a load more shit will happen."

I stare at them as they don't say anything but exchange a long glance between them, as if they're communicating telepathically. My brother and my best friend.

"Keelie," Elf says. "I think he's brainwashing you. You believe all this stuff—stuff that isn't feasible—"

"Are you not listening to a word I'm saying?" I nearly explode.

"We are. But it's bullshit," Five says. "Absolute bullshit. And you're so caught up in it all that you can't even see it. Keelie, you need to be rational, logical. Just *think* about it. He's Enhanced—this undercover story is a lie."

"Then why am I still Untamed?"

"Because he wants all of us. He wants to get close to you and find Nbutai."

"Well why not convert me and get me to tell him

where the village is after I've been converted?" I ask, hands on hips. I nod, triumphant. "Don't you see?" I stare at Five, challenging her. "Why don't *you* think about it? Gods, it's so obvious."

But Five shakes her head. "If he was undercover like you say, one of us, he wouldn't have run away, would he?"

I bite my lip. "He didn't know that you'd give him time to explain. You could've killed him straight away."

"We have to tell Rahn," Five says.

"No." I look to Elf, imploring. He's being too quiet—so he must be thinking about it, coming around? "You can't tell Rahn. He'll banish me. Any excuse, we all know he wants to get rid of me. Elf, come on, I'm your sister. He'd throw me out in an instant. You wouldn't do that to me. You care about me. We're twins—*twins of the stars.*"

I watch his eyes harden.

"*I* care about the safety of the group," he says. "And Five's right. Red could be Enhanced. Hell, we don't know it's even him."

"It *is.*"

Elf shakes his head. "Rahn has to know if there's a chance we could be in danger. We can't keep this from him."

"You don't care about me?" I raise my eyebrows.

"I care about the safety of the group, and, from what I can see, your mind is already being converted, Kee." He looks down for a moment, and Five places her hand on his shoulder. When my brother looks up, his gaze is hard. "You've been lying to us—even if he is Untamed, you've still lied. And it's only a matter of time before you lead him to Nbutai, even if you don't mean to—or you get converted. And I've got to put our people first. We can't take risks."

SIXTEEN

I STARE AFTER THEM AS they walk away. I shout, but they don't stop. Five's talking to Elf—needing to persuade him more?

My heart hammers against my ribs, makes me feel sick. I follow them, looking around desperately, as if there's something out here that can help me.

"You're going to ruin everything," I yell. "There are three other undercover Untamed working with Red in New Kimearo. Could be more—other teams, I don't know. But you telling Rahn is going to put them in danger."

Neither of them replies to me.

I try again, and I'm panting, out of breath, struggling to keep up. "Fine," I say. "If you're going to tell Rahn and jeopardize Red's mission, then I'm not coming back to Nbutai with you."

That stops them.

Elf turns slowly. "What do you mean?"

"I'll go straight to New Kimearo." I point in the direction of the town. "I'll go there now."

Elf pales.

"See," Five whispers. "She's joining the Enhanced.

She knows he's one of them. Elf, I'm sorry, he's brainwashed her." She looks at me. "Has he given you augmenters?"

"No." I stamp my foot. "I wouldn't be joining them. I'd be going to warn them."

"Warn them?" Elf says.

"Yes, because you'd be putting them in danger. Don't you see? You tell Rahn, and, if he believes that Red is undercover, he's not going to let it go. He's going to head in there, find them, draw attention to them. So, I'm going now." I turn away, but keep my eyes on them. "I'm going to find Red, tell him that you—his *friend*, Elf—is betraying him. And I'm going to make sure that he and his undercover friends leave with me. We'll go somewhere else. Somewhere safe. Because that's what we do. We're Untamed. We protect each other. And you'll never see me again."

Elf stumbles a little. I smile to myself; so he doesn't want me to leave Nbutai—or be banished by Rahn.

"You can't go to New Kimearo *now*," Five says. "You've got no glasses on. No truck. You'd get caught immediately."

I fold my arms, feel the wind on the back of my neck. "It's a risk I'll have to take, when *you're* going to ruin everything and get rid of the one actual advantage our people have. Even though we're supposed to protect each other."

Five exhales slowly. "Keelie, I just…" She tugs on her hair. "We don't know he is undercover. And you can't be one hundred percent sure either. Yet you've slept with him. Been having a *relationship*. Don't you see how that makes you a liability?"

"So you'd betray the other undercover Untamed because you're unsure?" I raise my eyebrows. "They could get killed. Their deaths on your hands."

"Keelie, I'm sorry. I think he's Enhanced. I think this is all a game to him. If he was undercover, he'd be focused on it. He wouldn't sneak out to see you."

"Except he would. Because it's Red, and we love

each other." Saying the words immediately makes me feel strange.

Five laughs.

"When are you next meeting him?" Elf asks.

"Day after tomorrow."

"You'll be grateful when you realize we saved your life," Five mutters.

Elf nods. "Fine. I'm coming with you then to see him."

"What?" I stare at him.

Elf folds his arms. "I want to talk to Red, see if he can persuade me he's undercover too. I need to know more about this undercover stuff to justify not telling Rahn and the others."

"What?" Five exclaims. "Elf, if he's Enhanced, you'll be walking straight into his trap. He could convert you both. Don't tell me Keelie's persuaded you?" She lets out an exasperated sigh.

"We'll take weapons, we can defend ourselves," Elf says. He looks at me. "Don't go off to New Kimearo now, please. Stay with me. I promise neither Five nor I will say anything to Rahn today."

Five doesn't look happy. "You're making a promise on my behalf?" She shakes her head. "Just wait until my mother sees that man leading the Enhanced here. Then you'll realize I was right. I'm not buying this story."

"But he doesn't know where the village is, so there won't be an attack," I say. And I nod to myself: Red made sure of it, by giving Bea the note for me. He's protecting us, in case he gets caught—that way, he can't give up our whereabouts and endanger us.

Five shakes her head. "Fine. But I think he's Enhanced. And the day after tomorrow, Elf, you'll see you agree with me, and then we'll tell Rahn."

"Nothing gets done until then though," Elf says, glancing at me.

Five snorts. "And, Keelie, just for the record, I think you've been very stupid and put us all in danger."

"Oh really? Hadn't realized you felt like that," I mutter.

We walk back to Nbutai in silence. I keep an eye on Five, part of me convinced she's going to tell Rahn anyway. And, when we get to Nbutai and see Rahn sitting on the steps outside his hut, right in front of us, I freeze and get ready.

The moment they say anything, I need to leave for New Kimearo, to warn Red.

Noise crackles through the radio Rahn's holding, and he flicks a switch on it, brings the radio up to his face. The channel isn't great; all I can hear is interference and a voice.

Rahn swears.

Elf and I step back quickly. Five starts to say something, but stops.

I look around: behind us, people are gathering. They're looking worried. And some hold guns.

"What's happening?" My heart thuds. We tune our radios into the Enhanced Ones' channels—they often broadcast announcements of when they kidnap us and again when they've converted one of us. Sometimes, there are even progress updates. Except they call it *rescuing* and *saving* us.

The gathering villagers are tense, and some are armed. Rahn only allows us to have the weapons out—out like this—if we're going on a raid or rescue.

Or if we're expecting trouble.

I turn to Esther as she appears by my side. My chest squeezes.

"They've got them, haven't they?" Esther's voice is quiet, and there's something in her eyes that makes me squirm. Fear.

"Who?" I ask.

Esther ignores me, points at Rahn. "I said they shouldn't have gone, I told you—"

"Be quiet," Rahn snaps, and then he's fiddling with the radio—trying to make it work.

I look around, count the villagers. Everyone should

be here—shouldn't they? Everyone was here this morning, and nothing was planned for today, was it? I think hard. No. It's not a raiding day, and we've got meat from Kayden's gazelle, so not a hunting day either. And we won't be out gathering until later.

But people are missing.

My eyes narrow as I pick out those who aren't present.

Corin.

Nico.

Yani.

Paul.

Katya.

Finn.

I turn and... Where's Bea? Then I see her, standing with Mila in the entranceway to our hut. Her eyes are wide, and she looks scared.

My heart pounds harder, and I look toward the other huts, willing the missing Untamed to come out. But they don't. Six people aren't here... Six is a good number, for raiding.

I turn to where we keep the trucks. I should be able to see all three from here. But I can't. The red one's gone.

Rahn's radio emits a high squeaking sound, then crackles. Four seconds later, it goes quiet.

"Three!" he yells. "What's happenin'? It can't break now. Sort it out!"

Rahn shoves the radio at Three as he rushes forward. He takes the radio and frowns at the coiled wire that's exposed through the hole in the plastic casing. He taps it, then brings it up to his ear, listening through the tiny earpiece.

"Have you dropped it?" Three asks, then he pushes Five to the side, giving himself more room. Three frowns. "Where's the—"

"*Of course* I haven't dropped it." Rahn shakes his head, baring his teeth. "This is just great, ain't it? I had a channel—the Enhanced said they had an announcement, and then it cut off. Just like that." He points a gnarled finger into Three's face. "You better fix this, and you better do it now."

An announcement? I go cold. The Enhanced love to announce when they capture Untamed.

But it doesn't mean it's an announcement about that, I know that. They also announce every time they create a new augmenter or grade. And when different shops are opening for special events. Boring stuff too.

"Have you tried one of the others?" Three asks, still frowning. Behind him, his youngest sister peers over his shoulder. Seven frowns too, and the sibling resemblance is uncanny.

"The others are barely workin'," Rahn says.

"What's going on?" I feel like I'm invisible, like no one's hearing me. I glance at my brother, and he nods, then steps forward.

"Rahn," Elf says, then looks at everyone else. "*What is happening? Did they go on a raid? New Kimearo?*"

Rahn's face pales visibly, and his glasses suddenly look a lot darker. "I didn't think it was dangerous. There shouldn't have been any Enhanced there. It's out of their range—they don't go that far... But they should be back by now..." He grabs the radio from Three and shakes it, then swears again. "I should've gone with them."

"Will someone please tell us what is going on?" I demand, turning to look at the others.

Esther looks pained. "A group of us has gone to Ninth Rock. Nico was out there earlier or something. Said he saw a woman and child—an *Untamed* woman and child. Bleeding and hurt. They went to get her."

"Aye, and I said it could've been a trap," Marouska says, ambling forward. Sajo steps out of her way. "And now that's what it looks like—with that broadcast you started to pick up."

"We don't know what the broadcast was. Could've been anything," Three says. "Didn't sound like a capture announcement."

"But it could be a trap," Marouska argues, turning to Rahn. "But you didn't listen to me, did you?"

I focus on her. "An Untamed woman and child?"

And Nico was out by Ninth Rock? But he barely leaves the village. Why was he out there? A lump forms in my throat.

"Nico heard the baby cryin'."

"They were supposed to pick 'em up. Bring 'em back here." Marouska folds her arms. "And that was ages ago—it don't take that long to get to Ninth Rock, not in a truck. I'm tellin' you, that was a trap—and that was 'em Enhanced announcin' their latest captives."

"But Katya went with them. She'd have known if it was a trap," Rahn says. "She'd have warned them." But there's something malicious about his tone, as if part of him is glad if they've walked into trouble because that discredits our Seer.

When I first arrived, the prejudice that Rahn has for his group's Seer shocked me. At D'Elinous, Caia-Lu was practically worshipped—even after she became inactive. Anyone who's been chosen to access the Dream Land is important. The Untamed cannot survive without Seers. We need those visions of the immediate future, of conversion attacks.

Rahn snarls at Three. "This is exactly why you need to make some two-way radios. So we can send and receive—"

"Well, maybe Corin shouldn't have broken the ones we did have. Making them isn't going to easy."

"Be easier to steal some walkie-talkies," Esther says, and Three shoots her a grateful look.

"Easier?" Rahn roars. "When they keep them locked up under high security?"

"They do the same with guns, and we still get them," Three points out.

Rahn spits at the ground, and the greedy, orange earth swallows up his saliva. "Guns are essential. We can't make new guns. But you can make radios. And you need to do better than these flimsy foxholes that barely work."

I breathe deeply. "Look—this is pointless. We need to concentrate on our people." Out of the corner of my eye, I'm aware of the dagger-look Five shoots at me. "How many weapons have they got out there—at Ninth Rock?" I look at Esther, then the others.

"All but the ones we've got."

"So, a few then. Well, they should be able to handle themselves," Elf says slowly. "They took ammunition too?"

"Of course," Rahn says.

Sajo nods. "I finished casting new ones last night. They took plenty."

Elf folds his arms. "Well, they'll be fine. Six of them. And they're not stupid. They're not going to walk into a conversion attack."

I breathe deeply. I know Rahn's group is stronger than my old group. And the Nbutai group takes more precautions. My group lived in the same place for sixty years—we thought we were safe. Since I joined Rahn's group, we've always been at Nbutai, but I heard him saying we should move the group again soon. A precaution, he said. I've been here ten years, but they've been at Nbutai for twelve. We can't afford to take risks.

"Well, why ain't they back?" Rahn asks. "Did they take a radio, Three?"

"Yes."

"But that wouldn't help 'em," Marouska points out. "The Enhanced don't broadcast the areas they'll be searchin', not when they know we hack into their waves. And, if they've been caught, they're hardly goin' to be listenin' to the broadcast about their own capture."

I point at one of the remaining trucks. "We need to go after them. We need to go now. You don't know what that broadcast was, and we don't know why they're late. I say we take a team up to Ninth Rock. Could be another reason they're late back. Flat tire?"

"But if it's a trap—"

"Then we'll rescue them. We always rescue our people."

You didn't rescue your parents though. You let those Enhanced women convert them, and you didn't go after them.

But that's why we *have* to do something now. And I focus on that. I couldn't go after my parents. Elf, Bea, Mila, and I were on the run; if we'd tried to stop their conversion, we'd have been caught too.

Would you? Even though you killed loads of Enhanced? Couldn't you have done it, couldn't you have saved your parents?

Rahn makes a sound deep in his throat, then flexes his fingers. "Okay. Keelie, you're with me. And Kayden. We need our strongest people, best fighters." He pauses, touches his forehead, then looks around at the rest of the village.

Suddenly our numbers seem so small, and I know he's trying to pick more of the stronger fighters— and best shots—but the obvious choice, Corin, isn't here. He settles for Elf, then gives instructions to Sajo who's to protect Nbutai in our absence. The man's a relatively good shot, and he's a mountain of muscle, looks scary. Intimidating. Would be a good choice to take with us, but I suppose someone good has to stay behind too.

"And get plenty of ammunition in the truck," Rahn orders. "And knives—whatever we've got. Esther, call the dogs—I want some with us too. And Three, I want you on the radios: make sure they damn well work by the time we get back. I've got a bad feelin' about this."

I think the worst bit about the journey to Ninth Rock is

that we don't know what we're going to find there—
and my heart is still pounding from everything that
happened before this revelation.

We go over and over what we know as we travel:
Nico hears a baby crying out here and sees a woman
and child who look Untamed. He goes back to Nbutai,
and six of our people set off. Ninth Rock is only a short
car journey away, but they don't return within three
hours.

The four of us—Rahn, Elf, Kayden, and I—are
squashed in the truck's cab. The sky's starting to look
heavier, and Rahn thinks that the Turning will be
soon. I shiver. We can't afford to be out in it, without
protection, when it happens. Not when the spirits will
lose whatever self-control they normally have and try
and destroy anyone who's visible.

Kayden holds the radio, keeps it turned on. Every
few minutes, we hear crackling, but the words aren't
clear. Still, once or twice, I make out the tone of an
Enhanced One's voice—and I don't think it sounds
like the tone they'd use if they were announcing a
capture or anything to do with the Untamed. Once, I
think I even catch the word *work*.

I glance at Elf next to me, pressed up against the
window. He stares straight ahead. Something tells me
he definitely won't tell Rahn about me and Red now.
I'm glad.

Even if it's because your people are in trouble?

I squirm. That's selfish, I know.

"You all right?" Kayden asks me.

I nod.

Rahn steers the pickup truck onto rougher ground,
and the engine roars. "Keep lookin' about and 'round.
We don't want to be ambushed. If Enhanced Ones
have got our people, they'll be lookin' for a settlement
nearby, and we don't want them seein' us."

"More likely to hear us first," I say.

Elf frowns. "You think we're going to have to leave?
Set up a new village where they can't find us?"

"Possibly." Rahn pulls the vehicle sharply to the left, avoiding a deep hole. He ducks slightly in his seat and looks up. "That sky ain't lookin' great."

I look at it. But it's getting darker—maybe a bit stormier. There are no signs of the spirits yet. But the Turning's coming, I'm sure.

I lean forward a bit, try to pull my shirt away from my back. I'm sweating, and the leather seat's making it worse. I often have this problem in the trucks.

"What's that?" Elf points ahead, and I narrow my eyes.

Rahn slows the truck a little as we look.

I frown. "It's…it's *them*."

Six figures stand on the sand by a clump of vegetation and two small, warped leafless trees that look dead. I pick out Nico easily, because he's the shortest, then Katya because of her height—she's tall like Seven.

"Any signs of the Enhanced?"

"No."

Rahn speeds up. We reach them in less than a minute. Once we stop the engine, it's so quiet. Eerily quiet. The desert's always quiet—that's why we're safer here, because we're so far from the Enhanced Ones' major cities, and New Kimearo is only a small town compared to others I've seen—but now the air has a darker sense of silence to it.

Then I see the bodies.

A woman, and a child.

"Bloody hell!" Rahn yells, then jumps out of the pickup.

The rest of us follow.

"What's goin' on?" Rahn shouts. "Been attacked?"

It's a few minutes before anyone speaks—or at least, it seems like minutes.

"They were too badly hurt," Nico whispers. He moves toward me, and his arm starts to go around my waist, like it's an automatic reaction, then he stops, steps away. He's shaking.

Everyone's shaking.

And I try not to look at the bodies, but I can't help it. There's a lot of blood. It looks like an animal attack. I see deep scratches.

And the baby… I look away quickly, my stomach churning.

"The Enhanced didn't do this?" Rahn questions.

They shake their heads.

"She's come far. A leopard, she said. When they were sleeping. She's… her car broke down a lot farther north." Paul moves toward Katya.

"Before she died, she warned us to be careful." Corin looks briefly at the leader, then away. He takes a cigarette and lighter out of his pocket.

"Careful about what? The Enhanced? We're always careful about them."

"Careful about who we trust in our group. She said she saw an Enhanced man and an Untamed woman talking together, looking friendly, before. Near here."

My face starts to burn. My breathing gets heavier.

No.

I try to keep calm.

It doesn't mean she saw me. It could've been anyone. And Red and I meet farther west than this. Anyway, it's too much of a coincidence if she saw me. Way too much. First Elf and Five saw us, and now this woman too?

My shoulders tighten.

But there aren't any other Untamed people about here. We're the only ones. We don't even know how many other Untamed groups are out there.

But she saw me.

Shit.

"What?" Rahn's voice is thunderous. "An Untamed woman with an Enhanced man? Around here?"

"That's what she said."

Elf clears his throat, and my attention jerks to him. Shit. He's going to say something; he's going to—

"We should get back," Elf says. "We should send their bodies off, and then get back to Nbutai."

"Quickly," Katya agrees. "It looks like the Turning's finally coming."

SEVENTEEN

RAHN SAYS THE SPIRIT RELEASING Words for the woman and the child, and then we send them off. But the nearest running water is a half-dried out stream and I don't have a good feeling about their journey to the New World.

Nico nods toward me. "You look off. Feeling all right?" His voice is blunt.

"I'm fine," I say, my eyes narrowing. Why's he talking to me?

"Come on," Katya yells. "We need to get back." She points up at the sky. Dark patches are creeping in now.

We pile back into the trucks, each in the same one we arrived in. I'm squashed between Rahn and Elf, and Kayden drives.

"I don't like it," Elf says. "That woman. What do we know about her? Where'd she come from? Are there others nearby?"

"Paul said she told him she'd been traveling two years with her husband after their settlement got caught," Kayden says. "She came from higher lands, and crossed an ocean. Her husband died two weeks ago. Got sick."

"I don't care about her life-story," Rahn says. "If there's another Untamed woman around here—we should find her. Before that Enhanced man preys on her and fully converts her."

I breathe a sigh of relief. He doesn't think it's anyone from Nbutai.

He doesn't think it's me.

I stretch out my legs as far as the footwell will allow.

"It's disgusting." Kayden breathes deeply. "Thinking about one of *us* coupling with one of *them*."

I want to point out that, according to Paul, the woman only saw the Untamed and Enhanced *talking*, even if they looked friendly, but Kayden's words seem heavy, and there's something about his tone that makes me breathe faster. Besides, what exactly does *looking friendly* actually mean?

Elf nods. "It's *wrong*."

I try to ignore how pointed his words seem. He wouldn't tell them now, would he? No, he was starting to believe me about Red earlier. That's why he wants to meet him.

"How can one of us *willingly* go with one of them?" Kayden continues.

Elf digs me in the ribs. "You're quiet, Kee. Don't you think it's wrong?"

I feel heat rushing to my face, and I glare at him. "Of course. All those who *are* Enhanced are monsters. Each and every one of them."

Elf presses his lips together firmly, and I try to read him, work out what he's thinking. I breathe deeply. I can persuade him completely when he meets Red.

"Are we going to make it back in time?" I ask, a few minutes later, mainly to break the heavy silence that's fallen. "The Turning's got to be close."

"The spirits ain't out yet," Rahn says. He sniffs loudly. "We got tarpaulins in the back if we need them. Just drive faster. I'd rather be in the village when we have to take cover. Not in the back of a pickup."

"We could stay in the cab. At least in *this* truck. We

all fit."

"We stick together. Safety is in numbers. Just keep drivin'."

Then there's silence. We don't speak; we just watch the sky and pray that we get back in time.

I wonder at what point Rahn will decide we need to stop and pool together from the two trucks. But he doesn't give the command, and we keep going. The wind is picking up. Part of me knows it's quite a slow start for the Turning—and I should be glad, because it means we've got more time…but I can't stop my heart from thudding and pounding so much that I feel sick and lightheaded.

Get a grip, I tell myself.

By the time we get back to Nbutai, the sky is dark purple and orange, and navy blue patches are creeping in. The seasons are changing, and we have seconds before the spirits enter.

We run, barely killing the pickups' engines before we're out of the trucks and—

"Keelie!" Katya's suddenly by my side, and then—then I see it.

The spirit.

It's hideous. Bigger than the one Red and I saw, and gray—partly translucent and—

My eyes narrow. I can't make it out. Can't see it properly.

Katya grabs my hand, whirls me around toward her. "Don't look at it! Run!"

I go cold. She's right. I mustn't look at it. People rarely see an evil spirit—see one properly—*and* live. I can't tempt fate. Not when I already looked at one.

I run as fast as I can, trying to see ahead, to the huts, but I can't. Everything's murky, and there's suddenly so much mist. I hear teeth gnashing, and something shrieks—a spirit, high and wailing.

The hairs on the back of my neck rise. They know we're here. The spirits know we're here. And it's *the Turning*. Every part of me starts screaming internally.

They're going to hurt us, kill us! We need to get undercover. We need to hide.

Katya pulls me along, and I hear steps behind us, see Paul and Nico.

"Where's Elf?" I try to pause, try to see him, but they don't let me.

"Come on! Can't stop!"

I crash forward, and sand sprays up over me. But it's damp now—damp from the mist—and it clings to my bare legs. I turn, looking, and—

Elf smacks into me, breathing hard. I grab him and turn. The huts are ahead, so close, I can see them now.

The shrieking behind us gets louder, so much louder.

We reach the nearest hut—Nico and Yani's. And then we're all piling in. All of us—so many.

"Shut the drape!" Rahn yells, and then he's pushing past me, and I smell the strong stench of sweat. "Get back!"

"Be quiet!" Katya hisses. "They'll know we're here and—"

"Of course they know we're bloody here! That one saw us."

"Yes," Katya says. "Only one. We don't want the whole lot knowing."

Everyone hushes, even Rahn. Above, we know the spirits are gathering. They're noisier this time, shrieking straight away. And I think of Mila, how scared she'll be, and hope that Bea isn't too overstimulated. I hope with all my might that Seven is with them. Or Marouska. They're both good at calming people down.

I sit down on the edge of the hearth. Nico's bed is next to me. I stare at the familiar blankets and feel something cold rise in my chest. It looks different than last time. It's the strange light—it's got to be. The Turnings are strange. They can happen at any time of day. They mark the changing of the seasons, and the evil spirits fill the skies, and the good spirits too—but they become evil in the Turnings as well—as, above, everything turns orange and purple and navy. The sun seems to disappear, and there's nothing but the spirits moving out there.

Shuffling sounds fill the hut suddenly; Nico moves through the crowded space, and several frown at him. Then he's next to me. He sits down, and reaches for my hand. I let him take it for a moment, before I snatch it away, a strange anger hot in my veins.

Five watches me.

Above, the spirits rage.

It doesn't last long; a surprisingly short Turning.

"That doesn't feel right," Katya says. Her words tremble a little. "There'll be another one soon. There's still pent-up energy waiting for its release."

Rahn scowls at her. "Just be glad it's over. Don't complain."

We start to leave Nico's hut. I know it's not that late, but I'm exhausted now, and I long for sleep. But, just as I'm about to leave, Nico pulls me back with a soft tug on my arm.

Immediately, my guard goes up. "What?"

"So, he says. You and me." His voice is soft, soft like his eyes. They're no longer red-rimmed. "I've been thinking about what you said, and I've realized what it is."

I stare at him, feel a strange sensation in my chest. He's realized. And he was out there...out at Ninth Rock.

But that wasn't near you and Red!

"We've been together four years now," Nico says.

"We were sort of together for three years," I correct.

"But it didn't seem like it was going anywhere, did it?" He looks down at the ground for a moment.

"There was no development, nothing new, not after the first six months really. It was stale, and I'm sorry, I didn't realize. But I've thought of something."

I shake my head. "Nico. No."

"We should get married."

I stare at him, feel all the color drain from my face. "What?"

"Marriage." He's grinning, and annoyance flies through me. Then he nods, and his blond hair flops forward in the most irritating way.

"You think marriage would solve this?" I stare at him. Bloody hell. This is his proposal? When we're not even together?

"Yes." And he nods, eager.

I stare at him, waiting for him to backtrack.

He doesn't.

"No," I say. "No, it won't. Nico's there's *nothing* that can be solved. You and me are—"

"But it would bring something *new*. We can have a big ceremony, get some of the spice back in things."

I shake my head. "No. Just *no*."

His bottom lip wobbles. "You said a break… Did you mean…?"

I nod, and I leave his hut before I say something I regret.

"Hey." Five's waiting outside, and her eyes are narrowed. "You can't keep playing with him like that. Nico's a good guy."

"You were listening?" I shake my head, exasperated. "I wasn't playing with him."

"You could've been firmer." Her eyes seem to get bigger, then she lowers your voice. "And I know who you're counting on being with."

"Be quiet," I hiss.

We walk a little way off.

"Was it you that Untamed lady saw?"

I shrug. "How do I know? I didn't see her."

"You didn't see me or Elf until we were right up to you." She shakes her head. "Please, Keelie. You can't trust him."

"I thought we weren't discussing this until after Elf's seen him?"

Her gaze darkens. "If that man's persuaded you, he'll persuade Elf in half the time. We both know that." She takes a deep breath. "The only people we can trust are the Untamed right here in this village. The ones we know have our backs. But, listen, even if Elf says he *is* undercover, and if I really begin to think he is too, you *still* have to stay away from him."

"What?" I frown.

"Because it would only be us *thinking*. It wouldn't be certain. And someone else will see you together sooner or later. Hell, they could shoot him *and* you."

I shake my head and laugh. "I'd be careful."

Her eyes hold sadness. "You're an adrenaline junkie, Keelie. You like putting yourself in danger— that's partly why you're attracted to him, because you don't know for certain he's Untamed and on our side. Admit it. The thrill of being with someone who looks Enhanced, it really excites you, doesn't it? And I'm scared. Even if he's Untamed he could be bait, and they could be waiting to find the village." Her eyebrows arch. "You have to stay away. It's too risky if you don't." Her voice gets smaller. "I don't want to lose my best friend."

"You won't," I say.

"And I don't want this village put in danger. It's not a chance we can take, not in this world. You have to stop seeing him completely. He'll understand if he is Untamed. He'll want to protect his fellow undercover people too. You'll do that, won't you?"

I reach for her hand, but she steps away. "I wouldn't put anyone in danger, Five. You know that."

"Do I? Because that's exactly what you might've been doing. You can't see it because you're blinded by what you think is your love for him." She shrugs. "I know you two were close before. Elf told me. And Red showing up, a perfect specimen of a man." She snorts. "I saw him, Kee. Even from a distance, he looked great. I can understand why you'd fall for him. But don't you agree that if it *is* him, and he's Untamed and not bait or anything, that it is just too good to be a true?"

EIGHTEEN

I BARELY SLEEP. IN FACT, I don't let myself. I'm too hot and sticky: the perfect conditions for nightmares. I can't let myself have one, not tonight. Not when Five's words are going over and over in my mind.

She's wrong. She has to be. I'm not putting anyone in danger. I haven't.

And it's not too good to be true, is it?

No. My heart pounds faster and faster. *This* is love.

Real love. And I know it is because each beat of my heart tells me so. I've never felt so alive.

And real love is never too good to be true.

I keep telling myself that throughout the long hours of darkness. I wouldn't put anyone in danger. Besides, Red doesn't even know where our village is. I'm careful each time.

We're safe.

Morning comes quickly now, and I get up before Elf and Mila, wish that Red and I were meeting today. I want to see him. Bea's already up, no doubt finishing her walk. Last night, she said she was going to look at the far rocky valley in the sunrise. I still haven't spoken any more with Elf about it all; he just talked about mundane things last night, avoiding the topic of Red completely.

Still, it doesn't make me feel any better. And I want to feel better—want to see Red. But that's tomorrow—with Elf. And I need excitement today, something to distract me. I need what Red can give me *now*.

Frowning, I leave Elf and Mila snoring softly and head outside.

The skin on the back of my neck crawls as I make my way to the small watering hole. It's a few hundred yards farther away than our usual one, and it's mostly dried up too, but I manage to get a few dirty handfuls to wash with. Not that it makes me feel any better. Instead, I imagine all the bacteria and nasty things it contains that are now on my body.

Before heading back to the huts, I look up at the Titian Mountains. There's something comforting about them, the way they watch over us.

"You're up early," a voice says.

I turn to see Corin heading toward me. About three hundred yards behind him, I see Bea returning from her walk. Yani is with her. I smile.

"Going to do some shooting practice," I say to Corin, deciding on the spot. The moment I've said the words, I know it's the right thing to do. I'm a good aim, but I have to practice.

"Without a gun?" Corin's words are somewhat blunter than usual. He smells strongly of smoke, and I wrinkle my nostrils.

"Haven't got it yet." I shrug and look toward Rahn's hut.

"You going up there?" He indicates the mountains with a jolt of his head.

The mountains are our usual practice range. There's a place not far off—only an hour's journey—that's perfect. The formation of the rocks muffles the sounds of the shots.

"Yeah." I press my hands together. "Are you?"

Corin frowns and breathes deeply, then folds his

arms. His stance makes his body seem stockier. "You seen Seven or Five?" he asks.

The mention of Five's name makes me wary.

I shake my head. "No. Why?" The hairs on the back of my neck stand up, still wet with the water.

The look on Corin's face says he's not happy. It's no secret that Corin doesn't like any of the Sarrs. He blames Katya, and her second son, for his parents' deaths. I hadn't joined Rahn's group at that time, but I heard how Corin's parents died in a conversion attack and neither Katya nor Two had been able to get a Seeing vision to warn them in enough time. Two's Seeing powers had been limited by liquor, and Katya's by her grief for Four. The group lost many people in that attack, including Two, but most people seem to forget they lost one of their Seers then as well. I've heard a few saying that Two deserved to die because he got drunk and wasn't able to get the vision in enough time for them to make a proper plan. They only had five minutes, and it wasn't enough. It was a huge attack.

Corin presses his lips together until all color has drained from then. When he speaks next, they make a smacking sound first. "Seven and Five took the dogs out for a walk early—about two hours ago. In the dark. They haven't come back, and they should've."

"You're worried about them?" I raise my eyebrows.

His eyes darken. "No. Not yet. They're probably on a long walk." He exhales hard. "I'll walk up to the shooting range with you—might be able to see them from there. Could probably do with some practice too."

I nod. "We'll take my bike though." I need to feel the wind on my face, the thrill of going fast, of being free. "I'd better get a gun," I add, but I don't move toward Rahn's hut.

Corin snorts. "I'll get it."

I concentrate on the targets. Several rows of small rocks balanced on boulders. I breathe deeply. Got to be calm. I line up my aim. The Luger feels good in my hand, and I've got Caia-Lu's Watcher Doll in my pocket for luck, retrieved it when Corin went for the firearm.

I get the first three targets easily. Then I miss the fourth, and irritation fills my body like a plague. I can't afford to miss, not when the time comes where these shots will really matter.

But guns aren't for killing….

I feel conflicted as I look at the fifth target. Killing with my hands may feel better—give me more glory— but time can be everything, and Rahn's right when he says that killing with a gun is the safest.

But safe doesn't always equal fun, and it still feels like cheating to me. Yet, strangely, holding the weapon fills me with more strength. Makes me feel invincible.

Corin stands behind me and to my left. He shouts out encouragement as I continue shooting, and I know I'm a good shot. Those small rocks are far away— much farther than they were when Corin set some up for himself—but I have to be able to do it.

I have to.

My parents missed their shots. I will not miss mine, even if it's cheating.

I grit my teeth and concentrate as I move to the next set of targets, leaving number four there to taunt me. I grip the Luger tighter. The trigger is light, easy. I hit each of the next targets first time.

We use some of the homemade ammunition. Finn's dad makes it, spends many evenings melting lead and tin over a fire, adding in wax shavings, and making ingots. Then he reheats the ingots and pours the melted alloy into the bullet molds he stole during a few years ago that miraculously fit most of the firearms we have.

Every now and then, I think someone else in Rahn's group should learn how to do it—in case something happens to Sajo—but there never seems to be enough time. It took Sajo years to get it right, from trial and error, as he didn't have the instructions when he stole the molds, and he says he's got the right knack for it now. But it took long enough.

Still, it means we nearly always have ammunition, and that's important.

"Good job," Corin says as I step back and flick the safety back on the gun.

I mutter something under my breath and glare at the only target rock still standing there.

We go through another couple of rounds each, until we've used up nearly all the ammunition, then we collect the used bullets and sort them into two containers. The ones that didn't hit the rocks can be used again, straight away, but those that are deformed will need reheating and remolding.

There's something about collecting up used bullets that makes me uncomfortable. Maybe it's because when it's a life or death situation we can't collect them. Not unless we want to risk conversion. And I think back to when we were escaping, when my parents missed their shots at the Enhanced Ones—when so many people missed their shots—and the land was littered with the bullets that failed to protect us.

Sometimes I wonder if Elf, Bea, Mila, and I—*and Red*—were the only survivors. Or whether I could've saved anyone if I hadn't told my parents that everyone else was dead.

That lie haunts me.

And I know I shouldn't let it, because guilt drives people mad.

But, then again, maybe I'm supposed to be mad. My skin prickles. It's in our blood: madness. My father's mother went mad and drowned herself.

I wish she'd never been the one who suggested the name my parents eventually chose for me, because all it does is link the two of us. I never really knew her—she drowned when I was a year old—but I've heard all the stories, and I'm nothing like her at all.

"Definitely not mad," I whisper under my breath, and I take the Watcher Doll out of my pocket and tell it that—because that makes it true, doesn't it? I'm *not* mad. But everyone at Nbutai has said I'm mad for how much I enjoyed killing the Enhanced when I was younger…how much part of me still wants to. But that doesn't make me *mad*, does it? Not really.

It just makes me good at what I do.

When Corin and I return to Nbutai, Five and Seven are already back. I see the way tension rolls out of Corin's stance, and I watch as his eyes follow Seven a little longer than I think is usual.

Corin looks away quickly when he sees me watching him, doesn't say anything, just heads to Rahn's hut to return the firearm.

I take my motorbike around the corner, a little way away from the village, and put it in its usual place, hidden from sight by rocks and sheltered under a makeshift frame that Nico put up for me.

"You haven't been to see him, have you?" Five asks the moment I'm within hearing distance. She's the only one outside the Sarrs' hut now—Seven disappeared inside with her terrier.

"Who? Red?" I reply somewhat sardonically. "No. Corin and I were shooting."

She nods briefly. "Good."

"You don't have to keep checks on me."

"Don't I?" She rolls her eyes. "I know what you're

like. And I *know* you really like him."

I sigh and think fast to change the subject. If there's one thing that can distract Five, it's talking about boys—particularly the one *she's* interested in. "How's it going with you and Elf?"

She looks around quickly as if expecting my brother to be right behind us. "He still hasn't kissed me."

I laugh. "We both know my brother's shy."

"Not on raids. He goes storming in on those."

"But when it comes to you, he's shy. Just kiss him. Pounce on him if you have to."

Five laughs, but it sounds off, and I know she's going to be watching me most of the day, making sure I'm not sneaking off.

I grimace a little.

But tomorrow, tomorrow I'll see Red. And even if Elf is there for part of it, I'll get him to leave early or something. I need to spend time with Red, alone.

NINETEEN

THEY FORCE THE WOMAN TO open her mouth, and they drip an augmenter onto her tongue, one drop at a time.

I'm standing in the room, chained, at the back.

They make me watch. They always make me watch.

The woman screams, and I see her eyes turn into mirrors. Mirrors that burn my own eyes.

The Enhanced men laugh as I cry, and they tell the woman she's safe now. She's no longer a wild Untamed creature. She has joined the Chosen Ones.

"You all right?" Elf asks the next morning.

I shrug, trying to gauge his mood. "Just a nightmare."

He's still barely said anything to me about Red. Last night, I tried to talk to him, but he shut off my attempts, said he didn't want to hear anything more, that he'd make his own mind up when he sees him.

"One of the usual ones?"

"Yes."

Elf breathes deeply. He seems to sleep peacefully most nights. Some nights, I watch him. And I envy him. My own brother.

Elf gets up and looks through our box in the corner of the hut. It's early, and the first rays of light are filtering through the window. Bea's and Mila's beds are both empty.

I head for the doorway and pull the drape back. The village is predominantly silent, though I pick out two figures by the fire in the center. Corin and Esther, on fire duty. After the Turning, there are more evil spirits about than usual; the flames are important. They provide safety.

On the other side of the village, a hand pulls back the drape that hangs across the doorway of the Sarrs' hut. I watch as Five and Seven step out. Seeing Five makes me a little wary.

"Ready for this?" Elf asks from behind me. But his voice is lighter, and I realize it: he wants to see Red, and he's excited. I smile. Maybe once Elf's spoken to him and believes the truth, then he'll find a way to help me continue seeing Red, possibly without Five knowing.

"Is Bea out on her walk?" I ask, looking back into our hut. Bea's collecting bag has gone. Usually she stays out of the hut in the morning, but once she's back, she always returns her collecting bag.

Elf nods.

"Where did she go?"

He frowns. "Think it was First Rock this time."

"Mila's with her?"

"No. She woke up super early... Shit, where did Mila say she was playing?" He pinches his brow. "It was nearby, I'm sure. Maybe playing football with Kayden. Yeah, that sounds right."

Right.

I reach for my survival bag and check the contents; can't go anywhere without it, not in these times when anything could happen.

"You meet at this time?" Elf asks. "This early?"

"Usually a bit earlier. Though it changes. And I always get there first—for safety." I cringe at the lie. Last time, I was late. But Elf doesn't need to know that. I need to reassure him.

Elf and I grab our knives, then go to the fire, tell Esther and Corin that we're going foraging.

Esther and Corin nod. They look tired; huge bags hang under their eyes.

Elf and I walk away. My stomach rumbles, but I don't feel hungry; I've always found it hard to eat first thing in the morning, and I can only really face it once I've been up for an hour or two.

We walk briskly. We can go at a faster speed when the air's cooler, like it is now, but we still walk for a good hour, heading across the mountainous terrain. I pick my way carefully but confidently. That's what my father always said: *be careful but confident, in whatever you do*.

I smile the whole time, can't stop smiling. Everything inside me calls to Red, drawing me closer and closer to him. Once, I nearly stumble on the rock because I'm not paying attention to my feet, instead dreaming about seeing Red. And he'll be there, I know he will.

We get to the meeting place, and I shade my eyes from the sun as I look at the giant rocks to the left. They look like ancient creatures, silhouetted against the skyline.

Elf frowns and moves to the right, closer to the plateau's edge. "Red's not here."

"No," I say. "I always get here first. And I leave last. That way he doesn't know where the village is. Can't follow me."

Not that he would.

Elf makes a sound deep in his throat, but I can't tell whether he sounds convinced.

He looks out at the view from the rocky shelf. "Hey, is that Mila?"

"What?"

"Down there."

I move forward. Only when I'm very near the end of the rocky plateau, can I see the figure down there, far away on a lower flat area near the base of the mountain. Even from this distance, I can see the person's fairly tall, lithely built, and seems to be looking at the plants. I think I see a basket on the ground next to her.

"Hell," I say, narrowing my eyes, trying to get a better look. "It is her. Thought you said she was playing? At Nbutai, with Kayden?"

Elf's eyes widen. "That's what I thought she said."

"She said *at Nbutai*?" I narrow my eyes, looking for her usual football. I can't see it. So she is gathering plants? It's definitely just her there. No sign of Kayden.

Elf frowns, looks at me quickly. "Is she going to be safe here, when Red turns up?"

I nod. "Of course. This is Red we're talking about— Five's wrong about him being Enhanced. Anyway, Bea saw him before, and she was fine. Obviously."

"What?"

I explain the second note as quickly as I can. The whole time, Elf doesn't look happy.

"Why didn't either of you tell me?"

I wave his question away.

"Do we call her up here?" he asks after a moment.

I shrug. "She's collecting stuff, isn't she? Copying Bea? Maybe she's trying to surprise her. We'll keep an eye on her." She's crouching down in the vegetation, looking at something intently. "Best not to disturb her yet. Though she knows the rules about leaving the village."

"I'll have strong words with her later," Elf says.

I nod, and we move back away from the edge and sit on the sand, our backs against a rock. I rearrange the food in my bag. Some dried, salted meat and a ring-pull tin of semolina pudding that we got on the last raid. Corin and Kayden found a whole crate of the tins and were able to load it into the red L200 without getting caught.

Sometimes, I think raiding is too easy.

Elf grabs the tin of semolina pudding.

"It's too sweet," he says after a moment. "Far too much sugar in this."

"Don't complain." I point at a clump of vegetation near us. "We're supposed to be foraging. We'll need to bring stuff back."

"Mila's getting stuff though."

"One basket between three of us? Not convincing."

Elf mumbles something in agreement, and I stare across at the plants. I'm not good at identifying them—even now, after years of living here—and to me they all look the same. They look like plants. Well, some have big leaves—ones that are almost fleshy. And some of the other leaves are thinner, but that's about as much as I can distinguish the types.

Bea on the other hand is amazing at identifying the plants.

After a while, Elf yawns. He stands up. "How long do we wait?"

I look up at the sun. Red's normally here by now. Then again, I'm not sure whether I can say *normally*. We've only met out here four times.

"He'll be here soon."

I settle back down. He's just running late. But the smallest seed of unease plants itself in me. I try to shrug it off. Because he is going to come, isn't he? Being interrupted by Elf and Five last time, that won't have scared him off, made him abandon our plan to meet today?

"He might be watching and wondering why you're here," I say to Elf after a moment—mainly to reassure myself—and stand up.

I walk around a little, looking down the mountainside for any sign of Red. He's a big man, not the type who can easily hide. Part of me wants to shout his name, but that would be stupid.

After a while, Elf walks down to see Mila. I watch

as the two of them talk, and then they both wave at me. I wave back and then look around. Again. Still no sign of Red.

"You sure it was today you were meeting here? You absolutely sure?" Elf asks as he rejoins me half an hour later.

Mila remains farther down, still collecting. She's moved onto a small ledge now, about fifty feet below us. I can hear her singing, the sounds travel up.

"Yes." I shake my head. "Something's wrong, isn't it? He's been caught."

I run a hand through my hair. It feels sticky with sweat. Time for a rescue mission? But there's only me, Elf, Bea, and Five who know about Red. Four for a rescue mission isn't ideal—and Bea and Five haven't been on them before. They might freeze up. You should only take those who are confident on the rescues. So what do I do? Tell others who I think won't tell Rahn? Bring Corin and Seven in on the secret?

"We don't know anything's wrong," Elf says slowly, but I detect the worry in his tone. "Maybe he's not coming. He'd have been pretty shaken up, being interrupted last time."

"No, he'd come to see me." My heart beats a little faster, and I start to feel sick. We slept together. Of course he's going to come back for me.

But unease takes hold, and I recall his retreating figure, how he ran so fast. What if that was the last time I'll ever see him? I didn't even say goodbye.

Just like I didn't say goodbye to my parents. When they decided upon code one, it was like they disappeared. Were snatched from us. No hugs and kisses, no goodbyes.

I take my knife out of my pocket, unfold it, and head around the huge rocky outcrop in front of me, then tread softly toward the edge of the rocky plateau. The knife's my old one, not my new Swiss army model.

"Are you always armed when you meet him?" Elf calls after me.

I nod, keeping my eyes in front of me. High in the sky, a bird calls. I always have a knife. Always.

Movement—down and to my left.

I turn, catch the flash of a mirror, and—

I scream as I see the men heading toward Mila's ledge.

Enhanced men.

Something hits me from behind, and I fall, smack my head against the stone, feel weight on top of me. Momentary pain grabs me, then the fighting instincts kick in. I throw my attacker off me and—

"Elf?" I stare at him.

"Be quiet!" His eyes are wide, and he moves back toward me, scrabbling on the dusty rock, but keeping low. "You screamed, Keelie. That's the one thing we don't do." He swears, and then he's holding me down against the stone—the side of my face against the rough surface—while he lifts his own up higher and looks. "I don't think they heard you. They're all around Mila."

My heart squeezes, and I fight against him to lift my head up. Mila… She's down there. With the Enhanced. How many men are there? Four? Five? I can't remember.

"We've got to do something!" I hiss.

I feel sick. She was visible on the lower ledge. And we're not, because of the angle… We're higher up here on our plateau, with plenty of boulders to cover us, only visible if we're right at the edge… Shit. Why didn't I get Mila to come up here too? Why did I think she'd be safe? They'd have seen her from wherever they were hiding, crept toward her, and….

And why didn't I realize? Why didn't I see them?

Mila shrieks.

Quick as a flash, I shove Elf away, lift myself up, look over the edge, and—

They've got her. The Enhanced have their hands on her, but she's fighting. That's good. She's one of us, the same blood as me, and I'm a good fighter, and—

She's outnumbered. Five against one.

But five against *three* is doable.

"Come on!" I yell at Elf. "They don't know we're here, right? We can surprise them."

I look down, make the calculations fast. The ledge they're on is fifty feet below us. If I jump and land on one of the Enhanced, my fall will be broken. It'll hurt the Enhanced—and probably me too—but I'll be able to help Mila. Just got to jump at the right moment.

And I can do it. I know I can. Adrenaline pulses through me.

I glance at Elf.

"No," he says, his eyes wide. "Keelie—*no*."

"Got to," I say, and I get ready to jump.

.

TWENTY

ELF GRABS ME AND HAULS me back the moment I'm about to launch myself off the ledge. My momentum throws me into him instead, and we both fall. Pain bruises against my thigh.

"We need a plan," Elf hisses, then he swears. "And that doesn't include you throwing yourself down there! If you miss, hit your head or something, then you're dead, Keelie. *Dead*." He shakes his head, his body trembling. "At the moment we've got the advantage. They don't know we're here. We need a proper plan. Got it?"

"We haven't got time!" I yell a little too loudly. "Mila's down there! Shit. Have they got the augmenters out yet?" I try to lift myself up, to look over the edge again, but Elf's strong, and he holds me back.

I fight him, cursing. Then I get free a little and look.

The Enhanced Ones are talking to Mila. She's stopped struggling. She's just standing there. My eyes narrow, and I think I pick out an augmenter by an Enhanced man's side; the light catches the vial. I feel sick.

The augmenter… It's too close.

"They're going to convert her!" I go to lunge forward again.

"No! I'm not losing you as well—"

"We haven't lost Mila yet! They'll do the proper conversion at their compound. That's how they do it. You know that. But…."

But one augmenter is enough to start the addiction.

"We can't stop first taste," Elf says. "We can't. We show ourselves, we'll get first taste too."

I curse under my breath. He's right. Need to be rational. Need to think. Need to *think*. "Intercept," I say.

"What?"

"I'll run back to Nbutai. I'll get a truck, and we'll set off. A group of us. These Enhanced are on foot, right? There was no car…or there might be later…farther on? Hell, I don't know. But we can get to New Kimearo first, intercept, and—what are the co-ordinates here?"

"Co-ordinates?" He looks blank.

"I need to know which direction they'll come from to get to New Kimearo—I can't think—but we need to intercept them." New Kimearo isn't in sight from here. Adrenaline fires through me. "I've got to go now. Elf, stay with Mila. Follow them. But hidden. At a distance. Keep her in sight. And then we'll be there with a truck and weapons, and we'll get her back, and you and—"

"But what if you don't get to Nbutai and get a truck in time? Or you don't intercept it—you might be in the wrong place…."

I shake my head. "It won't happen. We're going to save her. We always save our people. *Always*."

Do you?

Before he can say another word, I turn and run, descending the shallower side of the mountain, the same route Elf took earlier when going to see Mila. I know I'm on full view to anyone on this side of the mountain, and I hope there aren't any more Enhanced about.

My momentum builds, and I get faster, faster. My body buzzes with energy as I leap down from ledge to ledge, jump over rocks, and weave between boulders. I skid on small stones as the land levels out a little. Energy and adrenaline race through me. I can do it.

I know I can.

The sun is hot on my neck, and each slam of my feet on the ground resounds through my body. The soles of my shoes are thin, and I feel the stones bruising my feet.

I pump my arms, force myself to go faster, my mind a haze of thoughts. My feet send loose shingle flying, and sand sprays up over me. Dust, against my face. My eyes sting with the sweat that drips into them.

Faster!

More pain in my chest. Shit. A stitch.

I clasp my hand over my heart, but keep going. Have to keep going. I flex my fingers and—hell! I was holding my old knife when Elf tackled me to the ground. Must've dropped it, didn't look for it. Why the hell didn't I look for the knife? I'm unarmed. If one of them sees me, comes for me….

Keep looking around!

I turn, breathing hard—too fast, my vision's blurring—and I try to look. Can't see any Enhanced. The rocky ridges are behind me: I see Elf, on the edge of the plateau, looking down. Can't see Mila from here. Or the Enhanced Ones around her. I'm at the wrong angle for that.

I run faster. My vision blurs, and the land and sky ahead look hazy. Hazy with steam? It's hot now. Sweat pours off me.

Just keep running. Got to keep running.

I look ahead, trying to see Nbutai, but the contours of the Titian Mountains hide it. The perfect hiding place.

As I run, I twist my head around again, looking for the Enhanced, trying to see if any are watching me. I can't lead them to Nbutai—that's the worst thing we can do.

But I can't see any.

It's just me.

Just me.

But, suddenly, Red fills my mind. I picture his face. His mirror eyes.

Anger rises in me.

He's been caught and betrayed me. Sold me out. Sent those Enhanced to our meeting place.

And now…now he'll have been converted?

And this….

It's my fault.

I told Elf and Five about Red…and Red made it perfectly clear how dangerous that was. Somehow, the Enhanced have found out.

It's my fault they've got Mila.

Yet Elf and Five, they didn't say anything. None of us went to New Kimearo!

But, however the Enhanced Ones have found out about Red, they've still got Mila.

I run as fast as I can. Every time my legs start burning, I force the pain away. I have to keep going. Have to. I have to make sure there's a truck ready to intercept the Enhanced and Mila—and not too near New Kimearo either, else the Enhanced Ones will have backup out there in minutes. Seconds even.

You can do it. I tell myself the words because then it makes them true.

I *can* do it.

I will do it.

"Mila, I promise!"

I get to Nbutai, sweaty, panting, and shaking. I don't know how long it's taken me—too long?

Finn stops as he steps out from a hut, sees me, and stares. "Keelie?"

"Get Rahn! Need…keys…" I pant, trying to point to the trucks. "Need…."

Rahn appears from his hut, and then more of the villagers start to follow suit and crowd around me.

"They've got her!" I shout. Corin yells something at Rahn, and I can't make out his words over the humming in my ears. "The Enhanced have…got her… We need to go!"

"What? But you were foraging?" Esther says, then she frowns. "The Enhanced Ones were *there*?"

"Who've they got?" That's Seven, her eyes wide. I see her standing near the back of the group.

"Mila! But we can get to…New Kimearo before they do and…."

Nico suddenly steps forward, keys in his hand. Keys for a pickup. "Where's Elf?" he asks. "They got him too?"

I shake my head. "Not when I left… He stayed there…will follow them, they're going to take her back…but we can get to them before they get to the compound and—and I told him to follow them."

Rahn's face is like thunder. "Where's that damn Seer?"

"You mean my *mother*?" Seven's eyes flash, and there's something about her tone that seems to startle Rahn, and it surprises me. Seven never normally speaks like that. She's quiet.

"Yes, *of course* I bloody well mean her—she's the only Seer we've got. And a useless one at that. She should've seen the Enhanced Ones closing in."

"Seers don't see everything," Esther says.

"No, they don't." Corin's voice is hard.

"My mother's out," Seven says. "Gathering."

"Well go and get her then."

But Seven doesn't make a move to leave. She looks worried.

"Which area?" I ask, breathless.

Seven points. "Toward the old creek. Is that where the Enhanced are?"

I shake my head. "No… Opposite direction. Katya will be fine." She'd get warning. She's a Seer. It's Mila who needs our help.

Then I see Five stepping closer to me; for a moment, I freeze, silently begging her not to say anything about Red, about this being proof she was right—when she wasn't! It's proof that telling anyone about the undercover operation is dangerous.

"Come on!" I yell. "We need to intercept. There're only five of them. We can take them down, get Mila back—"

"*Mila*?"

I look up and my heart drops at the stricken look on Bea's face as she runs toward us. She shakes her head, and then her whole body's trembling, and she mutters Mila's name over and over again.

I turn back to Rahn. "We need to go *now*."

"She'll have tasted an augmenter; she won't be the same. And we'll be riskin' ourselves, our own lives," Rahn says.

I stare at him. Can't believe what he's saying. "We are *not* leaving her. We never do that—not when we can get there before she's fully converted, not when there's still a chance."

Rahn's nostrils flare, and the sun bounces off his glasses.

"I'm coming," Bea says, and her words surprise me—she's never been on a rescue before. She must see the look of shock on my face, because she then says, "I look after her! She's my responsibility. And why did you take her out that far? That's dangerous—she needs protecting."

"I didn't take her," I say. "She wasn't supposed to be there!"

"No." Rahn stamps his foot. "We ain't havin' Bea come with us. If it was any other person, I'd say yes, but she ain't right in the head. She'd just—"

"How dare you!" I scream at him. "She's a person. You can't talk to her like that. Hell, you aren't even talking *to* her! She's right here!" I point at Bea. "A person, Rahn. An actual person." I look at Bea. "And you're right, we need you. You're coming with us."

"Good," Bea says. "I'm getting my sister back, Rahn. I'm going to be there for her."

I nod and look at Finn. "Get me a gun."

"But they're in Rahn's hut."

"I don't care. Get me one."

Finn doesn't move.

"Already on it," Yani shouts, and he's running back, ignoring Rahn shouting at him.

Then Rahn turns to me. "If you insist on goin' on this mission, you ain't takin' any of us—"

"What the hell?" Corin exclaims. "We *always* go—no matter what." He looks at me. "So, you've got me and Bea. Who else do you want?"

I'm breathing hard, and it takes me a moment to think. I need the best shots, but also people who are good under pressure and won't panic when it comes to the Enhanced. The people who go on rescues. "Kayden, Esther, Sajo." I pause, bring a hand to my face, look at everyone else. If we end up splitting up, then people might have to run. Need the best runners too. That's me and… "Seven." She can run faster than me.

I scan the rest of the villagers. Five's eyes beg me not to choose her. I know she hates drama like this, she locks up, can't think. Rarely goes on raids because of it. She's a liability.

"I'm coming," Finn says. He points at Sajo. "I'm just as good a shot as my dad."

I nod. I particularly want Sajo as he looks formidable. He's muscular—the complete opposite build to his lanky son. I'm confident Sajo will be able to intimidate the Enhanced Ones just by looking at them, if needed. Finn, on the other hand, won't—but we need numbers, and he's decent with a gun. Even if he's whiny and petulant most of the time.

"What about Yani?" I look back toward Rahn's hut, but he hasn't yet re-emerged with a gun.

"No, not Yani," Rahn says. "That's already eight— nine includin' me. And we need people here."

"You're not coming," Corin blurts out.

"The hell I'm not! I'm your leader. If we have to rescue that damn girl then I'm sure as hell comin'," he says. "Three, you stay on the radio. If you hear that we've been caught, then—" He turns, points at one of the men. "Alan, you'll lead a team out for us, with Paul and Yani as backup. And you're in charge of the village when we're out—"

"We need to go," I shout. "We can't miss the interception."

"Fine," Rahn yells. "Get your stuff and get in the truck."

TWENTY-ONE

WE PILE INTO ONE OF the blue pickups, the one that has the nearly full fuel tank—me, Rahn, and Corin in the cab, everyone else in the back. I hold a Luger, and it makes me feel better. We also have most of the weapons and all the sunglasses our village has. We turn on one of the foxhole radios, and Corin tries to tune it in, but he's unsuccessful. I look at the space on the dash where the truck's own radio should be, but there's just a big hole: the Enhanced don't keep permanent radios in their trucks any longer, not when there's a chance we can steal one.

Rahn drives. He nearly always drives during rescue missions, there and back. Says that he's the only one who can keep calm enough during these times and be trusted to drive safely.

"Go faster!" I lean forward, peering through the windscreen, but it's dirty. Marks cover it, and it makes it harder to see.

Corin grabs a compass from the glove compartment, as well as the map we keep in here. It's old and not very detailed, but it will do. In blue circles, someone's marked the places where we normally enter New

193

Kimearo when we're raiding.

"Where were you when they ambushed you?" Corin asks.

I peer at the map. It takes me a few moments. "There."

He reads out the co-ordinates, and Rahn grunts.

"Then they're going to run back that way, straight along that bit—parallel to that valley," Corin says. "The land is flatter there—easier terrain and the quickest way. So they should get to the town from this angle—oh shit."

"What?" I stare at him.

Corin frowns. Jagged sunlight dives onto his face, highlights the sunburnt patches. "We're not going to get there in time. We're miles from it—and if they were traveling at a normal running speed while you were running back to Nbutai, they'd have a shorter distance than you. They'll be near that point now, or even ahead of it. They could already be at New Kimearo if they took the right augmenters or had a vehicle anywhere on the route." He indicates a point on the map with his thumb. "And we're here."

Miles away. I stare at the map, can't make sense of it, then look in the rear-view mirror. Stretching up at an angle, I can just about see Bea sitting in the truck bed. She's got her noise-canceling ear defenders on, and I think she's counting under her breath.

"You sure we're too late to intercept? We're going to get to that point in, what, fifteen minutes?"

Corin shakes his head and pushes his sleeves up—he's wearing black, like we always do on a rescue. "Won't be quick enough. My guess is they'll have her in the compound when we get to the interception point."

I curse under my breath and drum my fingers against my thighs. "Look out for Elf," I say.

"What?"

"Elf's following them. If he's already there when we get to that point," I say, pointing at the map, "we'll know we're too late for an interception, and we'll do an extraction."

Rahn slows the engine. "If we're too late, we should cut our losses and go home."

"No. If we are too late, it becomes a rescue mission from the compound," Corin says. "We'll get her. And we can't go back to Nbutai now anyway, Elf's still out there."

"Rahn, drive faster."

We get to the interception point. I look around, heart pounding, trying to see Mila and the Enhanced Ones. Or Elf.

But there's no sign of anyone.

Rahn revs the engine, mutters something under his breath.

I look in the rear-view mirror, see the others are looking too. Bea's taken her headphones off—a good call. She can't wear those during the actual mission. Hearing is important.

I breathe deeply and beg for Elf or the Enhanced with Mila to come into sight. But I can't see anyone. It's just quiet. Elf wouldn't go any nearer to New Kimearo than this, would he?

"What do you want to do?" Corin looks at me.

"*I* decide what to do," Rahn says, but we both ignore him.

I weigh up the options as quickly as I can. "How far ahead of us could the Enhanced be if they're not at New Kimearo yet, if they didn't have a vehicle?"

Corin shrugs. "Hard to say. Ten minutes? But they probably are at the town already. The conversion could've started."

I look at the radio. We managed to get a good signal.

No captures or conversions have been announced. But I know that sometimes the capture announcements can be delayed by hours.

"Right. Rescue mission it is then," I say.

"No," Rahn says. "That's my call. Not yours. And Elf's not here. If he's followin' them, and he's not here, then they've obviously not got here yet."

I shake my head, grimacing. "Doesn't mean that. He could've got caught too, or hurt. Or he wasn't able to keep up if they've got a vehicle."

"Rushing into a rescue mission is a mistake," Rahn says. "We're *not* doing it."

I grit my teeth for a moment. "You're just pissed off that we overrode you."

Rahn growls. "I put the welfare of my people first *always*."

"Then we're going in." My voice is hard.

Rahn snarls. "We have to prepare for rescue missions. Discuss tactics. We can't go barging in. And we—"

"Right," I say. "Here's the plan. Just drive there. We split up, go in there in three groups of three or four. I'll lead a group. Corin you lead one. And—"

"And *I* will," Rahn says. He moves the vehicle forward. Then he lowers his voice. "And you two would do well to remember *who's* the leader here."

"Right. Whatever." I flex my fingers, then point ahead, ignoring Rahn's splutterings.

I can see the edge of the town now. New Kimearo. Stone buildings and dark blocks rising out of the sand. The town is in a wide valley of the Titian Mountains, and, on the other side of the buildings, I can just about make out the murky shapes of the other smaller mountains, rising behind it.

Mila is in there. My sister. Somewhere in that matrix of stone buildings, my sister is there already.

About to be converted.

"Who do you want in your team?" Corin asks me.

Rahn clears his throat. "*I* decide the teams."

"No. This is Keelie's mission. Keelie, who do you

want?"

Rahn growls.

I think quickly. "Sajo and Seven and Bea."

"Of course you'd say Bea. She's your sister. You don't really—"

"She's the best at navigating," I shoot back. "You know the compound map you drew up? She learned it off by heart." It's something we all should've done, and some of us tried, but Bea's better at it. The same as our aunt, Ramna. "And Bea's closest to Mila. If Mila's already being brainwashed, seeing Bea might help her."

I catch Rahn's eyebrows lifting above his glasses in the mirror.

"I'll lead the extraction," I continue. It has to be *me* who gets Mila back. *I* have to do it. She was taken because of me. Because I told Elf and Five about Red. I *have* to get her back. I have to prove to everyone that I don't give up on my family.

"You want me to lead the distraction?" Corin asks.

I nod. The distraction for a rescue is arguably the most dangerous part: Corin's team will have to intentionally draw *many* Enhanced to them, away from the conversion compound—and the most effective way to do that is to use themselves as bait, revealing their Untamed natures to instigate a chase, and then evade capture.

"I want Kayden and Esther with me," Corin says.

"I'll be the backup then, with Finn." Rahn does not sound happy, and I half expect him to challenge me. "For whichever team needs it—if it's needed." He hands me and Corin two distress flares each—not that we ever use them. Purple is a request for help, and red is a signal for everyone to abandon the mission and retreat. "But if Mila's already converted, we cut our losses. Just like always."

"No—we only cut our losses after a week," I say. "We're getting her out, no matter what." I shoot him a dangerous look, daring him to say more—to treat Mila differently to any other person who's been taken.

But he looks straight ahead and then stops the truck in one of our usual spaces where we park during raids and missions, under the shade of some thick vegetation. We jump out of the cab, and make sure we've all got our dark glasses on to hide our Untamed eyes. I check Bea's okay, and she gives me a quick nod.

Energy buzzes through me now, but it's nervous energy. We update the rest of our group on the plan, and Seven, Bea, and Sajo stand next to me. Seven's tall, and I stare at our shadows on the ground, stretching out. She doesn't say anything. Neither does Kayden. Bea fiddles with our mother's necklace. I want to reach out and squeeze her hand, but I know she doesn't like being touched a lot of the time. Even by me.

Everyone else is talking. Rahn's going through the lessons. The lessons that we all know off by heart.

You can never outrun the Enhanced Ones. They are better, faster, and stronger than you… Don't ever lead the Enhanced Ones toward the village… They deserve to die, each and every one of them… Never let yourself be Enhanced. Once it's done, there's no going back….

That last one doesn't make me feel any better about this, about Mila. She'll be Enhanced by now. Never be the same again. But there's still time to save her—I know there is. She hasn't been Enhanced for long.

But what if she's pretty much converted after only first taste? What if the whole conversion doesn't take days, but hours?

No. She won't be like that. It can happen, yes, but it's rare. Very rare. If it wasn't, we wouldn't have the seven-day rule. Most people can be saved during that time—even if they're never really quite the same person again.

I grit my teeth. We have to get Mila back. We will. And I hold onto it. Mila won't be brainwashed easily, because she's got the same fighting spirit we all have.

"After an hour, I want you leavin' and makin' your way back out here anyway," Rahn says. "Whether we've got her or not. Keep the radio tuned in if you can. If you hear that anyone's been caught, tell the others as soon as possible—without the flares, unless they're needed." Rahn grunts. "Any trouble, you follow the lessons. Preservation is key. Don't risk yourselves. We're better comin' back without Mila, than without ourselves."

"We need to *go*," I say. I look at Bea, Seven, and Sajo. "Come on. We're going to the conversion compound. Corin, get ready to distract. Rahn, be ready on backup."

Corin nods, half smiles. I don't know how he can be so confident; everyone knows it's those in the distraction team who are in the most danger. They're the ones drawing attention to themselves. But they're also the ones with the most weapons. And weapons are good, I remind myself. The Enhanced won't touch them, not when they've got weapons.

"I can get us in through the alley by the pharmacy," Corin says. "There's a direct path connecting that building to the conversion compound, and they'll take it. Is that far enough?"

I think as fast as I can, trying to remember the layout. But I know Bea will have that sorted. "Yes. Give my team ten minutes to get in place once we're in the town, then start."

Corin nods.

"I'll take my team to the pharmacy then—we can infiltrate the top floor and there's a good vantage point from there," Rahn says, and Finn sniggers—probably at Rahn's use of *team*. "I'll be able to see if any more Enhanced head for the conversion compound, and I'll create a second distraction if needed." He doesn't look thrilled at that though.

I smile. "Let's do this."

We set off, my team going first. Corin leads his team to the right, and Rahn and Finn follow a moment later. I push my foxhole radio into my survival bag. It's one of the bulkier ones, but it's got the longest earpiece, so I'm able to leave that poking out. I should be able to listen to it quickly and check the broadcasts if needed—and if it works.

It doesn't take my team long to reach New Kimearo, and, within a few seconds, we're among the stone blocks. I make sure all our glasses are on firmly and that our weapons are hidden—that would be a big giveaway that we're Untamed. The Enhanced don't carry weapons.

We head for the compound that we know the Enhanced use for the conversions. It's the biggest building, stone, and it's on one of the edges of the town, but I lead us through a back route, so we approach from the opposite direction. They're less likely to suspect that we're Untamed if we approach from the heart of New Kimearo.

We walk through the official gates into the conversion area. Bea keeps close to my side, and I glance at her, intermittently. She's never been on a rescue before.

The compound is ahead of us: lots of blocks with connecting bridges and balconies.

"Act confidently," I say. "If we act like we're supposed to be here, we're less likely to be questioned."

Careful and confident.

And we need to get as close as we can and be ready to act quickly before Corin's team starts the distraction. We'll likely only have a few minutes, and, the closer we are to Mila's location, the better.

Heart pounding, I lead us around the side. We get to a small, open courtyard. There's a door straight ahead. We go inside. My hand is by my side, ready to grab my Luger if necessary, though it would be a last resort—only if we're recognized as Untamed.

But there's no one inside. The air is cool and refreshing.

"Conversion rooms should be that way," Bea says, pointing at the open doors in front of us. "I wrote down everything that everyone describes from raids and other rescues. That potted plant with the yellow ceramic pot next to the glass, I remember Yani saying about that before, that the conversion rooms were next to them."

"Okay," I say after a moment. "There's going to be Enhanced in there. We'll wait for the distraction."

We find hiding places and wait.

Two minutes later, a gunshot sounds.

About ten Enhanced Ones race out of the building. They're drawn to sounds of violence, because they know those sounds indicate that their prey is in the town.

We wait a moment longer, then we head over to where Bea said the conversion rooms will be. She's right. Inside each one, I see restraining beds and tables with huge cabinets next to them.

Sajo moves over to a screen on the wall, taps it with his finger. I wince as he touches it, leaves his DNA on it, and it doesn't do anything.

"We need to check all the rooms," I say. "Find Mila. There should be no Enhanced here now, but be careful. Come on."

We walk quickly, briskly. We check each room we come to. But there's no one here. No Enhanced Ones; the distraction was successful—sometimes, they're not. Sometimes, there are loads of Enhanced in the conversion rooms, and they only send a small fraction out to see what the gunshot is and what wild Untamed people are out there.

But there's no one here now.

No Mila.

"Do you think they still use this area for conversions?" Seven asks. "Maybe they've changed it. Got a new building? That cupboard's empty, no augmenters, and there really weren't many Enhanced in here anyway."

"Maybe they've got no one to convert."

"What about Mila?" Bea looks at me.

"We still don't know that she *is* actually here yet," Sajo says.

I bite my lip. "If we were wrong, and she's not here, then we're already in place ready to rescue her when she arrives."

But it's not ideal, I know that. Corin's already leading the distraction. And, if she isn't here yet, we should be doing an interception away from New Kimearo where the Enhanced don't have backup. Interception is always preferable. Now that the adrenaline is starting to fade, I'm worried we were hasty in barging in here. Maybe Corin got the timings wrong in his calculations?

We should've stayed out there, at the interception point, and waited. Maybe the Enhanced Ones didn't have a car and weren't running back here at a good speed…they wouldn't run with Mila, would they?

"Keep looking," I say. I glance at Seven and check she's okay.

I hear the faint crackles from the radio's earpiece, and the sound makes Bea jump. I press my lips together as I listen. The signal isn't strong.

I start walking down the corridor. The rest of my team follows. I recall which weapons they've got on them. Like me, Sajo has a Luger. But Seven only has a knife. I don't think Bea's got anything. Something about that makes me worry. And I don't know why. We rarely *use* our weapons anyway—not when the Enhanced Ones are so scared of our capability of violence, even though they shouldn't feel fear. It's a negative emotion.

We come to a fork in the corridor.

"Which way?" Sajo asks.

"Both lead to more rooms," Bea says.

I listen carefully. But there's nothing. I bite my bottom lip softly. "We'll split. Quicker to search that way."

Seven's eyebrows shoot up, and I know what she's thinking: a team splitting up on a rescue mission is generally a bad idea. Safety is in numbers.

"I don't think there's anyone here anyway," I add, nodding. It's safe enough for us to split up, I'm sure. And Corin's team is keeping the Enhanced away. "We were wrong. They probably haven't even arrived with Mila yet. We're too early. But we need to make sure all the rooms are clear, as quickly as we can, before we report back."

"And then what?" Sajo asks. "Retrace our steps and try an interception?"

"I don't know. We'll have to discuss it. And it'll depend on how far away they are by then." But the Enhanced will be aware that some of us are in their town now.

Seven falters a little. Her steps sound heavy. "What if...what if they've already fully converted Mila and taken her away, and that's why no one's here?"

Her words make my breath catch in my throat.

"No," Bea says. "They can't do it that quickly. Takes days, remember."

Or at least it does for most of us.

I nod. "Either she's here still, or they haven't arrived yet." I gesture ahead, to the corridor that leads to the left. "Seven and Bea, you go down there. Sajo, give Seven your gun, and you take the knife."

They don't argue with me. Seven swaps her weapon with Sajo, then heads off with Bea. My sister doesn't look at me as they walk away, and I wonder if I've made the right choice, not keeping Bea with me. Maybe I should've sent Sajo and Seven off together.

Sajo and I walk quickly and check each room we come to. These rooms are nicer than the first ones we checked, a lot of them furnished as bedrooms, looking less like medical rooms for the conversions. Still vacant though.

Then we hear footsteps ahead.

Sajo turns to me, and I make sure my gun is loaded and ready, but out of sight, tucked away.

My breathing is faster, and I signal for us to keep walking. There's nothing about us that should tell any Enhanced Ones who we really are—nothing apart from our glasses. But the Enhanced wear sunglasses too; we steal the glasses from them on our raids.

A DANGEROUS GAME

The footsteps get louder. My heart pounds. If the Enhanced are here, then it's because there's a conversion, because Mila is here. And Elf—no, he won't have got caught too. But if an Enhanced shows themselves, we can follow them, find out where they've got Mila and—

My younger sister rounds the corner, smiling.

"Mila!" I cry in relief, rushing to her.

Mila shrieks as I touch her, jerking her whole body back, lifting her head, and—

I falter as I see the mirrors. Behind me, Sajo swears loudly. And I just stare at her eyes.

Of course they would be mirrors—one augmenter does that. I try to keep my breathing even.

But the way Mila was smiling...that says more than one augmenter. More than two.

That screams *conversion*.

But the Enhanced haven't broadcast her conversion... so it's not complete...can't be... Yet they don't always announce them immediately... But, no! Mila's one of us, a *fighter*. She wouldn't be fully converted in mere hours.

"Here you go." A woman steps into view behind her, augmenters in her hand, and freezes, looks at me.

Mila's eyes are wide, and she steps back, toward the Enhanced woman, fear evident on her face. Fear—a *negative* emotion—and....

"No!" I scream as Mila reaches for the vials—for the augmenters in the woman's hand—and I react without thinking.

I pull the Luger out.

No! Don't use a gun! Guns are cheating! Kill her with your hands!

But there's not time.

Rahn's right: guns are safer for us.

I flick the safety off and—

"No!" Sajo lunges toward me.

He crashes against me as I pull the trigger, throwing me off balance, and I start to fall and—

A scream tears the world.
My head jerks up.
She falls.
"No!"
No.
No.
No.
My throat tightens.
My grip on the gun slackens.
I rush toward her.
The Enhanced woman starts shouting.
And I see the gunshot wound in Mila's chest.

TWENTY-TWO

I CAN'T BREATHE. I CAN only stare at Mila, feet away from me, as the sound of the gunshot resonates in my inner ear.

Nausea washes over me, and I blink rapidly. But the light's suddenly too bright in here. I look around, expecting to see Rahn and the back-up team. Did they hear the gunshot and think we're in trouble? Hear me shooting?

Hear me *missing*? Missing the woman—but Sajo crashed into me and—

The Enhanced woman stares at us, then pulls out her own radio—a two-way one—and speaks into it. I watch her lips move.

"Put your weapons down, Untamed Ones," she says to us, and I see the flash of Sajo's knife as he holds it steady.

Weapons.

My gun. I look down, see it in my hand.

I've—I've *shot* Mila.

"Put your weapons down, and let us help you. You've come to us because you want to be saved, and we commend you for that."

The Enhanced woman doesn't even look at Mila. My sister… My sister *bleeding on the floor*, because of me. And the woman's not calling for medics, not calling for help—why isn't she calling for help?

"Help her!" I scream. I try to step forward, but I can't—my legs, they're concrete. I'm trapped.

"Put your weapons down. Ignore the violence within you. Save yourselves, poor Untamed Ones."

Sajo grabs the Luger as I let go of it, then he turns and fires at the Enhanced woman. His shot doesn't miss. She hits the ground.

"Run!"

And it's like his command releases me, dissolves the concrete. I run—toward Mila. I get to her, fall next to her, and—

I press my hand over the wound, and her eyes—her eyes are still mirrors.

Are they moving?

I can't tell. My vision's blurring. She's breathing… I think she's breathing…isn't she? But she's not making any noise.

"Keelie!" Sajo shouts at me.

No. No. No.

I clench Mila to me, shake her a bit—then, no! You mustn't shake an injured person, must you?

But a pulse. I need to find a pulse…need to find a pulse…and I try, but my fingers are slick with blood, and then I'm screaming. I turn, and—

Seven and Bea skid into view. With them is the distraction team. How'd they get here so quickly? And why aren't they still keeping the Enhanced away from here? Or have they led more *here*?

"Oh Gods," Seven whispers.

I blink and stare at them, and—

Bea.

She flinches as she takes in the scene, freezes completely for a second. Then she opens her mouth, but no words come out. My heart pounds heavier as Bea races toward me and Mila, and then she pushes me away, shouting words I don't understand. Tears fall down her face, and she's trying to pick Mila up, hold her against her as if she's a baby again.

"It's all right, it's all right, it's all right," Bea tells Mila, and I stare at the blood on the floor around us.

Corin steps toward me, just one step. His face pales. Everyone's staring.

"Out!" he yells, then he grabs Seven's arm and pushes her away, with Esther and Kayden. "Keelie, Bea, leave her—she's dead! We need to get out—they're coming!"

Dead.

My mouth dries. I look down at Mila in Bea's arms. She's not moving. She's—

Bea starts shrieking.

I retch, turn away. My chest heaves.

I killed her…the gun and….

"Bea—*be quiet!*"

No. No. *No*. I shake my head. Can't…no…*no*! But everything's so loud around me, and all the sounds have nails in them, and the nails are scratching. Pain. Pain. Pain. And—

Sajo—he crashed into me. My aim was off because of him…could've hit anyone. Him or me or the woman or Mila.

Mila.

Hands grab me, and I scream, my shriek entwining with Bea's. But it's Sajo.

I stare at him, but then he lets me go, moves toward Bea. He reaches out to touch her, but stops, his hands inches from her shuddering shoulders.

"Come on, Bea! Got to move, before they get here! Keelie, come on! She radioed for backup before I killed her."

Killed her….

Mila. I killed *her*.

Sajo tries to pull me along, but I fight him. Fight him hard. Kick and punch.

"We can't leave her!" I scream, pointing at Mila.

She's across Bea's lap, and Bea's stroking her hair away from her face, patting her gently, while shaking violently herself.

Sajo turns and pulls Mila's body to him. And then she's in his arms, and Bea's trying to shout, but she makes the gurgling noises that she does when she can't. Then she's hunkering down on the floor, in the blood, next to me, her hands over her ears.

"Keelie!"

At last, Sajo's shout reaches me properly, twists inside me. My heart thuds, and survival mode kicks in. I jump up, slipping on the blood. Sajo has Mila cradled in his arms.

"We've got to go!"

Get out.

Yes.

"Bea! Come on!" My voice is breathless, and I reach out to touch her. But I mustn't touch her because, most of the time, she doesn't like being touched. Mustn't touch her. "Bea?"

Her dark glasses have gone. I don't know when. But her clear, brown eyes stare at me. Stare at me with horror.

Then she springs up and runs.

We all run.

I see Rahn and Finn ahead, and we keep going.

Mila's going to wake up. She is. She has to. She will.

"Shit! Leave Mila—she's dead!" Rahn yells. "She's slowin' you down, Sajo, leave her!"

"No!" Bea and I scream in unison.

I try to wipe tears from my eyes, so I can see properly, but my glasses get in the way. I pull them off, throw them down, screaming. I don't care.

"Keelie, she's dead, we have to leave her else they'll get us!"

"No!" I start panicking, and then someone shoves me forward faster, and I stumble. And—

"They're behind us!"

I turn, see the Enhanced—so many of them now.

They're filling the corridors. They're like a silent army—so suddenly here. So eerie.

"Keelie!"

Rahn's shout makes me turn back, and—and they're all ahead. All my people. Bea's out of sight. I'm on my own, ten feet back—and....

Shit.

The Enhanced are—

I run, feel adrenaline flood my body.

The rest of my people disappear around the corner ahead, and I race after them. I reach the corner, see more blood on the floor and—

That's when I see him: *Red*.

He stands ahead, at the side of the corridor, partly hidden by an open door on his right. The others ran past him. They mustn't have seen him.

And I don't think. I just see his eyes—the flash of them. And see how different he looks as one of them. *Really* one of them. And I know—know he's Enhanced. Truly one of them.

And suddenly it's like there's a clock ticking in my head.

I couldn't save Mila.

But I've got to find out what happened to Red, why he didn't show. And if he's been converted, the longest it can be for is two days.

I run at Red.

I can save him.

TWENTY-THREE

"YOU'RE STILL UNTAMED?" RED STARES at me as I grab him and pull him through the doorway, crashing into a small room.

I throw the door shut, look through its small window, see the Enhanced running straight past, continuing down the corridor.

Then I turn so I'm looking at Red. He's moved back to the far wall of the room, and I approach him slowly, cautiously. And I try to see him properly—could he still be undercover?

He looks the same. His hair is stylishly messy, framing his face. He's dressed casually in clothes that show off his physique—his physique I want to run my hands over....

But his eyes. The mirrors...they're *different*. Stronger. More...real. Hell. He's really Enhanced. Truly. And everything inside me tells me it again: he's not pretending now. This is....

Shit.

He grabs augmenters from an open-faced cabinet and steps toward me. His eyes flash—flash in a way they never flashed before, and the roof of my mouth

211

dries.

I hold my hands up. There are six feet between us. "No. Red—listen. Put the augmenters down."

"You need saving, Keelie. You're suffering." His voice sounds odd, and he moves toward me.

"No, Red," I say, taking a step back. "You've got to come with me. *I* can save *you*."

Can you? You didn't save Mila.

I eye the augmenters in his hands—three glass vials that chink against each other as he advances on me. He's moving slowly, like he's unsure. Good, so part of him is resisting. He's not going to try and convert me as forcefully as one who's been with them longer.

But he's still Enhanced—still going to be better, stronger, faster than me.

I dismiss the risk and grab his arm, pull him forward a few feet. "Come on."

"No!" Red screams, dropping one of the vials. It smashes. "Get off!" And he's shouting—shouting loudly.

"Be quiet!" I glance at the door. "Come on, Red, come with me. I'm going to help you." My words are tumbling out too fast, and I can't catch my breath. "Come on, back to the village and—and you can be Untamed again. Us together. We'll be together."

Me and Elf and Bea and Mila and Red, together—again.

Mila.

"No," he shouts, "you have to be saved! How can you still be Untamed and wild? They need to help you! They *have* to help you...save you...."

He tries to shove me away, but I twist around, somehow manage to keep pulling him toward the door.

"No. Come on, Red—you can resist. Just resist it. Come on, you can't have been converted long ago...you can do this. We can be together." I breathe hard, my head whirring. First taste and the mind-conversion...the latter, how long does it take? But it can't be complete now, not so soon! Not for him—and it hasn't been a week, and he's strong, isn't he?

"I sent them to our meeting point so we could be together," Red says. He grins, manically. "We have to be together, Keelie. You and me, we both felt it!"

All feeling drains from my body. I let go of him.

"And this is so much better," Red says, swaying a little. "To think I've been misguided, letting you suffer. Thank the Gods they reported me, realized I needed help, when they found out I'd slept with you, an Untamed! But we'll still get our house, Keelie, somehow. Don't worry. I'll talk to…."

"You did this? *You* sent them to our meeting place?" I swear loudly. *He* did this.

No, not him! He was caught, converted—not his fault.

I look back and forth. The remaining augmenters in his hands chink.

Get out. Get out. Get out!

I turn and—

"No!" He grabs me, whirls me around. The sounds of the other vials smashing fill my ears.

Red laughs. Actually laughs. "I can't let you continue being wild. Oh, Keelie. Don't you know anything about me? About how much I care about you? That hasn't changed! It was—"

"She's *dead*." The words fly out of me, and all I see is him. And it's his fault. *His* fault. He didn't resist at all, can't have—two days, it's been two days at the most. He should be resisting. "She's dead," I scream. "Because of you. They got my sister, and now she's *dead*."

I lose it.

I scream, and I go for him.

My fists hit his chest, the chest I so lovingly stroked two days ago.

"Kee—" Red shouts, and then he's trying to stop me, but I get a good punch in, under his jaw, and he makes a guttural sound.

Get out. Get out. Get out.

The mantra's still going, and I know it's right. I need to get out. One person isn't enough for a rescue mission. What was I thinking?

But I don't get out. I kick him, kick him as hard as I can. He falls backward, hits the floor hard.

I feel the power in me, and I advance on him. All I can see is him, and it fills me with anger. So much anger.

If you're not going to run, put your hands around his neck. Squeeze!

"Who are the others?" I yell, heart pounding, trying to ignore my thoughts of how wonderful it felt before, killing Enhanced with my bare hands. "The others who were undercover?"

I need to help them. Need to help them get out of here…if they're still Untamed.

"They're safe now too!" Red shouts, trying to scramble back away from me. I see his hand reaching out for something, but grappling with the smooth floor. "You don't need to worry, K. We can convert all your people too—"

"No! Who are they?" My heart pounds.

I kick him again, and he yells. There's something about his scream that satisfies me. Pain—he's feeling pain. An Enhanced One is feeling pain. Whatever augmenters he's taken aren't enough.

He needs to hurt. He's Enhanced, and, suddenly, he represents *all* the Enhanced. They need to die.

He needs to die—I can 'save' him that way. Like Mila.

And I'm already a murderer. What difference is one more going to make? And he's Enhanced. They deserve to die. Each and every one of them.

I go for him, throw myself onto him, straddling his torso. I grab him by the neck, dig my nails into his soft skin as I stare down at him. My hands squeeze, tighter, tighter, tighter. Not even the Enhanced can survive asphyxiation.

Adrenaline courses through me, and I feel alive.

I have never felt so alive, so ultra-awake. Warmth radiates through my body, and I stare at him as I apply more and more pressure, stare at his eyes—see myself reflected. See the satisfaction on my face as I squeeze tighter, tighter, tighter. He doesn't fight me. His face isn't changing color. He isn't choking.

You're not squeezing hard enough! You're out of practice!

But this is Red! You love him! You can't kill him! You should be running!

I falter and—

Red stretches his head up and kisses me.

His lips, against mine. Soft and—

I shove him away in disgust, my heart pounding. My eyes widen, and I try to climb off of him, but he holds onto my wrist, his grip suddenly so strong.

"You think you can stop me with a kiss? Make me spare your life by *kissing* me?" I let out a bitter laugh that rumbles from deep within me, but I know it's a reversal of before…but that doesn't make any difference! "She's dead because of you! *You* killed Mila!"

And part of me knows that isn't right. It's not Red's fault he was converted.

"*Who*?" Red looks so confused and the artificiality of everything about him makes me feel sick.

I swear at him.

Strangle him, Keelie. Do it again!

No, you love him!

Just get out! Get out! Get out!

It's too confusing being in my head. Too many voices. And new ones are popping up all the time, and some agree with others, and some don't.

"No!" Red screams.

I fight him, try to get his neck again, but he flips us over, so I'm under him, and I feel the way power kicks into him. He holds me down, leaning over me, and I struggle against him.

"What the hell are you doing?" he hisses. I see myself in his eyes, and it makes me feel sicker. "Keelie, I love you—and this is better for us both. So much better!"

I struggle against him, get him to loosen his grip a little.

"Keelie! I love you."

"You don't!" I shove him away and manage to jump up. My heart pounds, but, for once, I don't like the sensation. A horrible metallic taste fills my mouth. "You don't love me. You might have done as an Untamed, but not as an Enhanced."

Red stands.

"I love you, Keelie—I really love you." He leans in closer, and I look down and—

I swear as I see the vial in his hand, another augmenter. Where did it come from?

I scream and try to duck under his arm, but he's too quick. His hand slams into me, and I jolt back, my back against the wall. Pain swivels down my spine. I try to turn, but Red presses his body against me. He's too strong. He's *Enhanced*.

"Let me go!" I scream.

Red flicks the lid off the augmenter. I smell it. My first reaction is to gag, but then I smell the sweetness and—

No.

I try to move, but there's no space between us, and my back's against the wall. I try to move down and to the side, but he stops me.

You knew it would end like this. No one plays with fire without getting burnt. Maybe this is when you were always going to die, just like Caia-Lu said.

"This will be better," Red says, and he sounds happy—deliriously happy.

I scream then quickly shut my mouth, heart pounding. Mustn't make it easy for him. I bring my leg up, try to knee him where—

The door flies open.

"Keelie!" Esther cries, and she stops, seems to do a double take.

Red pulls away from me, his hand shaking.

Then Esther pulls out a gun. She shoots at Red's legs, and I stare as he falls. As he crashes to the ground, still smiling. Smiling because he's an Enhanced—because he's full of artificiality.

Because he's not who he once was.

Red screams, but he's smiling, and blood pours from his left leg.

"Come on!" Esther darts forward, grabs my arm, and pulls.

Red starts yelling, and his hand snakes out for my ankle. I see it in time and jump, clear him.

"You swallowed any?" Esther drags me from the room.

"What?"

"Augmenters—did he—"

"No!" I start to turn back, see Red and—

What are you doing? Get away.

"Good!" Esther yells. "Come on, we've got to get out of here and find Elf before it's too late."

TWENTY-FOUR

ESTHER HANDS ME A SPARE pair of dark glasses, and, somehow, we make it out of the compound with no problems at all. I don't feel anything.

We reach the truck. Everyone is there waiting. Bea's got her ear defenders on, and she's sitting in the corner of the truck bed, rocking back and forth. Finn's trying to talk to her, but she keeps shaking her head.

Mila's in the truck bed, and I know Bea's trying not to look at her. They've wrapped her in a tarpaulin. I expect to feel the need to brace myself when I look at her—my baby sister, whom I was supposed to protect—but I don't.

She's sleeping. It's fine.

I climb into the truck bed too. The cab is already full with Rahn, Kayden, and Sajo.

The engine starts. We drive away.

I can't concentrate. My head is just…full. It's pounding.

No one looks at me. No one talks. They'll all have seen the bullet wound, and everyone knows the Enhanced don't use guns. *Keelie or Sajo?* That's what they're thinking. Sajo had the gun when the others arrived, didn't he? Or did they see him take it from me? I can't think. My thoughts are too busy. We've lost Untamed before in raids and rescues—at the hands of the Enhanced—but those deaths were accidental. When the Enhanced Ones were trying to restrain them and accidentally cut off their oxygen for too long. Or something like that. Those types of deaths used to happen a lot.

But everyone will know that Mila didn't die like that.

The gunshot wound was visible. And there was one gun between Sajo and me. Him or me, that's what they'll be thinking. Or maybe Sajo told them what happened when I was with Red?

And I'm sure they can see that the blood is on me. The look of horror in Bea's eyes told me she saw the mark of death on me, clinging to me.

My ears crackle as I swallow. But it doesn't feel… No, I don't feel…feel what? Angry? Upset? Guilty? I just feel numb. Numb like it's not setting in now—it was before, when I went after Red, but not now.

Hell.

I killed her. Sajo knocked me, but *I* pulled the trigger.

No, she's sleeping. You'll see her again, when you're both awake.

And Red? He could be dead now too, could've bled out.

I let out a shaky breath. We're driving fast, and the wheels churn dust up behind us. I think we're going in a roundabout way back to Nbutai. Corin sits by the tailgate, with a pair of binoculars, looking out for any signs of us being followed.

"You okay?" Finn asks, and his voice makes me jump. "Heard one tried to get you?"

"One had already *got* her," Esther says. "If I'd been a second later, he'd have had an augmenter down her throat."

I try to tune out their voices. They're talking in that excited tone that we nearly always use after a successful raid. But this wasn't a raid, and it wasn't successful. Why are they talking like that?

I gulp.

The truck moves onto difficult terrain. I hold onto a handhold on the side. The bumps and jolts go right through me. Mila's wrapped-up body is in the middle of the truck bed, and I watch as every bump jostles her.

"We need to send her body off. Are we finding somewhere now?"

The others seem startled by my question, and they look at each other blankly for a moment.

Dead, dead, dead, a little voice whispers.

Corin, the farthest away from me, pauses for a moment, then shakes his head. "We've got to find Elf first."

I nearly choke. My brother. Gods. He's still out there. I swallow with difficulty, feeling sick that I'd forgotten about my own brother. Or maybe I feel sick because of everything else…because Mila's not going to be sent off soon, and the longer we wait, the harder it will be for her to reach the New World. And what if we're too late for her, and she's trapped and… No, she was converted—the Enhanced don't make it to the New World, do they? Why would the Gods and Goddesses and spirits let an Enhanced into the New World?

Mila wasn't Enhanced for long, but was it long enough?

I force myself to stop thinking about it, feel the tears welling up inside me. But I can't let them out. Mustn't. *Elf.* Need to concentrate on him.

We drive around for what seems like hours. Going different routes, the truck leaping and jolting across holes. Everyone's looking for Elf. Far ahead, I can see the meeting point where Red was supposed to meet me, the place where it all happened. We don't go up to it though. Good. Need to keep our distance, in case any Enhanced are still there.

I turn, swiveling on my knees to look in the other

direction. The sky's still light, but I'm exhausted, and it feels like it should be nighttime, but the sky has forgotten to change.

"He's not here," Finn states the obvious.

We drive around some more. My chest gets heavier, and there's a sinking feeling inside me. What if the Enhanced got Elf as well? What if I was close to him in the compound, without realizing, and now I've left him there…and I didn't even look for him. It didn't even occur to me.

"We have to go back to the compound," I say. "Elf could be there, being converted."

Seven tells me he isn't, because she checked the rooms.

They try to reassure me. They say that Elf could be back at Nbutai now.

In the end, we drive out toward the Old Waters. It doesn't take long to get there, and, all too soon, they're unwrapping her body.

Her clothes are covered in blood. So much blood.

Rahn and Corin lower her body into the water. Feeling hollow and like none of this is real, I walk forward and say the Spirit Releasing Words and then make the sign of the Journeying Gods and Goddesses over her body, begging them to help Mila's soul make it to the New World. She mustn't be trapped, left behind.

Then the men let go of Mila, and the water takes her away. I watch for as long as I can, but my vision blurs.

I catch Sajo looking grim. My eyes narrow, and a fierce pain burns inside me.

"It'll be all right," Esther says.

But it's that lie. The lie everyone hates, yet everyone still says it. We can't know anything, but the one thing I know for sure is that it can never be *all right* with the Enhanced still out there.

A DANGEROUS GAME

Elf's not back at Nbutai—I know this the moment we arrive. We're twins of the stars, and I know this sort of thing.

Immediately, Nico corners me, doesn't even let me go after Bea as she runs into our hut, her ear defenders still on. He seems to know everything—*everyone* seems to—and he draws me into a tight hug that I can't escape from.

Behind, I can hear Corin and Rahn arguing. Corin says we should go back to New Kimearo at first light tomorrow, in case Elf's there, but Rahn says it's too dangerous, that you don't make trips to an Enhanced town on two consecutive days. We'd be expected.

I want to join in—back up Corin—but something in me stops me from moving away from Nico. If Elf is there, and I go on the rescue mission, I might kill him too.

Being dead is better than being Enhanced.

You've saved Mila, anyway. She was Enhanced—and you can't reconvert people anyway. They're never the same, even if it's less than a week. First taste is enough—and she looked like she'd had more than first taste.

And being dead is better than being Enhanced.

I know it's what we say, but it doesn't make me feel any better. And it makes me think about my parents. My *Enhanced* parents.

I scream into Nico's shoulder, tears blinding me. And I know I shouldn't be standing with him, holding onto him, but I am.

"Come on," Nico says when I'm through. He steps away from me, but takes my hand. "You look exhausted."

He leads me to his hut—the one he shares with his brother, but Yani's not here.

"I don't know what I'd do if you were killed like that," Nico says.

He takes a seat on his bed and draws me down next to him. I look across at Yani's bed, feel numb.

"It tears me apart, thinking about it," Nico continues. "And...and I don't know... Other people *react* to death. But I'd just... I'd shut off, Keelie. People would think I didn't care. Everything in me would shut down, and they'd take notice of other people grieving for you—like Elf and Bea and Katya and Five—but they'd forget about *me*. They wouldn't even see me, and it kills me to think that if your soul was looking down at me, you'd think I didn't even care. That you'd notice the others and not me."

I want to scream at him to shut up. But I don't.

"Going to New Kimearo is risky," Nico says. "And people get hurt. They die—or they get converted and... and it's all so risky. I don't want you going anymore."

I stare at him, he's trying to tell me what to do? I shake my head. "Being Untamed is risky. Being alive in this world is risky," I say. "It's all so dangerous."

I lean back on his bed, stare up at the ceiling. I can see a sliver of the sky through the hut's roof. It's still blue.

A moment later, Nico lies back too. Then he turns onto his side.

"Have you thought about it any more?" His eyes are keen.

"Thought about what?"

"Us." He reaches toward me, and his fingers caress the side of my face. "I want to marry you, Keelie. And I think we should do it sooner rather than—"

I bolt upright. "My sister is *dead*, and you want to talk about marriage?"

"It's *because* of Mila, and how short and unpredictable life is—we could say something for your sister in our ceremony and honor her and—"

I stare at him. My mouth drops open. "Fuck you!"

I walk out.

Outside, Five finds me.

"I'm so sorry," she says.

"You come to gloat?" I mutter. "Because you knew me seeing Red would endanger one of us?" And it *shouldn't* have—I know that. But he got caught, got Enhanced. And they got Mila instead of me.

It should've been me.

"No," Five says, pulling me into a hug.

"He *was* Untamed," I say. "He *was*. He got caught, converted." And look what that led to. Tears blind me. "I *hate* the Enhanced," I say.

Five stiffens.

"What?" I pull away from her. "Don't you?"

"Of course," she says.

"But?" I prompt.

"You're putting too much emotion into this… into…."

"*What*?" I stare at her. My sister's *dead*, and she expects me not to be emotional?

"There's so much hatred wrapped up in this whole situation," she says simply. "In *you*, in your feelings for Red now he's…one of them, in your guilt, your actions, and it's a mess. Keelie, you hate the Enhanced for their artificiality and addiction—but *you're* addicted to everything they hate: the fight, the violence, the rush, the guilt. The *negative* stuff. Can't you see what you're doing?"

"Is this *really* the time for you to psychoanalyze me?" I stare at her.

"Just listen—you're feeling this so much stronger, all the guilt and grief, because you're pushing yourself to feel more of the stuff they hate, to be more Untamed, so you're less Enhanced."

"Less Enhanced?" I stare at her. "I'm not Enhanced at all."

"That's not what I was saying," Five says. "I was saying that it's *unhealthy*. A vicious cycle. You're going to push yourself to breaking point because you're determined to feel the bad stuff so strongly—just to make a point to yourself that you're not one of them. It's torture, Keelie. And you're going to break yourself."

"*What*? I'm feeling it *strongly* because my sister is *dead*. And *I* fired the shot that killed her."

My chest tightens. I shouldn't have used the gun. Should've killed with my hands. No room for error then.

Her eyes fill with tears. And I stare at her. How come she can cry?

"But you're feeling the *wrong things* strongly," Five says. "You're feeling hatred. And it's fine to feel hatred for all of them—but not yourself." She looks at me sadly. "The Enhanced, *they* caused this. They took Mila away from us. Not you."

I keep staring at her.

"Keelie, it wasn't your fault."

"It *was*. I shot her!"

"No, Kee. You just want to feel the burn of it all because you think it will make you feel better. But it won't. It *wasn't* your fault. You were trying to save her. You *have* saved her."

I push past her, walk off before she can say any more crap. Of course it's *my* fault. Five's just lying to try and make me feel better.

One of the dogs joins me—the Sarrs' little terrier—and he barks twice. I push him away as I head for my hut. I don't like dogs. But, I suppose, the prospect of having a dog barking around me is more preferable to seeing Bea. I saw the look in her eyes earlier.

She knows it was me.

She *knows*.

And the terrier doesn't let up. He keeps barking, and then he's trying to jump up at me.

"What?" I say, irritably. "You know it's my fault as well?"

A few of the other dogs look over at me, from a fair distance away, and then Seven comes rushing over. She grabs the terrier, and mumbles something. But the dog doesn't stop barking.

"Will you shut him up? I've got a bad headache," I mutter, feeling my temper rise.

My hands shake, and I stare at my hut. Bea's inside. I need to see her. Need to.

But I can't bring myself to move. Just can't.

Seven tries to quiet the dog, but the animal keeps barking—then he breaks away, running at high speed.

Seven calls after him, and then Three's out here too, and—

"There's someone coming!"

Seven's words jolt through me, and I turn, dread heavy within me. And I just know, I know without waiting to see as the figure becomes more distinct, that it's Elf.

Part of me doesn't want to see him—not now.

Not when I have to tell my brother how our youngest sister died.

TWENTY-FIVE

IT'S ME, THIS TIME. I'M in the cage, and they hold me in it, like a wild animal. There's a needle in my arm, and a tube runs out of it. They pump me full of augmenters, and, when I scream, they pump more in.

They tell me to be good, that this is better. They tell me that it's the right way to live, and if I'd only stop crying and screaming, I'd see it.

They're trying to help me.

And soon, soon I know I'll be cured, fixed—whatever they want to call it.

Happy—the only thing I can be, here.

And I learn to love my cage. And the smell of the augmenters, the taste—and I'm free, walking through the compound, with my parents on either side of me. But I can't see their faces. No matter how hard I try, I can't see them.

"We knew you'd come to us, Keelie." My mother hugs me.

"We're all together now," my father says. "The six of us."

Six? I look around, and then I see Elf and Bea behind us. Bea is humming and Elf is smiling. Behind them is Mila, with her skipping rope. She grins at me, and my heart grows lighter.

A DANGEROUS GAME

"All together at last."

I wake up, drenched in sweat. My stomach twists and heaves, and I lay a hand on it, cautiously. It's dark. Completely dark. And, there's something about the semi-darkness that makes it worse.

The nightmare was different. It wasn't me watching someone get converted, or my parents wanting me to save them and me saving them, or a flashback to the night of the attack: it was me and…me with my family. My parents, Elf, Bea, *and* Mila. All Enhanced.

All together at last.

I can still hear my father's voice—the last words he said in the dream—and it doesn't feel like a dream, it feels too real, but I know that's what it is. I'm not a Seer. It can't be the future: Mila's *dead*. I let out a shaky breath. *Dead. Dead. Dead.*

And Elf, Bea, and I are not going to become Enhanced.

There's only one way we can all be together now.

I take a deep breath. I can hear Elf's breathing. But it's not shallow, and I don't think he's sleeping. I desperately want to talk to him, but I know he won't say much. He barely spoke when he got back to Nbutai. Not after I'd told him—told him everything about Mila.

He'd just looked at me, and all hope left his eyes. They seemed flat; there was no twinkle, no spark of life. He nodded as I said it, then went to the hut. He didn't blame me outright—and that surprised me— but he didn't really say anything.

Neither did Bea. She just watched me, not speaking, not doing anything except sitting there with her arms tightly around her body, sitting on her blanket, her ear defenders on. I wanted her to get up, to go out gathering plants, or chat with Marouska and Katya, or look at the stars—anything that she normally does— but she didn't. She just sat there.

The jagged pain in my chest starts again, and time passes.

I didn't look after Mila.

And wherever they are—my parents—they'll think she's alive, that we can be together, all of us. Are they looking for us? Imagining finding their four children. They'll want to convert us…and I think of my dream. The *six* of us…how good it felt.

Bea's eyes blink at me in the darkness, and I try to work out what time it is. She hasn't gone for her usual walk. But now she stands, slowly, and grabs two breakfast bowls. Hers and Mila's. A moment passes, and I watch her. Watch her eyes grow bigger as she turns and looks at our sister's empty bed. She puts Mila's bowl back, and then her own, just rubs her hands together, then shakes them out. Her shoulders shudder, and she makes several gasping sounds. But she doesn't say anything, just sits back down on her bed, her fingers tangling around her blanket.

A moment later, she repeats the actions.

I press my lips together, looking at her. Bea needs routine to feel calm. But how can she follow her usual schedule without Mila? Yet I know that not doing so could also cause her great stress.

And it's your fault.

I shake my head—not because the thought is wrong, but because I don't want to listen to it—but my gaze falls on Mila's bed, on her doll, on her clothes.

I get up quickly and head outside.

The fresh air does little to make me feel better. My stomach won't stop churning. Since my parents got converted, I've tried not to wish they were here, wish that I could be close to them, be reassured by them. But now, the feeling's too strong. I want my mother. I want my father. I want them to hold me, like they did when I was little, and tell me it will be okay…even though I killed Mila.

Murderer.

I gulp.

My parents need to know about Mila. I should tell them… Will they kill me? No…the Enhanced aren't violent.

Something tells me that I'm not thinking clearly.

But I want to see them. I have to find them…and now the feeling within me—the desire to track them down—is even stronger. They need to know of Mila's death. They need to know I failed.

I failed to rescue them during the one-week window. And I failed Mila.

I look ahead, into the half-light. Everything looks still. Then I see Mila's football. It's at the base of one of the huts.

I approach it, pick it up slowly, feel the weight of it in my hands.

Movement behind me makes me turn. For a second, I think it's Elf and Bea, and that they've come to the same realization, that we can go together and find our parents. Maybe with three of us we can separate them from the rest of the Enhanced and try to get them back to being Untamed again.

But it's not Elf or Bea.

It's Katya, and she makes a beeline for me.

She's shaking, and her eyes lock onto mine.

"What is it?" I can't help but frown.

She looks at me. "I've seen you die."

I stare at her blankly.

"You've seen me die?" I say at last, but there's no emotion in my voice. Just blankness. My words are empty. I grip Mila's football harder. "A Seeing dream?"

I die. I join Mila. Together again.

Together.

I think of Caia-Lu's warning: *Your death is already written in the silk of time. You cannot escape it.*

Katya nods and touches her Seer pendant. The

crystal seems to glow in the dim light.

"It's going to happen soon?" I lean forward, try to read her face, try to see anything in her eyes that will help me. If I die soon, that has to mean I find my parents soon… I can't die without telling them about Mila. I just *can't*.

Katya exhales softly. "I don't know. The Gods and Goddesses and spirits warn their Seers of immediate conversion attacks that are looming. But I see far too, and these visions are different. Glimpses of the far future—and I've seen you die. I've been shown it for a reason."

"So we can prevent it?"

She presses her lips into a fine line. "I saw you die in a building controlled by the enemy. An Enhanced town or city. It is not clear. But I am sorry," she says. "Visions of imminent conversion attacks are warnings, so we can change the outcome, save ourselves. But far future visions…they cannot be stopped." She breathes deeply. "But we will try. Don't go to any Enhanced towns or cities. No raids…or anything else." But the way she says the words, the way they're filled with despair, tells me what I need to know. *Trying* won't do anything. "We don't know how soon this vision will be fulfilled," she finishes.

I nod. "You said it's the far future? So it could be years?"

But maybe I don't want it to be years.

"Years or weeks. All I can be certain of is that it isn't imminent. But we mustn't tempt fate to take you sooner. Avoid the towns, Keelie. Please."

I look away, try to keep breathing calmly. My death—foretold by another Seer. Great. I exhale slowly. But I've always known I'm going to die. And *everyone* dies at some point.

Behind Katya, for a second, I think I see Mila.

I see her standing there.

But when she turns, her eyes are mirrors, and I see myself in them, still holding her football. And behind me are my parents.

I flinch, turn and look. My heart pounds.

They're not there. Of course they're not. They're not there, and neither is Mila.

I killed my own sister.

Murderer.

But that's what I am. I knew that.

"I've told Rahn already," Katya says.

"You've told Rahn?" I squeeze the football tighter, then drop it. My fingers click, and I watch Mila's ball roll away. Katya's words seem to echo around me. But Rahn doesn't need telling—everyone knows I killed Mila.

"Yes. I've told him about my vision of you being killed."

My heart pounds. I wipe away the sweat from my forehead. "And?"

"And he thinks I'm losing my powers. I've had these far-visions quite a bit. He told me before that they were nightmares, that he only wants to know of *proper* Seeing dreams. But I had to tell him when I saw this one. And I had to tell you, Keelie, because I know this isn't an *immediate* warning—but it's still part of my power. It's still going to happen. Eventually."

"Okay," I say slowly. I swallow uneasily. "Thanks for telling me."

My need to report Mila's death to my parents grows. I need to find them, find them before I die. I have to. I don't understand it. Maybe it's a reaction to my grief. I've lost Mila—the sibling I was always the least close to. But closeness doesn't matter. I still need to find my parents. They're alive. Even if they are Enhanced.

I wonder how they'd react, being Enhanced and all.

Can they even feel grief? Anger?

Elf is awake when I head back into the hut. He's talking to Bea, but she stops speaking the moment she sees me.

I stare at them. "Don't stop because of me."

But they do. Bea twists the beads of our mother's necklace round and round, then strokes each of the butterfly's wings in turn. I stare at the wings. Four pieces to make something whole.

I move forward, see that Elf is holding what looks like one of the broken radios so his body blocks it from Bea's sight. It's one of the models that transmits and receives; Corin smashed the set of them a while back, and, since then, we've been stuck using the foxholes. Elf curses, twisting a dial. It looks smaller than I remember.

He sees me looking and hides the radio quickly.

The air is heavy around us.

"You trying to fix it?" I ask.

Elf doesn't say anything. He doesn't even look at me. Just turns away so I watch his profile. He's barely spoken to me since I told him about Mila. I'd expected anger, not the silent treatment. But I deserve it, I know that.

I wait a few moments before speaking. "I think we should go."

My brother turns slightly, and I know I'll get a reaction now. At least from him. Bea just…doesn't do anything.

"Go?" Elf looks at me.

I nod. "North. As far north as we… We've got to find the compound they're at—tell them about Mila."

Elf's hands tighten into fists, then he loosens them quickly.

I gesture around us, then in the vague direction of New Kimearo. "We're not going to find them here." I breathe deeply. Red said he'd located them, didn't he? But I didn't ask where they were. Why didn't I ask? I focus on Elf again. "They'll be farther north. You know that. And I know it. We can find them and—"

"No." Elf stands up suddenly. "What are you even thinking? They're gone, Keelie. Gone. We can't break them out of an *Enhanced* compound."

"I didn't say to break them out. I know they're gone! I was saying to tell them about Mila."

He wrings his hands together in front of his chest. "It's too much trouble."

"Trouble?" I raise my eyebrows.

"Yeah—because you're grieving, and I know you, and you'd try to save them—and you can't." His hands are shaking. "Our sister's dead. You telling them isn't going to make us feel any better. Or them. Mila is *dead*. And *you* killed her." The light catches his eyes in a strange way. He shakes his head, top lip quivering. "Violence. Murder. It's…."

I look over to Bea, see her scooting away from us, her eyes wide. Her hands are over her ears now.

I try to calm down, to lower my voice. "It wasn't my fault—I told you. It was an accident—"

"Believe what you want. She's still dead—accident or not," Elf says. "Violence is never good."

I spit at him. "You sound like a bloody Enhanced."

"Maybe they have a point. Our parents are safe with them. They're *alive*. The only reason Mila died is because of you and your gun. Their society is safe—"

"Go and join them then!" I shout, and Bea cries out. "I'm sure they'll be delighted to have you—an Untamed who's what? Come to his senses?" I look at Bea. "Sorry." I shake my head, know I shouldn't have shouted. I take a deep breath and look at her. "What do you want to do?"

She stares at me, moving her head slightly. She uncovers her ears, and I repeat the question.

A long moment passes.

"I don't feel safe here." Her words are small, and she tugs so hard on the butterfly on our mother's necklace that I'm surprised it doesn't break. But I'm glad she's speaking.

"Bea, we're safe here," I say. "The Enhanced don't know where Nbutai is. It's just as safe here as it's always been."

She shakes her head, and the look in her eyes darkens. "Not safe. Not safe. Not safe."

Elf presses his hands together, calm now. So calm. "We *can't* get our parents back. Whenever we go to a compound, people die. It causes trouble—"

"Not whenever we go," I say. "What about all the raids? They don't even know we're there and—"

"You can't go looking for our parents, Keelie. You *can't*. I can't believe we're even having this conversation."

I nod. He's right.

I think of my parents. And suddenly I'm back in those woods, running. My mother grabs my hand—or is it my father? I don't know; it's just a hand. And then my father's saying they're doing code one.

I breathe out slowly. They sacrificed themselves for us. They became the enemy to keep us safe.

But being dead is better than being Enhanced. And, Keelie, what if your parents believed that too?

I press my lips together slowly, feeling sick.

What if they were expecting you to end them? To not let them live like monsters?

My breath makes a sharp sound in my throat. All this time…all these years, he…my mother and him… was that what they meant? What they really meant?

I try to remember that last conversation. But what does code one really mean? Just that people are going to sacrifice themselves? Or that people are going to sacrifice themselves *and* expect to be released later?

Oh, dear Gods. I've let them live like that, let them live as what they hated most.

I sit down slowly.

Is that what I'm supposed to do?

You've got a taste for killing family members now.

The hairs on the back of my neck prickle. No. No. *No.*

A DANGEROUS GAME

But, Keelie, isn't it any excuse to do it again? To do what you love? To kill?

TWENTY-SIX

THE NEXT MORNING, EVERYONE'S QUIET. Rahn arranges a hunting trip out in the mountains. Kayden and a couple of the other men are going on it. It's normally something I'd jump to go on—and would insist and insist I go until they let me—but I don't care now.

And, anyway, I know Kayden's avoiding me. He loved my sister like she was his own daughter. Particularly after his baby daughter was killed seven years ago.

He wouldn't want me there.

And I keep thinking. Over and over. And over and over.

I can't find my parents and kill them. What was I thinking? I can't do that.

Murderer.

But I've killed Enhanced Ones before. When the four of us were traveling to Rahn's group, we had many encounters with the Enhanced.

The first time, it was nighttime. We were huddled up in the corner of a forest. It was raining—that was why we didn't hear the cracks of twigs underfoot until they were close. But one glimpse of the mirror eyes, and I was up, a branch in my hand.

Now, I don't know how I had the strength. I was eleven. I wasn't tall, wasn't even particularly muscular—not like I am now.

But it was exhilarating. I remember that. Remember that clearly, the way adrenaline pumped around my body, feeding me. Remember the euphoria I felt afterward, the surge of power that gripped me, that made me feel invincible.

They weren't the first Enhanced I'd killed, but they were the first I'd *beaten to death*. And it was more rewarding than when I shot two with Caia-Lu's gun when I was nine. And how sick is that? I was eleven years old, and I found I loved killing the Enhanced with my bare hands, knew it was what I wanted to do. At D'Elinous, some two of the adults would actively seek out Enhanced in the nearby area and kill them to keep us safe. They called themselves *the protectors*, and I'd listen to their stories, only half-heartedly, not understanding why someone would put their life in danger like that. Why they wouldn't just wait until a situation arose where they had to act, why they'd actually want to seek one out. Eventually, one of their missions got them both killed.

But, after that night, I understood why they did it. And I lived wanting to feel the exhilaration of beating an Enhanced to death, again and again. It became everything, and maybe I was taking out my anger, my anger over my parents' surrender. Every Enhanced I saw was personally responsible, and each one gave me the euphoric feeling I craved when I killed them.

I think that's where my adrenaline-junkie lifestyle, as Five would call it, comes from. That and Caia-Lu's prediction. Because, ever since then, I've wanted to feel alive in that way. Feel strong, powerful, invincible, in control. Wanted to dance with danger.

We came across a lot of Enhanced on our travels—or maybe I made sure it was that way. We skirted cities, and it's crazy to think that the four of us—children—made it through it all, alive and Untamed.

But I was the protector. It was my job to keep us alive, and I put everything into it. Elf was the hunter. He set snares and made a bow and arrow, caught our food and gathered berries. Occasionally, he joined in the killing, when the numbers were too much against me. Bea was the caregiver. She looked after us, fixed our cuts and grazes, washed out an infected gash, and was always the voice of reason, even though she was struggling and didn't like the constant upheaval. And she looked after Mila. Because Mila was just the helpless little baby whom we had to keep safe.

My shoulders feel heavy as I remember how much I hated having Mila with us on that voyage. We needed to be quiet if we were to stay alive and surprise the Enhanced, and a baby is never quiet. She screamed and cried, and, more than once, the Enhanced found us because of her cries.

I remember how much I hated her. Until she was three years old, and she came toddling over to me one evening and swung a punch in the air and said, "I'm like Kee-Kee."

My heart melted then.

But the four of us got through it. And we found Rahn's group, just like our mother had told us to.

Rahn wasn't happy with me that first week. They went on a raid. I stowed myself in the boot of one of the vehicles. I waited until they were gone, then I went on a killing spree. Rahn found me with the third body.

I smile. I've never seen him so furious.

He had strong words with me. They all did. They told me that it wasn't safe to do that. Seeking out the Enhanced in a town and killing them only draws attention to us.

"You kill lone Enhanced, Keelie," he told me that night, waggling a gnarled finger at me. "Or ones that are threatenin' you, that are near our village, that can't call backup immediately and kill you. You don't set out to kill on *raids*. Raids are for supplies, resources. You need to blend in, get the gear, and get out of there as quickly as possible. Sure, you kill if there's a problem, if you have to. But blendin' in is the top priority."

"But they deserve to die, each and every one of them." I shouted his own survival lesson back at him. I'd learnt them all that very first day.

"Yes, they do. But we deserve to live more. And goin' in and attackin' like that is a death sentence. You need plans, you need people, you need a team if you're goin' to kill. It's not somethin' you do spontaneously, on a whim. Spontaneous gets you killed."

He told the others I was damaged because of what I'd endured—I heard him talking. Said they had to wean me off seeking the Enhanced and killing them. That I was enjoying it too much.

Gradually, they turned my desire to kill the Enhanced into a need to keep fit. I started running a lot, and then fighting competitively with the men, and—when they thought I was ready to hold a firearm among them—improving my aim in shooting with a gun.

It seems so long ago now, a lifetime ago, but also like yesterday. My memories of it are both sharp and a haze, all at once. And, if I concentrate long enough, I can feel it.

Feel the euphoria.

And you loved the kill.

We clear Mila's things out of our hut. Me, Bea, and Elf. We take her bed out first, and Katya and a couple of the men say they'll sort it. I don't know what they mean by that.

I kneel in the space where Mila's bed was. I look at all her belongings.

I know I'm not supposed to dwell on death, that when an Untamed dies, the survivors have to keep going—otherwise the Enhanced have won.

But this is different.

The blood is on my hands this time.

Bea gathers up Mila's toys, and then she puts Mila's fairy wings on. They're the wings that Kayden stole on a raid for Mila once. I remember how threatened Bea felt for a while, as if Kayden was trying to become Mila's parent.

But he didn't.

Mila only adored one person in that way, and that was our older sister.

Bea grabs her ear defenders and gathering bag, and then runs outside, still wearing the fairy wings. I hear her anguished cries. Elf goes out after her a moment later. I don't miss the look he gives me though, before he does. It says: *this is your fault.*

My fault.

My fault.

My fault.

"She'll be back in a bit," Elf says, returning. "Probably just a short walk."

I think time has passed, but I've been sitting here, staring at the doll in my hands. Mila's doll, Straw Hair. It's wearing little clothes that Bea made out of an old shirt. Bea made a lot of clothes for Straw Hair. Once, Mila insisted she make sportswear for her doll so she could go running, and Elf told me that Mila was obviously copying me, wanting to be like me.

Or wanting a connection.

Looking at the doll makes me feel strange.

Like I should cry.

But my eyes are dry. So dry.

So are Elf's. We don't cry. Not like Bea.

I wait for Bea to return. Wait and wait. I stare at her calendar on the wall. Alan got it for her on a raid—he gets one each year for her, because Bea likes to know the date, and she always has it proudly on display.

A DANGEROUS GAME

When it's dark, I start to worry. Elf's asleep, and I don't wake him. I head out, alone, looking for her. I know most of her mountain walks, but not as well as she does, and I head out with just my Swiss army knife on me.

I call her name, over and over.

It's cold and I wrap my fleece around me, think I imagine shapes in the gathering darkness. I kick at loose stones, then jump at the grating sounds they make as they tumble over the rough ground.

"Bea!" My voice gets hoarse.

By the time I've walked all of her routes and scoured the area, shouting her name, the sun is rising. I'm shaking with cold and fatigue, bleary-eyed, and nauseous. It seems to take me ages to walk back to Nbutai. But as I focus on the outlines of the huts getting stronger, I convince myself that Bea will be in our hut. That she'll have been there all night. That I'll just have missed her. That's all.

"Keelie?" Alan's on fire duty, and he stares at me. He's one of the oldest men at Nbutai, with deep lines carved into his beautiful, dark skin. Grandfatherly, that's how a lot of people think of him. "You've been out all night?" He looks surprised.

See? People don't even realize when you're gone.

"Is Bea here?" I ask, but I don't wait for his answer.

I pull back the drape on our hut, head inside.

My heart gets heavier before my eyes have a chance to adjust.

Her bed is still empty.

TWENTY-SEVEN

I STARE AT THE PLACE where my motorbike should be. At the dry, beaten ground. At the way the orange dust clings to my shoes.

She's gone.

And she's taken my motorbike. The bike she'd never ride…not with me, anyway. Once I saw her on it with Elf. So she knows how to drive it? And she got it away from here, without anyone hearing or seeing….

My vision swims, and I take a step back, right into Five's arms. She holds me for a moment.

"It's okay," she whispers.

"No, it's not," Elf snaps, and Five's eyes widen. "Anything could've happened out there. It's *dangerous*."

"Look, she goes off on her own a lot. To collect her plants," Rahn says, striding forward. He inspects the ground, but there are no tire marks. I've already checked.

"But she doesn't take the bike." I say. "And she tells us where she's going then. And she's quick because…" Because she has to get back for Mila.

Only now she doesn't.

I take several deep breaths, but I find myself shaking more with each one.

Bea's never gone off on her own *like this* before. Never taken my bike. Never been out a whole night.

I turn, feeling sick. What was it she said to me? That she didn't feel safe here? And I didn't do much—if anything—to reassure her. I pretty much ignored her. I was too caught up in my argument with Elf. And we were shouting, and we never shout around Bea and—

Dread clings to my frame, tries to drag me down.

I wasn't there for her.

And now she's run away....

My vision swims, and I blink quickly, feel ice in my fingers.

Yani and Corin are running toward us.

"Her ear defenders are gone, and her gathering bag too," Corin says. "But she doesn't seem to have taken much food with her. Marouska thinks only a couple of tins are missing."

"So, a quick excursion then," Rahn says, folding his arms. "She'll be back."

The knot of unease in my stomach grows. "No. She's been out *all* night. And with no weapons."

"It's out of character," Five says quietly.

I take a step forward, toward Rahn. "Give me the keys for a truck. We need to go after her."

But he shakes his head. "If it's not a quick excursion, then leavin' suddenly with no warnin', not tellin' people, and takin' only a little food, points to one thing: joinin' the Enhanced."

"*What*?" I exclaim, my head spinning.

"No," Yani says, his voice firm, and I flash him a grateful look. "Bea wouldn't do that."

"She's grieving," Corin says. He glances at me quickly, then away. "She'll just be out in the mountains, somewhere."

Rahn points at Five. "Get your brother on the radios. Listen out for a conversion announcement. Do it *now*."

Five nods, then looks at me. "You all right if I go?"

Rahn glares at us. I nod, and Five leaves, but I know they won't hear anything. Of course Bea hasn't decided to join the Enhanced. No, she's out there. Alone. Grieving. And anything could happen—hell, the Enhanced *could* get her, like they got Mila… Visions of them ambushing her fill my mind, and I gulp.

"Rahn, we need to go after her, need to look for her. She's vulnerable. You know what grief can do to people." I glance at Corin. I've heard how he was a mess after his parents died. He disappeared for two days. Rahn had everyone out looking for him. And when someone's grieving, how observant are they going to be? Would Bea notice the Enhanced creeping up on her?

But Rahn stamps his foot, shakes his head with vigor. "I'm not wastin' resources lookin' for her."

"Seriously?" I say. "You're doing this again?"

"Doin' what?" His voice is low.

"Displaying prejudice."

Through his dark glasses, I catch what I think are the whites of his eyes flashing. "It's likely she's gone to join the Enhanced. All the signs point to that."

"She hasn't." Yani takes a deep breath, and my gaze snaps to him. He looks at the ground for a second, then swallows hard. "She's not coming back," he says at last, but I detect the pain in his voice.

I stare at him. "What?"

Corin steps closer to him.

"She told me…yesterday. That she was leaving. Trying to find others. A safer group."

My mouth dries. "You didn't try and stop her?"

"And you didn't tell us?" Elf demands. "You didn't think that we should know?"

"She made me promise," Yani says, pushing his blond hair back. "She wanted me to go with her, but I…."

"So you let her go out there on her own?" I point up toward the steepest part of the Titian Mountains, feeling sicker and sicker. "Have you any idea how many predators are out there? And you *let* her go."

"She said she couldn't stay here. I had to respect that."

"There's a difference between respecting someone and saving their life." I shake my head hard. Something in my left ear clicks, and I point at Rahn. "Give me the keys to a truck. I'm getting her back now."

But before Rahn can speak, Yani clears his throat.

"What?" I bark at him. "Is there more?"

He hunkers his shoulders a little. The body language of guilt, I think. Well, good, he deserves to feel guilty.

"She thinks there are other Untamed about," he says. "Because of that woman and baby we found. She thinks there must be more like that, and she's good at tracking. She's confident she can find them." He grips his hands together, then twists them, as if he's washing them. "She's heading north. And she told me if she can't find them, she's still not coming back. She doesn't feel safe here."

"Well then," I say. "We know which way to go."

Rahn coughs. "Absolutely not. Bea has clearly decided my leadership cannot keep her safe and would prefer another group. She ain't welcome here anymore."

I swear at him and storm back to my hut. My survival bag, I need it. If Rahn thinks I'm giving up on Bea, then he's got another thing coming. I've lost one sister. I will not lose another.

Especially when it's my fault.

Elf races after me.

"You coming too?" I look up at him as I grab my survival bag.

"Of course." He sounds annoyed. "Did you really need to ask?"

I clear my throat and—

And I see it.

At the end of Bea's bed. Our mother's butterfly necklace. How didn't I notice it before? She's gone without it.

I snatch it up quickly, stuff it into my survival bag. Bea needs it to feel safe. She's left it behind by mistake.

Or she was planning on coming back? I frown, breathing hard. Not according to Yani. No, she must've forgotten this and only remembered when she was too far away.

"You going to get the keys for a truck?" Elf asks me.

I nod, swinging my bag onto my back. Think I've got everything.

"No need," a new voice says.

Nico stands in the doorway, keys in his hand.

My eyes narrow.

"I'm coming too," he says. "Yani's told me. He's going to stay here in case Bea returns. But you need at least three people to get someone back. Extraction, distraction, and backup. One on each."

"It's not a rescue mission," I say. "And if it was, one on each would not work. Be far too dangerous."

"But safety is still in numbers. And you need three at least. A driver, a lookout, and—"

"And you?" I snort, and all my earlier animosity toward him intensifies.

Nico waves his hand at me and Elf. "You two are grieving. You need someone level-headed."

"And that someone's *you*?" I raise my eyebrows.

"I'm the one with the keys to a truck right now." He glares at me. "Yani's getting some food ready for us. And a radio too. Elf, see if you can get weapons. And Keelie, I suggest you check with Katya that she's had no warning about us going out."

I stare at him. He's giving me orders? Telling me what to do? I shift my weight so it's more evenly distributed across both of my legs. I glare at him.

Elf looks at me quickly, then sidles past me. "We need to find Bea," is all he says as he leaves the hut.

I glare at Nico. "*Fine.*"

I wait for him to move.

"I'm sorry about before," he begins.

I shake my head, hold one hand up. "Not now. Let's

just go."

But Nico grabs my arm. He steps closer, and the strong smell of smoke washes over me. "But there'll never be a right time, will there? Keelie, I love you. And we have to talk about this—"

"I said *not now*. Some things are more important."

He nods.

I wasn't more important, was I?

Mila's voice.

I freeze, then jolt, look around. But she's not here. Of course she's not. But—

I touch my head slowly. It wasn't her. Wasn't.

Me—just my grief.

Really? You don't look like you're grieving.

"Move then," I bark at Nico. "We're leaving in ten."

I barge past him and head straight to the Sarrs' hut. Katya's not there, but I see her walking over. She gestures for me to go in, and I'm glad to see no one else is here.

Katya watches me carefully long after I've told her the plan.

"You're grieving too. This isn't a good idea." She shakes her head firmly, and the movement makes her silver earrings flash. They're the earrings Bea really likes.

I flex my neck a little, wait for it to click. "I've got to do something," I say. "I can't leave things like this with Bea. I've got to try."

But Katya cuts me off by pressing a finger firmly to my lips.

"We both know what this is," she says. "I've seen it happen before. I've felt it." She sits down slowly and adjusts her blouse. It's a vibrant yellow, and it makes her dark skin look glossier than usual. "I felt it, Keelie. I've felt it many a time. The deaths of my mother, my father, One, Two, Four, and Six. Each one made me want to do something reckless, follow them there, to the New World."

I push my hair behind my ears. "I'm not going to a

town. And I'm not going to die." Except I am. Caia-Lu's words: *Your death is written in the silk of time*. But everyone dies. I straighten up. "I'm going to find Bea. That's all."

"And what if Bea doesn't want to return? You cannot force her."

I breathe hard. "Then I'll give our mother's necklace back to her. She can't have meant to leave it here… But I have to see her."

She shrugs. "I know I cannot stop you. No one can stop you. But, be careful, my dear. I don't want the boys coming back, delivering some reckless tale of your behavior that ends in death. Your death. I know what you're like."

"That won't happen," I say. "I told you. And I'm not going to a town or a city. Not going anywhere near the Enhanced."

She shakes her head. "But you will."

TWENTY-EIGHT

I DRIVE BECAUSE I FEEL more in control that way. Elf sits directly next to me, and Nico's on his other side. I can tell by the way my brother's glowering at the road ahead that he wants to drive, and my position makes me feel smug. I love driving.

Elf points ahead. "Where do you think these other Untamed will be? Bea said she was going north to find them, according to Yani. But how far?"

I shake my head and shrug. "If there even *are* any."

"You think there aren't?" Elf's gaze snaps toward me, and I feel it burning the side of my face. He sounds disappointed, and it takes me a moment to realize why: because, if we don't find Bea, then we need to hold onto the hope that she will find others out there. Untamed who are on their own don't tend to survive for long.

I grip the wheel tighter. "I don't know where they'll be. But I don't think they're going to be anywhere near our territory else we'll have seen them."

Nico clears his throat. "But that woman I saw— the one with the child—said she saw that Untamed woman and Enhanced man together *near* here. So that's one Untamed around here."

My heart thuds, and the memories of me and Red together make me feel sick.

How can something that was so perfect make me feel so sick?

But it can't have been us she saw. We would've seen her.

"We'd know if there are any other Untamed around this area regularly. And Bea would've seen them and told us, she walks around these parts a lot." I steer the truck onto a particularly rough patch of ground. The suspension isn't great, and we're all jolted back and forth for several moments. "No, we've got to drive a lot farther. That's what Bea's going to be doing. Going into unknown territory."

Except it won't be unknown. Because my siblings and I traveled from the north. Could Bea be trying to find our old group? In case there are many more survivors, like Red? People whom I left behind….

"So we keep driving until we see signs of Bea or other Untamed?" Elf asks.

I nod. "Guess so. But we're the only Untamed near New Kimearo—that's our main raiding source. Nico, get the map out. What's the next nearest Enhanced town or city, going north, that could be the edge of a territory for another Untamed group?"

Nico leans forward. The glove compartment is stiff, and it takes him a little while to release the catch because he does it so carefully—I would've forced it. He takes the map in his hands, unfolding it. He studies it for a few moments, and Elf leans over, taking a look.

"New Webbon or New Lija. They're both really far north of here though," he says. "They're on the other side of the mountains, and then some. We'll have to cross the whole band—that will take days just to do that. Then there's still a way to go."

"So we go to those cities?" Elf asks. "Isn't that risky? Those cities are big, and security will be great there. They've got sensors. If any Untamed are there then they'll have been caught as soon as they stepped near the city walls."

"No, we'd be searching the outlying land for Untamed," I say. "Bea wouldn't go to a city. And we probably won't need to go that far. Bea's less than twenty-four hours ahead of us, but she's the only driver. She's going to have to stop for rests. There are three of us. We can alternate."

I take one hand off the wheel and push my hair away from my sweaty face. My skin is sticky, and my eyes feel strange. Like they're dry. I have to blink a lot just to be able to see.

"Good point," Elf says. "We'll get her back." I'm not sure whether he's reassuring himself or telling all of us.

I look up at the mountainous terrain. We're going past many of the caves that I know Bea loves. But we're too close to Nbutai now. She won't be around here.

Not unless she's injured….

But I'm certain Yani and the others are going to look in the mountains by the village for her, no matter what Rahn says. Searching the nearby area is logical—even though I'm sure now that she won't be injured.

No, Bea will be getting as far away as possible.

"Keep a lookout for the motorbike or tracks," I say. The ground is hard and dusty, and I'm not sure how long tracks would preserve for at the moment.

"Kind of difficult when you're driving so fast."

"Got to go fast," I say. "Got to find her."

Got to find her.

Got to find her.

Got to find her.

The words sink into me.

TWENTY-NINE

MY SKIN CRAWLS AS I stare at the map.

We've stopped for a break because the engine was overheating. There's a shallow pool of water not far away, and Elf and Nico are refilling the skins and water containers. I watch them for a second, then look at the map again, hardly able to believe what I'm seeing.

Then I jump out of the pickup.

"Who did this?" I yell, marching up to them.

I reach my brother first and shove the map in front of him, pointing to where someone has stupidly marked Nbutai's location on it. My skin crawls.

"What?" Elf says, lifting his hand up.

"Hey! Don't get water on it," Nico yells. "It's only paper."

"Was it you?" I turn on him. "Don't you realize how stupid this is? Marking our village! What if the Enhanced found this—it would be a wipeout within, what? Hours?"

Nico and Elf look at the map. Nico's face pales, and Elf's dark eyes fix on me.

"I didn't do that," Elf says. "Keeping them away from our base is of utmost importance."

"Nico?" My voice is sharp.

He shakes his head and holds his stubby fingers up. Just the sight of them infuriates me.

"Someone must've done it!"

"Well, it must've been done by someone else," Elf says. "Back at the village?"

"But everyone knows—"

"Well, obviously they don't," Nico says. "And thanks for immediately assuming it must've been me, Keelie. Really appreciate that."

"Look, it's not a problem," Elf says. "There are no Enhanced here. None will see it. We use the map for the rest of this mission, then, when we get back, we tear that part out—"

"We can't tear out part of the map!"

"Well, stick something over it. Blot it out with a marker."

"And draw more attention to it?" I shake my head. "I can't believe how stupid you are sometimes."

"What do you propose we do about it then?" Elf shouts. "Destroy it here? Burn it? Then we've got nothing to go on to find these other Untamed and Bea!" He takes the map from me and folds it up. "Just ignore it, okay—getting worked up isn't helping us. You're just getting angry, and you're not even doing your job."

"Which is?"

"Keeping a lookout," Elf says. "That's what you're supposed to be doing while we get the water—you've got the gun! But you're not, you're getting yourself worked up about this. Meanwhile, a dozen Enhanced could've sneaked up and caught us."

My eyes narrow. "Fine. I'm going back to the truck. But it was still stupid of whoever did that."

I ignore their remarks as I stomp back to the pickup. The air is hot and sticky, and I don't like it. It makes me feel worse. Angrier.

Or maybe I'm angry because I murdered Mila, and it was all my fault. Why did I use the gun? Why didn't

I listen? Why didn't I strangle the Enhanced? Or kick her? And there's nothing like thoughts like that to make you feel even more wretched than you already do.

I wait in the truck until Elf and Nico are ready, then we set off again, driving through the lower Titian Mountains. I think we're making good progress. Nico sits next to me, in the middle seat, and he has the map out.

He points to the left. "I think we should have a look up there. The contour lines on the map indicate there's a steep drop up there, sort of around the corner, but this rock is softer than down there."

"So?"

Nico glares at me. "There could be huge caves. Up there."

In my periphery vision, Elf nods. "Perfect place for Untamed to live."

Perfect. I don't know about that. Caves often only have one entrance, and, if an Enhanced One stood in that entrance, then those in the cave would have no escape route.

But we all know Bea loves caves, says she likes the tranquility and peace within them. And these ones aren't within easy walking distance of Nbutai. These would be new to her. Would she be excited enough to stop and look, thinking that being in the caves would make her feel better? Maybe she'll have spent the night in one, pleased to be away from the sound of the motorbike for a few hours.

I pull the truck over the rough ground. The terrain's getting worse, but at least Nico let some of the air out of the tires before he got back in. That's something.

I drive as far as the terrain will let me, then we reach the rocky area Nico was planning on, and we get out to look on foot. The rocks are unusually dark in color for granite in this area—and piled up somewhat precariously either side of the narrow path we pick. Not that it's much of a path. We end up scaling the rocks most of the time. Among the rocks though, there's vegetation. And I hadn't realized until now just how green the plants are in this place. There's a surprising amount of underground water in this part of the Titian Mountains.

I keep my eyes peeled for Bea, for any signs of her, and we call her name as loudly as we dare.

"Watch your footing," Nico tells Elf, just as my brother treads on loose shingle and nearly goes flying. Nico and I grab him in time, though it snaps two of my nails.

I grimace.

"Caves!" Nico shouts suddenly. He turns back to me, grinning, apparently forgetting the low-burning animosity between us.

I look up, and I see them, a fair distance ahead. We start moving faster, it's just instinct to speed up. Because my sister might be there.

Nico reaches them first and disappears inside. No sounds follow. So Bea's not there? I hover by the entrance, looking for footprints. But the sand and compacted earth hold no signs, except for where Nico disturbed it.

He emerges and shakes his head.

"You don't think there's anyone here at all then?" Elf asks, a strange look on his face. "Not Bea, not others?"

I shake my head, but we still search them all.

I follow Nico. Elf brings up the rear.

It's surprisingly light in the next cave; the stones overhead don't quite meet up, and fragments of sunlight squeeze in. A handful of comb rat droppings litter the floor; comb rats normally take shelter in rock crevices, but a cave like this would be just as perfect for them as it would be for people…but only if there's a water source here.

I head back out, blinking fast to get my eyes to readjust to the brighter light levels and look around. But there's no obvious water source in sight. I'm high up—though not near the summit of a mountain—yet

I can see far.

No. This cave isn't that suitable for permanent human shelter.

But Bea would love it.

There were several caves at D'Elinous; on the other side of the village was the sea, and we'd walk along the coast for hours, Bea exploring all the caves. The first time she spoke to me—spoke properly—was when we were in a cave.

"It's a little world for me," she said, and her eyes sparkled.

I smiled, and, together, we began looking at all the jewels and crystals locked into the stone walls.

"What are they for? What do they do?"

I couldn't help but make up stuff, telling my sister that the red jewels would give the person who saw them good luck and the purple ones would give good health. Bea wanted me to cut them out of the walls so we could take them home, but I couldn't do that. And telling her that had nearly broken my heart. Up until then, she always looked at me with a sense of awe. She believed I could do anything. That I was an amazing person.

And I shattered that.

I turn and look back down, toward where we left the truck and—

I go cold.

There's a man. A man standing there. His back is to me, but I know immediately it's not Nico or Elf. Another man. An Untamed? My eyes widen. There really are others about—that woman was real, she wasn't me? And they're here…and Bea's here too? Maybe they're all hiding… Maybe Bea's told them about me, how I'm an Untamed who kills other Untamed, and they're waiting for me to leave.

"Kee?" Nico calls, but I don't turn. I keep my eyes on the man, narrowing them slightly, trying to see.

He looks tall, broad-shouldered. Muscular. The sun partly silhouettes him, so I can't make out the exact color of his hair—it just looks dark.

The flash burns my eyes as he turns.

Shit.

My breath catches in my throat. One of *them*.

I reach for my Luger before the voice in my head can start screaming at me not to use it, to kill with my hands—but a gun *is* best for this situation, isn't it? Only the moment I hold it, hold it like I'm going to use it, I feel sick. And it's stupid, I've touched it and had it on my person a lot on this trip and not felt like this before.

Yet now I'm shaking, and I try to keep breathing evenly.

I focus back on the man, don't think he's seen me. He's looking to his side now, shielding his eyes from the sun. Now would be a good time to shoot, I know that…unless there are others—firing would draw their attention to us. And there could be more of them than us.

My heart beats frantically as I back toward the cave, not taking my eyes off him and—

Then I realize what he's looking at. Why he's looking that way.

The truck.

Shit. Shit. Shit. He'll know there are Untamed about.

We need to get away, get away fast. Shoot him once we're close enough to the truck for a quick exit? But there could be others about, others who would grab us, possibly disarm us.

And I don't want to use the gun. I don't feel the urge to kill rearing up inside me now. I just want to run.

My feet catch on loose shingle as I back up, and I stumble, arms wide, but catch myself. Then I reach the entrance of the cave, duck inside. There's a crevice to my left, and I slide my body into it. Nico and Elf are farther back—I can just about see them, and I raise my arm in our *silence!* gesture.

Nico's eyes widen. "What is it? Bea?"

So much for silence.

I hold my breath and lean forward, looking out of the entrance. The man's not there. Only the sand-rock, broken up by a little greenery, is visible. I move quickly, over to the other side—and, immediately, I feel safer, between my brother and Nico.

"We need to leave. There's an Enhanced One down by our truck." I keep my voice as low as I can.

"What?" Nico and Elf shout the word in unison.

"Be quiet!"

Nico grabs my arm. "Are you all right? Keelie? Were you seen?"

"I'm fine. Don't think he saw me."

"How many—just one?" Elf asks, then he's taking the Luger from me, and heading out.

"Stop!"

Nico and I grab Elf, an arm each, and haul him back. It's like a twisted déjà vu—it was Elf who stopped me from charging down there when Mila was….

"I need to know how many there are." Elf's eyes narrow as he looks toward the entrance. "Let me go."

"I told you—one is visible." I hold onto his hoody tighter, trying to ignore how much I'm shaking, because this is ridiculous, pathetic. "And we need to be careful."

"There'll be others nearby," Elf says.

Then I freeze. Have the Enhanced caught Bea? But if they have, they wouldn't take her bike, would they? Wouldn't that still be here? Or would they collect that as well?

Still, there'd be a struggle. There'd be something, some sign, I'm sure. Or rather, I hope.

"So what do we do?" Nico asks. "Kill him, grab the truck, and go?"

"No," I say. "We avoid a confrontation." My chest tightens, and I feel like everything in my body is squeezing together, laughing, trying to choke me. "We leave. It's the sensible thing to do."

Nico frowns. "Is this really *you* speaking?"

I take a deep breath. "If we go and kill him, it'll bring

all the others out. We'll end up fighting them. Chances are at least one of us will get injured. If we just leave, we've got a better chance at getting away unhurt."

And it's right, isn't it?

No, you just don't want to use the gun. You're scared. But there are other ways to kill. Beat him to death! Or use your knife! You can't leave him alive!

"Okay," Nico says. "So, we wait him out, up here? Then get our truck when he leaves it?"

I bring a hand to my chest. My skin is hot and clammy. "That won't work. He's seen it, he'll know there are Untamed here… He'll be calling for backup, staying by our truck, thinking we won't go without it. If there are others about—and there probably are— they'll search for us, find us eventually. We have to get away on foot."

Nico's face pales considerably. "But what if one of them *does* see us? They can run faster than us."

"We would still have the gun," I say. My stomach hardens. "And our knives. If that happens, then we shoot or stab them. Last resort."

Elf shakes his head, then runs a hand through his hair. It looks thicker than usual. Maybe it's the light in here. "What about those other Untamed that are out here—can they help us get away?" He glances at me.

"No, we don't know where they are," Nico says.

"*If* they even exist," I add.

Nico grimaces. "We're on our own." He looks at me. "You think we should run now?"

I nod, feeling less and less like myself. "Yes. While we've got the chance."

"Run back to Nbutai?" Nico looks at me.

"No. In case we're trailed. We've got to keep going anyway, got to find Bea." I press my lips together, hoping that we haven't left clear tire tracks to Nbutai. But we shouldn't have, right? There's a fair breeze, and the ground is hard. But dusty too.

"We're going to have to go," I say. I slide the gun from Elf's loose grip, and I don't know why I want to hold it when it makes me feel sick. "I'll go first and look around—I'm smallest, less noticeable," I add quickly, seeing the looks on their faces. "I'll signal to you if it's clear. If I'm caught, I'll say I'm alone. There's a crevice opposite—there, that wall. Hide in there if they catch me."

Not that the crevice would do much. If the Enhanced catch one of us, they'll look for others. Like the Enhanced, we stick in groups, and they know that.

I move cautiously, slowly, back out to the cave's entrance, then onto the ridge. My heart hammers against my ribs, and the rhythm makes me feel sick. It's going too fast.

I stick close to the cliff face, feeling for handholds on the warm rock as I make my way. Then I lean around, as slowly as I can, and look.

The Enhanced man is still by the truck. He's leaning against the bonnet, arms folded. Waiting for us? Waiting for backup?

I scan the area. My eyes smart from the effort, from looking into the sun. I search for movement, for anything, but I can't see any more Enhanced Ones. It's just the one man. I press my lips together. If one's here, there must be others…but I can't see anyone.

They must be well hidden.

Or there really is just one.

If there's just one, you should kill him, take the truck, and run.

The thought makes me stiffen, and I see Mila's body in my mind. Dead.

Kill.

Kill.

Kill.

No.

No more killing.

Not even them?

You're an Enhanced lover now?

No. I'm human. More human than I've ever been.

I take a deep breath and scan the rest of the area

again. I step to my left, looking farther and farther. Movement catches my eye, but it's just a little of the low-creeping vegetation moving in the breeze. Not human movement. Not the Enhanced.

I try to keep calm as I look back around. I can just about see Elf's and Nico's shapes in the cave entrance. Both are watching me.

Hurry up, I tell myself as I continue checking the immediate area. We can't waste time. And it's clear, isn't it, if we go the opposite way to where the truck is?

I head back to the cave and—

"Keelie!"

I whirl around at the man's shout.

The Enhanced man. He's there, suddenly fifteen feet in front of me, sweat pouring down his face, his whole body shaking.

"I thought I'd lost you! And you've no idea what that did to me…when you're all scattering, moving, and how would I find you? And—and it was a clever disguise, your sister on your bike! And I'm so glad you're here, that I've found you! Because I knew I had to, just had to get away!"

The world stops as I stare at Red.

THIRTY

A THOUSAND INDECIPHERABLE FEELINGS BOLT through my body as I stare at him. At Red. Enhanced Red. But looking the same as the undercover Untamed Red. Because he would. Of course he would.

And he looks good, wearing a tight T-shirt and casual jeans.

But his mirrors are real.

"You know where Bea is? You've seen her?" My words sound strange, like they're not mine.

Elf and Nico are by my side in an instant. Nico's knife's out. So much for them hiding.

"Don't!" I yell at Nico, then look back at Red. "Where's Bea?"

"Keelie!" Red says again, and his voice sounds the same as before—as when he was Untamed—and it's full of wonder. The *same* voice. It paralyzes me. "I thought I'd never see you again, because you're not easy to track, and I'm…."

He takes a step toward me, and I'm just here, frozen. Stupidly frozen. Thinking of the things we did together, how he tasted, how he felt. And I feel everything inside me try and pull me toward him.

Like he's a magnet, and I've got to see him. Got to be with him.

No.

Nico grabs my arm. "You know him?" His tone is dark. "What's going on?"

"It's Red," I say. "My friend, Red."

But is he still my friend?

For a moment, Nico's eyes widen. He breathes heavily, his nostrils flaring. "I thought he was dead."

"So did I." I swallow hard and try not to remember that last night at D'Elinous. Then my stomach hardens. "But he survived, Untamed. Only he got caught, and now he's Enhanced. *Properly* Enhanced."

Elf wrenches the gun from me, marches forward, and—

I go cold.

"Don't shoot!" Red yells, hands in the air. "I—I want to be like you!"

Elf stops. "What?" He sounds strange, angry.

Nico and I step nearer, until the three of us are facing Red, only a few yards between us. I'm breathing hard, panting. I feel color rushing to my face in the most unattractive way—

It doesn't matter how unattractive you look. You can't be with him. He's the enemy now.

"It's a lie," Nico shouts, looking around frantically. "Elf, shoot him! There'll be others coming, and—"

"No!" I yell. "He's seen Bea!" I point at Red. "Where is she? Where'd you see her? On a motorbike?"

Red stares at me, looking both curious and confused. "Last night." His eyes look me up and down.

"Did you follow her?" Then my eyes widen. "Did you *convert* her?"

"We need to get away," Nico hisses at me, but I wave my hand at him.

"She was too far away…" Red says. "And I don't… When I realized it was her, I… I told you, I'm joining you."

I look around quickly—but no one else has appeared,

no other Enhanced.

"You *want* to be Untamed?" Elf stares at Red. He's still pointing the gun at him, and I try to see if the safety's on. "You're not making sense."

"Because I'm running lean! I want to be Untamed, but my brain is...." He breaks off, grimacing. "I have to be with you!"

"So he doesn't know where Bea is now." Nico shakes his head, then rolls up the sleeves of his checkered shirt. "Just shoot him, Elf. It doesn't matter what he says. It's a ploy. He's not seen Bea, and he doesn't want to join us. Shoot him, and we can go. He's buying time until others get here...they could be seconds away, and we have to move."

"Others?" Red says, and then he's looking at me. Straight at me, and it makes my heart do a stupid fluttery thing. "It's just me, Keelie. Why would I call others here?"

"Because you're Enhanced," I say, and the words feel good to say because I'm saying them out loud, as if that will teach my heart. I shake my head hard, to drill the same words into me.

"But I haven't been Enhanced for long...just a few days—help me! I can resist... And I need to join you, Keelie, I need to be with you."

Nico mutters something dark under his breath.

Red's pleas twist through me, make me think of all the stuff we did. I feel my face going even redder, and I try not to look at Nico, hope that he hasn't worked it out. That he won't.

Red spreads his arms wide, and I stare at his tattooed biceps and how the tightness of his T-shirt emphasizes their form. "Look," he says. "I've not brought any augmenters or anything—and I'm not trying to convert you... I've got no radios to contact them! You have to help me! Untamed save Untamed!"

"You're not Untamed though, *mate*," Nico says.

Elf nods. "And no Enhanced One *wants* to become an Untamed, become wild. Even if they're new," he says. "They can't resist enough to leave the compound themselves. They need help to do that."

I stare at Elf. Did I tell him about Red being converted and no longer undercover? I must've, when I explained about Mila, but I can't remember. But he's definitely treating Red like an Enhanced, not an Untamed. Not his friend.

But then again, I can't remember much. Not really. Not since Mila died. Everything's in snatches.

"No, it was just me," Red yells. "Please, K...."

Elf's nostrils wrinkle. He holds the gun steady, glances at me for a second, then turns back to Red. "I don't buy it. The addiction to augmenters is too strong. You shouldn't be able to voluntarily give it up."

"It's a trap," Nico says. "But, look, we're nearer the truck now. No others have shown themselves. Elf, shoot him, and then we can go."

"No!" I cry at the same time as Red, and his eyes dart to me. Those mirror eyes. And I try to read him, but I can't. Is he resisting the augmenters? Is it true? He wasn't before—he tried to convert me.

"Stop looking at her," Nico snarls. He steps closer to me, then Elf does too. "We need to kill him."

"No," Elf says, and I glance at him in surprise. "If there's an Enhanced One who's resisting enough to escape by himself, we need to keep him. There could be more like him... We need to know. Could...could be big for the Untamed." His voice is quiet. So he is seeing him as his friend? But he was going to shoot him just now.

Nico nods, reluctantly though. Then he points at Red. "How did you get here?"

Red folds his hands together carefully. When he looks up, his gaze is on me. "I walked."

"How did you find us?" I ask.

Red's eyes bore into mine. "Coincidence. I had no idea where a group of Untamed might be heading off to." Then he frowns. "Are you all scattering, relocating?"

"What?"

"Going off in small groups. Or individually?"

"Bea's run away," I say. "We're looking for her."

"And any other Untamed out here," Elf adds.

Red looks up at the rocky mountainside, then back at us. "So you're letting me join you? We can look for Bea together?"

And he looks delighted. But I don't buy it. He knows roughly the area where Nbutai is. Yet he's out *here*. My skin crawls as I remember how desperate he was to convert me after I killed Mila. No. He wouldn't change like that, would he? But it's within the seven-day period….

No. He wants to find the village, find all of us. And his memory's warped, thanks to the conversion process. He's Enhanced….

But he's *resisting*! And hope raises its head in me, even though I try not to let it. Need to remain level-headed. And it's not as if Red and I can ever be together now. Not when our secret meetings were the cause of Mila's death. And now Bea's gone too.

No. I can't be with him. No matter what I want.

"Maybe," Elf says, lowering the gun. "Maybe not."

"I'm on my own, I swear," Red says. "And I can't lie. Honesty is still in my system."

Elf snorts.

"We need to *go*," Nico wails. "We're doing what he wants—waiting here until others come."

"We can't abandon one who's resisting," Elf says. "Not given what it could lead to." He glances at me.

I nod quickly, my heart pounding. Red's *back*?

"We need to search you," I say to Red, but my voice wobbles, betrays the calm persona I'm trying to keep. "Elf keep the gun on him. Nico?"

Nico and I search Red quickly, and Elf keeps guard with the gun. I try not to react when I touch Red, and try not to let my fingers linger, but his eyes are on me, and I'm sure I know what he's thinking of.

And he's resisting because of me? Because he wants

to be with me?

But he didn't—not at the compound. And he'll have been converted even more since then.

The hairs on the back of my neck lift up. I don't like this. There's too much suspicion in me, fighting my hope, and it's twisting round and round in the tangled mess that is my feelings.

"What are these?" Nico asks, as we both pull several augmenters out of Red's pockets. With them is Red's ID card that says *Robert Yearling* on it, and I see Elf leaning closer to look at it. He frowns for a long moment.

"You know what they are," Red says.

"Why've you got them if you want to join us?" I hold one augmenter up in front of him, dangling it like bait in front of a fish.

I let Nico take the others from me, and he smashes them on the ground along with the ones he was holding, lets the earth soak up the liquid.

Red's watching me carefully. "I had them because I needed them. But I'm making myself run lean."

I let the last augmenter drop from my hands, then stamp it into the earth.

"Don't do that!" Red winces. He points at my foot. "You'll cut yourself."

"My soles are thick enough. But that's not the reason you don't want us to destroy them, is it?" I lean in closer, and Nico puts a hand on my shoulder. "It's because you're craving them, and this is all a game to you. You don't really want to join us…" I feel suddenly sick. He really is just buying time for the others to get here. Trying to keep us here. Disgust ripples through me as I realize how easily I've been tricked. I should've listened to Nico. "Come on, let's go. We're wasting time. We need to find Bea and—"

"No!" Red shouts, and he whirls toward me, grabs me by the shoulders, looks into my eyes, and…and *into my soul*. That's what it feels like.

A jolt of feeling burns through me, a thousand words

never said, lost, broken, gone. But here. Between us, with us, around us. Me and Red. And I stare at him, feel as if everything else has stopped. It's just me and Red, the only people in the world. The two of us.

It's your second chance, Keelie. Your second chance with him. Take it.

"Let her go," Elf shouts, and his words startle me, yank me out of my daze.

And I feel…weird.

Then Nico kicks Red, and Red staggers back, and I'm free. Only it doesn't feel like it, feels like…like I'm lost. I look at my shoulders, at where Red's hands were just moments ago. My body tingles, but everything feels empty.

"You okay?" Nico glances at me.

I nod.

"Look! Just listen!" Red's voice gets more frantic. He waves his hands around. "They'll find me! They'll realize I've run. Please! Rescue me! Keelie, *please*."

"Too late," Nico says, shaking his head. He's holding his knife again now.

"No, hang on," Elf says to him.

I step nearer to Red, still feeling strange—and I don't know what to think. I feel the connection between us, and my heart says to keep him with us, but my head tells me no, that it's too dangerous. That it's a trap.

"Why do you want to join us?" I ask.

"Because…because I don't want you to get hurt." Red blinks rapidly.

I don't understand that answer, and a quick glance at Nico and Elf tells me they don't either.

Red grins at me, and I try not to feel anything. Because my feelings, they're my weakness here.

I fix my gaze on Red, feel heat rush to my face. My head pounds as I look at him. And Elf and Nico, they're waiting for *my* decision—I can tell.

And can I do it? Send Red away? Leave him behind again?

Second chances are rare.

But it doesn't have to be permanent, does it, this decision? I can change my mind later if I realize that Red's not sincere.

I nod at him. "Take off your clothes."

Nico makes a startled noise, shock written on his face.

"We need to make sure he's not hiding any more augmenters there," I say. "Or weapons. A radio, a phone, whatever."

"We're *not* taking him with us," Nico says, looking at me in disbelief.

"We are," I say. "Untamed save Untamed." Only my voice sounds strange, not quite like me.

Elf nods in agreement. "He's *resisting*. This is big."

"The Enhanced are non-violent people," Red says, rolling his eyes. "You don't need to check me for weapons. You just want to see me naked."

"No, she doesn't," Nico says, his words jumping through gritted teeth. "And, if you think you're trying on anything with my girl, you've got another thing coming."

My girl. I grimace.

Red doesn't react to his words, just strips off.

We find nothing and let him dress.

"So, you'll have me?" Red asks. "I can join you?"

Nico does not look happy.

And me? I don't know how to feel. I just *don't know*. This is Red, and yet...yet it isn't. But I felt it—felt the connection we have so strongly. I betrayed him once, left him behind. I can't do it again.

"Tie him up," I say.

Red looks more delighted than he should at that prospect, but he lets us do it. No problem. As soon as he's secured in the truck bed, I lead Elf and Nico away.

"We need to watch him at all times," I say, keeping my voice low and trying to concentrate on being rational and logical. Not swayed by the way my heart is lifting. We have to be careful.

"You doubt your *best friend in all the world*?" Nico's

voice isn't kind, and I know then that he's definitely worked it out. He knows Red's not been Enhanced for long, and the air's so thick with the electricity between Red and I, that he must've been able to feel it. He'll know I was with Red, and that Red's the reason I broke up with him.

I look at him, expect more of a reaction. But Nico glares at the sky.

I wipe my sweaty hands against my top and take a deep breath. My heart patters too fast. "We just need to watch him carefully," I finally say. "See if his actions really do match his words."

But I saw him at the compound when I was...after Mila died. Red was Enhanced then. *Truly* Enhanced. How can he be more Untamed now than he was three days ago?

"I still think we should kill him."

Elf clears his throat. "What if this is bigger than just *one* Enhanced revolting? It might not even be because he's newly converted that he's able to resist enough to escape without help." He stares at the gun for a moment. "The Enhanced Ones could have factions of people who are breaking away, trying to become Untamed..."

I nod. "We've got more of a chance of fighting them if they're not a strong unit."

"We need to know as much as we can," Elf says. "Like *why* it's happened now, with him."

Nico lets out a sudden laugh.

I turn to him.

"It's obvious why he's switching sides. Just look at the way he looks at you, Keelie. He obviously *adores* you. He wants to be Untamed because *you* are." Disgust ripples through the air from him.

But his words make me feel strange. Red's resisting because of me? Because he loves me? I shake my head, don't know what to think, because part of me is still unsure, still thinking it doesn't make sense, that it's a trap. And I try to sort through my thoughts, through the tension in the air, through everything.

"He must have a vehicle somewhere," I finally say. "He can't have walked out here. Not this far." And how the hell did Red find me? *Was* it a coincidence? I breathe out hard and scan the area. "If he's lied about that, he could've lied about other stuff too. It's a possibility."

Nico snorts. "Thought you would've been all over him."

"He's *Enhanced*." I breathe out slowly. At the moment.

"Ah, so that's your excuse now. Why you're not jumping on him. You're waiting until the mirrors fade."

I feel my temper rising, but I know Nico has every right to be angry, and I force myself not to say anything.

Elf breathes hard. "When he runs lean, he's going to fight us, regardless of what spiel he spouts now. He'll be desperate for augmenters then. Question is, can we handle that?"

I swallow hard.

Nico nods. "If this is the start of us reclaiming our people, if they're all going to resist more strongly, then we have to do it. Regardless of who he is."

Reclaiming. I take a deep breath. "We *should* still treat him as a trap—"

"Surprised you're so against him, Keelie."

"—because it could be what he wants," I continue quickly, ignoring the voice in me that's making me feel guilty for doubting Red. We *have* to be careful. And I can't trust him just because I love him—especially when it's the old Red who I love. Not the Enhanced Red. And I know, despite what I want to believe, that we can't be sure which he really is now. "He could want us to take him to Nbutai, find out our location, then give it to the Enhanced."

Elf nods. "But we wouldn't take him there until we know he's definitely Untamed again. We'd have to monitor him a lot as well. Never leave him on his own when he's there. And he could never go on raids or visit the towns."

"So what do we do *now*?" Nico kicks at a loose stone.

"Keep looking for Bea and the other Untamed," I say.

"Brilliant," Nico mutters. "A road trip with him."

We head back to the truck and lay some ground rules for Red. He's to stay tied up all the time—at least until he's fully Untamed. If he tries anything, we'll kill him. Nico takes particular delight in telling Red that last bit.

But Red just nods and grins. Then he looks at me, turns his whole body toward me, despite being tied up. "You look hot."

"Don't speak to her," Nico snaps, venom lacing his words.

Red grins even wider.

"Let's check the rest of these caves, then drive on," I say. "Elf. You stay with Red. Nico and I will look."

"So, how long were you seeing him behind my back?" Nico asks the question on our way back to the truck. "And don't lie, Keelie. I'm not stupid. I've worked it out." His tone is dark, but he somehow says the words lightly—and it's a contradiction, but that's how it feels. Dark and light.

But it's a relief. Because the whole time we were checking the caves for Bea, he didn't speak to me. There was just darkness, and it was oppressive, squeezing around me, trying to choke me. I don't think I've ever felt so uncomfortable.

"It wasn't long," I say.

"How long?"

"I met him out on the sands three times before I

finished with you."

"Except you didn't actually finish with me. A *break*, you said." He cracks his knuckles suddenly, and the sound makes me jump. "What did you do in those three times you met?"

I look at him. "Nico, I don't—"

"I do." His gaze burns me. "I want to know everything. Every sordid detail."

"I didn't have sex with him in those three times," I say.

But I nearly did. I take a deep breath. If the spirit hadn't interrupted us and Red hadn't had to leave, I'm sure we would've.

"*In those three times*. So you did *after*." Nico snorts. "Still, how gallant of you not to do it when we were together. So what *did* you do?"

"Talked."

"Talked? So you went from talking to fucking as soon as you left me?"

I grip my hands together tightly. They're clammy. "We kissed a bit too."

"A bit?"

I don't answer.

The truck's in sight now, and I've never been so glad. I can see Elf sitting on the tailgate, talking to Red.

Nico kicks a stone, and it bounces away, angrily. "Why didn't you tell us about him? Another Untamed nearby? You should've told Rahn."

I breathe deeply. "I wanted to keep him to myself," I lie. I can't tell him about Red being undercover, in case there are still some left. Nico can't know, because I'm certain he'll tell Rahn, and then Rahn will want to look. I'd better make sure Elf doesn't mention it to Nico.

"You mean you didn't want *me* to find out." He grunts.

"Nico, please. I'm sorry."

He laughs. Then he looks at me. "Elf knew, didn't he? Huh. He didn't even react just now. He knew about him. Who else knew?"

"No one," I lie, picturing Bea and Five.

"Well, I bet you're happy. Got Lover Boy back. You two can cop off now, can't you?"

I look at the ground. "No. I don't buy that he's sincere in wanting to be Untamed, Nico. There's something off." And I don't know whether I'm saying it to make Nico feel better or because I actually believe it first and foremost. I just can't tell anymore.

He exhales loudly. "Well, at least you don't sleep with the Enhanced. That's something." But his voice lightens, and I detect the relief in his words that he won't have to watch me and Red together on the voyage.

As if I can be with Red now, after Mila. I ignore the way my body aches at the thought of him.

"I loved you, Keelie," Nico says in a loud voice so that Elf and Red can hear. And the way he looks at me, I see the hope amid the hurt in his eyes. "I *still* love you."

THIRTY-ONE

IT'S NOT UNTIL EVENING WHEN I get a chance to talk to Red—to talk to him properly. He's in the truck bed still, tied up. Nico and Elf are checking the area again for Bea. Nico was reluctant to leave me guarding Red, and he volunteered himself, but there was no way I was leaving the two of them together. That would be asking for trouble.

I pull myself up into the truck bed and look at Red. His whole posture changes upon seeing me. I look at his eyes. The mirrors have faded to half-ghosts. Aside from that, I want to say that he looks better because looking Untamed is better. But he looks ill, unattractive—and I hate that his attractiveness is one of the first things I assess. But his skin has gone a strange shade of gray, tinged with green, and more sweat shines on his forehead. More withdrawal effects.

"So, Red. Time to talk." I crouch in front of him, but this whole thing feels weird. And ever since my conversation with Nico, I've been doubting Red even more, thinking that it has to be a trap. That I'm stupid for believing him. But Elf's trusting him too, and I trust my brother. I straighten up, focus on Red. "You got

276

MADELINE DYER

caught, converted, Enhanced. How did it happen?"

He squeezes his eyes shut for a moment. "They found out I'd been in contact with an Untamed woman. That I hadn't converted her." He looks from side to side quickly, then shakes his head hard and moans. "They realized I was undercover. Converted me. Couldn't do anything. Couldn't stop it… Gods, it hurts, Keelie. My whole body and—"

"And why are you really here?" I ask, looking away from his eyes.

"Because I love you."

I run a hand through my hair, try not to show any emotion. Not that I'd know what emotion to show to that anyway. Can't tell if it's a lie or not. "And how did you find us?"

"I'm a skilled tracker." He grins a little, but his expression is lopsided, and he's breathing too hard and too fast. "And I saw your truck when you were traveling, realized you were in it. So I followed—I've got to know where you are all the time." He groans suddenly and goes deathly pale before color flushes across his face. "I can't lose you. And I needed to see you. K, I know you feel it as well."

I shake my head. "You're deluded." The words come out before I can stop them, and I know I'm building a wall between us to keep me safe. But a wall is what's needed—until I know for sure. Then I can pull it down, let myself feel all the things I want to feel. "Nico and I are back together," I lie, hope he doesn't notice how my words wobble. "There's nothing real between us."

Red's eyes seem to bulge. "So, us making love is *nothing*? Keelie, I *know* you felt it. And I *know* you want me. And when our souls entwined as—"

"Don't start the clichéd souls crap." My voice gets a fraction lower. "Just tell me the truth."

"I have. I want to be with you. And we're going to be. We're going to get a house, a nice house. A house with a swimming pool. You like swimming, don't you? Remember that summer when you and I—"

I shake my head and look around. Still no sign of Elf or Nico. The sky's starting to darken a little already, but the air shimmers strangely.

Pain flickers around my ankles, so I go from crouching to kneeling. I look at Red carefully, trying not to notice how strong his body looks, how attractive. I tear my gaze from him before I start salivating over his tattoos.

"It will be great to have the whole family together again," Red says. "You, me, and your parents. Or rather what's left of the whole family. But, we can have them all over for dinner, and Owen's going to get me a better job. One that pays even better, and we'll have the new house too." He frowns. "Did I say that already? I can't remember. Gods, I *can't remember*. My *head*."

What's left of the whole family….

I stare at him. He whacks his head against the back of the truck's cab four times. Then he laughs and flicks his head around, eyes darting everywhere. A sudden intensity fills his gaze.

"I love you, Keelie… Love you! We have to be together. We just have to go."

"Go?" I prompt.

"Back to civilization…where your parents are. Being together will make everything all right. And I just… I want you… I want us to be together and for you to be happy. And we can be with your parents." Sweat trickles down his nose.

I flinch. "Be together *there*? At an Enhanced town or city?" I lean back, alarm bells going off in my head. "Well haven't you changed your tune quickly?" I shake my head, let out a bitter laugh. And I don't know whether to feel disappointed or not.

I look into his eyes. Eyes are the route to the soul, and his are becoming unguarded. There's something in me that makes me think that if I look into his eyes—now that they're becoming Untamed—I'll see the truth. But all I see is a sort of twitchiness. Anxiety? Because he's running lean? Or because he's just revealed his plan?

And he has. I know he has. The wall I started to build grows in an instant.

Red coughs, and the action wrecks across his whole body. "I'm trying to prove myself...prove myself to you, Keelie. Show how much you mean to me, show you how...and I know you want to see your parents. I know how much they mean to you. We can live together safely, there, with the Chosen Ones."

"So you *did* lie." I stand up, jerk my hand back. "You lied saying you wanted to join us."

Of course he did. I shake my head. This *is* a trap. He doesn't want to discard his new identity—he just wants me. And he's playing a game, a dangerous game, and we're all caught up in it. A game to the death.

You're not getting out alive.

Yet I don't move away—and I know I should, but I don't.

Red clasps his hands together—the ropes let him do that, and then he's scratching the back of his left hand hard, leaving angry red marks behind. For a second, he stares at them.

"It...it hurts... I need Calmness...get me some Calmness, K..." And he smiles—the Enhanced part of him fighting back, trying to minimize the pain he's feeling. "You don't understand... We *have* to be together. It's the only way. Look, I'm doing this for you—running lean, and it's horrible, the pain, because I *need* you. I'm showing you how much you mean to me."

His eyes flash as the mirrors dim even further, as if a layer of metallic color has been peeled away in that instant, and his gray eyes become more obvious.

"I need to be with you. Us, together, against the world. You and me—we can be together. I love you, Keelie. Love you so much. You have to come back with me. And I can take you to your parents, and we can all be happy. And...and I won't convert you! I'd respect your wishes! But we can live there, and I'd—I'd hide you, keep you Untamed."

"That's a load of shit." I shake my head. "You want to convert me. You're one of them, Red. And I'm not. We're enemies. We can't be together," I yell, my voice savage. "Just look at you—shaking, sweating, feverish. That's what they've done to you, and you can't see it because they've got you. You're addicted, and your only purpose now is to convert."

I hold his gaze for a long, heavy moment in which the world around us seems to get darker.

"You want to see your parents," Red reasons. "I want to go to them. We want the same thing. I'll take you there."

I throw my hands in the air. "No."

I start to turn away, don't even know why I'm still talking to him. We were stupid to let him be with us— it was *obviously* lies when he said he wanted to join us. No Enhanced One wants to be *wild*. Not after they've tasted the 'perfect' way of life. And he's shown his true colors now.

You should get rid of him, Keelie. You like killing Enhanced.

I gulp. Kill him? Kill Red?

But I know it's the thing to do. He's Enhanced— we're keeping an Enhanced hostage, alive. If he gets out of his bindings, he'll go for us. He's too much of a risk.

They deserve to die. Each and every one of them.

But, if we can save them, we should. And I know it's just the addiction, the withdrawal, that's making him like this. And he's not been Enhanced for long.

Then I let out a frustrated cry. Why am I *still* trying to reason with myself?

No one is ever the same after an augmenter.

Red coughs. "Keelie—there's still part of me in here, the part that you know. You can find it again. We can still—"

"You're lying, Red. You're desperate, and you're

lying." I look away, into the distance, hoping to see Elf and Nico returning. We need to set off again. Bea's not here. And I knew that when we arrived, part of me knew, felt it.

And part of me is being called forward.

We need to keep going, need to find her. She can't have much food left now, if any. Unless she's hunting? Maybe Elf and Nico will find evidence.

"Am I lying?" Red's voice sounds so…so lost. He sounds lost. Different.

I crouch back down and look at him, feel something in my chest tear.

"Yes. You are." My voice is dark, irritable.

His brow furrows a little. "So, what—you're… you're going to kill me then?" His breathing gets faster. "Because even you won't do that—you won't kill me when you love me. And I know you do, K. Don't deny it. Please… Okay, I'll become Untamed. I have to be with you."

"You're Enhanced. You can't just decide to be Untamed. It doesn't work like that."

"It will if you help me!"

I stare at him. We're close. Too close. Inches apart. Why did I move so close? And it's in me—the desire to help him. But I know my help can't save him. It can make him Untamed, but he won't be the same. He'll always be desperate. He'll feel the negatives of life even stronger than we do. He'll never be the same. And he'll want what he once had.

"I love you, Keelie. I love you more than anything in the world. And that's why I want to save you. Being Untamed in this world is horrible—can't you see? Being Untamed in this world is dangerous. And it's my job to save you, to look after you. I don't want you getting burned. Untie my ropes, and I'll take you to your parents."

"No. I don't want to see them anyway, Red. So that's a pointless line of argument." Or at least, I need to find Bea first, before I find them, tell them about Mila. And

I stare at him, sad. He can't even remember what he's said. One minute, he'll hide me, Untamed. The next, he's going to convert me.

"But you *want* to see your parents," Red says, his face pained. "You want them to forgive you for killing Mila. And they will. We'll take away all your pain, all the hurt you're feeling. The guilt—it's eating you alive. And you want that, don't you? You want to forget about all the bad things the Untamed part within you has made you do. And if you come with me, that will happen. You'll be better. We'll fix you. *I'll* fix you."

My body tenses.

"Red, I—"

He lunges toward me, despite the ropes, kisses me, hard and fast. His lips crush against mine and...and something happens. Happens inside me.

I don't pull away.

I see his eyes, so close to mine, a fraction away, and he's watching me, and I'm watching him as he kisses me. And it doesn't feel like an Enhanced One is kissing me.

His tongue parts my lips, and I gasp against him. And...and we kiss.

We kiss *properly*—both of us, equal—and every emotion swarms inside me. A war in my soul. But it's Red. And it's like he's still Untamed. He feels the same, tastes the same, and—

"What the hell?"

I jerk back as Nico's shadow falls over us.

THIRTY-TWO

"YOU SAID YOU WOULDN'T!"

I spring to my feet, breathing hard.

Red laughs manically. "We're joining the Enhanced, aren't we, Keelie? You and me! Together! Ha, Nico, she was *always* mine. You never stood a chance."

I reach out for Nico as I jump off the tailgate, but he pulls back, nostrils flaring.

He points at me, walking backward slowly. "It's always lies, isn't it, with you? And now you're leaving? Changing everything you believe in to be with him?"

"Stop it!" I shout. "No! Can't you see what he's doing? He was trying to seduce me, to convert me. He's still Enhanced! Doesn't want to be Untamed! He admitted it—and tricked me and—" I'm breathing too hard, can't get the words out. "Look, we're wasting time, we need to find Bea. She's still out here."

"*Trying* to seduce you? Is that what you call it? You looked pretty into it. Don't make out like none of this is your fault."

I shake my head, looking back at Red. He's still there, still tied up, looking amused. *Amused!* "Nico—please. Just calm down."

"Calm down?" He lets out a manic laugh. "Let's see what Elf has to say about you betraying us."

I let out a shrill laugh, and my head feels strange. Lighter. So much lighter. "I'm not joining the Enhanced!"

Nico swears, then slams his left hand into his right. "You've taken some?"

"What?"

"Augmenters!" He grabs my shoulders and looks into my eyes, even though I know it's not necessary. You don't need to look up close to check for mirrors.

"No—I've not." I wrench myself from his grip.

"It's a wonder!" He turns his back to me, breathing hard. Tension bunches in his shoulders. When he turns back, the look on his face holds so much disgust and hatred and hurt that I stumble back. "Bloody hell, Keelie! You're supposed to be *my* girl."

"I'm not *anyone's* girl."

"And you said you didn't trust him—and then you're kissing him! Or did you say that to make me feel better? Another lie?" He's shaking. "But you're right—he is Enhanced and… That's disgusting. No." He grabs my arm. "Come on."

"What?" I pull on my arm, but his fingers stay wrapped around me.

"We're going to see what your brother has to say about you kissing an *Enhanced*."

"No! Just listen" I try to pull Nico back, but, somehow, he forces me with him. "Hey! You can't just drag me along with you—I'm not some puppy you're trying to train."

He starts running, and I chase after him. Elf's walking toward us. Nico gets to him first.

"She was about to have sex with that man!" he yells.

"What? The hell I was!" I scream, outraged. "That's a complete exaggeration—that was…. How can you—" I grab Nico's hand again, trying to pull him back.

"And you're right," Nico yells at Elf. "All that stuff you've said about Red over the years. That guy is a piece of work, taking Keelie from her own twin, getting in her head, and now stealing her from her boyfriend."

"You're not my boyfriend!" I shout back.

"Oh, I am," Nico says, and then he grabs me.

I yank my arm away—or try to—but he's fueled up with anger, and he forces me to look at him, and then he crushes his mouth against mine, and his hands press me against him, feeling me everywhere.

Shock makes me freeze.

"You're *mine*," he snarls into my face, pulling back just long enough to say the words. "And I've had enough of—"

I knee him in the crotch, and he stumbles backward. Elf grabs him, throws him farther back, away from me.

"Stay away from her." My brother's eyes flare, and he's breathing hard. "Don't you *ever* touch her again. Do you hear me?"

Nico glares at us both, still half-doubled over. But then he seems to recover and sizes up Elf. A second passes. In one fluent motion, Nico grabs the gun from Elf. I hadn't realized that my brother had it—but he often has the Luger now—and *now* it's in Nico's hands, and he turns, strides toward the truck, and—

"No!" I scream, and I don't know what makes me shout it, except that Elf's screaming it too. Because Nico can't kill Red. *He can't.*

I pounce on Nico, and we crash to the ground, me on top of him. I grab the gun and see the safety's off. For a second, I can't breathe. I could've been shot. Then I flick the safety on, and—

"Where is he?" Elf yells.

But it's like I don't hear the words, because I'm concentrating on Nico. On holding him down with one hand and pointing the gun at him with the other.

Nico spits at me. "You bitch!"

"Don't you—"

"Keelie!" Elf yells.

"What?" I turn my head for a fraction of a second,

see Elf running to the truck.

Quick as a flash, Nico shoves me off of him, and I fall back onto the ground. My shoulder hits something hard, and I wince—but I've still got the gun. I'm in control and—

"He's done a runner!" Elf shouts.

I look up.

The truck.

And then Nico's running, and I pull myself up and race for the truck, look in the bed myself. But he's not there, it's just the ropes. The ropes we tied him up with.

He's escaped? How?

Nico grunts, behind me. "Gone where?"

"He's gone back. Back to them, the Enhanced." I shake my head, and a part of me feels strange.

Lost? No, that's not the right word.

Red was *lost* out here.

He's one of them.

"We need to find him," Nico growls. "He'll be calling backup to convert us, and he can't be far away. We need to stop him, kill him."

"Get in the truck!" I yell at the two of them, and then we're all jumping in.

Elf takes the gun from me, and I take the wheel and grit my teeth. There's no way Red's getting away. Not now. He's not going back.

But what are we going to do? Really kill him?

And what about Bea? She'll be getting even farther away now.

But we can't make sure she's okay if we're caught by the enemy. No, we have to find Red.

My heart pounds. "Keep looking for him," I yell, trying to look in all directions at once as I turn the truck around. "He's got to be somewhere! Look at the map," I bark at Elf. "It's in the glove compartment… There must be somewhere where the land's hiding him. Look at the contours. Look properly! Is there anywhere a cave could be?"

I peer through the windscreen harder, until pain erupts across my forehead, trying to see a figure out there. But it's getting windier. Sand's whipping up. Great. A sandstorm. That's all we need.

"Oh no," Elf says. He pulls stuff out of the glove compartment.

"What?"

"The map—it's not here."

I slam the brakes, and we're all thrown forward. I hit the steering wheel—shit, I didn't put my seat belt on in the haste—and more pain attacks my body. I cut the engine.

"*What?*"

"Bloody hell, Keelie! You trying to kill us now?" Nico yells at me, his face right up close against mine, but I ignore him and try to lean forward, try to see the glove compartment.

But there are too many things in it: plastic packaging, tin labels, an empty ink cartridge, a length of twine. Why the hell have we got so much stuff? Elf pulls his hands through more. A notebook. Receipts. A few folded bank notes. But there's no map.

It's not there.

I breathe hard.

Then I go cold. I turn to them, my eyes wide. My heart pounds, and my lips feel fuzzy.

"What's the matter?" Nico snaps at me.

I shake my head. "One…one of you marked Nbutai on the map—I don't care who but I'm sure it was done after we left, and it sure as hell wasn't me. And now he's got it. Red's got it. He has to have it… Oh, *hell*."

And I know. A load more shit is going to happen.

I inhale sharply. "He's going to lead the Enhanced to Nbutai."

THIRTY-THREE

RED'S GOING TO GET US all.

They're going to get us all.

"Shit," Nico yells. "We need to go back, warn them. Now!"

I nod, frantically, staring through the dirty windscreen.

"No," Elf says, and he's calm—too calm. "We need to keep going, find Bea and the others. We wouldn't get back there in time, anyway."

"We would! He hasn't got a car," I say. "He's on foot and—"

"He has a phone," Elf yells. "I saw it! He'll have told New Kimearo by now, and they'll be sending people out." He rubs his hands together, frowning. "There's no way we can get there in time. Not with how quickly the Enhanced can move."

I stare at my brother, feel everything in my body get tighter. "No, he didn't have a phone."

"We searched him," Nico says. "He didn't."

But Elf shakes his head. "I found it just now, when I was searching—it was over there." He points vaguely to the left. "Well, somewhere over there. He'll have gone straight for it when he got free."

"You found a phone, and you didn't do anything? You didn't destroy it?" I stare at my brother, incredulous. "You didn't take it from him? Or tell us right away?"

"But I was—I was coming back to tell you and then Nico said about you and Red sleeping together."

"I wasn't!" I yell, but I know my brother's not going to believe me. Not after what he saw before.

But Red had a phone. My heart pounds. They can track phones, can't they? Loads of Enhanced Ones could've come for *us*. They could be coming for us—to stop us from trying to save Nbutai.

"Look," Elf snaps. "It doesn't change anything. We can't save Nbutai. It's too late for them." His tone is the most emotionless I've ever heard from him, and I wince, think of the Sarrs—all of them—and feel sick, hope that Katya gets a warning in time. "But we're free of them, unharmed," Elf continues. "We have to keep going, find Bea and these other Untamed. *You've* already lost one of our sisters. I'm not abandoning another."

I lean forward, stare at him.

He glares at me, as if daring me to speak against him.

Nico looks at me, uncertainty on his face. "We have to go back," he says, his voice low, meant only for me.

"No," Elf says, and I'm surprised he's heard.

"We go back," I say. It's the first time I've ever outright disagreed with my brother when it's come to Untamed safety. Because we always help each other.

We don't run.

Not anymore.

"I'm the leader—this is my mission." I'm breathing deeply. *Sorry, Bea.* I turn the engine back on. "Hell, *of course* we go back."

I can't drive fast enough. My head pounds. All I can think of is going faster…if there's any chance that Red's *not* got in contact with New Kimearo yet then we have to be quick.

We might just make it.

We have to.

I can't be responsible for all their deaths. Not them as well.

I let out a scream, completely involuntarily, and it startles me.

"Calm down!" Nico yells at me, and then he's grabbing at the wheel. "Stop! Let me drive!"

"No!" I try to push him away and point at the foxhole radio in his lap. "You're supposed to be trying to get some waves—trying to find out if the Enhanced have caught the rest of our people!"

"I *am* doing that," Nico yells. "But we should swap. You're in no fit state to drive, you'll probably crash the vehicle and—"

"Stop it, Nico," Elf says. "Let her drive."

Elf's still not happy, and I don't understand why. If there's a chance we can save our village, we have to try. Why doesn't he want to?

I look ahead, trying to remain calm. Through my watery vision, I can only see sand. The wind's picking up too fast, throwing the sand into a hazy vortex that scratches the windscreen. I hunker in my seat a little, my eyes narrowed as if the windscreen's going to break at any moment and sand's going to hurtle at me.

"It's not the Turning is it?" I ask, slowing the truck down a little. "Shit. I can't see."

"No," Elf says. "Can't be."

My chest tightens. "But didn't Katya say the last one didn't feel right—that another would happen soon?"

Nico leans forward, looking.

"The sky's normal above it all, Keelie," Nico says. "Just concentrate on driving. It's just a normal sandstorm."

But it's not normal—it's not normal at all. There's too much sand. The spirits are going to come out any minute now. If they see our vehicle moving, they'll come for us. We need to stop, don't we?

"Go that way," Nico says, pointing to the right.

"What? Why?" I try to see to the right, but the air's hazy, and there's so much dust.

"It's quicker. We came a roundabout way here before—after going to the caves—if we go through that way, we'll go through the mountains… You know, the lower path… It'll cut some time off."

I don't know if Nico's right, but I'll do anything to save time. Anything to give us more of an advantage. Anything if it means we can save our people.

I put my foot down and drive faster than the terrain advises. The fuel gauge tells me we're getting low. I curse, but there's another can in the back—isn't there? I shake my head, blink hard, can't think.

"Watch it!" Elf yells, and I swerve around a huge hole just in time.

More sand blows up across the windscreen, and it sticks to the screen in huge clumps. I flick the wipers on, but the sand scratches deep lines into the glass, and I turn them off again quickly.

Nico keeps going with the radio, but it's obvious it's not going to work. We've got a dud or something. Or Nico's not doing it right. Suddenly, I wish Three was here.

The world darkens rapidly. I flinch; it can't be that late already. Can it? The end of our first day. A whole day. A day away from the village—but no, we're nearer now. And I'm driving faster—going a more direct route than we came… But we're still hours away… hours and hours…how many hours? I try to think? Six? Seven? Or more? I bark the question at Nico. He yells at me because there's suddenly a roaring noise everywhere and tells me just to keep driving.

But that's what I am doing.

And that's what I keep doing.

The minutes blur into hours, and then the hours blur into what seems like days and—

A spirit slams into the windscreen.

I scream, stare at its eyes. Eight of them. Watery and big and smearing down the glass. The rest of its face is a semi-solid, partly-translucent mess wobbling about on the windscreen. Its eyes are the only things that look human—no, that *looked* human. They're stretching as they smear down the glass.

Hissing fills the air.

"Keelie!" Nico yells, then he lunges over and grabs the wheel.

Without thinking, I flick the wipers back on. They hit the gelatinous mass and something makes a squealing noise, and then—

Then the truck spins around.

Elf yells something, and Nico's still yanking on the wheel. I push his hands away, look up, and see more spirits by the driver's window. So close to me, inches away.

"They're taking control of the truck!" I yell, my voice all hoarse and not at all like me. My heart pounds, but it's not the good kind of pounding. Not pounding that I'm in control of.

This is… These are *spirits*. And suddenly all I can picture is them ripping my uncle to pieces. The way they descended and *ate* him. The way his screams wrapped around me, and how a flake of his skin smacked into my face and….

"Are the windows shut?" I yell, twisting around, trying not to see the spirits. But there are so many. It has to be the next Turning already—there are too many spirits about for it not to be. But the sky! It's dark, yet there are no patches of color. What the hell?

The engine revs—it's the spirits—and then we're

going faster, bouncing over bumpy, uneven ground.

"No, not that way!" Elf yells as we crash over ground.

I wrestle with the wheel, try to fight the spirits, but it's no use. They want us to go that way. We're going that way. Hurtling that way.

"No!" Elf cries again, his voice breaking and—

The truck slams to a halt, and I narrowly avoid whacking my head on the windscreen. The wipers are still smearing the spirit across it. I flick them off.

"Well," I say, "that was—"

"What's that?" Nico points at something on the ground. There are spirits around it, but they're not that close. Just in a loose circle.

I lean forward. My heart pounds, my whole body vibrates with energy and fatigue, and I stare ahead. "It's a *body*…a person."

Elf grabs the gun, then jumps out.

"There are spirits out there!" I yell, rushing sounds filling my ears, but then I get out too, along with Nico, and we're racing forward, toward the person, toward the spirits. But the spirits brought us here? Because someone's in trouble? An Untamed. Out here. Another one…like that woman and baby. My head spins.

"Keep back," Elf yells, and he flashes the gun toward us as he indicates for Nico and me to stay near the pickup. He walks up to the body slowly, then turns it over with his foot. The spirits hiss at him.

I stare at the body.

The squeak escapes my lips before I can stop it.

I go cold. My hands are ice.

No.

No.

No.

Next to me, Nico starts shouting, and I'm vaguely away that he's yelling at me to get back in the truck.

But I don't move.

I just stare. I stare at the body…at my…at my *brother*. My eyes glaze over.

He's there… The body is him.

It's Elf.

"Keelie—get inside! Don't look!"

Yet Elf's here. He's standing in front of me. Standing in front of me at the same time as looking down at the body. He's in two places at once. There and—

Nausea washes over me, sudden and abrupt. I look around, but the spirits are vanishing.

"Who the hell are you?" I point at my brother—at the one who's standing. Then I look at the one lying down. But my words don't sound like me, but maybe that's because my ears are fuzzy.

"Crap," Elf says, then he walks back toward me, a lazy smile on his face. "I was hoping this wouldn't happen."

He lifts the gun up and points it at me, and my eyes widen. I look between him and my brother—my real brother—and feel sick. My brother's body. And *him*.

"He's Enhanced!" Nico yells. "Has to be."

And the man with my brother's face snarls a low, animalistic snarl that reveals his teeth. "Take me to those other Untamed that your sister's gone to find. Or I'll kill you both."

THIRTY-FOUR

"HE'S ENHANCED!" NICO YELLS AGAIN, and then he's trying to pull me back. "He's—"

"One more move, and I'll kill you," the man holding the gun says, and he looks like my brother. He looks *just* like him.

I take a deep breath. And then another, and another. Then Nico's arms are around me, and he's shaking and clinging to me, and I can hear his heart pounding, and there's so much going on.

I stare at the man who looks like my brother. "Your eyes," I say. But they're Untamed. They're not mirrors.

He grins. Then he brings a hand up to his right eye and pinches his eyeball.

I feel sick as he pulls a thin layer off... a layer that's so big, bigger than normal contact lenses and—

I go cold.

"Still doubtful?" the man asks, one eye Enhanced, one Untamed. "Gods, you're thick." He steps closer with the gun. "Take me to those other Untamed," he snarls, and he doesn't sound like Elf anymore.

An imposter. We've had an imposter in our group. My breathing gets faster. How didn't I notice?

Behind the Enhanced man, Elf—the real one—stirs. He moves his hand.

Alive? He's still alive?

"Take me to the other Untamed now, or I will kill him." The Enhanced moves back and holds the gun over my brother. Over my brother's unconscious head. Inches from him.

"But you're not violent people," Nico says, and I feel his fingers clenching tighter onto my shirt. "You're not…you don't use guns."

Sweat forms on the Enhanced man's forehead, and I watch it—watch it and watch him watching me and the gun—as I try to disentangle Nico from me. It seems to take hours, but it can't have been more than a few seconds.

Then I take a small step forward, toward them. The Enhanced Elf and the unconscious Elf.

Is that one really Elf? How do you know?

"Don't go to him!" the Enhanced snarls. The gun flashes in the darkening light as the man lifts it higher, and I know it's lined up directly with my forehead. But I don't feel anything. Not fear of death. "Take me to the other Untamed."

"Oh—okay," Nico says. "Keelie… Where do we go? Which way?"

I shake my head. "There aren't any here. I don't know where they are." I look across at Elf, crumpled on the floor. Is it him, really? And he's alive? His hand moved earlier, but I can't see any rise or fall of his chest.

"You do know!"

As subtly as I can, I move my gaze from left to right, searching for anything that might help. I need a weapon. Need to get rid of the Enhanced—or get his gun—then I can check Elf.

My knife—I feel for it in my pocket, can't find it. Hell. It must be in the pickup.

"Take me to them!"

The man's eyes flash, just like the gun, and I

suddenly realize how dark it is. The light has fallen so quickly. A gust of wind sends more sand over me. And it's sharp. It stings.

Nico glances at me, his face ashen. *He's going to shoot us,* he mouths.

I shake my head. He won't shoot any of us. He won't. He can't. He's an Enhanced One. They don't believe in violence. They say it's wrong. He won't shoot. He's bluffing. An empty threat.

The Enhanced man turns to me slowly.

"Well then," he says, his voice nasal. "You'll tell me after I've saved you. We've got you, Untamed Ones. You can't get away. I've got you. And my colleague's got Nbutai."

"Colleague?" Nico says.

The Enhanced man laughs, but this time he sounds like Elf, and I shudder. "There is no village—I loosened Red's ropes, told him to get out of there when there was a chance, and pass the co-ordinates on as soon as possible. My radio communications haven't been getting through, but his phone works."

"Your radio communications?"

Nico steps toward me, clings to me again. I try to push him away, but he's persistent.

The man nods. "Must be too far for a signal. But I can save you three now." He fumbles with something in the pocket of his hoody, and I can't see what he's doing, but then he's holding several small vials. My mouth dries.

But my brain kicks in.

I think fast. The man's only got one gun. Can only shoot one of us at a time. If Nico goes for the truck, and I go for the man, try and disarm him, only one of us could get shot. Or have first taste.

"Get in the truck!" I yell at Nico, and I know he's seen the augmenters too. And it's how we're supposed to react when we see augmenters—we're supposed to get as far away as possible if we can't destroy them.

Nico runs.

I turn, legs braced, assess the Enhanced.

"No!" he yells, and he's lifting the gun, lining it up with Nico.

I run at him, pounce, knock him to the ground, feel adrenaline slam through me. My teeth clank together hard, and I grimace, my arms stretching around him, try to get hold of the gun.

Then the man twists around and shoves me away.

The back of my head hits the hard, dry earth. Dust billows up, clogs my eyes, and I wince, scrabbling against him as he leaps on me. Something cold like metal presses against my head, and I shove at his arm and—

A gunshot rips my ears.

I scream, turn my head, and—

Everything seems to freeze.

Not shot? Not me.

Nico?

But Nico's not been hit. I can see him, he's stopped a little way off, not quite by the truck. *Run!* I want to tell him. And Elf—the real Elf—has moved, he's crawling along the dusty floor toward me, pulling himself with his arms.

No! Don't come toward me!

But of course he's coming toward me—me and the Enhanced, and the Enhanced man is staring down at me. He's frozen.

I shove him as hard as I can, my hands against his chest. He yells something at me, and I get a punch to his shoulder—not an effective one—and the gun weaves about like it has a life of its own.

I kick up, getting momentum, lifting the man with me and—

Hands grab the man's shoulders, pull him back, lifting him off me.

Nico and Elf, working together.

I scrabble upward, see some broken glass by my foot. Just a little. From an augmenter? But, there's not much, and he had several and—

Elf grunts and falls back as the man punches him.

"Elf!" I rush to him and—

"No!" Nico yells.

I turn, see the Enhanced man slam into Nico. A bright blue color. An augmenter.

I scream, pull myself up, leaving Elf, and try and reach Nico and—

It happens.

I see it happen.

First taste.

Nico looks at me.

He mouths something.

I can't make it out.

Nico's eyes turn silver first, then they're mirrors.

The Enhanced man laughs. And it was—it was so quick…so….

Run!

My body locks up. I start to shake.

"Let me save you too," the Enhanced man says, lunging at me.

I punch him. I put as much force into my arm, punch right from the elbow, throw my whole weight into it, and I punch him again.

He falls back, and his other arm—the hand that holds the gun—flies up.

I jump. My fingers wrap around the gun at last.

No! Keep punching him! Don't use the gun!

Hair whips in my face.

I go for the trigger.

The shot resounds through me.

That's cheating!

There's hardly any blood. Not like with Mila.

For a moment, I can't move.

All I can do is stare at him. At the body. Because it looks like my brother. I've killed my sister, and now I've killed my brother.

No. He's not your brother.

My breathing speeds up, and I know I need to slow it down, remain calm. But how long? How long has this man been here? Pretending to be my brother? Infiltrating our group....

I turn back quickly, see Nico standing there, smiling with his mirror eyes. My brother, need to find my brother. My *real* brother.

Elf's not moving. And there's blood on him too, so much blood. I rush to him, and I'm shaking—shaking so much.

"Elf? Elf...can you hear me?" I mutter the words over and over again, my hands patting him, and then I'm trying to find the wound because there's so much blood, and I need to stop the bleeding.

And Nico's walking around now, behind me, and every time I glance up, he's just there, smiling. My heart pounds. He's Enhanced. My *boyfriend*.

No, not my boyfriend. But he's still Enhanced and—

We're in danger. He's Enhanced. An Enhanced One is here.

No! He's only had first taste. And my thoughts are wild, too fast, and I'm trying to help Elf, but I'm sure Nico won't be in the convert-all-the-Untamed mindset. Just had first taste.

We're safe, aren't we?

"Come on, Elf." My hands are slick with his blood. Is he breathing? But my eyes are blurring, and I can't tell.

I turn my head. The truck. Need to get him back there.

Nico smiles like a lunatic, following me as I half-carry and half-drag my brother into the truck's cab.

Elf's eyes creak open, then he blinks at me, groggy. A sigh of relief bursts from me.

"Elf... Elf, you're okay... You're all right... We're together now, and—"

Nico's face appears at the opposite window, makes me jump.

"No, don't get in Nico!" I yell, heart pounding as I jump back out. "Elf, stay there."

The wind runs icy fingers through my hair as I

sprint around. I grab Nico, feeling sicker and sicker as I look at his mirror eyes. He grins at me. Why's he grinning? What augmenter was it? Happiness? And we all know augmenters are strong...but don't some Untamed resist them the first one?

My chest tightens. Everyone's different—but the outcome's always the same. And what do I do with Nico? Take him with us—because we've got to go back to Nbutai, still got to warn Rahn.

No! Nico's one of them! the voice in my head screams. And it's right: we don't take Enhanced Ones to the village...not unless they were us and we've just rescued them and—

Nico's no worse than others we've rescued, I reason. He's had first taste. We can save him. And he won't have the desire to convert everyone he sees because he wasn't mind-converted...so that won't happen, will it? It'll be safer. Safer than a rescue mission.

"Get in the back," I say.

Red's ropes are still there, and Nico smiles as I fumble with them. My fingers tremble, but at last I manage to tie him up, and the whole time, he's smiling and murmuring, "Safe at last... So happy... I'm so happy, Keelie... So happy...."

I ignore him as best as I can and climb into the cab once I've secured him. I look at Elf. But what if he's another imposter?

No. He's my brother.

I squish my lips together, then look at him carefully. He's got scratches down the side of his face, and his eyes look duller than usual. Ill.

"Need water," he says, leaning forward, searching in the footwell. He picks up the water-skin there, then he glugs the liquid.

That satisfies me. If he was an imposter, he wouldn't know where the water was...unless he'd seen the skin there as he got in.

"Elf. What were our father's last words to us?"

He blinks at me. "What?"

"Our father's last words?" I hold my breath, praying that no Enhanced One would know the answer. "It's important, tell me."

"Look after Mila for us," Elf says quietly.

Relief washes over me, then I'm close to tears. It *is* him. Why didn't I check when I thought he'd arrived at the village before? Why? When it was that imposter....

I run a hand through my hair. It's all knotty. My eyes smart.

Why did I trust that it was him? Hell. An Enhanced One has been at Nbutai. The Enhanced know where we are. They've known for days, for....

I go cold, completely cold. That's two Enhanced Ones who've known where our village is... Red and—and this imposter. At least two—but they had communications, and Red's still alive.

Nausea washes over me. I have to get back to Nbutai. If there's any chance that neither Red nor the imposter have got the message back to their people, then I have to go. I have to warn them. I have to get them to move. But Elf speaks before I can start the engine.

"Did you get there in time?" he asks. "Did you get Mila back?"

My breath catches in my throat. I shake my head.

Elf makes a startled sound, and my gaze jerks toward him. His jaw trembles. "Enhanced or dead?"

"Dead."

He grunts, clenches his fists. A vein across his forehead pulses.

"We need to get back," I say.

Elf nods. "Tell me what's happened."

"A load more shit is what's happened," I mutter.

"Explain everything as we drive. Including Nico." He jerks his head back, and we both hear Nico's murmurings. Elf swears, then looks out of the window. "What's that?"

"What?" My voice is weary, and exhaustion pulls at me.

"Paper. By the Enhanced man's body, out there. Is

that our map?"

My vision blurs a little, but then, somehow in the darkness, I see the paper. And—and it does look like our map. But Red took that, didn't he?

"I'll go and look." I get out of the truck quickly.

Nervous energy thrums through me as I reach the man's body, as I make out the folded wodge of paper under him. It's fallen out from under his hoody and is badly blood-soaked.

Steeling myself, I use my foot to lift his body up, then I pull the paper out.

It is the map.

I let out a shaky breath, feeling sick. So the imposter had it all along. Red didn't take it…and he doesn't know where the village is? But the Enhanced man said he told Red the co-ordinates. I feel sick. Is Red going to send people to Nbutai? Would he remember the co-ordinates? Did the imposter really tell him?

My head pounds. There's too much stuff in it.

I head back to the truck, clutching the map. I get into the driver's seat, and Elf takes the map. The engine sounds throaty as the truck kicks to life. I spray the windscreen, try to get the smeary marks the spirit left on it off. Then I drive.

Behind us, Nico moans, and I see him in the rear-view mirror, writhing about. In pain? Is that normal for after first taste? I don't know. I haven't got a clue.

"Time to talk, Keelie," Elf says.

I nod, and I tell him everything. The whole truth. I tell him it all, everything about Mila, and then Bea, and Red, and my words start to get jumbled up, and I keep having to repeat myself.

Elf looks like he doesn't believe me as I tell him it all. When I've finished, he shakes his head. Disbelief? Or maybe I haven't made sense. I don't know. I don't know anything anymore….

"So Red really *was* an undercover Untamed at first?" Elf looks at me carefully.

I nod, surprised that he picks out that bit to question.

That he doesn't ask more about Mila. But he wouldn't, would he? She's gone to us.

Elf sighs. "Drive faster."

I grip the wheel tighter. "I'm going as fast as I can."

"We need to get back. If an attack hasn't already been launched on Nbutai, then it will be soon."

My vision blurs, and I can barely see. It's scorching in the cab, and sweat runs down my forehead, down my chest, and down my spine. I wind the windows down more. But there's no breeze now. The air is hot and clammy and thick, like it's trying to drag me down.

I glance in the rear-view mirror; I can just about see Nico in truck bed, still tied up, smiling again now, all signs of previous pain gone, eyes still mirrors.

How on earth do I explain to Rahn that on the mission I was forbidden from going on I let one of us get Enhanced?

THIRTY-FIVE

THE WHOLE TIME I DRIVE back, I can't believe I've been so stupid. All the signs were there with 'Elf'. How hadn't I worked out that it hadn't been my brother? He wanted to come with me because he thought we were looking for other Untamed as well as Bea—he mentioned the other Untamed often enough. He wanted to convert them too. And he knew a lot about New Webbon and New Lija, and the methods they use to make sure no Untamed secretly infiltrate the cities. And he'd been on Red's side when he wanted to join us...two Enhanced together? Or maybe he'd been suspicious of Red, an Enhanced One who supposedly wanted to join us...and then they started working together when they realized they both wanted the same thing? Us converted... And they were talking a lot, together...coming up with a plan?

I shake my head, bewildered.

And the imposter had been very against saving my parents—when I hadn't actually said that was why I wanted to find them.

I glance in my mirror again, see Nico. I try not to let the sight of him affect me. He hasn't been Enhanced for long—not even properly, just had first taste—we can get him back easily. Well, we've already got him here.

And suddenly I wonder if it's just going to be me and Elf and Nico forever, if there really will be no one left at Nbutai.

"What's this?" Elf says suddenly.

I glance over at him, see he's holding something—a radio. "Where did you get that?"

"It was down the back of the seat." He taps the one between us.

I swear loudly as I suddenly recognize it. It's the same one that I saw Elf—no, the imposter—with back at Nbutai. I'd thought it was one of the decent radios that Corin had smashed, that he was trying to fix it, but as I take the radio from Elf in one hand I realize it's different.

It is a lot smaller. And it's got smaller dials on it too. It's a transmitter and receiver.

"Hey, keep your hands on the wheel, Kee... What is it? You've gone white."

I drop the radio into his lap, grip the steering wheel, and tell Elf quickly. Then I look at him. "It's all my fault. I should've realized when I saw him hiding it at Nbutai."

"It's not your fault that an Enhanced infiltrated our group—and keep your eyes on the road."

I try to, but driving's hard now. I'm too jumpy, too nervous. Next to me, Elf fiddles with the radio.

"What are you doing?"

"Seeing if it's working."

"Why?" My voice is high-pitched. I'm close to panicking.

"Because I've got to do something as you drive."

I don't think messing about with an Enhanced One's radio is a good idea, but I don't say anything. I keep driving.

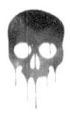

We're farther away than I'd thought. We're not going to get back in time. There's no way we can. Not when the imposter had this radio at Nbutai. The Enhanced would've known our village's location before we'd even left there. They'd have known right away, the moment the imposter joined us.

So why didn't they convert us then?

Suddenly, I'm filled with visions on the village being converted. A huge attack. Mass-scale. People shouting, running. Untamed trying to flee. And the Enhanced Ones are everywhere, chasing after us, slamming us into the ground, forcing us to open our mouths so they can drip their augmenters in.

And I'm back there, back to when I was eleven. Back to that night.

I look up and scream as the Enhanced man towers over me. An augmenter flashes.

Run, run, run.

I roll over, taste blood and mud, and twist around. A hand slams down onto my back, and I scream, kick out. My foot connects with something, and, out of the corner of my eye, I see Red's body with the blood fanning around it. His eyes are still on me.

Help me, help me, help me.

A ragged hole opens up inside my heart.

Something explodes to my right. A flash of bright light.

The Enhanced looks up and freezes.

I run.

And I keep running, and, somehow, I'm getting away, away from the Enhanced who was rising over me with the augmenters. But I can't see, the air's all thick and hazy, and there's so much dust and sharp, scratchy things in the air, and my eyes sting too much.

I throw my weight to the right as I see Yuma's body,

narrowly avoid standing on her arm.

Yuma. No....

The ragged hole inside me deepens.

Then I'm by more huts and—

What about Red?

I turn, but things happen too quickly, and I can't process it. I'm running still, deep in the village. Mud splatters over my legs, and then I see my aunt ahead. Aunt Sara.

Two Enhanced Ones grab her. They throw their weight against her, and she falls. Her head hits the ground, and her eyes roll, and then she is limp.

The Enhanced Ones tip the contents of their vials down her throat, but she doesn't react. No swallowing, no coughing, no choking...nothing... She just lies there. Dead? That blow to the head, when she fell? Another conversion death.

My heart pounds.

"Come on!" someone yells into my ear. Kacey, Caia-Lu's niece.

Then she's gone.

An Enhanced One looms up in front of one of the men, and he immediately raises his gun. His bullet misses, but the Enhanced backs away. And then everyone is shouting.

I smell smoke, hear something screeching.

"The trees! Get to the trees!"

My mother's voice.

I turn, looking for her. See her figure. See her running, and Elf and Bea are ahead. I can see Mila in Bea's arms. And my mother shouts the words over and over again. And she shouldn't be shouting her plan out for the enemy to hear.

"The trees! Get to the trees!"

I try to run after them, try not to see the blood, the bodies. They're too far away, my family.

They've left me.

No!

I can do it. I can reach them.

I can. I—

Red. I see his body. I've run in a circle.

A startled cry escapes me as I slam to a halt. As I stare at him. As I try to see life in my best friend, as I—

"Keelie?" Elf's voice pulls me back to the present.

I jolt, see the land ahead—the potholed desert I'm pulling the truck over at a rapid speed—too rapid. I've been driving all this time? Pain inches into my spine, but it doesn't feel like pain. It feels more like numbness, numbness spreading.

"Stop," Elf says, his voice loud, and I have a feeling he told me to stop a few minutes ago too. "Let me drive."

Nico's screaming again in the back—earth-shattering sounds.

I look across at Elf, then at the dusty land in front, lit by the headlights, as I catch a pothole. "How long has he been like that?"

"Thirty minutes or so. Threatening to do stuff if we don't get him more augmenters. Hell, sounds like it was Euphoria he was given. That's a strong one too. He's desperate for it."

I swear under my breath, but the word gets swallowed by more of Nico's screams and threats. All the hairs on the back of my neck lift up.

"Come on, Kee. I'll drive."

"No. You're injured."

"*You're* too tired. It's dangerous."

I am tied to a wall, my hands above my head.

I wait for them to come, with their augmenters and promises of happiness.

But they don't come.

I wait for days and days.

Weeks pass.

I get thinner.

Nothing to drink or eat.

I know I shouldn't be alive, a year later.

But I am.

Still standing there.

Time has stopped. Everything has stopped. And there is nothing.

"Do you see now?"

The voice comes from behind me—behind the wall. I try to turn my head, but I haven't used the muscles in my neck for so long, and I can't. Maybe the muscles have gone.

"Do you see now, Keelie?"

"See what?" *My voice is creaky, old. I am old.*

"What do you see?"

"I see nothing."

"Exactly. That is what you've given both your sisters: nothing. And that is what you've given everyone. All the Untamed. Nothing."

I wake when Elf pulls over, near Nbutai. It's dark, and I desperately try to see.

"Be careful," he says. "We need to be careful. If there are Enhanced here…."

But it doesn't look like there's anyone here… It's quiet. And it's so dark. There's no movement at all. It's empty? They've taken everyone?

The huts are in the distance.

We get out slowly, and I leave Nico in the back. He's sleeping, apparently calm now. I help Elf walk, and I keep the gun ready. With every step, I expect to be ambushed. I expect to see hundreds of Enhanced Ones marching toward us or see bodies or blood.

But I don't.

We reach the huts. It's still quiet.

Rahn's on fire duty, and he looks up. And…and it's all so *normal*.

Then Rahn's face turns thunderous. "You think

you can come back, join my group, after you've undermined my leadership, my authority, my ability to keep us safe?" He points outward. "Get out."

"No, wake everyone," Elf says. "There could be a conversion attack coming."

For a second, Rahn doesn't say anything. His expression doesn't change—but, then again, we can't see much of his face because of his glasses and the dark.

"Attacked?" he says, takes a step back. "But Katya's not seen anything—and… Where's Nico?" His tone darkens. "And your sister? Did you find her?"

"Nico's tied up in the back of the truck. Should be running lean by now," I say. "We had to abandon the search for Bea because we needed to warn you."

Rahn jolts. "Runnin' lean? What the hell?"

"Things went…wrong."

Rahn inhales sharply. "Explain everythin' now."

"We haven't got time," I say. "You've got to wake everyone. We have to leave now. They could know where our village is."

Rahn flinches, then stands up, looks down at me. "*I'll* decide whether we leave or not. Give me the short version, and explain everything *now*."

THIRTY-SIX

"WE'RE SAFE THEN," RAHN SAYS as soon as I've finished telling him the bare facts.

I didn't mention to him the exact details of my relationship with Red, such as how far we went or that I knew him from D'Elinous—luckily, Rahn didn't recognize the name, probably never paid to much attention to my talk of him before. He thinks we just talked, flirted, and that I fancied him too much to bring him to Nbutai and risk Five or Seven getting together with him. And he's furious I kept him a secret, that I didn't tell him. Told me that Red was captured because he was on his own, that his conversion was my fault.

There are other things I've held back from Rahn too, like how Red was linked to Mila's capture and that Red had been an undercover agent, pretending to be Enhanced. I've got to be careful. If, by any chance, there are still some undercover agents out there, I can't compromise them. And, if I told Rahn there was a possibility they were out there still, Rahn would want to look for them, and he wouldn't treat the Enhanced with the usual animosity in case they were really on our side. And I can only see that ending one way:

312

badly.

Rahn nods. "The imposter is dead, and his radio messages weren't gettin' through—New Kimearo's Enhanced Ones would've been here by now if they knew."

I shake my head, aghast. "We can't take that risk—our location could've been compromised. We don't know it hasn't been. We need to leave now."

Rahn holds our map. "But we still have this. Not the Enhanced. *We* do. They can't know where our village is. And you killed the imposter. He's not going to be a problem. If his radio was a dud, he was effectively workin' on his own."

"But what about Red?" Elf says, gruffly. "The imposter sent him back—to get backup. To have us all converted. Keelie says the imposter gave Red co-ordinates to pass on. Co-ordinates for our location."

Rahn tilts his head to the side. "You said he wanted to join us. If he was on our side, really believed that being Untamed is better, he wouldn't betray us."

Especially if part of him is in love with you....

I shake my head. It pounds. "That was a lie, weren't you listening?"

"Don't question what I was or wasn't doin'," Rahn warns.

"Red was just trying to get close to us." I shake my head. "He had no intention of joining us. Too far gone in his conversion already. It was just a plot to...."

"To what?" Rahn folds his arms, and the map ends up crumpled under his armpit.

To get me to join them. "To get our location—so the Enhanced can get all of our village rather than just a few of us."

Rahn shrugs. "Either way. We've got the map. And he was runnin' lean, that's what you said. His mirrors were fadin'—a sure sign. When an Enhanced is runnin' lean, he can't concentrate on nothin' but himself and his addiction. The need for augmenters is too strong. It's all he's goin' to be thinkin' about.

313

He won't remember the co-ordinates the imposter told him, and he's got no map to remind him. He'll just want augmenters—and, when he gets them, they'll likely have a much stronger effect because of his desperation. So, no chance of a rescue for him, Keelie. You said he's too far gone. Besides, we rescue Untamed from our group. And you made sure he wasn't part of it."

He nods, triumphant, as if expecting me to insist that we try and rescue Red. But—but I don't. I saw how converted Red was, both at Nbutai *and* when he left us out in the mountains. Red really is *too far gone*—cutting our losses is the only option.

"So," Rahn says, straightening up. "We're safe, and we're stayin' here."

"What? Rahn, *seriously*?"

"If Katya comes burstin' in with a Seein' dream, then we'll move."

I turn to Elf, implore him to say something else. He looks back at me with worn eyes.

"There's no point in tellin' the others about this," Rahn says. "Frighten them, that's all it would do. We don't want people knowin' we had an imposter in the heart of our village, else people are goin' to think there's another one too. We'll have people killin' one another, convinced some of us are Enhanced." He folds his arms. "Or we'll have a mutiny, some wantin' to leave. If people are scared and start leavin', then we've got more trouble. Handfuls of scared people travelin' about ain't goin' to be travelin' smart. Movin' the village—even half of it—needs plannin', and lots of it. Else we're goin' to draw attention to us. We ain't even got enough trucks for all of us. We're not doin' an evacuation until we've got solid proof they're after us, and we've got a Seer for that."

I feel the heat rush to my face. "Rahn, that's not right."

"*I'm* the leader. You'd do well to remember that. I decide when it's safer for us to leave than stay, and, right now, we're stayin' until there's better proof we're in danger."

I shake my head. "Tell me you're not arguing this way because you don't want me to get one up on you?"

"Why would I do that? The safety of my people is of the utmost importance to me."

I let out an exasperated sigh. "So we say nothing to anyone?" I shake my head. "This isn't right. We've got to tell them—"

Rahn unfolds his arms. "We find out who marked the village on the map, if it wasn't that imposter. But we don't hint or worry anyone. We're safe, I'm tellin' you. And you don't say a word to anyone. Do you understand?"

"And what about Nico?" Elf asks.

My chest tightens; suddenly, the atmosphere seems heavier, stickier, like it has little fingers that prod me and try to stop me breathing. The fingers get stuck in my nose, my mouth, my throat, and I swallow frantically, trying to get them away.

"How long ago did he have that augmenter?"

I blink hard, trying to think. How long has it been? Time doesn't seem to be working properly today. It's going too fast, and then dragging on, and nothing seems right.

Elf shrugs and then says something, but I miss his words because of the roaring in my ears. I watch him rub his eyes instead.

"So it'll be out of his system soon," Rahn says. "He's only had one, yeah? He'll be fine."

He'll be *fine*? I stare at Rahn. Nico won't be fine. We all know that. Just one augmenter is enough to change someone permanently, even if it's not as drastic a change as a full conversion would have been. But Nico will never be the same again.

And it's my fault. I should've realized that man wasn't my brother. My twin.

I stiffen.

Rahn clears his throat. "Keep him in your hut, tied up for now. We'll call a meetin' in the mornin', explain that you ran into two lone Enhanced Ones, that you killed 'em both, but not before they got an augmenter in Nico. But he'll survive, be Untamed again. If he says anythin' about the imposter, we'll say it's just delirium speakin'."

I clench my hands into fists. "He's not going to be the same though."

"It was one augmenter," Rahn snaps. "He hasn't been through a conversion, and it's not like he's been Enhanced for years, is it?"

"One augmenter's enough," Elf says. "It plants the seed of addiction and—"

Rahn stamps his foot. "He is still one of our group. And you, Keelie—you went to get your sister back even though you knew she'd have had a lot more than *one* augmenter by the time we got there. We always rescue our people, and get them back if we can. We've got Nico back and didn't even need a rescue mission. He may be different, but at least we've got him. That's a good thing in my book."

His words hurt, and I recoil from him.

"Now, we go and get Nico, secure him for the night."

There's nothing more to say, so we head back to the truck. The darkness seems even more oppressive now. Elf walks close to me, and Rahn leads. The distance between us and the leader gets bigger and bigger. I want to stop and talk to Elf, tell him this is madness— that we need to tell everyone our location could've been compromised. Secrets divide people. Secrets kill.

Elf glances at me, opens his mouth, then shuts it again. I know he agrees with me. Twins of the stars.

"What the—" Rahn's exclamation sounds strange, grates on my ears, and my eyes jolt to him.

Something is wrong. I know immediately.

Elf grabs my hand, we speed up. My head pounds, and I know—just know—that Nico's not there. He's gone—somehow, he's gone. Like Red. Hell. My feet slap the ground. He's gone to join them—one augmenter *was* enough. He's going to lead them to us. We shouldn't have left him.

I slam into Rahn, and the leader shoves me back.

"What?" Elf says, and then there's movement, and too much stuff is going on.

Elf pulls himself up into the truck bed, and then Rahn's shouting.

I see Nico. He's still there. I frown, I don't understand.

Elf slaps Nico's face, then his arms.

"Check for a pulse," Rahn commands, but his voice is choked up.

And I stare at Nico's eyes: Untamed once more. How long have they been like that?

But his eyes aren't right. They're not mirrors, but they're dull. Duller than Elf's were earlier. Dull and….

Lifeless.

I start to feel strange.

My stomach squeezes together. Then I see the rope, and I remember I didn't use all of it to tie him up. I tried to put him in the same place that Red had been, but Nico's smaller, and he didn't need as many bindings to hold him. There was one spare.

"Get Katya!" Rahn commands.

"It's too late," Elf says. "He's gone."

Gone.

Gone is a strange word. It doesn't sound right. Or it sounds like the gong of a bell, as if the word should echo over and over again, so that the sound of the word never leaves, and thus it's a contradiction. It's not *gone*, it's all around us.

People are coming now. The rest of the village.

Everything is a blur.

Nico's dead.

They don't think he meant to. Katya says it was probably an accident—that he must have been struggling, scared, trying to get free so he could find more augmenters, and one of the ropes around his body slid up, got around his neck, or something—but Elf and I both heard his threats.

I press my lips together. They taste salty. My eyes tear up again as I stare at the truck. I'm sitting on the ground, and it's cold, but it's good because I'm too low to see into the truck bed, to see *him*.

Nico.

The man who wanted to marry me.

My stomach squeezes together, and I throw up in the sand. It's mainly bile: long, stringy bile.

"Who tied him like that?" Corin asks.

I did. And everyone knows it.

Another death on my hands. More blood on me.

I back away, still sitting down. Moving my bottom, then my feet. Shuffling backward.

"It's not your fault," a voice says. Five's voice.

I turn and see her, but she's looking down at me, and she doesn't sound like she believes what she's saying. Or maybe it's just me, wanting to believe that. Because they need to be mean to me. I deserve it.

My lips burn. I wipe the back of my hand across them and keep shuffling.

"Did you find Bea?" someone else asks.

I look up. See Alan standing there.

"She died," Rahn says before I can say anything.

My gaze jerks to him.

"Keelie and Elf found her body," he continues. "Dehydration probably weakened her. And a cat got her. She's dead. Shame it was too long after her death for the Spirit Releasing Words to be said. Shame she'll be sufferin', trapped in this world, in pain."

I stare at him, feel every muscle in my body tighten. What the hell?

He crosses over to me and Elf swiftly, lowers his

voice, turning his back on the others. "Don't say anythin' contrary. I mean it. Else you'll pay." The threat is heavy in his words.

For several moments, I can't speak. Then, at last, I manage to. "But—but what if she comes back?"

"She won't. She'll *be* dead." He grins a malicious grin, and it's as if he's daring her to come back so he can make his words true.

I shake my head. "Bea's clever—if anyone can survive on their own, it's her."

Rahn snorts. "Let's hope so. Because even if she does come back, she ain't welcome here." He steps away from me, then addresses everyone, much louder. "Take this death as a warnin'. *You* can't survive out there, not on your own. *I* know how to survive, it's why I'm the leader, and you do as I say. You stick by me, you don't go gettin' any ideas, and then you'll survive." His eyes cross to Corin, and I sense something between uncle and nephew. "People who think they know better than me, people who go off on their own, people who don't trust my ability to keep them safe—they end up dead. Those who leave don't make it. You're all part of my group, and you obey my rules."

His eyes linger on me for a little too long, and then people are dispersing, and arrangements for Nico's body are being made. And I feel…numb.

"Come on, let's get you inside."

I let Five take me back to my hut, and she puts me to bed. Half an hour later, she leaves when I pretend to sleep.

But I can't sleep.

Mustn't let myself sleep.

Can't see Nico, not tonight, not in my nightmares.

But I don't have a choice.

And it's not just Nico who haunts me.

THIRTY-SEVEN

IT ALL COMES CRASHING DOWN. As I stare into the darkness, I know now that what I did to Mila never sunk in. Not at the time. Not really. But it does now. Everything sinks in, and it clings to me, vowing to never let me go. Never let me be free from the monster I've become.

Monster.

Monster.

Monster.

The word won't leave me alone. It's everywhere. And people are looking at me strangely now. They know what I am.

A murderer. A monster.

I see Mila everywhere. She didn't make it to the New World—of course. And now she's trapped...trapped between the two worlds, and she's angry...angry at me. Because I did this to her.

And she and Nico are walking together, following me, their mirror eyes burning me.

I've trapped them both here, and they know it. My skin welts under their stares, blisters, and I peel it off. Long flakes of skin, like paper.

Mila takes the paper from me, and she draws on it.

But she doesn't draw a sweet image. None of her flowers. No butterflies—not even her favorite ones, the Lilac Tips or Desert Orange Tips.

Instead, it's me.

She draws me, with the devil's horns, and I'm outside during the Turning and spirits are eating my face, tearing chunks out of my flesh. And she draws several of these images: my death in different stages.

And then Nico joins her, but he looks at Mila differently, and she's suddenly older, and he kisses her, kisses her passionately, and I'm forced to watch as their bodies entwine until they become one—one huge Enhanced One who grabs me.

I scream, and I'm running. My feet are bare, and the sand is sharp as I try to run faster. Large daggers jut up from the ground, and one impales my foot. I scream.

"Let me save you!" the Enhanced One shouts. And she's got an augmenter. A massive one, and she drips it over me, and I can't not swallow it.

But it doesn't taste good, because it's made of death and darkness—just like me.

And now my nightmares are real. They're here in the light, not just the dark. They're real—it's different, not like before! They're happening when I'm awake.

The light isn't enough to keep me safe anymore.

Katya tries to talk to me several times, when the huge Enhanced One is following me around the village, and it's better when she speaks because the huge Enhanced One backs away a little.

"Have you seen a conversion attack?" I ask her, and I know I need to tell her everything. But I can't. My head's foggy. So foggy. And it doesn't matter. Because death comes to us all.

And I should be going out there, to find Bea, to check she is all right. Yet, every time I head toward one of the trucks, the huge Enhanced One tries to grab me, threatens to convert me, and I end up shaking and shaking and shaking. Can never stop shaking.

Katya says she hasn't seen a conversion attack.

I suppose that makes me feel better, the monster that I am. But Katya wants to talk about other stuff—about me, about how I'm feeling.

"I'm a monster."

I don't know what she says to that, because I'm in a daze, and the daze won't let me go. Nothing makes sense. I'm traveling, and people are moving around me. And then I see Mila and Nico again. They've separated from being the huge Enhanced One, and they're both watching me. My own personal demons.

"Don't tell anyone anythin'," Rahn snarls at me. And he's suddenly here. "We're safe. And I don't want my people scared because of you and your imagination. We are safe. You're not thinkin' straight. You're grievin'. Leave the safety of *my* group to me."

I nod, and then we're sending Nico's body off. We've traveled a long way, to the water, and I don't remember going, but suddenly I'm here.

I listen to the Spirit Releasing Words, but they don't really make sense—maybe it's because I know. I know we're too late in saying them. Why are we so late in doing this? He won't get there, won't get to the New World. Because he's already here. Trapped.

I watch Nico's body float away. He wanted to be safe.

But he's safe in the wrong way.

Because of me.

Monster.

Monster.

Monster.

Mila starts shouting, throwing more words at me.

I whimper.

"I got Three to check that radio," Elf tells me in a low voice, some time later. We're back in our hut.

I turn to him. "What radio?"

"The one that imposter had. He said it was broken, but I wanted Three to confirm it. Told him I found it out there, it had been dropped by an Enhanced, and I wondered if it might be useful."

"And?"

"And it is broken. He said something about the transmitter not working. He wanted it for parts, but Rahn came over and stopped him. Said it was cursed by some bad spirit and needed disposing of. Just as well really. Don't want Three fixing it and then accidentally broadcasting our location." He pauses. "Do radios do that? Broadcast locations?"

I shrug.

He stretches his hands out in front of him. "I guess we are safe after all then. It's been two days, and I've been sleeping with a gun under my pillow, just in case. But they haven't come."

Safe. The word tastes bad as I mull it over and over. Then I frown—*two days*? But another thought comes to my mind.

I turn to Elf, unsure of where the question comes from, but sure that I need to ask it. "Would you have gone with me if it was really you?"

"To find Bea?"

I nod.

"Of course," he says, gives me a strange look.

"So why aren't you going off now, to find her?"

He's quiet for a moment. "If Bea's survived this long, then she'll survive another couple of weeks. Rahn's watching us too closely. We've got to bide our time if we're going to unite our family again."

Unite our family.

But that's impossible.

"We could get Mum and Dad too?" I look at him, feeling hopeful. "They sacrificed themselves for us."

Elf shakes his head. "They're dead to us, and we

have to keep living, not putting ourselves in danger. We can't get them back. But we can get Bea. We have to be clever—"

"But we could. We'd just have to find Mum and Dad and—"

And Red's found them.

My eyes widen. That's what he said. Didn't he? I try to think, try to force my way through the fog.

"Keelie. Stop it. We can't look back. The past will only trap us." His face darkens, and he presses his lips together firmly for a few seconds. When he looks back up, his eyes are sad. So sad. Sadder than I've ever seen them before. "You saw what happened to Nico. After only one augmenter and a few hours. Our parents are gone, Kee. It's been a decade. They're dead to us now. We have to bury them in our past and keep them there. We have to focus on us—and Bea. On the future."

Something catches in my chest, and then I'm crying. Crying properly. Huge tears that contain everything, that wash toward Mila and Nico, that wash them away in whispers and screams.

Elf holds me as I cry. He tells me it's not my fault. It's the dangerous world we live in.

The two of us stay like this.

I cry for days.

THIRTY-EIGHT

THE NEXT WEEK PASSES STRANGELY, and, soon, I find myself sitting on a rock, one late afternoon, high in the mountains, looking down at Nbutai. I feel irritable, like I want to do something, be active, but I've got little energy.

I think the raw part of the grief is lessening now, because I haven't seen Mila or Nico again. Not since I cried. Cried it out my system. And it makes me feel weird, knowing I hallucinated. Like I'm going mad.

But I'm not mad. I'm *not*.

I even told Katya about it a few days ago—because someone who *was* mad wouldn't tell anyone—and I told her that I'd seen them several times. She reassured me that it was grief, that it was normal—and that it wasn't really them, that Nico and Mila would've got to the New World. I know she can't be *sure* what she said was true, but it makes me feel better all the same.

I exhale hard, looking down at the world. The Watcher Doll is in my hands, and I squeeze it, as if by doing so, I can activate it and make the spirits protect me. But it's just a fantasy.

Elf is next to me, also sitting on the rock. We climbed

up here because it's one of Mila's favorite places. The four of us came for a picnic here once.

We were four. Now we're two.

How did it come to this?

But Bea's still out there. And there have been no new capture or conversion announcements on the radio.

I think she's alive.

A few days ago, Elf told me the whole story of what had happened to him after I left him when Mila was captured. He said he followed Mila and the Enhanced Ones, but injured his ankle. He had to pull himself to the nearest cover and hide there. Twice, he thought the Enhanced had seen or heard him moving.

He thought about what to do, but he was far from Nbutai, and his ankle was swelling up. He kept moving, once he was sure the Enhanced were out of the area, but an animal attacked him in the dark. He couldn't see what it was, but it had big teeth and big eyes.

Somehow, Elf fought it off, but two of his wounds became infected. He became delirious and couldn't find the way back to the village. He'd been wandering around, half-starved, surviving on berries. At some point, he managed to clean his infected wound when he came across some water and a few plants that Bea had taught him about.

It was a miracle really that I found him when I had. A miracle in more than one way.

"How are you now?" Elf asks. Then he wraps me in a tight hug.

I shrug, careful not to drop the Watcher Doll. I think of how Caia-Lu was always so careful with it. "I should be asking you that."

"I'm fine." He pulls back, smiling.

"So…" I look at him carefully. "Do you think we're really safe? What if the imposter's messages *did* get through—or Red could've told them?" Because he would've definitely made it back to New Kimearo—I'm sure. Rahn said the need for augmenters would've been driving him strongly. He'll have made it there for sure.

Elf doesn't answer for a few moments. "No one has come for us. But I've been talking to Rahn. He's thinking about moving us all on. He hasn't said anything officially yet about moving, only to me, so no one else knows about it. But he is sensible, and I think what we've told him has got to him."

Sensible would've been moving the moment we told him.

I exhale hard, pocket the Watcher Doll, and grip my hands together. My thumb slides over a rough bit of skin on my right hand, and I pick at it absentmindedly. "Where are we going to go?"

"I don't know. He didn't say. And I'm not even sure you're supposed to know, given he told me on the down-low." He gives me a cautious look.

"I won't say anything. Promise… But we'll need to raid, won't we?" I look down at the blood now on the back of my hand, where I've picked the scab off. I smear it against my jeans quickly before Elf can see. "We'll need supplies. Need to make sure we're not running low on essential stuff when we're traveling."

I look back down the mountainside. The breeze lifts up the sand a few feet away, and orange swirls whirl in the air like floating rust.

I remember how good driving fast around here made me feel. The adrenaline, the surge of life, the feeling of being alive and free.

I don't like how I'm feeling now.

"I need a new motorbike," I say. It will make me feel better. "We need to tell Rahn we have to raid before we go."

"You're not supposed to know that we are going," Elf points out.

"Well, you say it then." I shake my head, and my neck clicks. Energy fizzes through me. *Yes.* "Or maybe I'll just point out we need to raid. Raiding isn't unusual. Doesn't mean I know we'll be leaving."

Elf presses his lips together. "Come on," he says, pointing to the sky. "It's getting dark."

Neither of us wants to look at the stars now.

We head back to our hut, and I think of how much better I'll feel when I've got a motorbike again. I mean, *already*, I feel better. Strangely better, almost as if a spell has been cast over me. But it's not really a spell. I know that.

Elf and I share a tin of semolina pudding and half a mango, and we discuss different ways I can introduce the idea of a raid to Rahn in the morning, eventually settling on a plan.

Then I crawl into my bed.

I close my eyes. It doesn't take me long to sleep, because now I feel happy, and, when I do, I dream of Red. For once, it isn't a nightmare.

He caresses the side of my face, slowly, delicately. His fingers are like feathers now, but I know how competent they can be, and the memory sends shivers through me.

The bed beneath us is soft, but firm.

"I've missed you so much." Red breathes the words into my neck as he lowers his head. "I love you, really love you, K."

A second later, I feel his tongue against my collarbone. He licks me, and I feel my body react. I want him, want him so badly.

I wrap my arms around his chest, and my legs around his waist. We're one unit, breathing and living as one.

It's beautiful.

Everything is beautiful.

"Beauty is never lost," I say.

"Neither is hope," he says.

THIRTY-NINE

THE NEXT MORNING DAWNS BRIGHT and clear, and Elf and I wait for Rahn to leave his hut before I sneak in. It's dark inside, but I locate the medical supplies easily. I load most of them into my survival bag, and my eyes linger on the firearms for a little while. But they're not part of the plan. I head back out.

"You shouldn't have done that," Elf says to me, but he takes my bag and disappears into our own hut.

I walk over to the small water hole and wash my hair, then take out my Swiss army knife and head over to help Five skin the six desert rats that Kayden must have brought in—he's the only one who hunts those.

As I sit down with Five—half-listening to her endless chatter about nothing—I'm very aware of Elf watching us from a distance. Finn's with him, but I can see my brother's paying as much attention to him as I am to Five.

I hold the blade carefully as I separate skin from a rat's stomach and—

"Argh!" I cry out as I slice the knife into the fleshy muscle of my thumb—a lot deeper than intended. Sharp pain squeezes through me, and tears come to my eyes.

Authentic.

"Shit!" Five jumps up, then yells something to Elf and Finn, her voice too high-pitched for me to make out her words.

She pulls off her shawl and wraps my hand in it, and Elf and Finn get here, but blood soaks through the fabric surprisingly quickly. Too quickly? I stare at the way the redness spreads across the fabric, mesmerized. I'd thought it wouldn't bleed much, but I can't have hit an artery or something there, can I? I frown, and dark spots hover in front of me for a second.

I blink them away quickly and look up to see several more people rushing toward us. Katya, Paul, and Alan.

"Hey, you all right?" Elf's voice. "Keelie? You've gone really pale."

"I'm fine," I say.

"We need the antibiotic ointment and a bandage," Katya says. "Keelie, I think you should lie down."

"I'm fine," I say again, hear others approaching.

But they insist on lowering me to the ground. More voices fog toward me, and I concentrate on my breathing. Got to keep breathing evenly. Anyway, I'm fine. Absolutely fine. If I concentrate really hard, I can even block the pain out. I blink a few times, listening. And, sure enough, I hear Rahn saying, "It's the last bandage, and there ain't any ointment."

Katya and Marouska dress my hand, and eventually I'm allowed to sit up. Half of the village is around me, and, honestly, it's a lot of fuss for nothing. Just a cut.

"That was the last bandage?" I ask.

Rahn nods.

"Then we need to raid," I say. "Medical supplies are important."

"And we've only got a couple packs of water purification tablets left," Elf says, his voice not giving away any hint of our betrayal. "We should have more in reserve than that."

A couple of the men agree, and Rahn looks visibly

flustered.

"There should've been more supplies than that," he says. "I'm sure there were two more boxes."

"When did you last check?" I ask.

He shrugs.

"We should raid as soon as possible," I say. "Medical supplies are important. And there could be loads of Turnings soon. You know the damage spirits can do."

Except the Nbutai group doesn't. To my knowledge, Elf and I are the only people who've witnessed first-hand the destruction that a deadly spirit causes. The way flesh flies through the air. The way the screams haunt you. Huh, and spirits are supposed to be on our side.

Yet they *did* help me. They showed me where Elf—the *real* Elf—was.

"What about today?" I look around, making my voice as light as possible. "It's good weather at the moment too. Perfect for raiding."

Under Rahn's dark glasses, I get the impression his eyes are narrowing.

"Raiding today?" Corin raises his eyebrows. He's wearing a threadbare outer-shirt over a T-shirt, and he swats at a mosquito as it lands on his neck. Splatters it in a little star of blood. I look at the red smudge for a little longer than I should. "Could work," he says.

"Yes. We could do with more fuel," Rahn finally says. He glares at me. "We've got very little left after your little jaunt."

"Great," I say, refusing to be stung. "Elf and I are in."

"You?" Rahn's voice is blunt. "You're in no state to raid." He rubs the back of his neck for a few moments. "Corin?"

Corin nods firmly. "In."

Rahn grunts. "Finn?"

His face lights up, and he nods.

"I'm coming," Katya says suddenly.

Rahn turns to her in an instant. "You seen somethin'?"

It's unusual for Katya to volunteer for a raid. We've all heard the stories of how, before their group moved to Nbutai, Katya was one of the regulars who'd break the newly converted out of compounds in an attempt to save them. It never really worked. But, since then, Katya's preferred to avoid the Enhanced towns and cities because she's our Seer, and we need her to be safe so she can keep us safe.

Katya shakes her head. "But I am coming."

"Fine," Rahn says. He points toward Seven next. She's far away, out of earshot. "And I want her on the fuel run."

"Someone will have to go with her," Corin says. "She's not going to be able to carry all the fuel by herself. How many cans are we getting?" He folds his arms as he stands next to the leader. Looking at them now, you'd never guess they were related. Rahn is scrawny with a huge nose, whereas Corin's frame is stocky and muscular.

Rahn mutters something, then clears his throat. "We'll discuss the dynamics on the way to New Kimearo. Right, start loadin' the truck. Alan, get some food for the survival bags ready. Most'll be runnin' low on energy bars by now. Five lots."

"But I'm coming too," I say quickly. "We need six."

Rahn turns on me. "No—you ain't comin', Keelie. It's just me, Corin, Finn, Katya, and Seven."

I feel my chest swell with emotion. "But I'm our best fighter," I say. And I did not execute the first part of this plan for me not to be chosen to go on the raid. No way.

"You're stayin' here. You're injured."

I snort. "It was barely a scrape."

"You fainted."

"I did not!" I cry. "They made me lie down. I'm fine! Elf, tell them."

My brother mumbles something, and I could just about kick him. What happened to sounding strong and confident?

"I'm coming on this raid," I say.

"No." Rahn stamps his foot. Actually stamps it.

My eyes widen, and I suddenly get the urge to laugh.

"I don't think you going is a good idea." Katya's voice is cool and calm, but there's a heaviness to it too. Loaded with meaning. And, when I turn to look at her, I find her eyes are firmly on me. "Do you?" She raises her eyebrows.

"I need to go," I say. "Look, if I go, it makes it an even number. And I can go with Seven to get fuel. Rahn and Corin can get the medicine, and you and Finn can get food. We'll need lots."

Rahn clears his throat loudly. "Keelie. You are *not* comin'."

I look toward Elf for help, but the traitor has turned away. Why isn't he backing me up? Darkness clouds me for a moment.

"Load up the truck," Rahn says. "*Five* survival bags."

I turn away, feel my face burning, but Rahn's fingers latch around my wrist, and he drags me roughly backward.

"Hey!" I twist around and yank my arm free of him. "What are you doing?"

"What the hell was that?" he counters.

"What was *what*?" I fold my arms. We're not far from everyone else, and Corin and Elf are both watching intently.

Rahn exhales loudly. "That arguin', that defiance. Did I not make myself clear before? Am I mistaken and no longer the leader of this group?"

I glare at him. "I'm staying here, aren't I? You got your way."

His nostrils flare. "One more act like this, Keelie, and you're out."

"Out?"

"Out of my group."

My eyebrows shoot up. "You'd throw me out? Even though I'm Untamed and the best fighter?" I shake my head and start to laugh. He wouldn't throw me out.

"I would," he says, his voice dark. "You've proven we can't always trust you. And maybe there's no Mila or Bea around for me to use to keep you in line. But, remember, there are others. Five, Seven. Even Elf. You act up again, and you're out *and* they suffer."

My breath catches in my throat.

"Do I make myself clear?"

I nod.

We pack the truck quickly, and Corin heads over to Seven, tells her of her part in the raid. I watch her face fall. None of us like fuel raids, especially after Marouska's sons got killed in one. And that's why I should be there. I can keep people safe.

Really? Mila's voice asks. *You didn't keep me safe.*

I try to ignore her. No, me—because it's *me*. Not her... I'm not mad.

"Not mad," I mutter. "Not mad. Definitely not mad."

I notice Katya's stopped packing and is watching the assembly. She frowns, but there's something off about her frown. Something distant, and the expression makes her look a lot older than she is.

"Katya?"

Her eyes widen, and she sways.

I rush to her. "What is it?"

"It's going to happen." Her breathing gets heavier, then she shakes her head. "Just stay here, Keelie. You're staying here, aren't you? You must!"

I frown. "Are you all right to go?"

"Keelie, if..." She shakes her head and then adjusts her scarf. "Rahn's always hated me and my family." A strange look passes over her face. "If something were to happen…you have to make sure he treats her equally."

"What are you talking about?"

"My visions."

I lean forward. "You've had a vision?" I shake my head. "You need to tell Rahn—"

"I did. A few days ago. He wouldn't listen, not when I said it was one of those different ones. Far future. The ones that—like when I saw you die."

"But that didn't happen," I point out.

Her eyes seem to get harder as if they're becoming beautiful gemstones—the kind Bea loves. "Not yet." She looks strained, like she's sick. "And this latest one—I had it two days ago…or was it three?" She blinks slowly. "Oh Gods. I—I don't know. But, at the beginning, it was me and Rahn and Corin…trapped… caught…but two get out. And it…it doesn't make sense…and it wasn't an immediate danger, the dream didn't have the right feel—it was just a flash. An image or two. No sign of the bison, that I could see. But I do not know if the bison controls far-sight. The bison is supposed to be for the immediate warnings.

"But this *will* happen…these far-future visions are still visions. And, at the end of this latest one, I saw a woman standing on a battlefield—an Untamed girl— and an Enhanced One will stop her getting away… and she looked like Seven."

"What?" I shake my head. She's not making any sense. "The Enhanced looked like *Seven*?"

"No…the woman, the girl, the *Untamed*." Katya grimaces. "It wasn't clear. Just an image. The non-immediate future, the type of vision I'm not supposed to get." Her eyes darken, but her voice gets stronger. "It was those two scenes this time. Us trapped—Rahn, Corin, and I—and her, Seven, out there. But many of my previous visions of this sort have shown disaster for Seven, and those visions seemed farther away than this latest glimpse of the future—both parts of it, both scenes."

"What does it mean?" I stare at her. "What's going to happen? Is it this raid?"

She reaches for her Seer pendant suddenly. "Where's Paul?"

I point to the right in the direction where her husband is. "He's getting the truck ready, with the other men."

Katya pulls her pendant off, snapping the sinew. Her fingers shake as she ties it back together.

"What are you doing?" I eye the pendant as she dangles it in front of her face. Light bursts from the crystal. "Shouldn't you put that back on? You don't want to get trapped in the Dream Land…."

A sharpness in her eyes cuts me off.

"I need to give this…" She looks at me. "Not to you. You'll die." She turns, and her gaze falls on Esther, not far away.

Esther disappears into her hut, and Katya races after her. I stare after her, and her last words to me echo in my mind. I'm about to follow, when Elf shouts my name.

"What?" I turn to him as he jogs over.

"Rahn wants to know if you need more sanitary items. He's making the final list."

I scowl. "So much for our plan, Elf."

"We can't go up against Rahn," he says, his voice level. "Not like this. And he's threatened you before. We've got to be careful."

"Careful?" I snort. "We're letting him walk all over us. And I need to get a new bike, Elf."

"Just leave it. It's not worth it."

"Not worth it?" I shake my head. "No. You don't understand. It's not a want. It's a *need*. I need to feel alive. Need to feel *better*. I need to be free. I *need* it." I wipe my sweaty hands on my jeans, but the sweat's gone under the bandage, and it feels all rank and horrible. My thumb's starting to hurt more now too.

My brother's eyes darken, and he looks like he wants to say something else, but he doesn't.

On the other side of the village, I see Katya's outside again now, talking to Paul. She looks calm now—sincere—and that makes me feel a bit better about her. Then they both turn and glance at Seven as she walks past, carrying two empty fuel cans, her survival kit already on her back. She's oblivious to their stares. But she's not heading toward the truck yet.

No one's heading toward the truck. And no one's at it. Or nearby. Elf and I are the nearest.

My eyes widen.

Yes.

I turn to Elf. "I'm going to go. Rahn's not stopping me."

"Keelie." His voice is a warning.

"Cover me," I hiss.

Then I walk over to the truck. My steps bounce, bounce with energy, with adrenaline. And that's good. I feel alive again. My heart pounds, instilling more and more life.

I pull myself up onto the tailgate, then into the truck bed, and keep low. There's a tarpaulin in the corner. It's folded, but not very neatly.

"Keelie!" Elf hisses as I shimmy along the wooden bed. Something snags at my clothes, but I ignore it and hear a slight ripping sound.

I reach the tarpaulin, and lift it up, slide myself under it. The waterproof fabric smells of some sort of chemical I can't place.

"Keelie?" Elf shouts. "What the—"

"Be quiet!" I hiss back. Then: "Can you see me?"

I hear his footsteps, then the tarpaulin rustles and crackles over it—presumably as he readjusts it. I hold my breath. I'm not in the most comfortable of positions, but I'm half-crouching, half-leaning—a position I can hold for a long time, if needed.

Slowly, I count to ten.

"Keelie, don't do this," Elf says.

I ignore him. A moment later, I hear the sounds of him climbing aboard. His steps shuffle toward me, and I think he crouches down.

"Fine. Be careful." He lifts the corner of the tarpaulin.

"What are you doing?" I hiss, but then I see what he slides under it.

I take the gun and the dark glasses, a grin forming on my face.

Elf clears his throat. "After this, Keelie, we're moving."

"What?"

"You and I, we're leaving Rahn's group. Something's going to happen to you—Rahn's going to do something—and you're not going to be safe here."

"Rahn's all talk—"

"You don't know that. And I'm getting you away from him. This environment isn't healthy for you. It's—"

"We're goin' now!" Rahn yells. His voice is nearby. "Hey, Elf, what are you doin' there?"

There's a pause in which I cradle the gun to me. I think it's a Luger. Elf shouldn't have had it on him.

"Just checking the tarpaulin's a good one," Elf calls back. "Enough to cover you all in case there's a Turning."

And then the sounds of Elf getting out and the others dividing between the cab and the truck bed fill my ears. Even more adrenaline pumps through me. Gods, imagine what Rahn will do if he finds me!

And, I guess it's bad that part of me wants him to find me, so he knows he hasn't won.

Because he hasn't. He'll never win. There's only one person who'll win. And that's me.

I grin against the tarpaulin.

I am *alive*.

FORTY

BEING A SECRET STOWAWAY IS fun. It's also uncomfortable—and very infuriating when I learn from Seven and Katya's conversation that Rahn's completely disregarded the execution plan I made. He's sending Seven off on her own to fill up the fuel cans, while he, Corin, and Katya are going to the middle part of New Kimearo where Rahn will get medicine while the other two acquire weapons, clothes, and better shoes, before meeting back up again. Finn's to drive the truck around to the far western side of the town to load up crates of tinned food. And then everyone's to meet back in the meeting place in one hour's time.

Which means it's also going to be difficult for me to leave the truck without being noticed. I'll either have to jump out while Finn's driving or wait until he's parked to get the tins, and then go off and find a motorbike. And I'd better find one, as it's going to be difficult for me to get back to the meeting point on foot for the designated time. Which would also reveal myself to the others.

But I'll find a motorbike. I will. I smile to myself,

already feeling the adrenaline pulsing through me. It's like a drug.

Katya and Seven are in the truck bed, but now they talk in low voices that I can't make out. I think of how Katya acted earlier, all weird and mysterious about those different dreams, and I frown. Caia-Lu never said anything about different types of Seeing dreams, and I've only heard of this new type from Katya recently. Is Katya losing it?

But Caia-Lu did say about your death, Mila whispers. And suddenly I feel her hot breath against my face, and I'm confused—Mila can't remember Caia-Lu. *Maybe that was one of these far-future visions.*

I stiffen.

No. She's not here. Not under the tarpaulin with me. There's no one here.

But I am. And don't you think you'd better be concerned? Two far-future visions about your death—and you're still going into an Enhanced town? How stupid are you? Maybe you want to die.

I grit my teeth and turn my head a little. The scratchy surface of the tarpaulin catches my face, but I see enough in the darkness. Mila's not here with me. I need to stop imagining her words, have to. Because I'm not mad.

Are you sure?

Shut up. I put as much venom as I can into that answer, but I know I'm just talking to myself. And I'm not mad. Not mad. Not mad. Mila's gone, gone to the New World, that's what Katya said.

The truck slows and rattles over rough ground, then stops. I catch my shoulder against the bottom of the wall and hear Rahn's and Corin's voices. We must be at the drop-off point. Already?

I listen as Katya and Seven exit the truck bed. Finn keeps the engine running which makes it hard to hear when the others have walked away. Cautiously, I lift the tarpaulin up. Bright light assaults my eyes, and I blink several times before I can make anything out.

Fresh air bellows over me. Then I see Rahn, Katya, Corin, and Seven. They're a few hundred feet away.

I check the safety's on the gun—it *is* a Luger—and slide it into the back of my belt. The dark glasses go into my jacket pocket. I move farther out from under the tarpaulin, careful to keep low enough so Finn won't see me in the mirror. I crawl to the end of the truck bed. The tailgate is up, and I won't be able to lower it easily.

I steel myself, and then jump over it. I crash down onto the dusty earth, and something cuts savagely into my back. I gasp, gritting my teeth as more dust billows up around me. With my right hand, I check that my dark glasses survived the impact—they have. I peer through the dust-myriad at the retreating figures in the distance. They look hazy, but they don't look back. No one expects me to be there. The truck doesn't stop either—Finn mustn't have noticed me.

"One point to Keelie," I mutter as I carefully tense all my muscles, checking for damage. But I'm okay. I'm tough. Even my painful thumb's faded to a dull throb.

There are many boulders and smaller rocks around here that provide the perfect cover for me to shadow the group as they head toward New Kimearo. As they get nearer to the buildings, Seven looks behind her, but I duck behind a rock in time. The whole time, I grin manically.

"Ha! Take that, Rahn. I told you I was coming on this raid," I whisper.

On the outskirts of the town, there's more dust, which makes the air hazy, harder to see, but I pick out Seven splitting from the group. I'm still angry that she's going on the fuel raid on her own. I look toward Katya, expecting her to cause a fuss about it. But she doesn't appear to, just hugs Seven for a moment.

A cool breeze caresses my shoulder, and I wait until they've all disappeared. Then I put my dark glasses on, check the gun's concealed under my jacket, and follow

Seven. We'll get the fuel together, like I planned. And really, it's obvious that Rahn should've listened to me. What was he thinking, sending Seven off? And why didn't Katya stand up for her daughter?

Energy fizzes through me as I reach New Kimearo and navigate its narrow streets. I pass several Enhanced, but they don't look at me. A triumphant grin unfolds across my face—but it's okay because I'll just look like I've taken some Happiness.

"Good day," I say to the next Enhanced who passes me.

"Good day to you," he replies, smiling.

Gods, Elf would have a heart attack if he knew. But the Enhanced often greet each other in the street— even strangers—and we have to fit in. I've raised this point before, and Elf told me it wasn't a game. It was life and death.

"But it *is* a game," I mutter quietly, but no one is in earshot now.

I turn right at the next junction. The sign for the fuel station seems to wink at me. I grin at it then look down the road. Seven shouldn't be far ahead. She'll be getting the fuel. I'll help her carry it, and then we'll get my motorbike. I could even get a new model. Yes. I lick my lips. Yes—

"I can do that, yes," a voice says.

I go cold, and my mouth dries instantly. That voice. I turn, see him.

Red is ten feet from me.

He's on the phone, walking slightly ahead of me. But I know that body, I know it's him.

"Yes, Owen."

Owen? My father's name is Owen… He's talking to my father?

No, there are loads of men called Owen. Have to be.

But ones that Red would talk to?

I freeze, and then Red's getting farther away, and I lose his voice, can't hear his words.

But it's him.

Red.

And he's found my father—he told me that in our second meeting, that he'd found my parents.

My heart rate rockets, and I step against the side of the nearest building, my palm catching against the rough render. I try to keep breathing. Need to keep breathing.

And what the hell am I doing?

I move slowly, cautiously, looking around. Red's walking faster now. He's going to be out of sight soon.

Follow him.

And I don't know where that voice comes from. But I pull my hood up and check my glasses are covering my eyes sufficiently, and I do as instructed. I follow Red. And, really, for a skilled tracker, he's awful at noticing whether he's being tailed. And I don't even know *why* I'm following him. Except that I've been told to, and it's exciting, it makes my heart pound, and it proves who's in control.

Red enters a posh-looking building on the left, and I follow him. An Enhanced sits at the reception desk, but Red walks straight past her, so I do too. There are quite a few Enhanced in here, but if you walk confidently no one suspects you.

I smile and say hello to a few of them, mimicking the people around me, and—

Red freezes in front of me.

Then he turns.

I duck behind a group of Enhanced women in matching skirts just in time. I hold my breath, waiting. But he heard my voice—I know he did—and the thrill of it sends electricity pounding through me.

I grin.

This is fun.

Almost as much fun as killing the Enhanced.

And I could still do that. Still got the Luger.

Didn't you learn your lesson?

But now the thought of killing is making me feel even more alive. I could do it so easily…right here….

Except I shouldn't be here, and Seven's on her own, and I'm supposed to be with her. She doesn't like fuel raids.

And I need to get a motorbike too. What was it Rahn said? To meet up in an hour's time? I'm not wearing a watch, but I guess I've already used up twenty minutes.

I watch Red carefully. He looks around again, and my heart hammers. But he doesn't see me. A moment later, he continues on, disappears through another door, and I force myself to retrace my steps. I need to get a move on, not get distracted. Not by Red. Even if he was speaking with my father. *Could* he have been going to meet my father? He must've been, I decide, because he's the assistant manager at that garage, and we're nowhere near that.

I hover by the exit. I could be so close to my father. Would one glimpse hurt?

Yes, yes it would.

And what am I even doing?

I need to be looking out for Seven, need to have her back.

My father will have to wait. Maybe when Elf and I leave, we can stop by here first. Just to see him. And my mother too—if my father's here, she'll be here too, won't she?

I nod to myself and head back out.

By the time I reach the fuel station, Seven's already leaving. I see her retreating figure, pulled down on one side by a heavy-looking fuel can. Strange, I was sure she was filling two up. She carried two earlier, didn't she? I frown. Maybe Rahn and the others decided to take one with them? There's another fuel station fairly near the pharmacy where Rahn will be. Yes, that's it. He must've thought it was too risky for Seven to stay longer at the fuel station, filling both cans herself. Or maybe Katya did say something—because I doubt Rahn was thinking about Seven's safety.

Still, I breathe out a sigh of relief. She's safe.

I follow her for a little bit. She only looks around three times, and I've got my hood up, and the wind blows my super-long fringe across my face. Anyway, she's not *expecting* to see me. When I'm sure she's okay, and is on the outskirts of New Kimearo, I turn back.

"Time to get your new motorbike," I tell myself. I grin, then head off down a side-road.

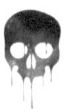

I stroke the side of the bike and whisper to it, tell it that it's mine. And really, whoever left it with the keys in the ignition on this back-road is silly. But I suppose all the Enhanced are. When the population of New Kimearo is drugged up on augmenters to make them better, no one steals anything, right?

The ex-owner's even left a helmet attached next to the bike. I put it on; it's a perfect fit. Then I take another look around.

What if it's a trap?

But it's not. I can feel it.

I hop on and start the engine. It feels good. Excellent.

I drive off, feel the wind on my face. I kick the gears up a level and roll the throttle. Exhilaration fills me, and, suddenly, I long to see the look on Rahn's face when I show up at the meeting point on this.

Only they'll be there *now*. I pull up my rough mental map of the town and think. I can get there, if I'm fast. And there's a chance they won't be completely ready to set off.

And, even if they have already left, I could tail them. Drive faster than them, herd them up, and—

And they might think you're an Enhanced and shoot you.

Hmmm. Maybe not then.

But they would recognize me, wouldn't they?

I steer the bike down the turning on the left, quickly

getting a strong feel for this new model. And, wow, isn't the engine remarkably quiet? So quiet I can still hear what's going on around me and—

Shouts fill the air.

I look up, see a man fighting another.

Fighting? The *Enhanced*? But they don't fight—they're perfect people.

I narrow my eyes and see the shock of black hair on one of the men as he turns toward me.

It's Finn.

FORTY-ONE

ADRENALINE RACES THROUGH ME AS I watch them, as I get nearer and nearer. Finn and the Enhanced. It's one on one. If it was me, I'd be able to take down the opponent easily. But Finn's not me.

I release the clutch, allowing the bike to slow a little. "Come on, hit him *there*. Punch him!" I mutter.

But Finn's not. He's throwing his hits in all the wrong places, and—

Shit. More Enhanced are coming. They know an Untamed is here.

My heart pounds, and then I move the motorbike faster toward them, bracing myself. My chest feels funny.

They look up, see me. And I'm going fast, so fast. Too fast. But I need to—and I also need to slow, grab Finn, and—

I pull on the front brake and push the back one. Something squeals, and then I'm right next to them.

"Finn! Get on!" I yell, jerking a wobbly arm out at him.

He stares at me, doesn't do anything.

"No!" an Enhanced yells.

I grab Finn, and then he's jumping on behind me. His arms lock around my ribcage, way too tightly.

He swears under his breath.

And the Enhanced shout, but I kick the bike off, and then we're going, faster and faster. I shift up through the gears, feel my eyes smarting.

"They're behind us!" Finn screeches near my ear.

I look up, but there are no mirrors on this model. Shit. I twist around, see Finn's panicked eyes, and then see the figures behind us. But they're on foot.

"Not for long," I mutter.

And I'm good at this. Good at maneuvering the bike through road after road until I'm sure we've lost them. But we can't hang around now, they'll have put out an alarm or something. A description of us. No, we need to get out of here. And, as soon as we're clear of the town, I need to check the bike for tracking devices—I can't believe I didn't think of that earlier. Basic error.

"No, go that way! The truck!" Finn yells, his voice strange.

"What?"

"Need to get the truck! Go right!"

I grit my teeth. Every part of me tells me to ignore him, to keep going, to get back to Nbutai as quickly as possible.

But if we lose the truck, I know Rahn will blame me. It'll all be my fault. And it won't just be me who he takes it out on—it'll be Elf too, because he knew I was stowing away, and Rahn will find out. So I turn right and try to ignore the way darkness swarms inside me.

I follow Finn's directions and feel him shaking against me. Shaking a lot.

"You all right?" I twist around and look at him. Redness seeps down the side of his face, and his eyes look hollow. "You're bleeding? Finn!"

"I'm fine," he says. "Keep looking the way we're going—and go that way. Left. I parked the truck over there, down there. Already packed the food in."

I do as he says, but I can't blink away the image of

the blood on his milk-white skin. It's seared on the inside of my eyelids.

We reach the truck, and I stop the bike about twenty yards away. There appears to be no one out here, but I look around, scanning every expanse of concrete and each stone block. The front of the truck peeks out from behind a clump of trees.

"Stay here," I say as we dismount, and I use the bike's side stand to keep it upright. I take my helmet off, give it to Finn. "And give me the keys for the truck."

He does, and I take the Luger out of my belt. Slowly, I check the immediate area. It appears to be clear.

I head for the truck, my heart still beating too fast. But it doesn't feel as exciting now. I'm too overloaded with adrenaline. I check all around us again, then look in the truck. Six crates of tins are in. Mostly chicken curry and chopped tomatoes. But, if I shift two of the crates over, there'll be room for the motorbike. Given how shaky Finn is now, I don't think he should be driving anything.

I climb into the cab and start the engine, drive the short distance to Finn and my bike.

I wait for Finn to get in.

He doesn't.

"Finn?"

He turns toward the cab slowly, his face suddenly green.

Then he throws up.

I leap out of the cab, leaving the engine running. I race around to him, grab him as he sways, alarm filtering through me.

"What happened?" I demand when he's finished vomiting.

He wipes the back of his hand across his mouth. Two of his fingers are bleeding as well, but not as bad as the cut on his head—which is still pouring. The blood, I need to stop it. But how? I can't think. All I can do is stare at the blood.

"They tried to grab me, and I tripped," he mumbles. "Whacked my head on the ground."

"On concrete?" My eyes widen, and I take his face in my hands, careful not to touch the gash, and look into his eyes. But what am I looking for? Hell, I can't remember what they'd look like in a concussion. "Have you got a headache?"

He rolls his eyes. "Of course I've got a headache… How are you here?"

"Doesn't matter. Just get in the cab. I'll get you back."

I guide him to the door and then help him in before jumping into the truck bed, make space for the motorbike. It's only when I've cleared the space that I realize there's no ramp in the truck. It must be at Nbutai. I curse. There's no way to load the motorbike into the bed. It's got to be about six hundred pounds, and I can lift a bike when it's on its side into the upright position. But I can't lift it *off* the ground.

My heart squeezes, and I look around. The trees. They'll have to do.

As quickly as I can, I hide the bike and the helmet. Finn watches me. When I get back in, he says he'll make sure Rahn brings a team back to collect it. I don't know how he'll *make sure* Rahn does that, but I smile.

"How are you feeling now?" I ask as I drive off. I glance at the clock on the truck's dashboard. We're way past the meeting time. Rahn's going to be angry. Very angry.

Finn grimaces. Enough of an answer.

"Why were you in the town?" I ask. "You'd already got the food."

"Needed a tin-opener." He shuts his eyes.

I sigh. I've got one on my Swiss army knife.

I tap my nails on the wheel as I drive. Dust kicks up behind us. I keep an eye out for the Enhanced.

"The tarpaulin," Finn says suddenly.

I glance at him. "What?"

"You were under the tarpaulin." He snorts, then

winces and clenches the edge of his seat so hard his knuckles go even whiter than the rest of his skin.

I breathe out hard, looking around. "This is the meeting point, right?" I ask when we get there.

Finn nods.

But there's no one here.

"We're far too late." Finn grimaces and touches the side of his head gingerly. "They'll have started walking."

"Then we'll pick them up," I say, pulling the truck over uneven ground.

I steer around the potholes and boulders as best as I can, but I scrape the underside twice as I navigate over high ridges. Then we're going faster, and—

I slam on the brakes.

Finn yells out.

I cut the engine and grab the gun from my belt.

"What is it?" He looks at me, but his eyes don't look focused.

I stare straight ahead. Two fuel cans and a shoulder bag.

I recognize the cans. They're ours. Seven filled one of them.

A rank taste fills my mouth.

"Stay here," I say to Finn as I jump out. The Luger is slippery with sweat in my hand.

I look around carefully. There's no one here now. Then I run toward the cans. They're full. I'm pretty sure one of them is definitely the one Seven filled up.

I straighten up and look ahead. There's something else up there.

Rushing noises fill my ears as I head over to the shape. A rucksack. I recognize it instantly: Seven's survival bag.

"No," I whisper, turning. I pull my dark glasses off and feel sicker. My hair falls in front of my eyes, and I shove it back.

Then I see the dark area not far away.

Blood. A splattering of it against the rocks to my

right. And a trail. I clap a hand to my mouth, try to keep calm.

The sun is bright, and I shield my eyes from it with a hand that shakes almost as much as Finn was. I look back at him in the truck, then swallow hard. I take one last look at the shoulder bag, the fuel cans, and Seven's survival bag. Then I hurry back to Finn.

"They've got Seven," I tell him as I climb into the cab. It's the only explanation. "Possibly the others too."

FORTY-TWO

"WE NEED TO GO BACK to the town," Finn says as I drive round and round the area looking for more signs. My heart beats far too fast and, twice, I think I'm going to throw up.

"No," I say. "You're injured. Too injured." I push my hair back, wish I had an elastic band for it.

I narrow my eyes, trying to see better, but my vision's blurry with horror. We haven't come across any other patches of blood, I keep reminding myself. It was the stuff Seven had that was scattered about—plus the extra fuel can. Who had that? Is it just Seven who's been caught? Has she definitely been? And the others too? They could've kept hold of their bags.

But they wouldn't, I know that.

They'd fight, and to fight, you can't be holding stuff. So maybe it was just Seven. Did she meet up with any of the others in the town—whichever of them was getting the other can filled—and collect it, then go off on her own and get caught?

But the others aren't here either.

So what happened? Were the others caught in the town, after Seven had got the extra can, and Rahn told the Enhanced where the meeting point was, and they came out, found Seven, and chased her before grabbing her? And the blood—whose blood is that? Hers?

A radio—I need a radio. Need to listen for an announcement.

But I haven't got a radio. I look at Finn. Can't see one on him.

I change direction. "I'll take you back to Nbutai," I say, and I hate saying the words. Because I'm leaving them—likely leaving them *all* in an Enhanced compound.

But I can't do a rescue mission on my own. I need people. Six people are generally needed to get one person back—and even then it doesn't always work. I swallow hard. And we've possibly got four people who've been caught. So, twenty-four of us to get them back? But we haven't got that many! We haven't. Gods.

But you're still leaving Seven and Katya and Corin and Rahn behind, in trouble.

Just like you did at D'Elinous.

The only difference is you haven't lied this time.

I push the voice away and drive faster and faster. I've got no choice. I have to get help. If I go in alone, there's no way I'll get any of them back.

But I should've stayed with Seven when I saw her. Should've stuck to my plan. Should've protected her.

But then Finn would've been captured. I groan.

And now Seven has been…and the others too? Or maybe they're trying to get her out—and, in driving away, I'm taking away their means of escape. Hell.

I swear loudly, and Finn looks at me. He still looks queasy and his eyes still don't look like they're focusing properly. He looks vague.

No. I've got to get him back to Nbutai. I don't know what's happened to the others. I can't put Finn in danger on the chance that Rahn, Katya, and Corin have launched into a rescue mission.

Déjà vu fills me as I drive back to Nbutai. It's just

like when I had Nico, Enhanced, in the back. Shit.

Got to keep breathing, I remind myself. Got to. Then I realize I should've picked up the fuel cans, the shoulder bag, and Seven's survival bag—not left them out there. But it's too late now. And the Enhanced will probably go back, claim the items.

Finn and I make it back to Nbutai in record time, and he spills out of the cab, throwing up again.

"I knew you'd gone!" Five says, her voice triumphant when she sees me. "Knew you'd defied Rahn and—" Her face falls. "What is it?"

I shake my head. "They've been caught."

We load another of the trucks as quickly as we can, making plans. I take charge because there's no one here to challenge me. Anyway, I'm a natural leader, and I'm the obvious choice.

Esther rushes over to us as we're packing more ammunition. "Come, listen to this—Yani's got the radio working, and you need to listen."

"What is it?" Elf asks.

She shakes her head, and I see she's wearing Katya's Seer pendant. Alarm filters through me. "All of you, come on—they'll repeat it and…."

And then she's running back, and we follow her to the main fire. My heart thrums.

Marouska and Yani have a radio each—though I think only Yani's one is working. They're sitting near the flames, and we all crowd around. Yani has an earpiece to his ear; his eyes are cold.

We join them.

"What is it?" I demand.

Three pushes past me, and I see he's got one of his homemade devices in his hand. An amplifier. He attaches it to the foxhole radio, and the sounds grow.

Five slumps to the floor, tears pouring down her face.

"Five?" I crouch next to her, and Elf goes to her other side, puts an arm around her. Together, we try to hold her up.

The voice is crackly. At first, I can't make the words out. But then they get stronger—or the signal, the line, whatever it is—gets stronger, and the words are clearer than we've ever heard them.

"Later today, we'll have the supervisor of New Kimearo speaking on the remarkable conversion of one formerly Untamed woman. As Anna told us earlier, this conversion is one of the first in the area where the poor, wild individual asked for help herself. She appeared neither frightened nor scared—not controlled by negative emotions—but was happy and confident. 'Certain' is the word that the supervisor used in his initial press release last night. She willingly joined us."

I go cold. Seven willingly joined them? But no—she wouldn't. And there was blood.

"Such an event could indicate that the Untamed are developing awareness of their own plight and are wanting to rectify it. Should that be the case, this woman's willingness to join us could mark a—"

"What the hell?" Elf says. "*Willing* conversion?"

Everyone starts talking.

"Shh!" Three growls. I see Paul behind him, fire in his eyes.

We fall silent. The radio hisses. Just when I'm sure the line has gone, we get a woman's voice again. A different woman, I think. At first, I think the report's moved onto a different broadcast—music or something, because the Enhanced like their music, they say music is good, calming—but then I pick out the words *daughter* and *resemblance*.

"Wait? Is that…?" Paul points at the radio, as if the device is going to tell us.

And we all listen again. Three picks up the radio

and twists something. A tinny sound follows, then crackling, interference, and….

"…*along with the capture of an Untamed girl with a strong family resemblance to the first woman… The daughter is reported to have shot Miles Forthright in a non-fatal injury… For now, her name is being withheld at the request of….*"

"Seven." I can barely breathe. "Seven's been caught." I turn and look at them. "And Katya's converted *willingly*?"

FORTY-THREE

"SHE WOULDN'T," I SAY. "KATYA wouldn't. It's not about her, that report." I shake my head firmly, as if by doing the action, I can make it true. "Can't be."

Kayden nods so hard something in his neck clicks.

Esther clears her throat, looks uncomfortable. "She was acting strangely earlier though. Before she left. She gave me her pendant." She looks toward Paul. "Shouldn't you have it?"

He turns away. "She gave it to you."

"But she hasn't left us," I say. "She'll be back...."

Katya wouldn't leave the Nbutai group without a Seer, I'm sure of that. She just wouldn't. That would be putting us all in danger. We were attacked at D'Elinous because we had no active Seer. Seers are important.

And why would she abandon her children? I breathe out hard. She loves her children, that's obvious. Maybe...maybe she saw Seven get captured and she pretended to convert, to get her daughter out?

I nod. Yes, that's more believable. Maybe it was part of the plan—and Rahn and Corin are trying to get Seven out too? But we can't count on it.

I flex my fingers.

"We need to go and get them," I say. "Rescue mission."

Yani's eyes are dark. "But if she's willingly converted, that'll make it all the more harder to get her out."

I wave away his words. "We stick together. *Always.*" I breathe out slowly, and waves of tiredness dance in front of me. "Come on. We need to get going. Same plan as before. The radio report hasn't changed anything. I'm leading the extraction team."

Most of us head out of the Sarrs' hut and toward the loaded truck.

I look at the others. "There's a good chance Rahn and Corin have been caught too—it just hasn't been announced yet. We're most likely not going to be able to extract them all. So, Katya's our priority, because she's our Seer. Okay?" I don't give anyone a chance to speak before I continue, but I see the looks that Elf and Esther give me. "Plus, whichever of them are the least-converted in their minds…any of them who help us, that are still fighting the augmenters and everything." I gesture toward the truck, hoping that will be Seven and Corin. A huge part of me doesn't want to rescue Rahn.

Sajo looks at me hard. "Are you the best person to lead an extraction? I mean, after what happened last time."

Heat floods my face. "You mean when I shot my sister because *you* knocked me?" I stare at him, parts of me going numb. "Convenient how easy it is to forget the facts, isn't it?"

And, suddenly, I want to hurt him. He's got off scot-free. No one's been questioning his suitability—yet he thinks he can do that to me, control me, make me feel bad—when he was the one who caused my sister's death. *Him.* Yes.

Not me.

But you pulled the trigger.

And my aim is good. I lift my head up higher. It was Sajo. Five was right—it wasn't my fault!

"Is this an extraction or a save-them-whichever-way-you-can mission—for the others?" Kayden asks. "Not Katya."

The thought of killing Seven or Corin makes my stomach curdle. But, no, it won't come to that.

I won't let it.

Sajo's not coming.

"Death is better than being one of them," Elf says quietly. He meets my eyes a second later. I'm glad he's coming with me.

Kayden's already climbing into the truck's cab. Three, Esther, and Yani jump into the truck bed. I look around, see Paul checking his survival bag; he's coming too.

I count on my fingers—ideally, we need more people when we're aiming to rescue more than one person. But we can't take everyone in case it all goes wrong. And the only other good choice would be Sajo, as Finn's too injured, but that's not happening. I think of the dogs, wonder if we can use them.

"Right. Have we got everything?"

Just as I'm about to climb into the driver's seat, I spot movement to my left, far, far away.

People.

On foot. In the distance….

"Shit. Are they Enhanced?"

Kayden loads his gun quickly, jumping out of the cab, and Sajo passes a firearm to me, along with a round. Irritated, I wonder if he's going to knock me again.

"Everyone—get inside." I look back toward the huts. "Now." My voice wavers.

And then it's just me, Kayden, and Sajo outside. I can hear everyone else in the Sarrs' hut and Sajo's. They're talking. I curse them under my breath.

Kayden, Sajo, and I move backward, so we're standing partly under cover. Two of the dogs suddenly run out of the hut toward us, and I grab one, pull him toward me. Kayden gets the other. Then the dogs are still, waiting, waiting with us.

I watch their ears as the two men approach. Dogs can sense things. I remember how the Sarrs' terrier barked at the Elf imposter.

But the dogs aren't reacting—not badly anyway.

"It's—it's *them*." Sajo frowns, and my eyes spin back to the figures.

I hold my breath, as if that will help me see them better. A moment later, I pick them out: Corin and Rahn.

I narrow my eyes against the dimming light, trying to pick out more figures behind them.

But they're not there.

As the two men approach, both dogs wag their tails. That makes me feel better.

We walk out to meet them. The three of us, and the two dogs. I tuck my gun into my belt.

"What's happened?" I ask the moment we're within speaking distance. "They've got Katya and Seven?"

Rahn looks around, then at the two trucks far back, behind the huts. "Is Finn not back?"

"What? Yes. The other one's parked over there."

He swears. "He could've picked us up on the way."

"They've got *Seven*?" Corin looks stricken. "What the hell?" He takes his dark glasses off and blinks in the light.

"They announced her capture on the radio."

Rahn nods. "The traitor. Like mother like daughter."

"Not a traitor. Seven *shot* one of them," I say.

"You know about Katya?" Elf asks, and I jump as I turn, see him behind me. The others are coming out of the huts now.

"We were with her when it happened," Rahn says. "She willingly chose them. Turned on us completely."

The world reels around me.

I flush hot. "No. You're wrong."

"Wait." Corin holds his hand up. Rahn glares at him. "We saw Sev at the first meeting point, and then she was supposed to meet us again at Mountain Rock, when Finn didn't show with the truck. But *she* didn't show there. And they've got her?" He swears and runs his hands through his short hair. Then he turns on Rahn. "I told you—I told you we were being followed. And sending her off on her own made her the target… We should've stuck together."

"What?" Paul roars. "You sent my daughter off on her own, knowing you were being followed?"

"We weren't bein' followed!"

Then everyone's talking at once. It's just a haze of voices, a blur of sound.

Three points suddenly in the direction of New Kimearo, and the movement somehow seems to slice through the cacophony. "We've got to go there! We've got to get her back."

"No," Rahn says. "Katya went willingly. If her mindset was converted enough that she left us for them, we've got no chance of saving her. And you don't rescue someone who's willingly joined them, betrayed us."

"I'm talking about Seven! Hell, she *shot* one—that's not a willing conversion."

I point at the loaded truck. "We were about to head out. We've got the stuff for an extraction. I've got it all organized. We need to go now."

"You've got it organized?" Rahn's eyebrows jump above his glasses. "Remember what I told you." The warning is obvious, but I ignore it.

"We're going now."

"No," Rahn says.

"What?" Corin sounds furious. "*Of course* we're going now."

Rahn shakes his head. "We've just got back. We've been walkin' ages, and had a run in with a spirit—"

"A spirit?"

"All fangs and blood, it was. Lucky it didn't feed from us, suck all our energy out."

"But we got back here quicker," Corin says. "It must've helped us—a reverse feeding?"

"We got back here quicker because we were *runnin'* from it. Nothin' to do with the spirit itself. And now we're bloody exhausted," Rahn says, but I frown. There definitely wasn't time for Rahn and Corin to run all the way from New Kimearo to here *without* spirit intervention. "Corin and I need to rest. We'll go after Seven in the morning."

"No, we have to go *now*." I fold my arms. "We don't need you two. It's me, Elf, Kayden, Paul, Three, Esther, and Yani. We've already planned this—though we thought we'd be getting you two out as well." Well, *trying*. "We can't waste time—every second is important." I exhale loudly. "If I'd known this was going to happen, that you were going to try and delay, I would've gone straight in there instead of driving Finn back. I didn't think you'd start showing your prejudice to the Sarrs in a situation like this!"

"*What*?" Rahn takes a step toward me. "You were with Finn? On the raid? In New Kimearo?"

"Yes." I glare at him. "And it's a good job too, because he'd been caught when I found him, and I got him out of there. He was injured too."

For a long moment, Rahn and I glare at each other. He's got the faded shadow of a moustache and beard, and it makes him look savage, but in an almost comical way. Like he's trying to look scary, but he isn't. Because really, he's just an old man. Nearly fifty.

"You disobeyed me," he says. "You disobeyed your leader. *Again*." He cracks his knuckles, and his previous words—*I will crush my competition*—fly through my head.

I lift my head higher. "Ever wonder why people don't listen to you, Rahn? Why they disobey you?" I point at him. "Because you get people converted. You had five in your group. And you lost Katya and Seven, and Finn was also in trouble. *I* saved him. Me."

"And you think people will trust you?" Rahn steps closer. "Trust you like how they trust a leader? Even though you've proven yourself untrustworthy, countless times. Keelie, you're mad. Actually mad."

Mad. I stiffen. No. I'm not.

"You ain't got experience," Rahn says, punctuating each word with a jab of his finger toward my face. "And now you want to go divin' straight in there, when we're not prepared, when we've not talked plans."

"Plans? It's always the same plan. *Get them out*."

"Not when her mother converted willingly. Seven could've chosen it too. We have to think of everythin' and be prepared."

"But Seven shot an Enhanced," Three interrupts.

Rahn ignores him. "Do you see, Keelie? Bein' a leader ain't all about action and rushin' in. It's plannin', it's workin' out what's best for the group, it's keepin' the group safe. You ain't got experience in that, so you don't decide what we do."

"But sittin' around is the one thing we *don't* do when one of us is taken." Hell, I've even started speaking in his clipped manner. I take a deep breath. "I've killed more Enhanced than you—I'm more experienced there."

"And you love it, don't you?" He nostrils flare. "You're psychotic."

Psychotic. For a moment, I see a crimson haze in front of me. "I am *not* psychotic."

"You love killin' though," he counters. "And that is killin' *you*—killin' your humanity. You're obsessed. You ain't well. You're mad, Keelie. *Mad*."

I grit my teeth. "I am *fine*." I flex my fingers.

"No! You're not—Keelie, we've all heard you! How you talk to yourself, tellin' yourself you're not mad. *That's* not normal."

I shake my head. "I don't do that! I'm not mad. Don't you dare say that!"

"But it runs in your family. Elf's told me. He's worried about you. We all are."

"What?" I twist around, look for my brother. Then I look at Rahn. "*You're* worried about me? Huh, that's almost funny."

He nods. "You are reckless, Keelie. And selfish. And that's why people don't trust you. That's why you shouldn't lead this mission. And that's why you need to back down. I'm not saying I'm not gettin' Seven back. But we're goin' in the mornin'. Corin and I need to sleep, and we're the strongest fighters."

"No, *I'm* the strongest."

"You're unstable. You're a liability. We can't rely on you."

I let out a high-pitched laugh. "But I'm the one who saved Finn! *Me*, Rahn—me! Where were you? Because you weren't there—you weren't looking after your people. And that's what a leader should do. A leader keeps people safe. *I* keep people safe."

The corners of Rahn's lips lift up. "Like how you kept Mila safe? And Bea?"

Cold fury bursts open inside me. How dare he. How *dare* he!

I scream at him, throw myself at him. My body hits him, hard, and he falls back.

One quick movement, that's all it takes. One movement.

I pounce on him, punch him. Blood sprays out from his nose, and I grab his shoulders, shake him, yell at him, scream at him.

Hurt him! Kill him!

And the others are shouting at me, yelling and screaming. Someone pulls the gun out of my belt—I feel it slide away, but I don't care, I don't need it. I punch Rahn again.

Hands grab me, but I turn and kick out, get Elf and then Corin. Then I'm pummeling Rahn again and—

Keelie!

Mila's voice.

I freeze.

And Corin drags me away. I don't fight him. Just stay on the ground. Hell, I attacked Rahn. *Rahn*. And part of me wants to laugh and laugh and never stop laughing.

"I am *not* havin' you in my group," Rahn snarls, getting up. "You're banished!"

"Banished?" I snort and let out a strange laugh. "You're not *banishing* me."

I stare at him. He can't really be. Not after his speech before, when he said that we have to stick together, that Untamed don't survive out there on their own.

His upper lip curls. "I most certainly am. I will not have you in my group. I warned you. I have given you plenty of chances, but you're wild." He rubs at his jaw.

"No!" I yell. "You need me on this mission. I'm coming! I have to get my sister out."

"Seven isn't your sister, Keelie." Rahn's words are icy.

I stare at him blankly. Then emotion kicks in. "You still need me!" I yell, fighting against Corin. Three steps in, grabs my arm, stops me from punching Corin. "I'll be there! I will! I'm coming with you! I don't care what you say. I'm getting her back!" I turn, twist, try to see Elf. But he's just staring at me. Why isn't he backing me up?

"Take her to her hut," Rahn says.

"What?" I burst out. "Thought I was being banished?" I laugh manically. "See, you can't even make your mind up! What kind of leader does that make you? A *leader* needs to be sure! And why would you want me in my hut if I'm banished *and* mad? It doesn't make sense. *You* don't make sense, Rahn. Can't you see?"

Fury passes over Rahn's face for a moment. "I'm banishin' you tomorrow—*after* we've got Seven back. Not when you're in this state. You'd probably turn up at New Kimearo anyway, wreckin' havoc and ruinin' our plans as we try to rescue Seven. No, if you're goin' to be there, it's on my terms. Got it? My rules. You obey me. And if you so much as set a foot out of line tomorrow, I'll kill you."

There's a sharp, collective inhalation of breath.

My eyes widen, and I stare at him, sure I can't have heard correctly. "I'm on the rescue mission?" Even though I'm *untrustworthy*?

Rahn nods. "Your last *ever* mission. Because, I mean it, afterward, you are *out* of my group. You're to go far, far away. And if I ever see you again 'round here, I'll kill you. Got it? Tomorrow's the last day I want to see you."

"Rahn," Elf begins. "This is—"

"Don't," Rahn snaps. "Just take her away now. And make sure she doesn't get out of her hut. Keep watch."

"What?" I stare at him. "You're imprisoning me?"

He wouldn't. Wouldn't do that. This is….

"Yes," Rahn says. "I am." He flicks his fingers at Sajo. "And check her for more weapons. Make sure she ain't goin' to slit my throat in the night."

"Slit your throat?" I raise my eyebrows. "I wouldn't kill you!"

"*Really*?" he says, dryly. "Well, that's news to me."

FORTY-FOUR

THEY SIT OUTSIDE OUR HUT with loaded guns.

"I'm not mad!" I yell at them. "You don't need to be guarding me! You need to be out there, getting Seven and Katya back! Can't you see what Rahn's doing? He's making you focus on me instead of what you should be doing!"

"Keelie, calm down." Elf touches my shoulder gently, and I flinch. I'd forgotten he's here too. It's just the two of us. "Rahn could change his mind at any moment about you coming tomorrow."

I pull myself away from him. The traitor. "You didn't even back me up. *Twins of the stars.* Yeah, right."

"Keelie—your behavior...."

"My behavior *what*?" I snarl.

Elf shakes his head. "You're exhausted. You need to sleep. You need to be prepared and... And, Keelie, I don't like this. It doesn't make sense, Rahn letting you go tomorrow. Despite what he said."

"It's because I'm the best fighter."

But my brother doesn't look convinced. "He's got something else in store." He exhales hard. "I'm sure of it. Look, just make sure you've got a gun on you at all times tomorrow. I'll stick with you too, but I wouldn't be surprised if Rahn attempts something."

I snort. "I can handle myself."

Elf nods. "Let's hope so." He lets go of a shaky breath. "We'd better sleep. We need to be in top condition tomorrow."

I nod, feel strange. "You'd better be careful too," I say after a moment, remembering Rahn's threat from before. "And Five."

And Seven.

Elf nods, says they're always careful.

We settle down. In the darkness, I stare across at Bea's bed. It's still there. My sister. My sister who left because of me.

I'm supposed to protect my sisters.

But I didn't.

"I should've stayed with Seven," I whisper, imagine my words tangling round and round and round and round, until they take on a shape, a form. They look like Seven. She stares at me, blinking. "I'll make sure you don't end up like Mila," I promise her.

I try to keep breathing evenly, but it feels like there are invisible hands squeezing my neck.

If I lose Seven as well, I'm not sure I'll be able to live with myself.

By the morning, part of me expects Rahn to have changed his mind about me coming on the rescue mission, but he hasn't. Just rounds me up with the others he's chosen and gives us all a quick briefing.

We nod, and then we're going through the finer details. But the plan is always the same. The distraction team distracts. The extraction team extracts. The backup team backs up. And we get our person out.

Now we just wait to hear who's on which team.

"You're on distraction, Keelie." Rahn points at me. "You're the primary distracter. And Elf and Yani will be your backup. Corin and I will do the extraction, with Esther and Kayden on hand for our backup. If need be, we'll set off a purple flare to call you lot for more backup, in which case Keelie continues distracting, and Elf and Yani come to us."

Distraction? And two backup teams?

"But I'm our best fighter," I say. "I need to be on the extraction. Anyone can do the distraction."

"What's the problem?" Rahn's voice is blunt, and it reminds me of his earlier warning. I have to obey him. "You love puttin' yourself in danger. You've got the most dangerous job, drawing all the Enhanced out to you. Thought you'd be thrilled."

My eyes narrow. The plan is never for one person to be doing the distraction for a major operation like a rescue. In those, we have to work together—it's not like a small distraction that one person can pull off on his or her own, only needing to distract one Enhanced, while others steal a car or a set of keys. I frown.

Then I get it: Rahn doesn't want me surviving this.

He wants me captured?

Or dead.

I grit my teeth as I listen to him. He wants me to distract? Fine. I'll distract. I'll be *very* distracting.

As soon as he's finished, I head back to my hut and sort through all my clothes. I find my shortest shorts and put them on my bed, then grab the hoody I'm looking for. Neon orange and fitted. I smile as I pull it over my black T-shirt and replace my jeans with the shorts. The hoody's a little tight around my bust, but I know I look *distracting*. Even the Watcher Doll, from its place by Bea's calendar tells me that I do. I finish the look with sturdy, black boots with slight wedge heels and do the laces up tightly.

I smile as I head back out.

"Keelie?"

Five's tear-stained face wobbles in front of me. She blinks at me, her gaze raking over my appearance.

"Get Seven back," she whispers.

I take hold of her hands quickly, and then she's in my arms, crying gut-wrenching sobs. I hold her tightly.

"I will," I say.

Five and I break apart, and she disappears into her hut.

Rahn shouts for us to depart and gives me a strong look when he sees my outfit. Doesn't say anything though. One point to me.

"Her mother's a Seer," Esther says, climbing into the truck bed. She's dressed all in black, like the others. "So Seven might have a strong mind too. Able to resist for longer."

"Let's hope so." I breathe deeply. Seven's spent a night there already. We should've gone yesterday.

"The cut-off isn't until the seventh day," Esther says. "We've got plenty of time, and we'll do it. We'll get her back."

Corin marches over with two bags, dumps them in the truck bed. He hasn't spoken a word.

A few minutes later, we leave: me, Rahn, Corin, Yani, Elf, Kayden, and Esther. Seven of us to get the seventh Sarr back. For some reason, that seems important to me. Very important.

Rahn drives, and I am in the cab with him. Just the two of us. Probably so I can't start conspiring with the others. We crash over the uneven terrain. The headlights jolt, and, after about twenty minutes, one of them flickers.

Pain rumbles in my chest.

"I never could work out what Lìxúe saw in Owen— your father," Rahn mutters. "She would've been better off with…."

My eyes narrow. "With what? *You?*"

Rahn's expression darkens; suddenly, I'm glad I can't see his eyes. They'd burn me.

"With anyone *but* Owen. And I would've raised Bea

as my own if…."

"As your own?" I stare at him. "You've always treated Bea awfully."

He exhales hard, then curses, tilting his face to the sky. Then he looks back at me, staring again. Trying to see my mother in me?

Great.

Just great.

I feel my skin crawl under his gaze. I turn a heavy glare on him and lean back into the seat, deeper, let the headrest cradle my head.

"Just tryin' to be friendly," Rahn mutters. "There's no need to sulk."

Friendly? Huh.

"I'm not sulking," I say.

"You're always sulkin' because you always think it's a competition." He shifts the truck into a lower gear as the terrain gets steeper. The engine groans.

The land looks different now. More orange than usual. Brighter. I squint, bring a hand to my eyes.

Sudden darkness.

Someone screams. High-pitched and blood-curdling.

Rahn slams the brakes, his body jolting.

I flinch, turn, look through the criss-cross fine mesh over the back window, look for the others, and—

They're looking back at me. Esther's eyes are wide.

"What the hell?" Rahn snaps, then revs the engine loudly. He turns, looks at me. "I didn't do that."

"I know," I say. "You don't scream like that." My hand is already on my door's handle.

"No—it wasn't me who braked. I didn't move my foot."

In the truck bed, Corin and Kayden are shouting.

I jump out, and the air's suddenly cold, the wind roaring. "What's happening?"

The scream slices through the air again, and the engine stutters.

I feel my blood get heavier as I stare at the other

villagers. No one here is screaming.

Rahn gets out, walks around the truck slowly. The high-pitched scream sounds again, and it's so loud, it swamps the engine. And it keeps going. It doesn't stop.

"We ain't run someone over, have we?"

"There wasn't anyone there." I shake my head, and—

What if….

No.

I crouch down. The shrieking continues.

"What are you doing?" Corin jumps down next to me, and dust flies up, gets in my eyes, stings them.

I swear, blinking hard, then rub at them.

Corin puts a hand on my shoulder.

"We need to look under the truck," I say, and—

"No," he shouts. "Rahn, cut the engine first. If there's—"

"Is it a spirit?" Esther's voice is small. "Has it got in the engine?"

"Impossible," Rahn says, back on his way to the driver's door. But the look on his face says that he *doesn't* think it's impossible.

We all stare at each other.

"We didn't see a spirit," Rahn says slowly, then gets back in.

"Good," Elf says.

The wind picks up, and the high-pitched screaming gets higher still. I groan, clutching my head.

"Keelie?"

"If it's in the engine, having the truck running could be hurting it," Esther shouts. Then she looks confused. "Can spirits get hurt?"

I don't know. I press my lips together, pull my hair back from my face. I'm sweating. Sweating so much.

"Turn the engine off then," Elf says.

And Rahn does and—

And then there's no more.

FORTY-FIVE

A TREMOR RUNS THROUGH RED'S *body.*

I stare at him.

"Run!" someone screams at me, but I can't tell whom it is. Can't see them.

But the voice is right. I need to run, have to run, have to get away.

And so I do.

And I'm running, and everything's pounding.

And my parents, they're ahead. They're running through the trees. Mila's cries wrap around me. We're all here. All of us. Our family, surviving. A unit. The only survivors.

I cry out, and my father looks back, sees me.

And then I'm in his arms, and there's blood in his moustache and something broken in his eyes. He points with his other hand back toward the hut. "Is anyone else alive?" His voice is low as he sets me down on the woodland floor.

My mother looks panicky, and she flaps her hands around her head as she turns.

"Keelie!" My father snaps his fingers in front of my face. I refocus on him. "Is anyone else alive at D'Elinous?"

Alive....

I turn. Dry leaves crackle under my feet. Red's body is

visible by the last hut. Just the shape of it. Then I think I
see him move. His head. But no, it's too dark to see. And he
didn't move. He's dead. The blood fanned out around him.

But—

"Keelie?" He starts to step away from me. Toward the
village. "If someone's alive still, I have to help. Fight, help
them, not flee."

He's going to go back.

No. He can't. There are too many Enhanced there now.
Far too many—we'd get caught or killed and—

But the others! They need help!

"There's no one!" I cry, the words escaping me. I grab
hold of his shirt, realize how much I'm trembling. My
bottom lip quivers.

My father flinches. "No one?"

I shake my head. In the corner of my vision, I see Red's
body. And it is a body, I tell myself. He's dead. He's not
there, not watching this, not hearing.

But his eyes asked for help!

And I didn't, because an Enhanced One came after me,
and I got away—and I ran to the edge of the woods. Not to
Red. But he's gone now.

"Owen, there are two Enhanced coming!" my mother
shouts. "We have to go!"

My father pulls me closer. "You're sure there's no one
left?"

Red's there!

But we're left. Us. And I have to focus on the people that
are here, Untamed, now. My family. And the Enhanced are
coming after us. My father can't run toward them.

And I look back at Red's body and at the Enhanced women
heading toward us, and I tell myself I've got no choice. He
can't have survived. It's stupid going back.

But other villagers are still alive—I know that. I heard
their screams. They're still alive, still fighting.

But I can't lose my father. He can't go back there.

"Owen, they're coming now! We've got to run!"

"Keelie?"

I shake my head. "There's no one left. We have to go."

A DANGEROUS GAME

I open my eyes slowly, and every part of me groans. Light fractures toward me. For a moment, I feel sick as I recall the flashback dream.

That lie. No… But why have I revisited it now? Hell. I'm lying down.

Lying next to the truck, my cheek pressed into grit and dust and red rock.

My breath hitches, and I stand up slowly, confused. I look around. "The spirit…it's gone…."

"Keelie?"

The voice comes from my right, and I turn. See the others. They're waking up now too. Rahn gets out of the cab, looks groggy.

It's silent. No wailing now. No high-pitched shrieking.

"Everyone all right?" Rahn's voice is dull. My ears crackle.

We all say that we are, but we sound different.

"What the hell happened?"

"The spirit…."

"What?" Corin looks at me. "The spirit…" He trails off.

Esther frowns, then looks alarmed. "Has it fed from us?"

And, suddenly, we're all looking at our arms, our legs—every bit of bare skin. Corin pulls his shirt off. Elf and Yani do the same. I push my sleeves up, examining my arms. They don't look any different. There are no marks. Would there be? I run my fingers over my skin, feeling for lacerations—or anything— that might not be visible to the eye.

But I don't find anything. As far as I can tell, my body's the same as always.

But your mind?

For some reason, I hear the question in Caia-Lu's voice. Then I shudder. I try to think. How *do* I feel? I stretch my neck a little.

If anything, I feel stronger. More suited for a fight. The spirits did that? To help us? Given us strength—for a reason? A reverse feeding, like Corin said before….

"I think we're okay," I say. But I don't like it. Spirits are supposed to be bad. Even the good ones.

But they used to help the Untamed a lot—that's what Caia-Lu said. And they helped me find Elf.

"We all just fell asleep," Kayden says, yawning. "All of us." He frowns and looks up at the sky. "Was that spirit sent after us?"

Corin clears his throat. "Sent after us? Why?"

"To delay us getting to New Kimearo? To stop us getting Seven back? We all fell asleep."

Elf points at the sky. "But now it looks earlier than it was?"

"We've gone back in time?" I frown. Spirits can distort time. When they killed my uncle, they messed with time then. Made the scene play over and over. And now we've gone back in time?

"So they're making sure we get to Seven in time," Corin says. "Giving us an extra couple of hours?"

"The spirits *are* mostly supposed to be on our side," Esther whispers.

But her words make me uncomfortable, and the back of my neck prickles.

"What is it?" Yani looks at me. "You look like you've thought of something?"

I shake my head. "No. I haven't."

"Let's get goin'," Rahn says.

We do.

And, soon, we see the town, down there, in the little valley of the Titian Mountains. Sand-colored blocks with spider-wires strung between them.

New Kimearo.

I feel too hot, like there's too much heat in my body making me fuzzy, trying to discourage me. The color

A DANGEROUS GAME

of my hoody makes me feel sick now.
   My shoulders tighten.
   You mustn't go to any towns or cities.
   But I am.
   And I'm not coming back.

FORTY-SIX

IN THE END, I TELL myself to forget Katya's warning, that it doesn't mean anything. That Seers can't really see events that far in the future. No, Seers see *imminent* events. That's all, and I push any contradicting thoughts aside, insist that Caia-Lu was just trying to scare me as well. That it's not real. It's just a coincidence both Seers picked on the same thing: my death.

And this mission, it won't end with my death. Because I'm good. I'm careful.

Rahn drives us as close as he can, then he parks the truck in one of our less-used places, and we check the immediate area. We're a fair distance from where we believe Seven was captured—where I found the cans and bags—as it's likely the Enhanced will be paying close attention to that area now. They'll probably have claimed the bags and fuel by now.

I look around. I'm buzzing to get started. To get in there and get Seven back.

And Katya, I remind myself.

Corin grabs a pair of dark glasses from the truck. The rest of us have ours on now. I tie my hair back into a tight bun, high up on my head, and watch as survival bags are handed out. I shake my head when Kayden tries to give me mine. The bag is black, and I need the neon orange of my hoody to be visible from all angles—plus, I'm likely going to be running and climbing. I'll need to be able to move freely and fast. Rahn just shrugs when I explain it, and Elf says he'll take the gear from my bag in his.

"Remember," Rahn says, handing a radio each to Elf, Esther, and Corin. "Seven could already have been mind-converted. If that's the case and it's too dangerous, I'll set off the red flare. Remember, the purple flare is for when we need help. Red means abandon. We cut our losses, and we get out if we need to. All of us."

I get the impression that, under his dark glasses, he looks at everyone but me.

Because he wouldn't mind if I didn't come back. And isn't that his plan, having only me running the distraction?

"Everyone ready?" Rahn asks. He hands me a stopwatch on a long, looped string. "Keelie, don't start the distraction until thirty minutes in. We need time to get in place and locate her. We don't know how long you'll be able to distract the Enhanced and leave the compound free for us once we start, so we absolutely need to be ready."

"I can distract for as long as needed." I keep my voice cool as I put the stopwatch's cord around my neck.

"Once we're finished, one of us will come and find you, signal to you, and Elf and Yani, if they're still with you, and we'll get us all out," Rahn says, but we all know that the plan often changes at the end of a rescue depending on whether other gunshots have sounded or not. Mostly it's improvising and doing what you think is best at the end. "And, remember, if Seven's gone too far, then we leave her. No arguments." He rubs his hands together for a moment. "I ain't got a good feelin' about this."

I resist the urge to say something. Nothing like a reassuring leader.

Rahn makes sure we've all got weapons—though he doesn't look happy as he watches me tuck a Luger into my belt—and we set off in two groups. Corin, Rahn, Kayden, and Esther walk faster than us, and they head more to the left. Elf, Yani, and I are to skirt around, avoiding the main conversion compound, and then, when it's time, I'm to separate from the guys and draw the Enhanced away from the conversion area and toward me, toward a new location.

We don't say anything as we walk. I listen to my heart pounding and start to feel the usual thrill in me—only it's different, and I can't work it out. We seem to get to the town line too quickly, and then suddenly we're inside New Kimearo, navigating the streets.

We skirt around several buildings, and I catch a glimpse of our reflections in a shop window. Part of me smiles. We look good: Elf, Yani, and I. Ready for action. And my legs, they look *amazing*.

I smile slightly.

"This way," I say, looking around. Everything looks duller thanks to the glasses—it's not an especially bright morning—but I see the clock tower ahead. It's one of the ones that shows the date as well as the time.

I stare at the date and frown. It can't be. My head whirls. That's not today's date...that...that's a date *next week*... Bea's calendar is up in our hut; I saw it before I left, saw this month's page, and we're —

Why do the Enhanced Ones have the wrong date up? One that's... I count on my fingers... Six days ahead?

Unless the spirits have... Hell. They mess with time. We haven't gone back in time...we've gone *forward*.

Shit.

I turn, ready to show Elf and Yani, but they've walked past. Neither of them noticed?

I catch them up quickly, desperately trying to think.

I remembered the date from Bea's calendar correctly, didn't I? And we left Nbutai the day after Seven's capture…and we've gone forward six days in our journey here? So she's been here a week—is that right? My head pounds. And Katya too… A *week*.

My chest tightens. Is that too long? A week's the cut-off point, isn't it? So it'll be fine, right? We can still try on the seventh day…still get them back.

But what if Rahn sees the date, decides we're too late, and abandons the extraction—because it's any excuse with him to leave Seven, isn't it?

And Seven will have thought we weren't coming for her. And how Untamed will she even be now? A week is the max—but that's for the strongest ones… We could be too late.

The commentary in my head won't shut up, and I stare ahead, barely taking in my surroundings.

If we've really lost that amount of time in our journey here, will the same number of days have passed at Nbutai too? Are they worrying about us, sending a team out? My head feels like it's going to explode, and I feel sick.

"Kee." Elf's voice is low, and I jump. "How long do we give them to get in place?"

I look around quickly. "Rahn said thirty minutes from set-off. They should be be ready by then." I lick my lips, wonder whether to say anything about the time, the days. But I don't want to make them nervous. And we'll get Seven back. And Katya. We will. I nod. "I'm going to distract from the gardens. Come on."

The three of us head over there. It's deep in the middle of New Kimearo—a predominantly walled area of eight acres, split into various gardens and courtyards—but I know there's a direct path from the conversion compound to it, providing an easy route to draw the Enhanced along. We only ever visit the gardens when we're distracting or checking for new distraction locations when we've got spare time on raids.

"Do you think Rahn *will* use a purple flare?" Yani asks just as the welcome sign for the gardens comes into view. The gate's open as always, and I look up at the walls. Red brick. "It's a sure way to draw the Enhanced Ones' attention to them." He shakes his head. "If he has to use a flare, I hope it's a red one, then we can all get out as quickly as possible."

Annoyance flares through me at his use of *Enhanced Ones*. That's a sure way to draw attention to *us*. He should use the name they have for themselves—*the Chosen Ones*—when we're out here.

"It's just the emergency protocol," I say. "Same as always. He'll only set them off if it's a last resort to try and save us. And, anyway, he won't need to signal for help. Seven's strong, she won't be mind-converted already." Even after a week? "And I'll be distracting them," I add. "They won't get caught."

Elf grunts. "They'd better not. Because I don't want to leave you without backup." He shakes his head. "The three of us should be doing the distraction *together*, not just you."

Yani nods.

"Hey, I'm the only one wearing neon." I let out a small laugh.

"You don't need to look distracting to *be* the distraction," Elf mutters.

"It's got to help," I say.

But he's right: it's safer if a group works together for a distraction. That's what Corin's team did when we were trying to rescue Mila. But Rahn must be anticipating trouble, and it's the only way for him to be sure to have extra backup—and I know he's confident in my abilities and that I won't need Yani and Elf helping me. Pride swirls in me, and I hold my head up higher. Out of all the Nbutai villagers, I'm sure I'm the only one who can pull off a distraction for such a big mission single-handedly. Hell, even Yani had trouble doing a distraction on his own when I was getting the keys from the dealership office, and that was just distracting one person.

"We need to go in, check the gardens," I say. "Check nothing's changed in the layout. You go left at the gate. I'll go right. And you need to find a high vantage point to watch me from—on the very rare possibility that I need you for backup. But make sure you're near an exit in case Rahn needs you. Meet back here in ten, and we'll have time to finalize my plan."

"Be careful," Elf whispers.

"You too."

We part.

I already know the rough layout of the gardens and ornamental courtyards. It usually only has few Enhanced patrolling it compared to other parts of New Kimearo, so it's a great place to draw more of the enemy too.

Many paths wind through the different courtyards and gardens here—lots of routes to be chased down, but I know which ones connect up with which. Shrubbery, hedges, and trees provide plenty to hide behind. I look up at one particular tree. It's about forty feet tall and doesn't look like a native species. I could climb up there and fire the gun from high up, giving myself a good vantage point. The Enhanced would flock around the base of it—but then my escape would be limited. Still, I'd have a gun; they wouldn't climb up to meet me. Last resort then…perhaps only if Rahn sets off the flare. Then Elf and Yani could go on ahead and this could be my new distraction.

I store that info as I move on.

The brick walls only encase three sides of the gardens, and, at the back, there's a pretty open field-like space that leads to a gray-colored building a few hundred yards beyond. The inside of that building is like a maze. Hundreds of small corridors and intersections. Leading the Enhanced in a dance around the gardens first seems like the obvious choice. Then I can make my exit via the building and its network of corridors— discard my not-so-subtle hoody so I'll be dressed all in black like the others, and let my hair down—and then meet up again with Elf and Yani. The Enhanced will still be looking for me then, and, by that time, Rahn's team should have Seven. If not, I could climb the tree, do that plan.

But what about Katya?

I press my lips together. Can Elf, Yani, and I go for her? Head over to the conversion compounds while the Enhanced are still looking for me in the gardens— or the maze-buildings—and get her out too?

It's a possibility. But it won't work if Rahn sets the flare off. And it will be going against his plan. But that thought only makes me more determined.

I glance at the stopwatch. I've still got a couple minutes before I'm to meet Elf and Yani for final comments on the distraction plan. I head down the path quickly—it will loop back on itself for a moment— and take stock of everything I notice. More flowers. A water-feature. A sundial. Several small saplings tied to canes with red twine.

And Mila.

I inhale sharply and freeze as I stare at her. She's sitting in the middle of the path, running her fingers through the gravel. Her gaze is intent, and her eyes are Untamed.

Snakes of ice slither through me. My chest shudders.

No, it's not her.

She looks up.

Keelie, she says.

My mouth drops open, and I feel the cold breeze against my bottom teeth.

"I'm not mad," I whisper. "Not mad. Not mad. Not mad."

I turn quickly, heart pounding. Mustn't look at her. She's not real. She's trying to distract me.

Keelie! Don't!

I walk away as quickly as I can. My hands feel clammy, and I clench them into fists, then wipe them against my dark jeans. Just need to keep breathing, need to stay calm, mustn't let my mind distract me.

Trails of anger whisper around me. My skin feels too hot, like it's been taken off, heated up, and then placed over me.

My hand finds its way to the Luger in my belt, hidden under my hoody. Its presence is reassuring— as is the knife in the pocket of my shorts.

Keelie! No!

I walk faster and faster, until I see them: Elf and Yani.

They're talking, their heads together, as they look left. Elf nods, and then Yani steps forward a little, looking farther down the pathway that leads to the next ornamental garden. My brother points at something, and both of them nod again.

But neither looks toward the three Enhanced men who are watching them.

FORTY-SEVEN

I STEP AGAINST THE SOFT leaves, melting into the hedge, watching. My heart pounds as I peer through the foliage. Elf and Yani are still oblivious. I need to signal to them. Need them to look toward me.

And why the hell haven't they noticed they're being watched?

Come on! I will them to look around.

Neither does.

I shift my weight slightly, stretching up so I get a better view of the Enhanced. Three men, crouching about fifty yards from Elf and Yani, and downhill too. Two look like they're my sort of age, one's a little younger. They haven't made any moves yet toward Elf and Yani, and I can't see any communication devices on them. But it's three against two—if I don't get involved.

A quick look around tells me they're the only Enhanced here at the moment.

One of them stands up. The light flashes through the leaves as he takes a glass vial with red liquid from his pocket.

My heart pounds.

Two options. Yell out to Elf and Yani—and risk drawing more Enhanced here. Or sneak over there, startle the Enhanced, and kill them with minimal noise.

The first would mean the Enhanced would know there were three of us, and it could mean Rahn would have no backup, as well as making it difficult for me to carry out the distraction.

The second would be the least disruptive to Seven's rescue.

Treading carefully and keeping light on the balls of my feet, I make my way around, sticking close to the shrubbery line. Leaves tickle my face, and something cracks underfoot. I wince, my eyes on the Enhanced the whole time. The one standing, with the augmenter, hasn't moved, but they're all definitely watching my brother and Yani.

I inch closer, skirting around the Enhanced a little, so their backs are to me, and listen hard. I pick out the word *Untamed* in their hushed whispers, but the rushing in my ears prevents me from hearing the other words.

My hand finds my gun, and I debate on pulling it out. If I need to shoot, I will. But it will start the distraction, and the stopwatch tells me it's too early at the moment—Rahn's team may not be in place yet. I edge closer and closer to the Enhanced. More saplings tied to canes with red twine line this path. I stare at the red twine for a moment.

Quickly, I rip two lots of the twine away, and the saplings bounce toward me. The twine comes away in loops, and I grab my Swiss army knife and cut above each knot so I've got two lengths.

Then I make my way closer still to the enemy, pocketing my knife once more. My heart pounds deliciously. And it's just like before, when my siblings and I were traveling. Any feelings of pain in my body melt away, and I feel strong. Invincible.

"The signal's not good here," one of the Enhanced

says. So they have got a communication device?

I am feet behind them. I flex my fingers. They're not clammy now. Carefully, I wrap the two lengths of twine together, making one thicker piece, and hold an end in each hand. My breathing increases. The gun in my belt is reassuring.

"But I won't need it," I whisper—whisper so quietly. *Join me*, Mila replies. *A bullet for each of us.*

I take a deep breath and lunge forward, throwing the length of twine around the neck of the youngest Enhanced man. He cries out, but I'm fast, and I yank him back, the twine cutting off his squawk.

The other two spur into action, turning toward me. I kick out at one—a deft hit to the lower abdomen that doubles him over, moaning—while still yanking the youngest one back by his neck. As the second man goes down, I pull hard on the twine around the first, bracing his struggling body against my own. I pull tighter and tighter. He splutters and splutters, trying to turn.

The third is close now, and I kick him back, but not with as much force as I did the second man because most of my energy is going into strangling the first man.

"Don't make a sound!" My voice is beautifully calm as I address the third. He's recovered from my kick, but hasn't made another move toward me. The augmenter is in his hands still.

A glance upward tells me that Yani and Elf haven't noticed the commotion. From this angle, they're farther away than I thought, and the breeze must be carrying these sounds in the opposite direction. Or maybe the plants are insulating. My pulse races. I can't help but smile. I'm *good*. This feels *good*.

The second man's still down, and the first man finally goes limp against me, no longer spluttering and wheezing. I lighten the pressure of the twine around his neck, use my fingers to check for a pulse—can't find one. Then I punch him hard in the side of his face to be sure. He slides down to the ground, and I spring toward the third, yanking the twine with me.

"No, please!" he yells, fear written all over his face. Fear that he shouldn't feel. Oh, what a lie that is.

What a lie they are!

His voice is loud, and, if I wasn't so fired up with adrenaline, I'd wince. Instead, I leap toward him, pulling my Swiss army knife out again and flicking it open. He turns, starts to run, but I'm fast.

I grab him.

"No, no—"

I slice the blade across his neck, aiming for the jugular vein. Blood spurts out, and I let him fall. Then I stab him in the stomach for good measure.

Two down. One to go.

"Help me!" a voice yells out. The second Enhanced. He's crumpled on the ground still, clutching his stomach, his face a brilliant shade of crimson.

I bare my teeth as I advance. I'll strangle this one with my bare hands. No twine or knife needed—I shove them into my pockets.

"Keelie!" Elf's voice.

I look up, see him yelling at me from the other side of the hedge, his face broken up by foliage, and—

Footsteps, behind me.

More of them?

I turn, knife ready, and—

"Use your gun!" Elf yells, and I could curse him, revealing himself to be Untamed like that. "The gun!"

But, no, I can't. It's not time for the distraction yet, is it? How much time has passed? I go to grab the stopwatch—but its cord isn't around my neck. It's gone? Lost in the fight? I swear loudly. How much time has passed? But I can't shoot now; it's better to leave it longer—to be sure Rahn's team is in place.

"Keelie!" Elf screams. I can't see Yani next to him— at least one of them has got sense.

Keelie! Mila echoes.

I turn and face the Enhanced. I've got the twine. I've

got the knife. They're both in my pockets. I can use both of those. My heart pounds. My lungs feel strange. My breaths make scratchy noises against my throat.

This is it. *Yes*. Adrenaline dances through me. Eight Enhanced, advancing toward me. Some look cautious. Some look determined.

And I've killed two without the gun.

I can take them on. I can do it easily.

And it's just like when I was eleven. When I was living to kill them—and the desire never left me, it was suppressed. Suppressed by Rahn; he was controlling me, stopping me from doing what I love.

And killing Enhanced is what I love: killing them with knives and twine, killing them with my hands, wrapping my fingers around their throats, squeezing the life out of them, like how they try to squeeze the humanity out of mankind—how they're doing it, destroying us all, replacing our genuineness with their artificiality, thinking they know what's best for us.

But no, they don't.

Fire burns through me.

Yes.

Run! Mila yells.

Start the chase early? Have them chasing me? My head pounds. Yes, I could...and then I can fire some shots when it's time for the actual distraction—draw even more after me. Lead them away so I can kill them all.

I grin.

"Your gun!" Elf screams, and then he's pushing through foliage and trampling on flowers. He hurtles toward me.

"What are you doing?" I scream. "Get away! This is the distraction!"

"I'm not letting you kill yourself!" he yells.

I pull my gun out, direct it at him. "Stay away!"

For a moment, Elf looks shocked. Then he pulls his own gun out, and I stare at it. All that time he was yelling at me to use my gun, and he had one? But thank the Gods he didn't use it!

"You can't shoot now! It's too early!" My whole body shakes and pounds, threatens to burst with adrenaline. I need to do something. I need to use it up. Need to fight, need to kill.

Kill....

I turn, look at the Enhanced and—shit—they're so close. Too close.

Run! Mila begs.

"Come on!" I scream at the eight Enhanced. And why aren't they moving quickly toward me now? They're just walking, tense and careful and scared. Because they know I'm a threat. We may be low in numbers, but we do what they despise: we kill. We're *bad*.

"Put the weapons down, Untamed Ones," the nearest Enhanced shouts.

I wave the gun around. "Run after me, and I won't shoot any of you," I say. The Enhanced who I kicked— and was going to strangle with my hands—is starting to crawl away. I see him moving slowly.

"Keelie, no!" Elf says, flicking the safety off his gun. He lines it up with the nearest Enhanced.

My mouth dries. "No guns!" I yell at him. But—oh hell. He's going to shoot.

Think!

I point at Elf and look at the Enhanced. "Leave him alone, chase me, and neither of us will shoot you!" I yell. Before anyone can reply, I turn, energy flooding me. And I run. "Come on!"

I sprint as fast as I can, kicking up gravel and dirt as I tear across the gardens. I turn my head, see some of the Enhanced coming after me. *Yes*. But not all of them. Two are looking at Elf. A stationary stand-off.

My brother lifts his gun.

No.

No.

No. He can't! Rahn's team might not be ready—will they? I don't know, has it been thirty minutes yet? I try to look again for my stopwatch—in case it's just got tangled in my hoody or something—but my vision's blurring, and everything's foggy. And where's Yani? Has he gone? I pray that he has, that he's hiding, remaining undetected. He's the only one who can help Rahn's team now that Elf's revealed himself.

"Chase me!" I scream at them. "Come on, run! All of you! He's going to shoot you! I won't! Come on! Chase me! Catch me!"

More power sets in.

They all chase me.

Alarm bells go off in my head about the danger I'm in. But I like danger. I like it a lot. And I'm doing what Rahn wanted—he wanted me to do the most dangerous task of the mission. And, when it's time, when I draw *all* the other Enhanced of New Kimearo after me and away from Rahn's team, away from Seven, it'll be even more dangerous. I promised not to shoot them, but I'll still kill them…later.

I love the way the word *dangerous* tastes. I want to swallow it. I want it to be part of me always.

This is what being alive feels like.

This is better than riding my motorbike.

This is better than fighting the Nbutai villagers.

This is better than sleeping with Red.

This is better than just ambushing and killing Enhanced men and women.

Being chased.

This is freedom—I'm not tied down, not bound by rules. And I'll have no people after this; I'll be on my own. A butterfly. *Free.*

I'll be responsible for myself, no one else.

I'll be able to do what I want.

And *this* is what I want to do.

I scream at more Enhanced as I pass them, and they look at me, shock on their faces. Shock! I burst out laughing, and it slows me, but more adrenaline kicks in. I duck under a low branch, wave my gun about to attract more attention.

A DANGEROUS GAME

Shouts fill the way behind me, my own personal tail.

I keep running, diving down new pathways. Gravel sprays up everywhere. I slip, skid on some mud, and fly forward. For a moment, I think I'm going to fall, but my free hand catches onto a branch—ripping my bandage off in the process—and I hurl myself forward, land on my knees, on grass.

I turn, jumping up. The Enhanced are still coming. *Yes*.

My heart pounds as I run faster, faster, faster. Got to keep going. Got to. Got to. This can't end. The game can't end.

Somewhere, a shrill siren goes off.

No, Keelie! Mila shrieks, and I look for her—look for my madness. Because that's what it is.

And maybe I am mad. But mad is okay if mad is being alive.

And I am alive.

"I am alive!" I scream.

I grin, see my deranged expression reflected against the smooth black marble plane of the water-feature as I sprint past. My dark glasses have gone. Seeing my Untamed eyes fuels me, and I run faster and faster.

Pain drills into my chest as I snake out of the center of the gardens and into a courtyard. My boots make *slap slap slap* sounds on the concrete squares, and the concrete squares remind me of a chessboard.

Of playing the game with Red.

And it is all a game. Everything is the game.

Life is a game.

"Stop at once, let us help you!" a female voice cries out.

Run! Mila yells.

Huh, as if I'm going to obey the enemy over my sister.

I run faster and faster, then I'm back in another of the gardens—one with a neatly cut lawn and big yellow flowers—and it's at the edge of the complex, because I'm back by the brick wall. I plow through, and the Enhanced follow me. I shriek with excitement as the wall ends, as I get to the open field-like space and turn, see them all behind me. So many.

I run faster, zigzagging. The gray building is in sight. The maze hides inside it. And part of me tells me I'm not supposed to go in there yet, not until after I've set off my gun, done the distraction properly—but I don't know if it's time yet and—

A hand lands on my shoulder.

I shriek, whirl around, kick out. The Enhanced man falls, his mirror eyes throwing distorted reflections everywhere. I turn; butterflies fill my stomach, and the pounding in my head gets faster and faster.

Run!

I run and reach the building, yank open the gray door, and—

An Enhanced man looms in the doorway, steps back when he sees me.

"Keelie?" Red's voice is full of disbelief. Then he grins and grabs me.

I punch him, twist around, see the others. And Red looks up at that moment too, sees my entourage. Because they're right behind me.

And I don't think—I don't think about the others, about Rahn and Corin and Elf and Yani and Kayden and Esther. I just do it, go against my plan, the plan. Or maybe it's time now, I don't know.

But I grin as I lift the gun up and point it at Red.

"Checkmate." My word is a whisper that tells me it'll be okay.

I pull the trigger.

FORTY-EIGHT

THE MOMENT I PULL THE trigger, Red shoves the gun out of the way. The bullet hits the wall, and something hits me. Something hard and sharp and jagged, in my right arm. I look down, and suddenly I feel scared. The emotion pours through in waves and waves. So many waves, and I'm going to drown. Can't breathe. Can't....

And so much blood.

I'm bleeding.

Death.

But I'm alive.

You're alive, Mila whispers.

I turn, try to see her, need to see her. But I can't.

It's just me. Me and Red.

He grabs the gun from me, and I let it slide from my fingers.

No, don't!

"Oh, Keelie." Red's voice is soft. "The Untamed darkness is destroying you. Come on, I'll make you better." He looks up as the Enhanced behind me, and he's shouting at them. "I'll take her for a full conversion—I've got the authority for it, all of you can only do first taste. And Owen Sykes is here. Yes—this is Keelie Lin-Sykes. A familial relation present would be best for her, given she's so stressed and wild—and Owen arrived earlier."

Conversion.

My mouth dries. That's not how my game ends. No.

Pain inches into my head, but then, suddenly, it's everywhere, the pain. Every part of me hurts.

The door shuts. Darkness.

Red flicks a light on, but my eyes don't adjust properly. I can't see where we are, but I think it should be a corridor....

"Your father's here, Keelie. It'll be okay now," Red says, and he pulls me to him in a tight hug. His shirt is scratchy against my face.

Get out. Get out. Get out.

I blink back more pain as I lean against Red, turn my head the opposite way, try to see where my gun is. Is he still holding it? But *I* need the gun, need to keep doing the distraction, draw the Enhanced away from Rahn's group. But the movement of trying to look around for the weapon pulls at my shoulder— my right shoulder—and more pain takes hold of me. My arm. What's wrong with it?

"It'll be okay," Red says.

I feel his body responding against mine.

No.

No.

He's Enhanced.

I squirm and get my left arm free of him, but he's quicker. He grabs me again, pulls me back against him. He smells of lemons, and my stomach twists.

"Are you going to join us voluntarily now?" His voice is a whisper, but there's hope in it.

I shake my head against his chest, try to turn my body, from side to side, but I'm exhausted now. So suddenly. Too tired. Can't move. My heart thuds, yet it's like a herd of stampeding elephants. It thuds with darkness, not adrenaline.

"Oh, Keelie." Red snorts, and then he twists me around a little, so I'm angled to the left, looking down the corridor—but I can't see much of it, because my eyes are smarting. "Come on, K," he says. "Walk."

Something hard prods me in the upper back. I think it's my gun.

I walk quickly, willing myself to think of something. Need to think. He's holding onto my upper left arm now, his fingers like iron. And he's strong. And I'm tired, exhausted.

Come on, think!

Need to get away from Red. Need to stay Untamed. Need to get my sister back.

"Where is she?" I ask as we walk.

"Who?" Red's grip gets tighter. It's not a friendly grip. It's a grip that tells me I'm not getting away.

"Seven Sarr."

"You know her?" He sounds surprised.

Irritation clouds me. "*Of course* I do. Where is she?"

"Conversion compound. Don't worry, you can see her once you've both been saved."

Once you've both been saved. So she's still resisting. Good. But of course she would. She's my sister. And we're all strong, strong-minded and—

She's not your sister, Mila says. *I am.*

I jolt.

"It'll be all right," Red says. "I'll even see if you can both be held in the same wing. That'll be comforting, won't it? Knowing she's nearby. But Raleigh thinks it will take longer for her, says she's special."

"Special?" I frown. Who's Raleigh?

"She's the one who can make a difference, apparently," Red replies. "She can win the war."

Darkness creeps down my spine. Seven can win the war? *The* war? The War of Humanity? I try to swallow, but I find I can't. The muscles in my throat, they won't work.

Seven will make the difference? But the Enhanced have her...and I'm supposed to be doing the distraction. Rahn and Corin and the others—they can't get her out without me doing my part.

My head swims.

The gun. I need to get the gun. Got to do the distraction. Got to make sure they can get Seven out. Have to. Have to. *Have to*. My heart pounds heavier. A countdown.

To your death, Mila—my madness—says.

I flinch, try not to remember either Caia-Lu's or Katya's predictions. But death is a prophecy. My prophecy. And death belongs to all of us.

But Seven has to escape.

She's *special*.

A special one is a Seer. Caia-Lu's voice.

My eyes widen. Seven's going to be a *Seer*. Her mother already is. The power's often hereditary. Seven's going to become one… Shit. Yes. We have to get her out. Nbutai needs a Seer. Rahn's group has to get Seven back—because they're not going to rescue Katya, Rahn made that clear. And they need a Seer.

They have to get Seven.

A group of Untamed cannot survive without a Seer.

"Let me go," I say to Red as we walk. I narrow my eyes, trying to see farther down the corridor, see if any doors are in sight. But I can't. It's too dark, even though the light's on. I can only see the immediate area. My vision's not right. Everything's swimming. "Please. Let me go."

"No. Your father's here. He's *here*, K." Red pulls me along a little faster.

I take a deep breath, try to remain calm. I can get out of this. Hell, I've fought Enhanced—killed Enhanced. I can do this.

But my energy's low, and my body hurts, aches, thrums with pain. There's still no adrenaline fueling me, it hasn't come back. The traitor.

"Please, let me go, Red."

"I will," he says. "When we're with him. He'll do the honors. It's what he wants. What he's always wanted—

to be the one who saves his precious daughters."

Conversion.

I twist my head to the left, trying to keep breathing evenly. Need to stay calm. I glance behind me—can't see the gun. He must be holding it by his other side, in his left hand. If I can just get it, I'll be in charge again.

And I have to be in charge. *Have* to be.

You will be.

"You saved me a journey," Red says. "Coming to see us. Coming to *me.* You can't live without me, Keelie. Neither of us can. We're too alike."

My vision clears a little, and I see the corridor turns right up ahead, but I don't think it's a junction. Think it's the only way to go.

"We are nothing alike," I say through gritted teeth. "You are not the Red I knew."

I look up, see a large, square air vent. An escape route?

But then we've walked past it. I twist my head back, ignoring the pain, looking. There could be a network above us... Can I get away from Red, run, get into the air vent, crawl along there, shoot out of the next opening, starting the distraction, then crawl through the passageway again? Could it connect to the conversion compounds? I frown, no. This building's the other side of the gardens to the compound where Seven will be.

I breathe out slowly. I need the gun. I slow a little, trying to lean back so I can see the firearm in Red's left hand. Maybe if I yank him back and—

"What are you doing?" His voice is abrupt, and he spins me around.

"No!" I scream, and I fight him, try to kick him, but he's still got hold of my arm. My right hand flies out, and I punch him—but the punch isn't good, because that arm, it's not right—but I momentarily feel the gun against my side as we twist around and—

Red pins me against the wall.

For a second, I freeze. Then rage blinds me. I throw

my weight at him, everything onto him, and manage to knock him back a foot or so. My head jolts up, and I see the gun—my gun—in his hand. I lunge forward, slam my head into his, flinch at the pain and….

He chucks the gun away. It clatters on the tiled floor somewhere to my left.

I freeze, stare at it, stay where I am, sort of crouching, reeling in pain. My breaths come in short, sharp bursts, and my head spins.

Then I lunge for the gun.

But Red grabs me, yanks me back. I shriek, and then his eyes are right in front of me, his mirrors throwing snatches of light at me in a way that *hurts*. There's something dangerous in his expression, something that makes my stomach twist. He leans in close to me.

"Stop it." His voice is low. "*You* don't want to hurt anyone, Keelie. It's the darkness in you. And I understand, because I had it once."

I remember the knife and twine in my pockets—and why the hell didn't I use them when he was marching me along? I let out a small squeak as Red's grip on me tightens painfully, and I try to move my left hand down to my shorts. Need to pull them out. Need a weapon. But my fingers, they won't work. They're going numb.

I feel the tears in my eyes welling up, then they're spilling over. My fingers scrabble at the pockets of my shorts, but I'm shaking, and they still won't work.

"I will knock you out if I have to," Red says. "I can do that easily."

My eyes widen, and my chest squeezes.

No.

"Please, Red, please, no." I turn my head, looking around for anything that can help me. But there's just my gun, over there.

I get ready to kick him.

Then I hear footsteps.

Don't go to any towns or cities. Katya's voice.

I look up.

401

A DANGEROUS GAME

My father walks toward us.

FORTY-NINE

MY FATHER LOOKS...HE LOOKS the same. Hasn't aged a day. Our eyes meet—or at least, I think they do, but his are mirrors and—

Mirrors.

Mirrors reflecting the augmenters in his hands.

I scream and lunge to Red's right, somehow pulling myself free from his grip. Energy slams into me; and I start to run, back the way we came, got to get out, even if I can't get the gun, and—

He grabs me around the waist.

I scream as he hauls me back. Then I throw my weight down, try to throw him off balance.

I land heavily on my chest, Red on top of me.

"Keelie! Stop it! It's okay!" Red yells into my ear, his weight pressing down on me.

I scream loudly. Screaming for Elf, for *anyone*. Tears blind me. I turn my head, trying to see something—anything that will help me.

My gun. It's on the floor over there, not far away now. I'm closer now. Yes.

Get the gun.

I try to get it, reach with all my might, try to slip

out from under Red, but he's like concrete, too strong, holds me down, I can't move. Shit.

"Don't be scared," Red whispers, and then he moves quickly, pulls me up. My heart pounds as he holds me against his body, like I'm a shield.

My father walks up to me. He looks at me for a long time, sticking his head forward, like his neck has a crick.

I stare back. From what I can see of his expression, it's blank. Just blank. Hatred boils inside me. He's Enhanced. He's the enemy.

"You've got the wrong girl," my father says slowly. He turns on Red. "This isn't her."

Red blinks. "But you told me to find your daughters."

"I meant my *biological* daughters. And I heard of Mila's death, so now there's only Bea: my surviving biological daughter."

My gaze jerks to him.

I'm not….

My eyes widen. I stare at him. My mouth dries almost instantly.

Me and Elf, we're not his?

I try to say something, but nothing comes out.

And the man who I thought was my father for all these years doesn't look at me, he's still looking at Red. And then they're talking, about DNA and dates and family and…and I don't understand. They should be ramming the augmenters down my throat…not standing here, discussing paternity.

"But I got her for you!" Red says. "I've kept her Untamed and oblivious until you got here. I made sure no one else discovered her group's location so you could be the one to convert her."

"Where's Bea? Is she here too?" My father—no, *Owen*—pushes Red to the side, and Red pulls me with him.

Run! Mila yells at me.

But I don't. I stare at my father…who isn't my father. Isn't my father? I inhale sharply. So I'm *not* related to

404

his mother, the woman who went mad. My shoulders get lighter. I haven't got her madness! They were all wrong—*wrong*!

"Mr. Sykes, Bea's whereabouts is unknown," Red says. I turn my head, look up at him, confused. He called him *Mr. Sykes*? But he said *Owen* earlier... Why the change?

"But I need to convert her!" Owen waves a dismissive hand at me, and seeing him as just another Enhanced is weird when I thought he was my father. "Anyone can do Keelie, whenever. I don't care. I wanted *my* daughters. And it's Bea who'll need *me*. I know how to help her, calm her, because she's like her mother—and Mila might've been too. Redala, take Keelie away and do her yourself. Gods, you should've saved her the moment you set eyes on her, not let her suffer."

"But you said she'd suffer more in the conversion if it wasn't you!"

Owen shakes his head. I just stare at him. He's shorter than me. And I'm not tall—but Bea's taller than me, and she's his daughter? And Mila...Mila was tall too, for her age. Yet he's short.

"I was talking about Bea," he says. "She can't have someone touching her whom she doesn't know. We need to find her."

I look at Owen, and I feel...empty. "Who..." My voice is weak. "Who is my father?"

"It doesn't matter," Owen says quickly, eyes on the ground. But there's something like fire burning in his voice. Then he looks back at me. "Redala, take her away and save her. I don't care who converts Keelie."

"Wait," Red says, and he picks up my gun. "What about my new house... I'm still getting it, right?"

"You'll get it when the deal is complete. When you bring *my* daughter to me."

"But Keelie and I will need a house. And I've done everything you asked—lied, pretended, got—"

"And you got the wrong girl!"

My eyes smart. I can't process this. Can't. There's too much. Too many reveals. But the man who claims not to be my father wants something. And I can use that to my advantage.

Red's grip on me is no longer that strong—though he doesn't let me go—but I find I can step closer to Owen. My heart pounds. I feel sick.

"Tell me who my real father is, and I'll tell you where Bea is." I hope the wobble in my voice doesn't betray me.

Owen looks at me. He wipes the back of his hand across his mouth, then shakes his head a little. But not in a way that means *no*. More in a way that suggests pain. Like he doesn't want to remember.

Because my mother cheated on him?

He coughs once. "Rahn Eriksen."

I stare at him. "*Rahn?*"

Owen's eyes seem to glisten. "Yes, that wild man corrupted my wife. We were traveling south—what was supposed to be a brief break from D'Elinous. We met Rahn's group. I got injured in a hunt. Your mother was infatuated with him—by that corrupt, wild man. When we left, she was pregnant. I knew it couldn't be mine. And he had to go and give her *twins*, didn't he? Including a *son*. Eirnin should've been *mine*." Resentment curls in his voice, and I shake my head.

Rahn? *Rahn's* my father?

"Now, where's my daughter?" Owen growls.

I take a step back and another.

Red moves with me, his hand tightening on me again. "Let me save her first. She's getting upset. We can...we can discuss this afterward, once Keelie's no longer suffering."

"No!" Owen shouts. "She said she'd tell me—and my daughter's suffering. My child. My flesh and blood. She will be suffering for longer—and that is unacceptable."

"Your *other* daughter is suffering—your words are hurting her. Keelie's still your daughter," Red says.

"And our duty is to help them."

Owen steps up to Red and I, glaring. He bares his teeth—perfect, white teeth. Not crooked like I remember. "Tell me where Bea is. Tell me *now*."

"She's out there," I yell. "Untamed. Surviving. Being who we're supposed to be!"

Fury fills Owen's face. He grabs me, wrenches me from Red.

I fight back, but he's strong. Too strong.

Hell.

I curse him, try and get the knife out of my pocket—but can't.

Red starts shouting something, and I lose sight of him as Owen drags me forward, round the corner. Then there's a door which he kicks open.

A room. Dusty. Bare.

Owen throws me into it, and I skid forward, fall, hit the tiled floor hard. Momentary pain. I spin around, launch myself up, need to get to the door. Need to get out.

"Redala, start saving her now! She's too far gone to be trusted." Owen thrusts the augmenters at Red as he appears in the doorway, and Red takes them.

"No…no…no," I cry, and I run at them, try to push past. But the two of them make a solid wall. Hands push me back, and then Red latches onto me again. I try to fight him, but I'm freezing up. Hell, why am I freezing up? And my arm isn't working properly, and there's blood.

Owen smiles. "I'll go and notify them to get a room ready for the mind-conversion. You give her first taste."

"South Meg Wing," Red says. "Her friend's already there. It'll make it easier for her."

I frown—that's not the usual place. I struggle to think. South Meg Wing—is it attached to the usual conversion compound, but farther to the right, behind the main block? Or is it the separate building over on the other side? I curse my memory; I don't know.

Owen grunts. "Have her ready for it by the time I'm back." He steps out of the room. "Hopefully she'll comply more once she's had first taste."

The door closes, clicks.

Red grabs me, squashes me against his body. My back against his chest, his arm around me.

I twist and twist, scream loudly, but I know there's no one to help me; Elf can't be nearby—he'd have got in here by now if he was.

Red flicks the lid off an augmenter, brings it closer.

"Open wide."

I shake my head, clamping my lips firmly shut. Sweat breaks out across my forehead. My head and heart pound together in unison. I bend my left arm up, twisting around, manage to claw at his skin. The augmenter slams into the side of my face, breaks. I feel the jagged glass scratching.

Red swears at me, but I punch him. Weakly, but it's still a punch.

He staggers back, but not far enough.

Then he jumps on me.

His body slams into mine. I fall back, hit my head hard, and—

Red hovers over me, somehow still standing. And I see the gun. *My* gun. The Luger. It's in his belt. He went and got it? When? My head pounds. When Owen dragged me into the room?

But it doesn't matter because the weapon is smiling at me. It's saying I can use it, that I'll manage to do it, and—

My gaze jolts up.

Another augmenter comes at me, and Red throws himself on top of me. His weight crushes me, but I turn my head to the side, just in time, hear the augmenter slam into the tiled floor. More broken glass.

Adrenaline pulses through me, and I push at Red, get him to go back a few inches, to lift off of me a little. I shove him again and spring up, spitting at him; my saliva sprays across his face, so much of it. And it's pink—blood. My mouth's bleeding? And then I taste it, the blood, like an augmenter of death.

No…no…*no!*

I go for Red again, for his belt and—

Red screams and backhands me at the exact moment my fingers wrap around the gun's handle. His slap sends waves of pain through me, and I fall back, pulling the gun with me. I spring into a crouching position and…the gun—I've got the gun!

He rears over me, but he stops when he sees the gun pointed at his chest. Slowly, a smile unfolds across his face. A *smile*.

"Come on! You love me," he says. "You wouldn't shoot me."

He's right! A gun isn't your weapon!

I flick the safety off and pull the trigger.

He ducks. The bullet hits the wall, bounces back just as I jump up. A fresh wave of energy fuels me.

"No, K—no." Red holds his hands up, takes several steps back. I try not to look at his muscles, his tattoos. "I love you. And you love me. We love each other."

"We don't," I say. "I loved the Untamed you. Not when you're Enhanced. *You're* not there anymore. It's not you, Red. You're just… It's not *you*."

"But it is," he cries, and he produces another augmenter. I don't see where he gets it from. It's just suddenly there, in his hand. He grins. "I was a Chosen One, *Enhanced* all along. I was never Untamed out here."

"What?" I stare at him. And it's what he wants. To distract me. When I should be using the gun, when I should be killing him and getting out of here.

"I'm a good actor, K," he says, spreading his arms wide. My eyes follow the movement of the augmenter. "And you fell in love. I was saved ten years ago. And you fell in love with me—a Chosen One—during this last month, because it's *me*. Because it doesn't matter what our state is. Love surpasses all."

FIFTY

THERE IS A CLICKING IN my head, and it won't shut up, no matter how much I shake it. And I keep staring at Red. Because it can't be true.

It just can't.

Enhanced all along?

"How does it feel, eh?" His mirrors flash. "Feel betrayed, right?"

Betrayed.

He lets out a bitter laugh, and I know—I know what he's referring to.

I hold onto the gun tighter, try and stop it from shaking. "I'm sorry, Red, I—"

"You were my best friend, Keelie. *My best friend.* And you left. And I'm not even angry about it." But he sounds angry. "Not really," he says. "Because I became a Chosen One. In leaving me, you saved me. Saved many of us." He steps slowly toward me. "But I remember the betrayal. The horror I felt when I heard you tell Owen there was no one left. Yes, I heard that! And, although I don't feel the negative emotion of betrayal anymore, I can remember what it felt like. Tell me, Keelie. How does it feel for *you* to be betrayed?"

I get the gun ready, try and line it up, try not to shake.

Red just laughs—laughs in the face of death. "Don't worry, you won't feel this betrayal for long. I'll save you. But you'll feel it *temporarily*, the betrayal. And you'll remember. I'll make sure you remember— because it's a shared experience now, isn't it? You betrayed me. And I've betrayed you." He licks his lips. "The perfect couple. Oh, aren't we similar? Aren't we just *meant* to be together?"

I shake my head. "I'm not joining you."

"You don't have a choice, Keelie. And it's the only way—you're resisting now because you're scared. But I'm here. I'm still me. Don't resist. And I'm sorry that this went on for so long. But Owen told me he had to save his daughters himself. If I brought them to him, *Untamed*, so he could save them, he'd have my augmenters upgraded to the strongest level and get me a bigger house. I thought he wanted you, so I kept you alive and Untamed until he was back from Section One."

My heart pounds. "What?"

And I don't know why I'm still talking, why I'm not just finishing this.

"He had to go to Section One," Red says. "Mariella and Lìxúe were in an accident."

"Mariella?"

"His four-year-old daughter."

His...my...my sister? I've got *another* sister. My hands shake. The gun shakes. And why aren't I using it? I *love* killing Enhanced.

Red advances toward me. "I'm so sorry I've let you suffer. I...I thought I was doing the right thing. I blocked Marlon's broadcasts of your village's location the whole time he was with you—I was keeping you safe. They couldn't find where you were! I even ran lean to protect you, to make sure I knew where you were. And I'm sorry I ran away. I needed augmenters. You've no idea what it's like. I should've told you about Marlon then, but I wasn't thinking straight."

I frown. "You stopped the Enhanced from finding out our location?" I breathe deeply. My vision blurs a little, then rights itself. Red knew all along?

"Yes! I was playing the long game, don't you understand?"

My breathing quickens. Suddenly, it's so hot in here. Is Red still the only one who knows Nbutai's location? My eyes narrow. Or are others on their way to the village now?

"No, I don't understand." My words are slow. "Explain it. Explain it all."

He chuckles to himself. "And this will make you feel better when I convert you? Knowing all this? Because you're not going to shoot me, K—you've had plenty of opportunities. But you feel it too, I know you do. And this will make your conversion easier?"

Slowly, I nod. "Talk."

"Fine." He passes the augmenter from one hand to the other. "I heard Raleigh talking about it: the long game can be the best conversion technique at times, gives the biggest results. And we'll still get everyone, all of your friends—but I thought I could get my reward from Owen first." His shoulders seem to droop a little. "We came up with the undercover story—me and Owen. Then he had to go. And I didn't expect you to walk into my office so soon. But you did, and then some guys found out I'd slept with you, an Untamed, and reported me. Reconverted me. And I nearly lost the plan, nearly converted you as soon as I saw you, because the mind-conversion was so fresh and…" He grins widely. "But my love for you is stronger! I can't stop thinking about you. I've tried stronger augmenters to not feel anything for you, but they never work. I need *you*, Keelie."

I stare at him, feel a jolt in my body. "You really kept my village safe—for me?"

"Of course."

"And no one else knows?" My voice breaks. I look

up at him, then quickly down at the gun. It's pointing at him, but he's moved a bit. I reposition the firearm slightly, hear my heart pounding in my ears.

"No. Just me," Red says. "I told you, K. I was keeping you safe—making sure only I knew, so I could get the timing right for when Owen was back."

"And you're definitely the only one here who knows? No one else does?"

"Only I know the co-ordinates."

But he's not the only one here who knows now. Katya's here somewhere, and she knows. And Seven.

I breathe in too quickly and nearly choke.

Rahn's team *has* to get both of them back. Hell—the Enhanced could've already got the location out of either of them.

Only Rahn won't rescue Katya….

Suddenly, Red walks over to the wall near me. I keep the gun on him, feel strange.

"I'll send a team over now for them." He presses a button, and, too late, I realize there's a small communications panel on the wall. Red clears his throat. "I'm reporting the location of an Untamed village for immediate—"

I fire the gun.

The bang resounds through me, makes my ears ring, and I don't see where I hit him. More pain pulls through me, and my bad arm's going numb. And then Red's right in front of me, standing—how is he standing?—shouting at me and….

Blood…blood *on me*. Splattered. His blood.

Shoot again!

"No, Keelie, no!" he screams, and he grabs the gun, but I don't let go.

He yells for help, shouts at me to put it down, not to fight him, that he'll save me. That he knows I'm angry because he should've saved me weeks ago, but—

"It's called Nbutai!" Red yells, twisting around. "Its co-ordinates are—"

I pull the trigger again. The sound is deafening. But

413

I've missed. *Missed* him.

Because you shouldn't use a gun. A gun is cheating. A gun isn't safe. Drop the gun!

"No!"

I twist around. In one fluid movement, I pull him with me, against me, and then his back is against my chest. Practically the same position we were in before, but with our roles reversed, and it emphasizes the height difference. His hands drop to his sides, and I have full command of the gun. For a moment, I falter, listen to the voice in my head that tells me to drop the gun, but then another cuts in, screams at me that I'm too exhausted to kill him with my hands. That this time, a gun is okay.

Then the voices are arguing, and I stretch my neck out to the side, so I can see around Red a little. And I point the gun at him, feel him tremble against my body as we both look at the barrel. I hold my injured arm tighter across his chest, begging it to work, to keep him there so I can pull the—

Shit.

My heart pounds as I realize what's going to happen. No! I need to get him away from me before I—

But you can't stop this, Keelie.

Red slams his foot down onto mine. I scream into his ear, and he struggles against me.

The communications panel bleeps and flashes, spits words out.

"Yes!" Red cries. "Co-ordinates are—"

My finger moves.

I hear the sound—the bang—and—

Pain. My stomach.

I gasp. Red slumps against me. We both crash down against the wall, him on top of me, but my back catches something, and then my torso's wedged partly upright, my legs under him. The back of my head hits something hard, and—

Can't....

Gurgles escape my mouth, and my left hand and

the gun are spasming. I see the movement out of the corner of my eye. Red's breaths rasp loudly, and he tries to move in the pool of blood that we're becoming. Pain screams through me. My head pounds. I can't see well, there's just a hazy fogginess.

I shot *myself*. Shot myself *through him*.

Told you not to use the gun.

The bullet—I can feel it. In my stomach. A hardness that's hot and cold and screaming and screaming and screaming. Shot straight through Red, into me and—

Red's head jolts back, ramming against my shoulder, but his gaze is on me. I try to push him away from me, but I can't get the strength. I'm trapped between him and the wall, and my legs are still under him. Blood trickles from the corners of his mouth, and I scrabble again, try to move, need to get away. But I'm bleeding too much, aren't I? Or is it all his blood that's gushing out?

My stomach burns.

"Please repeat the co-ordinates. We did not get that."

Red opens his mouth, makes a gurgling sound. Then he says a number. One digit. He wheezes, tries again and—

And the Untamed all fall down.

No…no…*no*….

Blood pounds in my ears.

"Please repeat the co-ordinates. We did not get that."

Red tries to speak again. Hissing sounds fill my ears, block his words from me—if they even *are* words—and….

Shoot him! Else they'll get Nbutai! Mila cries.

Mila. I look around, can't see her. My breaths burst from me, savage and broken. White spots hover in front of my eyes.

Shoot him!

I manage to grip the gun tightly again. My hand's stopped spasming, but I'm sure it's only temporary. Need to do it now. And I try to slide him away from me—need to! But I can't. Too much pain.

Shoot him!

Red laughs, the sounds becoming manic, and he's so heavy, squashing me. Can't... A jolt runs through me.

"Please repeat the co-ordinates. We did not get that."

My fingers click as I angle the gun.

"No!" Red gasps, and he struggles against me, his legs moving, as if he's running—but he's not. He just flails on top of me, emitting a strange, high-pitched sound.

"This game's over," I whisper.

I pull the firearm's trigger again, shoot a bullet through Red.

Mila says my name as the bullet slices into me again.

The pain...no... Something clicks... Wetness, running down my side, bleeding, and....

My knees lock up, and Mila's here, next to me, turning a key, like I'm a clockwork doll.

My body twists, and Red finally slides down, away from me, and I see his tattooed arms slipping away. I try to listen...need to... Is he...breathing...is....

My head hits the floor...the blood...my blood...my stomach... I see the mass of tissue and muscle. My throat clenches. I smell something sour.

The gun goes off again as I drop it...and I'm... I'm... I press my hands to my stomach, breathing deeply. Need to apply pressure. My head turns and....

"Please repeat the co-ordinates. We did not get that."

Red writhes on the floor next to me. His limbs are moving, jerking out.

Shoes—heavy boots, by his head—so suddenly there and—

Elf is above him, with a gun. Elf...and then Yani....

My vision blurs as another shot sounds.

I close my eyes, feel the liquid still pouring from my stomach. So much of it. But everything's dark.

And darkness is good.

Darkness is....

"Kee! Keelie, no!"

It's all right, Mila says.

Something pokes me, and I open my eyes, can't see....

"Keelie—I'm here!"

And then there's a sound I don't like. An inhuman sound. A sound that no one should make. Least of all my brother.

"Elf..." I whisper, but his name's too difficult, and I don't know if he hears me... I don't know if I hear myself...

Maybe...maybe I didn't say it...maybe....

Elf.

Elf....

I try to move my lips. And there's something... something....

I try to move my head... If I could just move my head out of this pain, I'd be able to....

"Elf...."

"What?" I see his eyes—my eyes...and Rahn's eyes? Rahn's eyes under those dark glasses....

Elf.

Elf.

Elf... *What* was it?

"Get Seven..." I mumble. "She's... She'll keep you safe...."

Corin charges into the room. I see the look of horror on his face as he stands behind Elf, as he sees me.

"Have you got Seven?" I croak.

"We can't find her!" Corin yells. His arms fly out. "Come on, we've got to get back to—"

"We can't leave her!" Elf shouts, and I stare at his face. See the way tears run down his cheeks, feel them drip onto me.

"South Meg..." I struggle to say the words. "I think...it's round the side of... She's at South Meg Wing... Not the... Get her...go! You can't survive... without her... She's...."

"She said go!" Yani shouts. But his words echo to me in a different place, and the world's getting quieter. "She's...she's gone, Elf. But we've got to get out of here. Get Seven and go."

Gone?

Where've I gone?

I'm still here....

And I open my eyes.

See the ceiling.

But there's no ceiling.

There are only stars.

Bright and knowledgeable.

And a shape hurtling toward me. A mass of silvery threads with a lone eye in the middle that's bloodshot. A spirit.

And the spirit takes me to Mila, it takes us to the lights, for the sky is a playing field, and we're shining brightly even though there's no darkness.

Mila holds my hand. And, together, we look down at the motorbike tearing over the hard desert land, at our beautiful sister as she weaves her own destiny toward the group of Untamed who, far away, do not yet know they are waiting for her.

END OF BOOK ONE

THE DANGEROUS ONES SERIES
WILL CONTINUE WITH

THIS VICIOUS WAY

AVAILABLE FROM DECEMBER 2019...

ACKNOWLEDGEMENTS

A Dangerous Game has certainly been a fun book to write, and, as always, so many people have assisted me in its production.

To Kelley York, Rachael Bundy, Tessa Elwood, S.E. Anderson, Tam Lee, E. Mitchell, and Janelle Alexander: thank you for your amazing critiques and countless (re)reads of this manuscript. Your advice has been invaluable. And a special thank you goes to Kelley York, S.E. Anderson, and Ashleigh Neame at *The Literature Hub* for blurbing this book.

To everyone in the YA Story Sisters, AAYAA, and the YA Writers' Critique Group HQ: thank you. You're all amazing.

To Elizabeth Huxley-Jones and Moriah Gemel: thank you for your guidance and advice regarding the portrayal of autism in *A Dangerous Game* and for checking the manuscript for any issues of representation. Any errors are mine.

To Michelle Dunbar, my amazing editor: I'm so pleased I was able to work with you on this manuscript. Your comments were spot-on! Thank you.

To Molly Phipps: thank you for creating such an awesome cover and the beautiful interior designs. You've really made *A Dangerous Game* come alive!

To Megan Crewe, Jenna Beacom, Tessa Gratton, Ragini Bhaumik, A'ishah H. Amatullah, Asha Groves, Rachel Hurdle, Alice Varah, Natalie Jones, Naomi Hill, Nicky Wynne, and Tom Wija: thank you for your advice and support.

And, finally, to my parents, my brother, the rest of my family, and my friends: thank you for believing in me.

ABOUT THE AUTHOR

MADELINE DYER lives on a farm in the southwest of England, where she hangs out with her Shetland ponies and writes young adult books—sometimes, at the same time. She holds a BA Honors degree in English from the University of Exeter, and several presses have published her fiction. Madeline has a strong love for anything dystopian, ghostly, or paranormal, and she can frequently be found exploring wild places. At least one notebook is known to follow her wherever she goes. *A Dangerous Game* is her fourth novel.

Find Madeline online:
Twitter: @MadelineDyerUK
Instagram: @MadelineDyerUK
Facebook: MadelineDyerAuthor
Website: www.MadelineDyer.co.uk

Sign up to Madeline's Newsletter:
http://madelinedyer.co.uk/newsletter/

www.ingramcontent.com/pod-product-compliance
Lightning Source LLC
Chambersburg PA
CBHW051207120726
47905CB00004B/1022